Kerry Sanderson is an exotic dancer, former military brat, and aspiring fashion designer, but believes he's much more than any of those labels imply.

As his relationship with transgender boyfriend Jamie falls apart, it's Kerry's gender identity and sexual preferences that become the real issue between them. Left questioning whether he's been living under everyone else's terms, and none of his own, Kerry sets out to discover who he really is. Desperate to escape his dangerous neighborhood and redefine his life, Kerry vows to start making some changes. One of the first is accepting what seems to be an innocent offer from allegedly straight security guard, Ewyn Garrity, after a long shift dancing at gay club Blaze. Safety isn't the only thing Ewyn tempts Kerry with as sparks fly and lines are crossed. The more acceptance Kerry finds in Ewyn, the more he's tempted to let go of the fear and self-doubt that had been hampering his ability to be himself. But the more honest Kerry is, slowly accepting the feminine aspects of his identity and becoming vulnerable, the more deadly threats he faces when blind intolerance threatens before he's barely bloomed.

Becoming Kerry

Lynn Kelling

ForbiddenFiction
www.forbiddenfiction.com

an imprint of

Fantastic Fiction Publishing
www.fantasticfictionpublishing.com

BECOMING KERRY

A ForbiddenFiction book

Fantastic Fiction Publishing
Hayward, California

© Lynn Kelling, 2017

For more information, contact publisher@forbiddenfiction.com.

CREDITS
Editor: Lon Sarver and Rylan Hunter
Cover Design: Siolnatine
Cover Art: Adapted from photos © Visivasnc & © MinervaStudio at Dreamstime.com
Production Editor: Kaye O'Malley
Proofreading: Emma Williams
Font: Wellrock Slab, by Manfred Klein

SKU: LK1-1.000267-01 FFP
ISBN: 978-1-62234-332-4

Published in the United States of America

DISCLAIMER

This book is a work of fiction which contains explicit erotic content; it is intended for mature readers. Do not read this if it's not legal for you.

All the characters, locations and events herein are fictional. While elements of existing locations or historical characters or events may be used fictitiously, any resemblance to actual people, places or events is coincidental.

This book depicts one perspective on the diverse and complex matter of human gender identity. Real people are necessarily more complicated than fictional characters; this depiction is not intended to be exhaustive or typical. The author makes no attempt to describe every possible combination of sex, gender, and orientation. Many, many variations on gender, orientation, and identity exist in the world than can be included in any single work of fiction.

This story depicts fictional BDSM; it is not intended to be used as an instruction manual. It contains descriptions of erotic acts that may be immoral, illegal, or unsafe. The characters are not models for the Safe, Sane and Consensual forms embraced by most current practitioners of BDSM. The author takes license with the use of BDSM for dramatic effect. Do not take the events in this story as proof of the plausibility or safety of any particular practice.

Such content should not be read as a depiction of the desires, opinions, or fetishes of the author or the staff of ForbiddenFiction.com.

Dedication

For those who live outside of boxes,
May you find your truth and own it, gloriously.

Contents

Chapter 1: In the Spotlight

"So, you've been working exclusively at Savage Men for the past year? No private parties?"

"No," Kerry Sanderson replied, trying to be as professional as possible. "I had a few bad experiences with the private party aspect. I prefer the safety and security of a club, especially one that enforces policies on touching and nudity."

The 'bad experiences' involved clients who expected to get more for their money than just a dance and a tease. Boundaries and rules had always helped Kerry feel more comfortable in a job that constantly put him in vulnerable positions.

The guy across the desk, a glamorous, locally famous aging queen named Cory Lesh, gave Kerry the once-over. Kerry had come to the interview wearing a kilt, with a tight black t-shirt, his combat boots and plenty of eyeliner. The look seemed a little goth on him because of his pale skin and naturally inky black hair, but the eye makeup helped highlight his violet eyes. Some subtle contouring set off his bone structure. He hadn't been sure whether the outfit was a costume or not, but he liked it.

Cory owned Blaze, the most popular gay nightclub in the entire surrounding area. For weeks, Kerry had obsessed over the looming interview-slash-audition. The initial idea had been to keep the gig at Savage Men until he had a better one lined up, but like many things following the break-up with his ex, Jamie, the job simply hadn't fit anymore. At Savage, the problems for Kerry were many: the atmosphere, the management, the endless crowds of women expecting only the most macho of men to take the stage, flex, and dry-hump them into a fleeting state of delirious, orgasmic bliss. For a while, it had been great, the perfect way to rebel against his

1

conservative, military-brat upbringing. Now, he knew he'd outgrown it in ways he still couldn't quite put a finger on, but felt way down to his core. Being able to live with himself wound up being more important than financial security.

"And obviously you know we're a gay club?" Cory chuckled, scratching at a spot on his sleeve with a fingernail painted a glossy, cherry red.

"Yeah. Not a problem," Kerry said. He'd expected the question. After spending the entirety of his life doing everything in his power to project a hyper-masculine, heterosexual appearance, Kerry had become an expert at it. So much so that even wearing a kilt and makeup did nothing to convince Cory that Kerry hadn't made an embarrassing mistake by applying for their opening for a new exotic dancer.

"Have you ever danced for men before?"

"No," Kerry replied honestly, "but I don't see how that matters. It's not like I have a problem with guys looking at me. From what I've seen, they can be a lot better-behaved than the women I've dealt with at Savage."

"Mm," was the noncommittal response. "Did you bring your music and a costume?"

"Yeah. Should I go get changed?" Kerry asked.

"Show us what you've got, Tommy Gunn."

Kerry grabbed his duffel bag and headed for the backstage area. It only took him a minute to strip down and suit up in the tear-away clothes he'd hand-sewn and tailored himself. The clothes helped him transition immediately into his stage persona. Leaving Kerry behind, he became Tommy instead.

He let the staff member waiting by the side of the stage know he was ready. A moment later, his music track started to play. The drums and bass line were heavy and thumping.

Chin up, posture straight, mirrored aviator sunglasses on, he strode onto the stage, then directly to the end of the runway. He did a sharp, proper salute, standing at attention. After an about face, he glanced back over his shoulder and began to slowly swivel his hips, gyrating to the beat. It was a slow melt from the sharp military position to the smooth, liquid flow of the dance.

He tossed his hat first, then began to work the buttons of his dress shirt. The uniform was similar to the dress blues which had always hung in the closets of his home, since his stepfather and two of his brothers were Marines, though it was not an exact replica. Kerry wore a long-sleeved choker-collar midnight blue blouse decorated with an assortment of completely fake medals and ribbons, a white cover(hat), blue trousers, and high gloss black shoes. He'd left his replica Mameluke sword behind this time, but sometimes he used it in his routine.

Kerry's body wasn't bulky, but he was cut, and his body was waxed perfectly smooth, everywhere. His skin wasn't tan, but the creaminess of it had never worked against him. He'd always been told there was something sensual about his features, his lips formed in a natural pout, his eyes brilliant and expressive, hinting at innocence and a bad boy streak at the same time. Kerry was a walking contradiction, playing both sides at the same time. His strong jaw gave him a distinctly masculine appearance women had always appreciated.

The shirt off, his chest bare, he inched the pants down, opening them just enough to show a hint of his shimmery gold shorts. Rolling his abs, using the pole, thrusting in smooth full movements against it, he swooped around, shook his ass, then ripped off the tear-away pants.

Working the whole stage, he touched himself, caressing from his chest, down his stomach to his package, using his pout to lure in the spectators — all three of them.

Kerry teased the back of the shorts down to show his bare ass. He got low, rolling his hips to the beat, then came up smoothly, curving his back, sticking out his ass, and ripped off the shorts. It left him only in a barely-there gold thong. Holding the pole with both hands, he shimmied, shaking his bare cheeks as the music's pace quickened, building to a crescendo.

Turning to face his audience, he gave a wide, brilliant smile, as if he was having the time of his life. Bouncing, pumping his arm, thrusting hard, Kerry crouched lower as he got back into the dance, using his hips and everything he had to sell himself.

When the music faded out, he stuck around instead of heading offstage, like he usually would.

The trio in the mostly barren room were clapping.

"Tommy," Cory told him. "Congratulations, you're hired. You start tonight."

Kerry lived in a shitty neighborhood. He knew it. There was always trash on the streets, blowing around as litter or stuffed in overflowing trash bags that never left the curb for long. The humid weather and unending sunshine scorched all of the asphalt and concrete. The buildings crowded together, close to the road, as if cowering in fear of the danger Kerry sensed nearby whenever he was going to and from his car. People were so desperate to get by or get high, muggings and robberies were commonplace. The windows that weren't boarded up had weather-beaten bars on them. Next to the old converted home he lived in — a Queen Anne style, poorly aging beast with sun-bleached, chipped salmon and white paint, and an interior which had been carved up into tiny apartments — there were plenty of abandoned structures. They'd been left to fall apart, decorated with obnoxious slashes of colorful, sometimes offensive, graffiti.

Kerry's building had a wide front porch ringed with groupings of columns and centrally-located steps which always seemed to be occupied with a random assortment of people, and not necessarily tenants. Some were waiting for the public bus that stopped right out front. Others were friends of people who lived there or nearby, just looking for a place to get lost in shadows and wait for opportunity to strike.

As uncomfortable as the lingerers made him, those abandoned places all around them bothered him most. Anyone could be in there, squatting, pushed hard into a hopeless sort of desperation that made them capable of anything. If they got hungry enough for food or their next fix, who knew what they might do to get it?

Sometimes he saw people peeking out at him from behind grungy curtains, or through gaps in shabby blinds or the boards covering shattered glass. He didn't make eye contact. He kept his head down and his body tensed, ready for anything.

It was because of his neighborhood that he sometimes wore things he wouldn't otherwise. He dressed as someone he wasn't, for safety. If his oppressive, fear-clouded childhood had taught him anything, it was that intimidation and presenting an unruffled appearance went a long way.

Kerry was thankful he'd changed clothes after his audition at Blaze, dressed now in old jeans and a beat-up, patched-up leather jacket, when he was stopped on his way up the sidewalk that sunny Thursday afternoon. He generally didn't like the constricting feel of pants, but at least they had pockets, and discomfort was a small price to pay for drawing unwanted attention, especially from people like the one standing right in his path.

"You owe me, Sanderson," was the clipped, angry demand. The shrill voice belonged to his landlord, a woman named Dorothy Hammerstein. She was somewhere around sixty years old, with gunmetal gray and black hair pulled back in a bun and a permanent frown on her face, turning down her mouth almost comically. To Kerry, she'd always just been The Hammer. He wasn't sure who pissed in The Hammer's coffee each morning, but it was the only explanation that made sense for the furious, puckered expression she always wore. Maybe her good-for-nothing son, Victor, did it. He didn't live in the building, but he always seemed to be there. He liked to treat the tenants as if he was the one they should be thanking for having a roof over their heads. He'd hang around, demanding rent payments, then "accidentally" forget to pass the money along to his mother.

In fact, a few yards away, leaning against a post on the porch, Victor watched the exchange on the sidewalk with a dark, malicious sort of expression, his gaze locked onto Kerry. Not wanting a longer conversation, or any more attention from The Hammer or her son, Kerry answered, "It'll be in an envelope under your door tomorrow, just like every other month, Ms. Hammerstein. I haven't been late on rent day once."

She leaned in closer, squinting. Her nose wrinkled in disgust. "What is that on your face? Are you wearing makeup?"

"It's dirt. Excuse me." He skirted around her, shifting the strap of his duffel bag higher on his shoulder. She kept trying to get a closer look, so he turned his face until he was clear, adding, "Have a good one."

"If you're late, we're going to have a problem!" The Hammer yelled at Kerry's back. "That girlfriend of yours is gone now. Probably left your ass for a real man." She laughed at her own joke. "You don't make rent, you're out! You hear me?"

"Loud and clear, thanks!"

There were so many arguments he could have or should have had. So many ways he should have stood up for himself or Jamie, who hadn't been his girlfriend at all but was still a friend deserving of respect. Sometimes when a sour woman like The Hammer insulted you, it was a safer bet to ignore it than risk eviction.

He didn't blame her for the bad mood; it wasn't like she could lift the building and move it someplace nicer. She was stuck there, just as much as the rest of them, if not more so. He had a feeling Ms. Hammerstein realized there would be no one looking to buy the building from her, even for the privilege of knocking it down. She tried to call the cops on the trespassers and loiterers, but it didn't do any good. The bus drew pedestrians and the cops had bigger problems to solve.

There were many aspects of Kerry's life that had become empty spaces filled with nothing but false hopes. He should have had a lover, a supportive family, and more confidence in himself. Lacking those, Kerry had no wish to move, even if it meant dealing with a grumpy landlady. The consistency of where he slept each night was one of the only things getting him through.

Kerry had dreams of someday moving somewhere less dangerous, but he and Jamie had lived there together for two years without much trouble. It was close to work, and it had too many good memories. Jamie had only been gone for a few months; the ongoing process of making peace with the breakup and learning to live on his own for the first time, ever, meant he wasn't ready to go anywhere else yet.

He climbed the rickety outdoor stairs that were located around the side of the building, zigzagging upward and leading up to the door to his attic apartment. There were things he needed to do, preparations to make. Getting hired at Blaze had been a huge accomplishment — the first of many, he hoped with likely foolish optimism.

Ewyn Garrity always felt conspicuous at the big, wild parties thrown by his old, trusted friend, Trevor. His complete inability to relax or drop his guard, as well as the rumors constantly circulating about his lengthening string of failed relationships left him standing in corners alone, unable to blend in or let loose. Curious glances in his direction from small groups of whispering onlookers reinforced his certainty that his dirty laundry was still being aired. Everyone knew everything about him, which was fine. It just made getting by in light of it all more challenging.

For all of his love for law, order, rules and safety, Ewyn wasn't a particularly private person, even about his sex life. Still, he found it was better to be careful. His exes were still around, as were their mutual friends and all of the gossip stirred following a few tense, dramatic separations. They all blamed Ewyn for things going south, and maybe they were right. For a while there, immense personal tragedy had made him morose and needy. He realized he'd held on too tightly to people who only wanted him to let go. But the world had the tendency to shrink down at inconvenient moments. It had the possibility of making things really awkward, especially since lately it wasn't the women catching Ewyn's eye.

Trevor was into BDSM, and he helped run things for the local community. Ewyn asked Trevor to let him know whenever there were men-only events. Those appealed to Ewyn because there was no chance of running into his exes, or their gossip-happy girlfriends. But navigating around his reputation for being hopelessly uptight wasn't the only thing on his mind.

The party was at Trevor's home, confined mostly to a large open-concept living space. The lighting was dim, giving the space a cozier atmosphere as people hooked up. Doms found willing, eager subs. Ewyn, along with a few others, hung back, preferring to watch the show rather than join in.

Leaning back against a wall, Ewyn was quickly enraptured with a cute, nervous-looking sub who was shackled to a spanking bench. Behind the sub, a well-endowed Dom was getting ready to fuck him, slicking lube onto his rigid cock. When the Dom fed the sub's hole two thick fingers, the sub cried out, his voice quivering as much as his body. As the Dom replaced the pair of fingers with the head of his dick, pressing it gently through the sub's rim, Ewyn throbbed with arousal. Palming his erection, he let out a low moan of approval as the sub's ass gradually swallowed the full length of the large cock.

It had been several years since Ewyn had been with another man. When he had fooled around with guys, it had never gone as far as sex. That was something he now regretted, but it wasn't possible to go back in time and make different choices. He'd thought wanting to get touchy-feely with other men had been a phase he could purge from his system so he could settle down in a real relationship with a woman who'd give him kids and a traditional marriage.

Laughing a little at the memory, and how stupid he'd been, Ewyn couldn't tear his gaze away from the male sub. The slick length of the Dom's cock pumped in and out of the sub's slim, tight body, his ass tipped up for better access. When the Dom pulled completely out before finishing, the sub glanced back over his shoulder, begging, "Please, more, sir?" in a lust-roughened, youthful voice. He looked like he was in his early twenties, whereas the Dom was pushing forty.

Ewyn gave his rigid cock a squeeze through his pants as he watched the Dom thrust, hard, back into the sub's flushed, wet, tight hole.

There were subs nearby trying to catch Ewyn's attention. His size and build always attracted attention at the parties, but he was there to watch, not play. What he needed wasn't more fucking around with strangers, or letting more friends of friends date him only because they thought they could be the one to finally break him of his habits. They thought it would be so easy to finally get past his walls, to get him to relax and stop taking things so seriously. They expected he was only so uptight because of the quirks of his exes, and not because of his own shortcomings. There was no understanding that he'd become the man he was for valid reasons, and couldn't change his personality on a whim. It would take a special person to appreciate him as-is as he kept taking steps to break his habits on his own. A partner only to fuck around with was just not going to cut it. He wanted something completely different — to build a long-term relationship in ways he'd never dreamed possible when he was a younger, more naïve man.

An attractive, dark-haired sub came closer and seemed about to get on his knees at Ewyn's feet.

"Sorry, not interested," Ewyn told him, and kept his attention fixed firmly on the one thing he wanted most of all. It wasn't play he was after, or another girlfriend, and it was time to do something about it.

Chapter 2: First Impressions

On his first night dancing at a gay club, Kerry's nervous unease was tempered by the reality of his empty bank account. Luckily, there were so many men packed into Blaze on the dance floor, at the bar, near the stage and backstage as well, there was plenty to keep his mind off his troubles.

Mostly, the hours passed in a blur. The chorus of voices around him overlapped, working to drown each other out. They were lower in pitch, but similar to those he'd always heard at Savage Men. Kerry made sure he didn't really focus on anyone in the audience, even when he was acting like he was. Everyone who knew him outside of work found it impossible to believe he was a dancer, since he was the shyest, most private person most of them had ever met. The nerves would get the best of him if he didn't rely on a few cherished coping mechanisms. He went into his head and happily became the character Tommy instead of himself.

They had him on the main stage, but the setup at Blaze was different than at Savage. He didn't have to do a show, since it wasn't a strip club, per se. He was eye candy, on a platform way up above the crowd, standing under red lights which hid flaws and sculpted the body in flattering ways. They sent him out in only a thong and silver boots with a stacked heel. That was the outfit he stayed in for the whole night, showing off his goods. He had similar makeup to the other dancers — wide, glittery silver-winged eyeliner painted around his eyes and huge false eyelashes that were also silver, with silvery lip gloss too. Body glitter was dusted over him from head to toe, and he knew it was going to be a bitch to get off later. He thought the makeup looked great, even if the eyelashes did weigh down his eyelids, so it helped boost his confidence in sorely needed ways.

No one got out of control. There weren't any fights. It turned out to be much more fun than he'd expected. It seemed possible he was really starting to figure out a better path for himself.

He hoped so, at least.

When the night ran into the morning, and his shift was ending, Kerry headed backstage. He was sweaty, sore, and out of energy. Dancing for hours-on-end, in heels, was a lot more draining than doing a few shows a night, plus lap-dances in the crowd.

Security guards were stationed at the doorway to the backstage area. Kerry hadn't met them yet, so they were a mostly faceless type of reassuring presence. The guy on the left caught Kerry's eye almost right away as he got a closer look. A startling but distinct physical attraction sent a low tickle down to caress Kerry's balls, tripping him up right away. The guy was big, built, and badass. He looked to be a few years older than Kerry, with thick, black plugs in both earlobes and a thin silver nose ring. He had short, sandy colored hair, a short beard, intelligent dark brown eyes and a ruggedly handsome face. Basically, he was hot as hell.

Though watching gay sex online got him off during uncomfortable dry spells, like the one he was currently experiencing, Kerry wasn't used to being attracted to guys he encountered face-to-face. Most didn't do anything for him, and as far as it went with the ones who did turn him on, it was an instinct he'd conditioned himself to bury. So, as soon as he became aware of his attraction to the guard, Kerry felt hugely embarrassed, and instantly tried to push the feelings down.

In fact, Kerry was so distracted by trying not to react, he forgot to watch his feet in the ridiculous platform boots and tripped over some discarded, wadded up, sweaty clothes.

The hot guard caught Kerry by the arm.

"Careful. You okay?"

"Yeah. Thanks," Kerry answered, feeling his blush spreading and overly aware of the guard's gaze focused right on his near-naked body. There was nowhere to hide and everything was on display. "Been a long night. Not used to these shoes."

The guard's gaze slipped momentarily lower, to places Kerry knew he should be used to people looking, especially after hours of it. Standing so close to someone who was looking down there — maybe measuring the size of his bulge — made Kerry feel profoundly self-conscious, like he was under the spotlight again. Not to perform or please the crowd, only to allow some up-close-and-personal, perverse scrutiny. It embarrassed him and caused him to doubt all of the choices leading him to wear only a thong in public. "You new here? I don't recognize you."

Kerry tried to straighten up and reclaim his arm, but he wobbled again, so the guard held on a little longer. Very much aware of how little of his body was currently not on display, Kerry had no way to disguise any physical reactions that might be provoked. When he continued to find the guard to be unspeakably sexy, Kerry tripped over his words like he'd tripped over the shirt on the floor.

"I-I, uh, yeah. First night. First gay club too, so, uh...."

Cool and calm, the guard smirked, just a little. He didn't look like he smiled easily or often, but preferred to smolder instead, which was honestly just fine with Kerry.

"I'm Ewyn," the guard said. He let go of Kerry's arm and extended a hand to shake with him.

As they shook hands, Kerry tried to decide whether he should say he was Tommy or Kerry. At Savage, he'd always used the stage name, no matter what. His legal name was only connected to him through paperwork locked up in the owner's office. Honesty had become his main, driving goal, though, and the worrisome ways he was attracted to Ewyn tempted Kerry to make a different choice, for once.

As soon as Ewyn had Kerry's hand, easily enfolding it with a firm, impressive grip, Kerry felt Ewyn guide him to the side of the walkway with his other hand bracing Kerry's bare side. The skin-on-skin contact gave Kerry another jolt and he flinched a little at first.

Letting himself be moved, Kerry saw a few other dancers impatiently slip past them, looking more than ready to get changed and get out of there.

"Oh. Thanks. Nice to meet you, Ewyn. Up there I'm Tommy, but I'm really Kerry."

The guard was watching him intensely, with more than just passing interest. It was making Kerry profoundly self-conscious.

11

What was going on there, anyway? He was clearly measuring Kerry up, but for what?

"Kerry. Welcome," Ewyn said. "You seem a little overwhelmed. It does get a little chaotic in here, doesn't it? If you'd like some company for the walk out to your car, I'd be happy to make sure you get there safely."

"Sure," Kerry nodded, smiling awkwardly, biting at his bottom lip. It was strange how the longer he stood there, faced with the impressively confident guard, Kerry felt an odd sense of balance. "That's nice of you to offer. Just give me a minute to get dressed."

Ewyn's gaze slipped downward again, tellingly, over everything Kerry's thong wasn't hiding. A light shiver made Kerry's skin pebble and his nipples stiffen.

"Absolutely. I'll be here."

"Hey," Kerry asked the dancer getting dressed beside him. "You've been here a little while, right?"

"Sure," the guy shrugged. Kerry had caught the dancer chatting with a lot of the staff during the night, his comfort level there apparent. At first, he'd caught Kerry's eye because some of his features reminded him of Jamie, like the shape of his eyes and his height, but the tone of his skin was a deep mahogany, richer that Jamie's. He also had a shaved head and some tattoos, setting him apart even more. "I guess so. A few months."

"You know the guard out there? Ewyn? What's his deal?"

"Oh, him? Good at his job. Pretty reliable. Keeps to himself. I think I heard he used to work for some corporation, doing private security until his brother got beat up at a club. Not this one. That club was a few miles away. It shut down pretty quick. Ewyn started working here to do the good guy thing, protect other kids."

"Oh. Cool," Kerry said, a little surprised. Maybe Ewyn had just been doing the same with Kerry — trying to be friendly to someone looking a little rattled. He paused to think it over, then finished pulling his kilt around his waist so he could pin it. "But does he ever, like, flirt with anyone, or..."

The dancer laughed. "Dude's totally straight, man. If you've got a crush, you best give it up now."

Confused, since he'd gotten definite signals, Kerry asked, "Seriously?"

"Seriously. Used to see his last girlfriend around here, before or after his shift. Fine piece of ass, too."

"Oh. Okay. Thanks." He extended a hand. "I'm Tommy, by the way."

"Jaz," the dancer smiled, shaking with him.

Like so many other things in Kerry's life, it should have been a relief to hear that Ewyn was straight and hadn't been coming onto him. Instead, it only left him feeling strangely disappointed and bewildered. Clearly, Ewyn hadn't been looking him up and down out of interest, but maybe just amazement about Kerry's outfit, seen up close. Were his instincts really that off? If so, what did that say about him?

He told himself he was better off without worrying about the guard's attention. What Kerry needed was more stability, not a wild card guaranteed to cause chaos and distraction.

The thoughts weren't as comforting as he would have liked.

Feeling discouraged and down, Kerry finished dressing and packed up his gear. Tiredness sank into his bones, making him weary and foggy-headed.

Ewyn was waiting out by the exit when Kerry got there. Dancers streamed out, and club patrons lingered, reluctant to end the night just yet.

"Hey," Kerry said in greeting after catching Ewyn's eye. "I think I'll take you up on that offer so I don't get mugged on the way down the block, if that's okay with you. I'm parked over there." Kerry pointed at his beat-up old sedan, barely a speck in the distance.

"No problem," Ewyn said. He looked around as if to ensure the coast was clear. His hand touched Kerry's back again, as it had before. Leaving it there, Ewyn ushered him along.

"You have a thing for watching out for the new guys, or what?" Kerry asked as they walked. The kilt swung with each step, the cool night air blowing up his legs. He'd brought it to wear home, thinking it was dark enough out to be safe and the most comfortable choice given how sweaty and tired he knew he'd be after his shift. If there was any time he was less likely to get hassled for what he was wearing, it was in the middle of the night.

13

"Not really," Ewyn replied. They moved in and out of the amber pools of light cast by the street lamps. "You just looked a little like you were in over your head back there."

"Ouch. That bad, huh?" Kerry winced.

Ewyn held Kerry back, bracing his chest this time as a car sped past, going at least twenty miles per hour over the speed limit. Once the road was clear, Ewyn's hand returned to Kerry's back and they crossed.

"It's not bad," Ewyn explained. "But when you work somewhere like this, and you've got that look about you, it can be dangerous."

"Dangerous how?"

They reached Kerry's car. He turned to face Ewyn, who stepped only slightly into his personal space, but maybe just to stay out of the way of speeding traffic. He gazed down at Kerry curiously, with an unreadable expression.

"Vulnerable people tend to attract predators," Ewyn explained quietly. "I've had... friends... get hurt that way. I don't intend for it to happen again, especially on my watch." It sounded sincere, and like there were painful memories behind the sentiment. Kerry wondered if he was talking about what had happened to his brother, and if he was trying to protect Kerry in a similar way. It would make sense, especially if Kerry was younger, just like Ewyn's brother had been. He could see how, if he looked distracted, someone might try to get one over on him. Living in the roughest part of town for years had taught him as much, if not how to constantly stay on edge like he needed to.

"I can handle myself," he assured Ewyn. "Even if it doesn't look that way. This isn't my first time dancing, just my first time dancing *here*."

A few more cars sped past, and Ewyn shifted even closer to Kerry. It might have been to avoid getting hit. Or not. The coziness of their positions was making Kerry's blush rise again, especially since he was feeling guilty about his attraction to someone who obviously didn't feel the same way.

He became distracted by the ways he was physically drawn to someone so different than any other person he'd ever been with, in any sense. Ewyn was bigger than him, more masculine than him. With his scruff and his piercings, not to mention the handsome face beneath all of that, he was making butterflies flutter in Kerry's stomach. Being attracted to a guy like Ewyn was a reminder of how fucked-up Kerry's instincts were. All his life, those who loved him most had steered him deliberately away from where he felt inclined to go, whether it was his behavior, the way he dressed, or who he liked. Private desire and learned self-doubt clashed inside him. He began to sink back down into the depths of despondency.

While lost in his head, Kerry didn't have the chance to realize how close Ewyn actually was.

Ewyn's hand came to rest on Kerry's hip. The touch was a jolt, causing his breath to catch and tensing his body. As another car zoomed by Ewyn's back, he leaned down a little more. Instinctively, Kerry bent his head slightly to the side and down, hiding his embarrassed expression, feeling Ewyn's warm breath on his neck. There was no instinct telling him to throw off Ewyn's touch. Much to the contrary, Kerry's heart pounded as he froze in place.

He didn't understand. That touch by his hip was a spark of danger, the source of all his problems. But he liked the dangerous thrill he got from feeling it.

Kerry was breathing harder, frowning slightly. He knew he should ask Ewyn to go, so why wasn't he?

"If you can handle yourself so well, why'd you ask me to walk you back here?"

"Because I'm stupid," Kerry murmured. That seemed to be the reason for everything, actually.

Shocking the hell out of Kerry, Ewyn took hold of him by the jaw, tilting his chin up.

Eyes widening, breath coming even quicker, Kerry knew he was way out of his element and unsure of anything. But Ewyn didn't look like he wanted to hurt Kerry. He actually looked concerned.

"You okay?" Ewyn asked.

"It's been a rough couple of years. Sorry. That's not your problem. I guess I'm kind of overwhelmed right now, which probably does make me a target, so thanks for looking out for me. People would be a lot more intimidated by you than me."

"You want me to go?"

"Not really."

As soon as he glanced at Ewyn's lips, wondering what it would be like to kiss them, Ewyn moved, like that was the signal he'd been waiting for.

15

Lynn Kelling

It was the most gradual, slowly advancing kiss Kerry had ever experienced. Ewyn leaned down little by little, giving Kerry every chance to pull away or say no. But Kerry didn't do either of those things. In fact, he leaned in. When their lips did touch, the kiss was soft and light, just a brush of lips against lips. Kerry felt himself start to get hard, right away. A tingling sensation raced out through his body as the distinct ache in his balls only grew.

Gasping soundlessly against Ewyn's mouth, Kerry frowned. He paused to breathe, but didn't pull back. So Ewyn kissed him harder, more firmly. His tongue licked lightly at Kerry's mouth, and Kerry felt the jolt of it shoot right down the center of his body to help stir his cock. Pushing into the kiss, Kerry only wanted more, and he knew it showed.

Ewyn's fingertips were pressed lightly against the side of Kerry's neck, beneath his jaw. It took him a few moments to realize Ewyn was feeling his pulse, which was racing. Gently, Ewyn said, "Easy... If I'm scaring you, I'll stop."

Kerry didn't want to stop. He grabbed hold of Ewyn's shirt.

Wanting to hide from the recklessness of what he was doing, what he was feeling, Kerry turned his face more toward Ewyn as he tried to calm down. He couldn't, though. Not with the warmth on his lips from their kissing. He'd *kissed* Ewyn. It had actually happened.

The fingertips pressed harder at his pulse, measuring it, measuring him. His heart pounded away. He had so many questions.

Do I apologize?

Do I run?

What am I doing?

Ewyn's thumb stroked Kerry's lower lip. Closing his eyes, Kerry felt the rise and fall of his chest, the press of those fingers, the heat of Ewyn's larger, broader body shielding him from the night, trapping him against the car.

"Easy," Ewyn hushed, his lips hovering by Kerry's, not quite touching. That slight space drove Kerry mad, so he chased forward, kissing Ewyn back.

Ewyn broke the kiss first, looking down in a measuring way at Kerry, touching his lower lip again. Kerry's grip on Ewyn's shirt tightened. Slowly, maintaining eye contact, Ewyn came in again, giving Kerry even more time to anticipate it this time. He felt the tip of Ewyn's tongue trace the curve of his lower lip. Kerry moaned.

16

Ewyn's hand followed the curve of Kerry's waist to his lower back, then to his ass. He pulled Kerry's hips flush against his own. Ewyn was as hard as Kerry. He realized it at the same moment as Ewyn slipped his tongue into Kerry's mouth, feeding it to him with a hungry growl.

Pulling hard on Ewyn's shirt with one hand, bracing the other against Ewyn's broad chest, Kerry could only open up to the deep, searching kiss. Head spinning, he let Ewyn tongue him for a while. When he did pull back, he bit gently at Kerry's lower lip. His hand palmed the curve of the underside of Kerry's ass.

For a moment, they paused. Ewyn's eyes closed and a small frown creased his brow, like he was making decisions, choosing what would happen next. Head spinning, body tingling, Kerry could only hold on and ride it out.

"All I want to do right now is slip my hand up this kilt, but I'm not going to. I'm gonna step back, okay?"

Kerry breathed out a sigh filled with relief, regret and anxiousness as Ewyn did as promised, giving Kerry some space.

"I'm sorry," Kerry said. There were still people everywhere. He couldn't help wonder who could see them, or what they thought.

"Why?"

"I'm... really confused. I don't do stuff like this."

"Stuff like what?" Ewyn still seemed concerned more than anything, as if he knew how much Kerry was prone to fucking things up and was trying to swoop in to save him by bringing a secret wet dream to life. Ewyn was a stranger. He had no reason to care, even if he did have something awful happen to his brother.

"Kissing guys," he said sheepishly with a brief upward glance. Self-consciously, he tugged at the kilt, wishing he was wearing something else and afraid his erection was noticeable.

"Really?" Ewyn grinned wickedly, breathing out a faint laugh. "Can I be honest with you, Kerry?"

"Sure. Please."

There was no one else close by. People were clearing out of the club even faster now. The night wrapped around them, its darkness cool and concealing them from everything Kerry didn't want to face.

Ewyn took one step forward. One of his hands clasped the side of Kerry's neck again, the thumb caressing the underside of his chin. It felt nice. Soothing. Steadying. The other reached down low, the back of his knuckles stroking down, deliberately, over the tip of Kerry's hard-on through the wool of the kilt.

"Fuck." Kerry bit hard at his lip, bowing his head when Ewyn only continued, tracing the head of Kerry's dick, blocking them from sight with his body. The longer it went on, the more Kerry wanted, and the more he didn't understand why.

"I like that you don't usually kiss guys. I know the feeling. You want me to back off?"

"No," Kerry answered quietly.

"Hmm?"

"No," he repeated, a little louder.

"Why not?"

Turning toward Ewyn's neck, Kerry tried to swallow a hard moan. The rub of those fingers just felt so dirty, so forbidden, and so good...

"You getting off on it?" Ewyn asked.

Kerry nodded, not trusting his voice. He let his forehead rest against Ewyn's neck. Ewyn's fingers clasped Kerry's cockhead through the kilt, squeezing slightly.

"What were you..." Kerry released a soft moan, the sound breaking. "What were you going to say?"

"Maybe you'll think this is a line. It's not. I don't screw around with guys either. Not since I was a kid. But there's something about you that's fuckin' irresistible. Never seen someone with eyes that color before. I saw you dance tonight. You stood out. Stood out to me, at least. I was glad I had a chance to introduce myself. The ways you move?" The fingers followed his shaft, stroking down it, then back up. He was achingly stiff. "How hard your dick is right now?" He leaned in so close, his lips brushed against Kerry's ear. "Let me make sure you get home okay."

There was nothing Kerry wanted more than to get the damned kilt off and enjoy more of those lazy, exploratory touches until he really did get off on it.

"I shouldn't. I don't even know who you are," Kerry said, trying to fight for sense.

Strangely, Ewyn seemed pleased with the rejection. He held Kerry's gaze, radiating gratitude Kerry didn't understand.

"Okay. I'll let the offer stand. If you're dancing again tomorrow, I'll be here. I'm happy to make sure you get home safe. I'll let it be your call." Amazingly, Ewyn stepped back. "Have a good night, Kerry. Get some rest."

Ewyn turned and walked toward a Harley nearby. When he got to it, he gave Kerry a faint grin from over a shoulder as he reached for his helmet.

"You're really going?" Kerry asked. The quiet of the night was the only reason Ewyn heard him.

"I really am. Take care, all right? Be safe."

Kerry unlocked his car. Ewyn drove off on his bike.

"Holy shit. *Holy shit*," Kerry breathed, gripping the door of his car and trying to calm down.

Chapter 3: Private Show

The next night, Kerry asked more of the dancers about Ewyn. All of them swore he was straight, that he was a reliable guy and good at his job.

Ewyn was there, but on the door instead of in the club, so Kerry didn't see him until it was time to go.

It wasn't really the rough nature of the neighborhood that made Kerry want to ask Ewyn to follow him home, just to make sure he got there okay. Kerry was pretty used to living where he did, and accepted the risks. But there was just something about Ewyn that was as right as it was wrong. Needing to figure it out, Kerry decided to let Ewyn walk him to his car again. He didn't make a move, but he did keep his eyes out for all of the shadows stretching around them. It reminded Kerry a little about the good parts of his childhood, and how the military element lent a sense of safety Kerry had come to miss once it was gone. Maybe Ewyn had served, and that's where those instincts came from.

After Kerry had gotten in behind the wheel of his car, he'd asked Ewyn to follow him to his place, if he didn't mind.

A few minutes later, they were there.

The sight of Ewyn, big as life and twice as hot, walking up to Kerry's car in his side view mirror, was kind of amazing.

Rolling down the window, Kerry said, "I really appreciate you doing this."

"No problem," Ewyn replied. "Happy to help."

"I'm dancing again tomorrow, if you're around."

"Yeah. I'll be there." Ewyn smiled, then glanced warily around Kerry's street. There was a clatter in the alleyway nearby. The shadows seemed to crowd in closer. It was the middle of the night, but there were two people on the porch of Kerry's building, sitting there in the pitch dark. The glow from a dim lamp lit inside one of the first floor apartments suggested the outlines of the figures waiting there. He couldn't make out who they were, if they were tenants or not, but it looked like one of them might have been Victor. "It okay with you if I stick around until I see you're safe inside your place?"

"Of course. Thanks." Kerry gathered his keys, his bag, and got out. The night was warm, the air barely moving. Ewyn held the door, then shut it for him. He kept walking to avoid any public displays of affection, not knowing who might be watching. With a wave, he said, "See you tomorrow."

Ewyn kept scanning the street as Kerry climbed the stairs, then unlocked his door. Kerry gave another wave as Ewyn climbed on his bike and drove away.

The next couple of nights were more of the same. Kerry got lost in dancing, letting go of his worries and cares for a few precious hours. He kept glancing Ewyn's way, seeing him by the front entrance now and then. Ewyn didn't often look directly at Kerry while he was dancing. But, when he did, Kerry felt like he danced even better than usual and had a better time doing it.

Each night, Ewyn offered to walk him out at the end of their shifts. Anticipation for those moments energized Kerry. At the end of the week, he realized he wasn't nearly as tired as he'd been before, so he said to Ewyn, "If you're not doing anything, I wouldn't mind company after you follow me home."

Everything Ewyn seemed to be had held true. And, most importantly, Ewyn hadn't made a move once. He was waiting on Kerry's lead.

"Are you sure?"

Kerry was wearing a different kilt — black instead of evergreen. Ewyn hadn't given any sign that he was put off by them, so it helped Kerry feel more comfortable wearing them around him. Around his parents, Kerry always had to wear the uniform of khakis and polo

21

shirts. With Jamie, Kerry had been pressured in a different way to become the man's man Jamie craved. The whole time, what Kerry personally wanted never seemed to matter. Now, his tentative first steps towards honest self-expression were being witnessed by a man Kerry wanted to impress. It was both a thrill and a terror. He felt the night breeze creeping up his legs, cooling him off. He sensed that Ewyn wanted to touch, but was holding back. Kerry, on the other hand, wasn't sure he had the balls to make the first move. The most he could do was step closer to Ewyn, savoring his body heat and running his thumb down the teeth of the zipper on Ewyn's leather jacket.

"Yeah. I am. Nervous, but sure."

When Kerry stayed close, Ewyn took the hint and clasped Kerry's hip. "Okay then. No pressure, okay? If you change your mind..."

"I won't," Kerry told him, glancing up with a dark sort of hunger. It was the same desire to act out, to do something he knew he shouldn't, that had gotten him in trouble time and time again. Still, he couldn't resist. The temptation Ewyn posed was too great.

It was obscenely late when they reached the apartment, closer to dawn than sunset, so Kerry didn't worry too much about his pain in the ass landlady catching him bringing a guy home. After all of The Hammer's closed-minded, bigoted comments over the past two years, he guessed he'd be out on the street if she ever caught him with what she called, 'a real guy.' Her opinion of Jamie was something they had chosen not to debate, for the sake of having a roof over their heads.

Drained but shaky with apprehension, Kerry led Ewyn upstairs and to his door, fumbling for his key. He'd thought he'd glimpsed Victor on the porch, but it might have just been paranoia making him see things that weren't there. All around was quiet and still. While he unlocked the door, Kerry felt Ewyn gently lift the back of the kilt. He wasn't wearing underwear, since he'd figured he was headed right for a shower anyway.

Cool air brushed his bare ass as it was exposed and Ewyn took a look.

Kerry's cock twitched. He hadn't realized how hot it would be to have a guy like Ewyn make overt sexual advances towards him. It felt extremely taboo, in all the right ways. Everything about letting

Ewyn touch or look at him was a symbolic 'fuck you' to everyone who'd been making Kerry question himself.

Out of his element, heart pounding, thoughts in a whirl, Kerry just went along with it. He didn't push the kilt back down, but just finished unlocking the door, then swung it open.

From directly behind Kerry, Ewyn said, "Even better without the thong, gotta admit. The glitter's a nice touch, too."

Fighting a powerful blush, Kerry stepped into the apartment and flipped the light switch.

"Come in."

The living space in his studio apartment was located at the top of the apartment building's corner turret. The high ceiling reached up into the turret's point, while narrow windows ringed the circular space. The pleasant, almost storybook charm was what had initially driven Kerry to rent the place.

Right away, despite everything and how disjointed his thoughts were, he glanced at the candle on the windowsill. The deeply ingrained obligation was a pull in the core of his body, reminding him of old, familiar responsibilities. Kerry had been breaking so many of his old rules, doing even something small to honor his commitments helped set him at ease.

He shut and locked the door behind them, throwing the bolt, just in case. His guilt was running away with itself.

"Just gimme one second," Kerry said, going for the lighter. He'd set out a fresh candle that morning, painstakingly carving an elaborate script J into the white wax, finding comfort in the ritual. The shavings still lay scattered on the sill. After setting the wick alight, seeing the flame start to dance, Kerry was able to breathe easier.

The light, the hope — it made sense.

"Mood lighting?" Ewyn asked.

"Not so much. It's just something I have to do. Long story." He changed topics quickly. "Look, I really don't do this. I'm coming off a complicated breakup and I've been trying to find myself, I guess. I'm not a one-night stand kind of person, and I've never done more than fool around a little with a guy. I mean, I've wanted to do more, but..."

Ewyn was watching Kerry patiently, and glancing around the small studio to get his bearings.

"Go on," he encouraged. "Sounds like you need to get this off your chest. I've got time. And, for the record, no one said anything about a one-night stand. I don't do those either."

That stopped Kerry short.

"Oh. Okay. Um." He ran his hands through his hair, then set his bag down by the wall. It was a lot lighter now that he didn't need to cart multiple costumes back and forth from work. Blaze provided matching outfits for all its dancers. Feeling frantic and dead-tired at the same time, Kerry tried to remember his manners. "Can I get you something to drink? Or — "

"Just talk to me, Kerry. What's got you so wound up?" Ewyn was standing in the center of the small apartment, just waiting. Everything about his posture and expression was patient and steady. He seemed to be listening intently and entirely present in the moment. It was a nice counterpoint to Kerry's internal uproar.

"Well, full disclosure," he began, squeezing his eyes shut briefly, then just stared at the floor. He hated having to explain things. Words came hard when he had to talk about his life. "I'm twenty years old. My birthday was just a couple of months ago. My ex — we started dating almost two years ago, before he transitioned. He's transgender. Pre-operative, doing hormone therapy now, and had a few surgeries, though not the big one. Sexual reassignment. I don't actually know if he's going to do that one, but it's not my business anymore, so... Yeah. He can pass, even though a lot of people, like my bitchy landlady, still say he's a chick. And I feel really fucking bad about having this, like, fantasy of being with a guy who has all of his equipment, but Jamie's the one who dumped me for not being enough of a man, so I'm working to get over it. Unlike me, he's only into guys. Like, *guy* guys. He wanted someone alpha and hyper-masculine, and figured since I was a military brat, I'd be perfect. Once he found out otherwise, we cared about each other too much to walk away. Before Jamie and I dated, I thought I was straight. Or straight but confused. I thought guys were hot, but being gay was just not an option in my family. Dating Jamie during his whole transitioning process only made me more confused. But I'm on my own now, for once, and I'm doing my best to listen to myself, and make choices for myself instead of other people. Which is why I'm here with you, I guess. Sorry. I don't know if any of that made sense." Kerry blew out a breath and let his head fall back on his shoulders. The words had, surprisingly, come easier than expected.

"Better?" Ewyn asked with only a hint of a grin.

"Yeah, actually. And you're not running out the door, so, good sign, I guess."

Ewyn stepped closer. With one bent finger, he tilted Kerry's chin up again. Looking down at him, Ewyn scrutinized Kerry's expression.

"I'm not running."

Chapter 4: Nowhere to Hide

"You're sweet as hell, you know. It's a big turn on. I'd like to tell you a little more about me, too, if that's okay."

Kerry protested, "I think I should shower first, or — "

"No need. But, will you sit with me? Relax a little. I can tell how tired you are."

"Okay."

"You want me to keep hands off, or can I touch?"

Kerry breathed out a laugh, blushing again. "You can touch," he said softly.

Ewyn brushed Kerry's thigh, his hand skimming up, under the kilt, all the way to his hip. He palmed Kerry's right butt cheek and pulled him forward, walking them both a couple of steps toward the couch. Ewyn seemed to consider, then sat down directly across from the tall, narrow mirror propped on the opposite wall. He pulled Kerry down with him, so that he was straddling Ewyn's thighs, facing him and sitting on his lap.

"This okay?"

"Yeah."

"If I do anything you're not okay with, just tell me. I'm told I'm a great listener." There was a little extra twist to the way Ewyn spoke that Kerry couldn't quite put his finger on. It just made him want to listen closer and distracted from the brazen ways Ewyn kept touching him.

While Kerry's anxiousness cranked up more, though not as much as his lust, Ewyn pulled at the kilt, gathering it up around Kerry's waist. Ewyn shifted his legs apart, spreading Kerry, who leaned forward instinctively. His arm was braced on the back of the couch, his heart pounding again, knocking hard against his ribs.

Kerry's bare ass was completely exposed, and he suspected that the mirror's reflection showed Ewyn everything. Next, Ewyn arranged the front of Kerry's kilt, rolling it back so Kerry's erection curved up, freed and also exposed, his balls hanging heavily.

Simply being naked like that in front of Ewyn was so arousing it made Kerry's dick jump, getting wet as his desire turned a sharp corner, leaving his anxiousness behind. A hard shiver raced through Kerry's body. He had goosebumps. His skin felt too tight, but he loved it, even if he didn't understand why. He writhed a little, equal parts shy and turned on in response to what he was allowing Ewyn to do.

"Very nice," Ewyn praised. He slowly traced the underside of Kerry's dick with a finger, watching it twitch. "Well, I'm twenty-nine. Worked in private security in a few different places since graduating high school and doing some training. I own a small place on Oakwood Drive down in Newport Beach. All my exes are women, but there were a few guys I just had to get my hands on, way back when. Hook-ups, not relationships. Lately, after coming off my own breakup, I just started feeling... curious, again. About men. So I applied at the club. No one's really caught my eye until you, though."

He reached behind Kerry with both hands, palming both cheeks, squeezing, then spreading them. Ewyn watched him, not the mirror, studying Kerry's expression rather than the view of his backside. Kerry was suddenly breathless. There had always been so much hesitancy between him and Jamie after a few disastrous initial attempts. Sex was awkward. Even just fooling around left Kerry suspecting he wasn't giving Jamie what he was really looking for. Jamie wanted sex to be hard, fast and passionate, without any of the careful search for answers that filled the rest of their lives together. Kerry just couldn't get there and be that. He wanted intimacy to be more explorative, lingering, and thorough. The way he craved the ability to yield and submit to another man was something he had regretted for years. Now Ewyn was playing off of that desire in a huge way. He touched, looked, and acted without uncertainty, but wasn't looking to get in and out either. Kerry craved more of Ewyn's persistence.

He leaned forward, resting his head on Ewyn's shoulder, hoping if he gave off signals that he would happily give whatever Ewyn wanted to take, Ewyn *would* take. Meanwhile, Ewyn kept Kerry spread. Had Ewyn's gaze shifted to the mirror, looking down at Kerry's spread cheeks from over his shoulder? After a moment, a pair of fingertips caressed directly over Kerry's hole, teasing it lightly.

Kerry whimpered, just a little. Ewyn hummed in appreciation and rubbed a little more firmly. Shivering, Kerry wanted to writhe or grind against Ewyn's body. He arched his spine more, pushing into the touch of those fingertips. The more Ewyn encouraged Kerry's submissive instincts, the less Kerry was able to hold them back, even though that's all he'd been doing for years. Suddenly, all of his willpower and ability to act differently was gone.

"I like to watch, if you couldn't tell," Ewyn told him. "Big perk of the job, and big part of what I look for with people I'm interested in — man or woman. You're nervous. You want me to stop?"

Kerry was breathing hard and having trouble staying still. Pre-come dripped down his shaft. He rested his left hand on Ewyn's chest and just tried to steady himself. "No."

A single finger touched the center of his knot. "You gonna let me in here?"

Kerry nodded.

"You wanna get fucked? Try taking a cock?"

Again, he nodded. It was safer than trying to speak. The suggestion alone was pushing all of his buttons. Fear couldn't keep up with his aching need to cross some lines.

"No, tell me. Let me hear you. Please." The fingers were pulling at his hole, like they were coaxing it to open up. The terrifying intimacy shattered Kerry's control.

"Yeah." He gasped audibly, frowning and embarrassed beyond belief to have to admit it aloud, though not nearly enough to say no. "I want it."

"That's why the ex left?"

"Part of it."

"Just meant he wasn't a good match for you, right?"

Ewyn's left hand sought Kerry's dick. When he found it, and how wet it was, Kerry hid his face, lips parted, breathing harder.

Ewyn wrapped the shaft with his hand and began to pump it slowly. His right hand kept playing at Kerry's ass, stimulating the skin at his hole, keeping him spread.

Ewyn's lips brushed the shell of Kerry's ear. His teeth scraped lightly, and it was so good, Kerry couldn't help but thrust into Ewyn's hand. After that first push, he couldn't stop moving, circling his hips, riding Ewyn's fingers. "Well, you know what? I can tell how much you like all of this attention. Got the proof sliding in my hand. And I think you like the idea of what I want. That makes us a *great* match."

"You're really... intense." Kerry managed.

"Is that okay?"

Kerry nodded.

"Good. All the little ways you're reacting right now? Playing shy, feeling nervous, giving me cues that you want me to keep touching you, bowing your head, baring your neck... they tell me a lot about you. I like to be in control, Kerry, but I don't think you do. No, I don't think you like being in control at all, and that works just fine for me. I'll take good care of you."

Ewyn spread Kerry's hole with the two fingers of his right hand. It pulled Kerry's attention right to that spot, causing a new flush of heat to rise all over his body, his dick twitching inside Ewyn's grip. Feeling it, Ewyn rubbed over Kerry's cockhead.

"You ever touch yourself? Jerk off?"

"Yeah." He hummed, restless, feeling like he was dancing, giving the ultimate lap dance to someone he had no intention of denying. He couldn't think past that touching, the prying of those fingers and everything he suspected it was leading to. It was making him crazy.

"You finger yourself, too?"

Kerry started to push counter to each tug a little harder, riding Ewyn's hand more obviously. In small circles, Ewyn rubbed Kerry's opening a little harder, seeming to encourage Kerry's rocking thrusts.

"Sometimes."

"You ever take a cock? Or a toy?"

"No."

The tugging got faster. Then, Kerry was shamelessly humping Ewyn's fist, grinding on his lap. He couldn't stop, even knowing what Ewyn could see, or where he was touching.

"That's it. Gorgeous. Just a little more. A little faster."

Kerry moaned and quickened his pace.

Still speaking slowly, taking everything in, Ewyn said, "You can let go with me, Kerry. I'll take care of you. I like safety, and some basic rules to keep things in order, but what gets me off is testing limits and seeing just how far I can get you to go."

Ewyn's thumb swiped over Kerry's tip, soaking wet. Kerry's hips stuttered on their next thrust, his balls drawing up tight.

"I would never hurt you, okay? All I want is to make you feel good."

"Feels a little more complicated than that," Kerry breathed. He bowed his head a little more, feeling Ewyn's scruff against the side of his face.

"It is." He tapped Kerry's hole. "This? The way you're trusting me right now? That's important. I'm just trying to read your cues, and not do more than you're ready for. Like I said, I don't do one-night stands. I'm fine with having some fun, like we're doing now, but I'll warn you before we go further — it won't be enough for me. I like you. I want you. Now that I've had a taste, I want to see where this could lead. Is that all right?"

Kerry nodded, grunting softly as Ewyn continued to fondle and stroke.

"I like to take care of my partners. I want to take care of you, too. You interested or should I excuse myself and take my leave now?"

"*Stay,*" Kerry begged, so close to the edge, just a few more thrusts and he'd tip over.

Suddenly, Ewyn was shifting them. While Kerry was half dazed with his anticipated orgasm, Ewyn quickly brought both of Kerry's arms behind his back. Pinning them there, spreading his knees even more to pull Kerry's ass open even wider, Ewyn forced him to bend even more sharply at the waist. The helplessness of being restrained like that was something he'd never experienced before... but he loved it instantly. The pressure and immobility helped him feel calm, like there was less for him to worry about.

"That's it. Good. Stick out that ass. Stay nice and open now. Show me what ya got."

Moaning, needing to come, Kerry obeyed, pushing his ass out sharply, curving his back, resting his head on Ewyn's shoulder. He felt like he'd do anything Ewyn wanted, just to be able to come, to keep feeling as keyed up as he did. It was a high unlike any he'd felt.

"Good boy. Just a little pressure now."

Ewyn's middle finger pressed, dry, through Kerry's asshole. It happened fast, going into him firmly and up to the hilt.

Kerry grunted, frowning heavily at the pressure. His lips were parted and gasping. The violation of it made him quiver.

"How's that?" Ewyn asked.

A flash of heat washed over Kerry from head to toe. Tension in his chest, clenching inside, then a tingling in his scalp, making his hair stand on end, was chased by another breathy gasp. That finger sheathed in his ass was creating pressure there, burning a little. It made him really bashful. He clenched on the finger and tried to speak past the shock of having a man like Ewyn fingering him. For a few moments, his mouth worked soundlessly, the words not coming.

"Kind of makes me... self-conscious."

"No problem. We can work on that."

Kerry's ass relaxed again as the finger pulled slightly out. The friction made him moan and thrust, humping air.

"You like that?"

It pulled out a little more, then pressed all the way back in and twisted. Kerry thrust again, shuddering. He hid his face and tried to stop panting so hard.

Kerry grunted his assent.

"Can you be clearer for me? I don't like there to be any confusion or misunderstanding."

"*Yes*. I like it."

"Good. Good boy."

Ewyn's thick finger gave Kerry's ass a slow, thorough ride, with deep, complete movements. The longer it went on, and the more he thought about Ewyn watching it all in the mirror and felt how tightly Ewyn held him in place, the more Kerry needed to move. He started pushing back on the finger, humping it. His pushes got more and more pronounced, until he was bouncing on Ewyn's hand, his cock straining, trying to come.

Kerry's soft, rasping cries grew more desperate, and just when he thought he'd never get relief, Ewyn let go of Kerry's arms. Instead, he fisted Kerry's dick, giving it a tight, squeezing tug. Kerry came with a hard, rough cry, keeping his arms behind his back where

Ewyn had left them. Shuddering, leaning his forehead against Ewyn's shoulder, he came slowly down.

Pulling out, Ewyn wrapped his arms around Kerry, hugging his tired form to his chest. Comfortable, spent, held close, Kerry closed his eyes, just for a moment.

He slept for hours.

Chapter 5: Awakening

As Kerry slowly woke, he realized he was in his bed and he wasn't alone. Someone else moved around in the tiny studio apartment, opening drawers in the kitchen, setting something on the stove, each of their steps causing floorboards to creak. It felt familiar, tapping into memories of the old routines of many other sleepy mornings. The weight of loneliness he'd carried for months lifted. Hope sparked.

Had Jamie come back?

In a minute, he thought, *I'll smell the burnt toast and start laughing. Jamie will curse and make some rambling excuses for the horrible cooking, then start laughing with me. He'll come kiss my cheek and say, 'Up and at 'em, soldier,' just to give me a reason to curse back at him and keep laughing.*

Whatever we'd been arguing about will be forgotten.

I'll roll over and catch his scent on the other pillow — equal parts Old Spice, cheap cologne and coconut body wash.

At any moment he'll start singing Three Little Birds, almost too low to hear, but right on key.

The more Kerry woke up, the more he realized it was just a dream.

The glossy bubble of fantasy strained, then popped.

Before things had turned sour between them, it had been truly good. Sweet. Their young, foolish hearts kept them anchored to each other for so long, growing into adults had been a rough process for both of them. Most days, the only one who'd really understood had been Jamie, and for Jamie, Kerry. Details didn't matter when you had someone watching your back and holding your hand.

Morning was when they had their chance to start over, every day. The fights would be forgotten, forgiven. There would be another chance to try and fix things. To open his eyes and see his chances had run out was an awakening he never wanted. But Jamie was really gone. Jamie had been the one to leave, without warning, months ago. The initial pains of being abandoned had faded, in their wake a dull certainty that Kerry was a mess when he was alone. There was nothing to distract him from issues he'd been running from since childhood. Now that he didn't have to face Jamie, he had to face himself.

Fleeting, warm happiness melted away, replaced by a guilty pit of dread and stark confusion about the continued sounds of someone cooking in his kitchen. He lay there for a while without the will to make it to the bathroom and a shower, unwilling to face what would be an awkward encounter. Listening to the percolating coffee pot, the gentle scrape of a spatula over a pan, Kerry's head was slowly filled with the scent of sizzling eggs, not burnt toast.

Jamie was a diehard vegan and couldn't stand the smell of eggs. Kerry had always liked them, though, so a selfish, small thrill warmed him to the trap he'd been caught in.

Ewyn was still there. Kerry couldn't understand why he would be. More than that, he didn't know how to face what they'd done together in the harsh light of morning.

His desire to submit to other men had always been the most shameful part about who he was. Relationships with his mother, stepfather, and three older brothers were strained to the breaking point over that particular facet of Kerry. It had threatened over and over again to ruin his relationship with Jamie, since Kerry couldn't quite let go of his preference for things other than what he was getting. Jamie had always wanted Kerry to take charge and be dominant in ways that had never appealed to him. There had been no room at all for Kerry's desire to be taken and overpowered by a male lover. Meanwhile, Jamie's status as a trans man kept him far from Kerry's family — an arrangement that ensured the comfort of both Jamie and Kerry's family. Each slice of Kerry's life stayed disjointed for years.

Now, there was a man in the kitchen who'd seen him naked, digitally penetrated him and made him come. Kerry knew he'd fucked everything up yet again, getting intimate too quickly with someone he didn't know well. He had a talent for doing things that seemed like great ideas at the time and wound up biting him right in the ass later.

Hiding in bed from his predicament, Kerry's pessimistic side warned that the embarrassing ways he'd behaved with the guy he'd brought home would only destroy the meager scraps of good he had left. How he was going to get out of that bed and look his consequences in the eye was far beyond him. Kerry groaned and turned his face into the pillow.

There was a nudge against the mattress. The intoxicating scent of freshly brewed coffee strengthened.

"Mornin'. Figured you took your coffee black, after looking through your cupboards."

Kerry lifted his head and stared up, wide-eyed, at Ewyn. He was an unlikely sight, dressed in the clothes he'd been wearing the night before, though a slight damp patch hinted they'd been hand-washed in spots. Visions of coming over Ewyn's shirt a few hours back only hurried a flush of embarrassment. At first, Kerry only gazed into Ewyn's dark eyes, which held no overt judgment, coldness, or scorn. They were ringed with long, light brown eyelashes, and it felt like Kerry could just fall into them, as they seemed to welcome his scrutiny so openly. Then his gaze snagged again on the nose ring and dime-sized plugs in Ewyn's earlobes. The impressive size of Ewyn's body was overwhelming, as well as the air of daunting masculinity the likes of which Kerry knew he'd never attain, much to his stepfather's displeasure.

Ewyn was holding out a mug and wearing a subtle grin, hidden beneath his dark blond beard.

"Thanks," Kerry said, sitting up and carefully reaching for the mug. "I appreciate it."

"Careful. It's hot."

"Could you, um, a splash of milk would be perfect if you don't mind grabbing the carton. That's how I usually...."

"Oh, no problem. Coming right up."

Ewyn hurried to the fridge. Something about it made Kerry smile, despite himself.

Lynn Kelling

Returning with the half gallon carton of milk, Ewyn added the requested splash to Kerry's coffee.

"There's egg white omelets if you're hungry. Healthy eater, are we?"

"Yeah, gotta stay in shape if I want to keep dancing. No sugar, no salt, and avoid fatty foods."

"Yeah, my ex was the same way," Ewyn murmured, running a hand through his short hair like the memories unsettled him.

Kerry was staring. He knew it. Couldn't help it.

"What?"

"Sit with me?" Kerry asked.

"Breakfast in bed?"

"Sure. Why not."

Plates in hand, Ewyn returned. He passed one to Kerry before reaching for his own coffee, setting it on the floor by the side of the bed.

"You seem surprised I'm still here," Ewyn observed.

"I am," Kerry admitted. "I can't imagine why you would be."

"I don't do fuck and run. Not my style. Though my persistence and compulsiveness hasn't won me many favors in the past. The last two exes left for those specific qualities, actually. Said I moved too fast and didn't give 'em enough space. Don't be afraid to tell me if it's too much for ya. I'm trying to learn from my mistakes, not repeat 'em over and over again." He caught and held Kerry's wandering gaze. "You're doubting yourself. It's right there in your face. I don't like to be someone's regret either. Just because I've got a dick doesn't mean I'm gonna fuck you over."

Kerry wasn't sure what to say to that, so he took a bite of his omelet. It was good and surprisingly well seasoned, so he said so.

With a thoughtful expression, Ewyn said, "Anyone ever tell you, you have this Liz Taylor thing about you. Like you could be her kid or something? It's in your coloring, I guess. The pale skin, dark hair, violet eyes. I don't think that's it entirely, though. She was so elegant and knew how to make an impression. I think you've got some of that, too."

The words just wouldn't come. There was so much that didn't line up, so much Kerry didn't understand and of which he was terrified. The submissive, feminine aspects of his personality had always turned Jamie off. They drove a wedge between them. The longer

36

they were together, the more Kerry had learned to combat his natural instincts in order to keep the peace. Essentially, he'd tried to figure out who Jamie wanted him to be, then tried to only be that. Now, with Jamie long gone, faced with Ewyn, Kerry began to glimpse the type of lover Ewyn sought in him. If he was to follow his own pattern, and work to become who Ewyn wanted him to be, Kerry was startled by how close that might take him to everything he'd been running away from.

So much about Ewyn made him nervous in dangerous, wonderful ways. It left Kerry afraid to say or do anything, but he had to start somewhere, so he began with an apology. "I'm sorry about last night. You didn't get off. It was selfish of me not to — "

"Hey," Ewyn cut in. "That was my choice, not yours. Like I said, you're worth more than a fuck. I've been listening to you. I know this is new. Scary. If I made you feel good last night, that's all I could ask for."

"But I thought you wanted...." He couldn't finish the sentence. Instead, he chewed at his lip and dropped his gaze.

Luckily, Ewyn understood anyway.

"I do," he said. "But just because I know what I want, doesn't mean I'd ever force myself on you. Okay?"

"Okay," Kerry said, after a thoughtful pause. It hit him then, how very little he knew about his companion, so he tried a question next. "I keep hearing an accent, but I can't place it."

"My parents are both Irish. I grew up in Wicklow until my teens, when we moved to the states. Last name's Garrity. I've tried to lose the brogue, but it sticks with me, just a little."

"It's nice. I like it." He took another bite of breakfast, then asked a tougher question. "Why me? I mean, if you've been working at the club to scope out the guys..."

"That makes me sound like some sort of predator," Ewyn objected.

"Sorry."

"I'm picky. I know what I like and I don't settle for less. Sometimes it gets me in trouble, but other times it works out well. When you're looking for something more lasting than a blowjob, you tend to wait for someone special to come along. I've just been following my instincts. That's all. If you like to cook, you become a chef. If you find it rewarding to protect vulnerable people, you work in security."

It still didn't make sense, not when Kerry took mental inventory of all of the hottest club patrons and dancers he'd seen.

"But you could have anyone. There are a ton of guys you could have approached."

"I could say the same to you, you know, only I guess you wouldn't do the approaching if you could help it. I like you, Kerry. There's a sweetness about you that's very rare to find, in my experience. A sort of delicacy." The brogue was there in that last word, making it ride over hills and swoop into valleys Kerry didn't anticipate. "The way you move, your passion, your body — it's so damned sexy. I've watched you get lost in dancing, just feeling the music and letting it move you. I've seen others watch you dancing, too. You draw them in, whether you know it or not. But I can tell you're someone who needs protecting. It's like when you see a beautiful, exotic flower. You appreciate its loveliness, but know there will always be cruel people out there who will want to crush it, just because they can. That's what moves me — standing in the way of anyone with those kinds of instincts."

"Because of your brother," Kerry said softly.

Ewyn sighed. "Yeah. I know rumors go around at the club. That's a story for another day. Bad memories."

"All right."

"It's true though. My brother opened my eyes, showed me there's risk in waiting and hoping you'll get another day after this one. Sometimes in order to do right by yourself, you have to take a chance and act, even if you look like a fool. I don't tend to question my instincts. They've served me well, even if they've left me lonely at times."

"Then I guess we're opposite that way," Kerry said, "because I question all of my instincts. I can be terrible at resisting strong impulses. Always have. It's landed me in trouble plenty of times. I'm still learning how to take chances in smarter ways. It's not as easy as it seems. But I'm glad I took the chance with you."

"So am I."

Chapter 6: Laid Bare

They both fell quiet, just eating their breakfasts. Some of the street noise filtered in, unwanted — horns, yelling, the thumping of a trashcan's lid from nearby and distant bangs.

"Are you dancing today?"

"Yes." Kerry glanced toward the closet, where his running shoes and workout gear were stashed. Sitting with Ewyn was disrupting Kerry's routine in more ways than one. Going without exercise caused an itch under his skin and a restlessness in his bones. The benefits were mental and emotional as well as physical, tempering his anxiety and stress, and boosting his mood. Speaking to that, he said conversationally, "I need to get in my morning workout."

Ewyn nodded, then thumbed at the metal pole bolted nearby. "I saw the bar. Bathroom doorway." Kerry had installed it himself. "You do pull-ups?"

It was a welcome change of topic. So much so that Kerry smiled despite himself, and surrendered to a fleeting sort of want for wickedness. It was part of his innate love of doing what he probably shouldn't, which had led to so many unlikely detours, like his dancing, and Jamie. If there was something off-limits, something impossible, Kerry would want to have it, just out of spite. Instead of awkward conversation, showing off for Ewyn had much more appeal.

"Why, you don't think I could?" Kerry countered.

He set aside his plate and mug, climbing out of bed still wearing the kilt and t-shirt he'd worn home from the club. The bathroom doorway was only a few steps away. Grabbing the bar bolted within the doorframe above head-level, he easily pulled himself up with one arm.

Dropping back down, he saw with a quick glance that Ewyn was watching. There was heat in his eyes.

There was a full beat before Ewyn said anything.

"I'm impressed." Ewyn took a bite of his omelet, drank some coffee. "I can't stay much longer. Got a job to get to."

"But the club doesn't open for hours."

"Not the club. I do private security, too. Got a client contract for this afternoon."

"Oh." Kerry hesitated, watching Ewyn eat while sitting on Kerry's bed, breathing his air, charging the room's energy and causing so many different reactions. "I really desperately need a shower. You mind if I take one while you eat?"

Ewyn set down his plate, then his cup. Slowly, he stood, eyeing Kerry up and down. That lingering look sent a tickling thrill twisting through Kerry's stomach. He stood still while Ewyn approached, and Kerry knew why without needing to be told.

"Not at all. As long as you get undressed out here." Heat rose quickly to the surface of Kerry's skin. Ewyn was right there, close enough to touch. "I need to see you. Didn't get to enjoy the whole picture last night and now I can't think of anything else, honestly." When Kerry stayed silent, Ewyn added, "Is that okay?"

"You just want to look?"

"To start. But if we come up against a boundary, just tell me."

"Okay."

Ewyn began helping Kerry lift his shirt.

"Why dancing, though? You seem so shy."

Kerry's shirt was pulled off. He let it fall, sucking in his stomach as Ewyn's bent index finger skimmed down over Kerry's left pectoral muscle to his nipple, then down the center line of his abdomen, across his six-pack. It was nothing like undressing for customers. Kerry knew there was no out. No safety net. There was only this intimidating, sexual man exploring all of his senses, and none of Kerry's doubts were speaking up to stop him.

"Guess I have my exhibitionist side," he admitted, his voice fluttering softly. "For so long, I was told I couldn't do this, be this, so it feels good to give in."

"Mmm," Ewyn grinned. "A little rebel, are we?"

"Guess so," Kerry admitted, reaching for his kilt's buckle. While he worked it open, Ewyn tugged on Kerry's nipple. It sent a bolt of heat straight to Kerry's dick, which instantly made him nervous of being obviously erect by the time he was nude.

Kerry's hands faltered when he began questioning his motivation for giving in. Was he only rebelling? Or did he actually want what Ewyn offered, for his own sake?

The answers wouldn't come, but his gut told him to give in and see where it would take him, tempting him with the possibility of clarity if he crossed a few more lines.

He knew how to put on a show, and part of him wanted to tease as he stripped. It would be easy to do it. The instincts were there. But his more personal, private side was too self-conscious to dream of doing so for a lover he barely knew, and especially for someone as intimidating as Ewyn.

The outcome of his inner struggle was a slow build into the tease. Unfastening the kilt, Kerry inched it down instead of letting it fall. As the wool slipped lower, showing more and more, Ewyn twisted Kerry's nipple, causing Kerry's eyes to flutter closed. His lips parted on a sigh.

"That's it. Nice and slow," Ewyn said, his voice deep and rich.

Very gradually, Kerry peeled off the kilt, helplessly wearing his anxiousness right on the surface. All of the ways he tried not to give in to these particularly *homosexual* instincts screamed at him, a formless raging no one else could hear. The child he used to be and still was, deep down inside, was afraid, expecting punishment.

The kilt fell, leaving him without any way to hide. He wanted to cover his groin with his hands, but Ewyn moved to touch before Kerry could.

"May I look at you for a moment?" Ewyn asked. He caressed down Kerry's side, then around to cup his balls. His thumb brushed up the underside of Kerry's swelling cock, which stirred quickly with the attention.

Jolted with nerves, Kerry nodded in answer. He didn't trust himself to speak.

"Widen your stance. Stand straight. Lace your fingers behind your head."

The commands helped him calm down, giving him something to focus on, other than his doubts. At home, in the upper-middle class gated community in Fallbrook, in a household run by a Marine strictly raising four young men — future soldiers in his eyes — there'd been commands too. Kerry had developed the instinct to obey without hesitation.

He got in the position, eyes closed tightly after he noticed how Ewyn had begun to walk in a circle around Kerry, taking in the view from every angle. It felt like one of his old, dirty fantasies of some hot young Marine giving him orders.

The touching stopped, but it didn't matter. Knowing Ewyn was there, seeing him, his arousal and his nervousness, was a heady experience.

Soon, Kerry was completely erect, just from knowing Ewyn was there, wanting him. All of Kerry's private, filthy fantasies of getting butt-fucked by a big, domineering man only fed his lust. Between the pair of them there were two perfect puzzle pieces. Ewyn's strong, commanding desire to dominate Kerry in every way imaginable was countered by Kerry's quiet need to trust someone absolutely, and give himself over to be cared for. The particular way those two conflicting needs fit together was startling.

For how long had he fantasized about this? An alpha male like Ewyn, wanting not only to fuck him, but willing to tend to other needs, too, if only Kerry would swear to be loyal and obey.

But what did that mean, really? Being expected to obey could become a nightmare depending on the person delivering orders.

Nervous caution was no match for Kerry's lust. His dick strained upward, a manifestation of all of his discomfort.

When something brushed the sensitive skin of the tip, Kerry made a soft, plaintive sigh.

"I like this, seeing how hot you get from being watched, imagining what I want to do to you. You do know what I want to do to you, don't you?"

Ewyn's thumb slowly traced the crown's ridge. It was almost impossible to stay still, to not make a single sound.

"Funny how, with some of my ex-girlfriends, they didn't like to be touched unless they were really in the mood for it, you know? Their preferences were more distinct than mine, so it didn't work. But there's just something about a cock that begs to be played with. And I can see *exactly* how much you're in the mood for more."

42

For a long moment, they stayed just like that, with Ewyn so gently stroking, and Kerry coming more and more unraveled, just wanting it *not* to stop. Wetness slicked the end of his cock, making him even more embarrassed at the state he was in.

"What do you want?"

"More," Kerry answered honestly, on a gasp.

"What else?"

"I want to see you, too."

"See what I'm packing, you mean?" Ewyn asked with amusement. "Since, sooner than later, I'll be packing it into you?"

Kerry bit back a moan. Ewyn rubbed through the fluid gathered at Kerry's slit, as if he was letting Kerry know he was aware of what that muffled moan meant.

"Eyes open."

The touching stopped again. Ewyn had stepped back.

Avidly, still holding the position Ewyn had ordered him into, Kerry watched Ewyn open his fly, sliding the zipper down. Before he showed any more, Ewyn pulled his shirt over his head. Kerry's breath caught at the sheer size of him — the muscle mass of Ewyn's chest and arms. His nipples were pierced, his chest hair plentiful and blond. His pectoral muscles flexed as he reached again for his fly, parting it. He inched the pants down, then pulled the waistband of his boxers below his erection. Cradling it in a hand, he began to stroke himself.

A subtle shiver raced through Kerry's body and his next exhale left him sharply. Staring at how thick, flushed, and long Ewyn's cock was, Kerry clenched up at the thought of being made to take it. A gleaming silver piercing was fed through the head, and another through the skin of Ewyn's scrotum.

"Well, you're not running, so I'll take that as a good sign," Ewyn teased, wearing a crooked, faint grin. He began to walk around behind Kerry again.

His breath quickening and roughening, Kerry felt Ewyn press up against his back, fitting his thick cock between Kerry's butt cheeks. Kerry moaned, desperately, though the word *stop* was right on the tip of his tongue.

"Such an amazing fucking ass on you, boy."

43

Lynn Kelling

He caressed the sides of Kerry's ass, then around to his hips while thrusting shallowly through his crack. His thickness was spreading Kerry. It was obscene. It was irresistible.

Kerry cried out softly at a flood of realization. He bowed his head, gasping as Ewyn's hand found Kerry's cock. Fondling it, Ewyn gave Kerry some time to adjust to their positions as if he could tell just how rattled Kerry was.

"How's that feel?" Ewyn asked patiently.

Breathing even harder, tempted to thrust but overwhelmed with bashfulness, Kerry wasn't certain how to answer. It was too hard to deal with the tempest of shame battling excitement. When Ewyn pressed harder against him, then tugged more sharply, and tenderly kissed the side of Kerry's neck, some of Kerry's walls came down.

"Please," Kerry begged.

"Please what?" When Kerry couldn't answer, Ewyn said in a whisper by his ear, "It's okay to like it, a *mhuirnín*."

Instantly, literally, the soft tumble of the Gaelic endearment moved him. Kerry broke out of the pose in which he'd been frozen. He reached back to touch Ewyn's hair, arching into the next shallow thrust, loving the forbidden friction of the cock riding his ass crack. He undulated into the next long, tight stroke of his dick and offered his neck for more kisses that trailed up to below his ear.

He sighed, shivered.

"Gorgeous," Ewyn said, playing Kerry so easily, it was just as scary as anything else. "God, I want you."

"Ewyn," Kerry breathed, his voice breaking.

"Turn and grab the edge of the doorway."

Kerry did it instantly, and Ewyn followed right along, barely breaking contact as Kerry braced himself against the doorframe, ass out, feet planted widely, back curved. Ewyn fit perfectly there, better than Kerry could have dreamed. As soon as Ewyn touched Kerry's dick, Kerry began to ride Ewyn's fingers. Circling his hips, rubbing back against Ewyn's thick cock, Kerry moved, letting Ewyn guide him. He rocked forward to chase the grip of Ewyn's hand. Ewyn's thrusts got sharper, quicker. He steadied Kerry with a tight hold of his hip and was grinding against his ass. Ewyn's cock felt so thick, warm, stiff; both wrong and right.

Kerry was on the edge, gasping roughly, quivering on each down-stroke.

44

But then he felt how it was too easy, too sweet. All of those times he'd given it hard for another's sake, he'd wanted the tables turned. Now was his chance to finally have that.

If he really wanted it, he had to ask.

"Give it harder," he rasped. "Don't be gentle."

Ewyn stopped stroking him, grabbed hold of his balls instead, and pulled down on them.

Kerry cried out, straining against the pressure, feeling more acutely the wet slide of Ewyn's dick between his spread cheeks. He clenched around it, moaning.

It was good, but it wasn't quite enough. The temptation to over think, to analyze and doubt was there, creeping closer. He needed to shock his system and get lost in the moment in less tender ways.

"S-spank me?" Kerry stammered. "Please?"

Ewyn growled. The slap of his open hand drove a gasp from Kerry. His cock jumped in delight. The hand pulling on his balls pulled even harder, forcing Kerry to bend over more to try to relieve the pressure as cramps formed low in his belly. Ewyn kneaded Kerry's thickly muscled ass, then slapped it again.

"Fuck yes," Kerry panted. He clenched, grunting, hanging his head, trembling. Ewyn's thrusts riding him were quick, hard, and dirty.

Another slap. Again, even harder, and again. The whole side of Kerry's ass stung and he stayed clenched. Ewyn gasped as he came. Hot come splashed over Kerry's lower back, then dripped downward.

Chest heaving, feeling frantic as he feared the sensations would begin to soften too soon, Kerry managed to grunt, "Don't stop."

He cried out as Ewyn's thumb pressed hard to enter him, sheathing in his ass.

"Beautiful. Good boy," Ewyn praised with an audible grin. Fireworks exploded in Kerry's nerve endings, from his head to his toes.

Ewyn rolled Kerry's balls, squeezing gently, keeping him deeply impaled on the thumb. He'd barely grazed Kerry's tip with his palm as Kerry shot, quivering with orgasm and making rough, primal sounds.

It took a long time for him to come down from the high he'd achieved. While catching his breath, Kerry savored the gentle caress of Ewyn's hand, and the decadent feel of his light kiss below Kerry's ear. Ewyn took hold of Kerry's face, turning it slightly to the side and kissing him. Ewyn's lips were warm, soft. Kerry made a hungry, faltering whimper, frowning against the pressure of the thumb pumping shallowly inside the clenched muscle of his sphincter.

Ewyn bit at Kerry's lip and pulled out to rub his rim before plunging back inside. Another shiver shot all the way down to Kerry's toes.

"Say I can have you." He caressed the frowning pout of Kerry's lips. "You're safe with me. I promise."

Kerry hesitated, then looked over his shoulder to study the man who'd already gotten inside him in ways no one else had. It would be so easy to give in to the ingrained instincts telling Kerry what he was doing was wrong. That he was just trying to hurt others by doing something shocking. The pressure, the ache, the twinge of humiliation and reluctance to trust so completely so soon... it twisted him up.

Ewyn pulled out, caressed Kerry's tensed, throbbing rim, then pressed back inside like he needed to be there, was desperate to be there. "You're safe."

After a heavy exhale, Kerry surrendered. "Okay," he said. "Yes."

Ewyn moaned with need, licking into Kerry's mouth and kissing him deeply for a long time.

Chapter 7: Loss' Lesson

Ewyn unlocked his front door and punched in the code on the keypad inside the doorway to deactivate his home security alarm. He'd never had a break-in, and his neighborhood was a nice one, but 'better safe than sorry'   had been his personal motto ever since he was a scrappy kid dodging fistfights in the back alleys of Wicklow. He shrugged off his holster on the way to the single story, cottage-sized home's second bedroom. Walking through the room's maze of exercise equipment, he slipped the gun safe's key from around his neck. With it, he unlocked the cabinet and set his holster inside, along with his Glock. Unloading the rest of his gear — the knife strapped to his ankle, as well as the one on his belt — he thought about how the years since he'd traded in one country for another had only heightened his certainty that paranoia was sometimes warranted.

A natural tendency to attract danger didn't make him fear for his own safety as much as that of others. Most of the people he cared about didn't share his pessimistic outlook, but fear could be a good motivator when trying to avoid tragedy. When other, bigger kids began to pick fights with him when he was a boy he'd learned to fight back, just to scare them off long enough to get away. If he saw the bullies picking on smaller kids, he'd step in and try to help. As a teenager, he'd developed a fondness for weapons, martial arts, physical fitness, and basically anything that enhanced his ability to feel more in control of any given situation.

Exploring power dynamics in sexual and romantic relationships had been an extension of the same passion. It just wasn't in him to lay back and give over control to his partners, though he never instigated anything without complete trust, respect, and consent that ran both ways. He was always 'on', always looking out, and derived much more pleasure in doing for others than having things done for him. His most persistent fantasies involved exploring the vulnerability in beautiful, sensual mates.

He knew what worked for him, but he'd struggled to find a match with someone looking to totally let go. Because he'd never push someone to violate their own clearly drawn personal boundaries, he usually found out quickly if a relationship was going to work or not. It left him going through girlfriends at an alarming speed, draining his hope of ever finding the right person. The longer relationships he'd enjoyed had ended for one reason in all cases — deep down, they'd expected him to loosen up eventually. They had enjoyed all of the caretaking Ewyn provided for a while, but then it became tedious, his mannerisms too close to being paranoid. They began asking him to lighten up, to break his own rules for the thrill of it, to change basic qualities of the way his life was structured. While he had no interest in changing a lover to suit his needs, he also knew he wouldn't change either.

It left him lonely and dispirited.

Ewyn had learned a lot from his friend Trevor about creating safety and control in sex and romance, though he didn't have the interest in following through with a strict BDSM lifestyle. The kink didn't draw him as much as the order and sense of it all. Unlike his tutor, who practiced for profit as well as pleasure, Ewyn had only been looking to enhance his ability to enjoy a richer relationship with lovers of a more submissive temperament.

His most recent and successful relationship had lasted two years with a woman named Isla, who was at the time studying to be a doctor. The only time Isla had been able to truly relax was during sex. Then, Ewyn had assumed full responsibility for her pleasure, asking only for trust in return. But when Isla got a promising internship at a hospital three hours away, she'd relocated without warning Ewyn. His first clue she was leaving had been the suitcase in her grip being wheeled out of the house, and the car driven by her father parked in the driveway. The relationship suddenly was over. Ewyn had truly cared for her, but he understood her motivation to prioritize her career, even if he hadn't initially understood why she hadn't trusted him with forewarning. It was only later, after much reflection and pestering from his mother that he saw how his determination to safeguard their relationship had robbed Isla of comfort in standing up to him. She hadn't thought Ewyn would let her go easily.

It had been a massive wake-up call, instigating much self-reflection and drive to recommit to a deeper kind of trust with his lovers in the future where listening and clear communication came first.

Ewyn locked the cabinet again, then lingered, his gaze catching on the large home gym that took up most of the space, and in particular the padded bench. He couldn't help picturing Kerry there. Ewyn's place offered a whole lot more than just a pull-up bar mounted in a doorway. Shirtless, sweating, muscles aching, breathless from a few reps with the dumbbells, he'd be beautiful.

Kerry.

Almost as soon as Ewyn had first laid eyes on him, he'd felt an eerie, unsettling tickle in the pit of his stomach. That feeling felt like a warning, drawing him to Kerry, or else.

Ewyn's pessimism and training had honed his ability to sense trouble. It was what kept him gainfully employed and useful to his clients. So far, he'd never lost anyone on the job.

The same wasn't true of his personal life.

There, he knew fate was against him.

Watching Kerry up on that stage, next to naked, seducing the whole damn room with a slight twist of his hips, a hint of a heated glance or an upward tilt of a grin — it had made Ewyn's heart leap into his throat. It was fear, not lust that had driven him at first.

Ewyn had been working at Blaze for a while. Countless men of all ages and temperaments flooded the place night after night. Kerry had stood out in a big way, but it was hard to say why. Sure, he was beautiful in a somewhat androgynous, but intensely sexualized, way. He was a great dancer, but that wasn't it either. Mainly, it was a feeling, a sense that the bravado Kerry wore onstage was as thin as gauze. Underneath, he was so emotionally exposed, craving comfort, acceptance, and companionship, Ewyn was certain something bad was on its way, lured to snuff out a soul so innately sweet-hearted.

"A *mhuirnín*, Kerry," he murmured. The endearment, Gaelic for sweetheart, honored both Kerry's innate fragility and Ewyn's stark fear for him.

The fear never went away, but that wasn't the problem. What plagued Ewyn was his inability to find a comfortable balance with his control mechanisms. Something was always getting away from him, and people kept getting hurt.

"Fucked in the head, eh, Darcy?" he said, leaving the small bedroom behind.

Maybe it was Darcy's fault. Seeing his dear baby brother lying under a plastic sheet, a bloodstain spread over the pavement below him, the dark pool seeping outward past the sheet's reach — it had hit Ewyn brutally hard. In one moment, all of his lifelong paranoia had been proven correct. There were monsters. There were victims, and the hero didn't always save the day.

Ewyn walked to the kitchen, wanting a swig of bourbon but settling for coffee instead. He scooped some grounds into a filter, trying not to remember the musical sound of his brother's laughter, or the magic of his dimpled, careless smile as he danced just out of reach.

Darcy had been good. There was nothing cruel in him, nothing jagged or tough. He'd been an artist, a dancer. He loved color and life, poetry and the sound of raindrops tapping on the roof. He'd brushed things off instead of worrying about them like his too-serious older brother. Paintings he'd done in bits and pieces over the course of years covered the walls of his apartment, much to the distress of his landlord, though more so to Ewyn and his mother, who weren't able to save those treasures once Darcy was gone. Darcy would go to clubs every night, dancing until dawn. He was incredibly embarrassed by flattery and would have eagerly gone to the ends of the earth, climbing mountains and swimming oceans, all for the sake of his family.

He'd lived only twenty-five years.

In Ewyn's mind, his imagination, he heard a gunshot cutting through all ambient, joyous noise spilling from the club, cutting through Darcy as well.

He might have lived if they'd just driven off, but they stopped, kicking and stomping Darcy while he was down before finally leaving him to die.

A hate crime. It sounded so cut and dried, to label it in so few words.

But Darcy had been a beautiful spirit, the light of Ewyn's life, and now he was gone forever because of a stranger's blind hatred for someone they didn't even know.

The little lights on the coffee pot's display blurred, smearing.

Ewyn groaned, wiping a hand angrily over his face.

He knew sometimes his worry wasn't warranted, and that he tended to take on too much blame when things beyond his control went wrong, but he also knew it was bad Kerry reminded him of Darcy. Ewyn had learned there were all sorts of people in the world. Some were thorny, with hard shells and rot underneath. Some were soft as flowers, easily crushed, quick to wilt and fade if denied sunlight long enough.

Ewyn hated that he could see so much of Kerry's vulnerability because it meant others would be able to see it as well. Kerry wasn't safe. Ewyn didn't think it was paranoia telling him so, but real insight.

It was clear Ewyn had been given a choice. Kerry had been placed in his path. There had to be a reason. It was his chance, perhaps, to right a wrong, to safeguard someone in danger and be there as he hadn't been able to for his brother.

Maybe it's all shite. Maybe bad things will always happen to good people, no matter what.

He didn't want to believe it. He'd never forgive himself for sitting back and doing nothing. Following instinct had driven almost everyone from him so far, leaving Ewyn isolated and questioning his choices, but he had to take the chance one more time for Kerry's sake.

The coffee percolated, dripping into the pot, and Ewyn pictured Kerry. Those strange violet eyes, ringed with thick, black, curled eyelashes. The sad pout of his lips, the tousle of his inky black hair against porcelain skin, a body carved from marble by a master, and just a hint, in every gesture, every glance, that Kerry had already been hurt. In some ways, Ewyn was too late. He didn't know why, or what had happened, but he knew. Someone Kerry trusted had scarred him, badly. It had left a psychological wound, a timidity, so Kerry always second-guessed himself, fearing more hurt, suspecting it was unavoidable.

It was rare, in Ewyn's experience, to find beautiful men who thought so little of themselves.

Who hurt you, boy?

He needed to know, to understand, so he could develop the appropriate strategy of protection. No one else was there for Kerry. He seemed entirely alone, devoid of basic support. Even if Kerry decided to keep Ewyn at arm's length, maybe there were still ways to watch out for him as a friend.

In Kerry's past there was pain. Ewyn had no doubt at all. But Ewyn also had no doubt that, unlike with Darcy, it wasn't too late for Kerry. There was still hope.

Ewyn had seen it, felt it, in the way Kerry had clung to him, lips pressed to Ewyn's shoulder, letting himself be spread and seen. Even in those first moments together, there had been trust. It had come so quickly.

Kerry had the makings of an exquisite lover. Ewyn felt the yearning in him for simple tenderness and honest praise. There was a void in Kerry, starved for attention, and it had hypnotized Ewyn, drawing him in. Even if it took everything he had and more, it would be worth it to see Kerry smile.

Scrolling to Kerry's number, already saved in Ewyn's contact list, he selected it and pressed the green button to make the call.

A moment later, Kerry's unusually hushed, soothing voice, which always sounded as if a volume dial inside him had been turned way down, asked, "Ewyn?"

Most of the men and women Ewyn worked with in security had powerful, commanding ways of speaking. The subtle lure of that constant quietness only worked to pull Ewyn in, making him want to press the phone closer, or seek Kerry out in person.

"Ya go on shift at nine?"

He heard a soft, rolling chuckle. "Your accent's stronger on the phone."

"Been reminiscing, I'm afraid. That always does it." He cleared his throat, tried again. "Is this better?"

"I like the accent," Kerry protested, with all the ferocity of a kitten batting at a scrap of yarn.

In a couple hours, Kerry would be nearly naked again, oiled and writhing under lights for a roomful of horny, drunk strangers. The thought of that drove Ewyn mad. Yet, he knew he had no right to object to Kerry's chosen profession.

"Is that all you like?" Ewyn teased.

"Mm. I think you already know the answer."

"Christ, boy. Yer killing me already and ya've barely said a word." It had been a long time since anyone had managed to drive Ewyn as crazy so quickly. He was almost completely hard, gripping the phone, cursing their circumstances. "I'm on at eleven. I'd like to make sure you get home okay, even if it's just to follow ya on my bike. Dancers have been targeted before, thieves wanting the cash they carry from tips. I'd feel better about it if — "

"I've been dancing for over a year," Kerry put in. "I'm not as naïve as I seem, you know. But if you're asking to see me later, then yes. I'd like that."

"Good." He paused, then tried to read between Kerry's lines, asking, "You don't regret anything, now you've had a few hours to think it over?"

"Not regret, but... guilt, maybe. I mean, I know I want this. I've wanted this for years, but just because it's right to me doesn't mean it's not wrong to everyone else."

"Someone's been getting in your head," Ewyn guessed, getting angry. "Telling you there's something wrong with you for wanting other men."

Kerry sighed. "It's not one someone. It's just how it is. But something you need to know about me, Ewyn, is that just because instinct tells me I'm wrong, doesn't mean I'm going to let it stop me. Honesty is important to me, so I'm just letting you know. There's a lot that scares me — you, me, what we did, what I still want to do, what I think we might do once we're alone again — it's an endless list."

"I'm not scared. You might say it's my job to not be scared, so just try to trust me, okay? Whatever you can't handle, I will."

Liar. You are scared. Everything about that boy scares you, in one way or another.

"Why do you care about this? About helping me? We only spent one night together, and most of that you spent sleeping on my couch. Just help me understand here?"

"You need someone to care. I like to be needed. You felt safe with me, didn't you?"

"I did," Kerry admitted, though he sounded embarrassed to do so.

He fell asleep in your arms. That had to count for something, too.

"Do ya trust me?"

"I shouldn't, but yeah, I do."

"Then stop doubting yourself so damned much."

"Not that easy," Kerry said, trying to laugh it off, sounding frustrated.

"Save me a dance later?"

"How about a private one?"

"Perfect."

They ended the call. Ewyn stared at the phone, trying not to get ahead of himself, to over-plan, over-anticipate, but all he could think of, all he wanted, was Kerry.

Chapter 8: Defensive Maneuvers

Slowing to a jog, Kerry pulled out his phone. It was buzzing like crazy. Breathing hard, wiping the back of his hand over his sweaty forehead, he debated answering. Curiosity, and a desire to react maturely, prompted him to do it. He pressed the button to pick up the call.

"Thank you for answering. I know you probably just wanna be done with me."

Where there used to be heartache, Kerry found there was mostly calm acceptance. Maybe part of that was due to Ewyn helping him take a chance and test himself, or maybe that wasn't it at all.

"I don't blame you for bailing," he told Jamie. "Wish you would have given me a chance to respond or ask you to wait until the lease was up, but it's over. I get it. I just didn't think we'd be able to stay friends, which sucked the most, to be honest. I thought we'd always at least be that. But I'm not who you expect me to be, and that's not going to change."

"I'm sorry it ended the way it did, okay? After I left, I couldn't believe it had really happened, like I'd watched it instead of done it, but it was too late to go back. Maybe it was my pride talking, but I just needed to own it. I know it hurt you, and I know it wasn't fair."

"Nothing's ever fair. We both know that."

"Yeah," Jamie quietly agreed. "Look, I, I need you to know, it wasn't even about you, Kerr. I was angry, and frustrated, and those names I called you were the first stupid things I could think of. It was fuckin' mean, and I just need you to know I know. No one should ever tear you down like that. Especially not someone who's supposed to be your support. Whatever makes you happy makes me happy, too. I feel so bad, Kerr."

"It happened," Kerry said, speaking at a measured, lazy pace. "It's done. But I'm good, and I hope you are too. I worry, you know." He laughed a little. "Of course you know. I always did the worrying for both of us. Who's going to watch your back now? Keep you from saying the first stupid thing you think of to the wrong person? Not everyone in this world is as understanding."

"Yeah, and you worry too much. Living in a bubble isn't going to save you. It'll only hold you back from living your life. The whole reason I'm here right now is because I didn't let anything hold me back. Nothing and no one. We've gotta believe in ourselves first. I own my mistakes, but I can't live in fear of making more."

"Just promise me you'll be smart. That you'll take care of yourself? Please?" Kerry asked. "I'm serious."

There was no one else near him on the path in the park he'd driven to for his run. He was thankful for the relative privacy. A few hundred feet ahead was a woman on a bike getting farther away by the second, but besides her they were the only ones around.

"You kiddin'? I'm smart as hell," Jamie said. "Quick as a whip. Stronger than steel."

"Where are you living now? With a guy from the gym? I know you're not back with your mom. You wouldn't do that to yourself just to get away from me."

"A guy," Jamie echoed. "Right. You're right. I am. He's a friend."

Kerry shook his head, gazing up at the bright blue sky streaked with wispy clouds. "And yet, here you are, calling me. Go hang out with your new guy, Jamie. I hope he makes you happier than I did. I really do."

"I still care about you. I always will."

"I'm trying to move on," he said adamantly.

"What's that mean? You're already with someone new? Who are they?"

They. Neutral pronoun. So Jamie knew, at least subconsciously, that Kerry might wind up swinging back the other way now that Jamie had given the push. Plus, now Kerry finally didn't have family peering over his shoulder to judge his choices. Hard-won freedom had its perks.

He never would have been able to make the step of dating a man if not for Jamie. The chance to be with someone as alive and confident as Jamie, who naturally, effortlessly broke barriers that had always scared Kerry shitless, had opened up the whole world to him. Jamie had taught him to listen to himself, no matter what he might hear if he tried. He'd shown Kerry that gender wasn't something the world could impose upon him if he didn't want it to. He'd proven that anything was possible if you wanted it badly enough.

Jamie's presence in Kerry's life had been a blessing and a miracle he never would have wanted to do without, but their relationship had run its course. They both knew being together had begun to hurt more than it helped.

"Someone careful, and kind, and almost as fearless as you," Kerry said, not without tenderness. "I forgive you, Jamie. We just want different things, and that's okay. Love you."

He hung up and finished his run.

Once he was back at his apartment with the door bolted, his ass planted on the floor and his back against the side of the bed, Kerry made another call. He dialed his slightly older brother Kent. They were two of four. Kurt and Kipp were the oldest, in that order. Both were Marines like their stepfather. They had absolutely nothing in common with Kerry besides their initials. Following orders, respecting the chain of command, and driven by an unshakable sense of duty, they questioned nothing and had always seemed satisfied with the way things were. Kent was another story. He worked for a tech company in Silicon Beach, raking in enough money to afford not only a sprawling house of his own, but a vacation property, too, out in scenic Sedona, Arizona. He wasn't as uptight as Kurt and Kipp and, out of everyone, he was the most determined not to give up on their eccentric, screwed-up baby brother.

"Hey. Knew I owed you a call, so I just wanted to let you know I'm doing better now."

"You sound better," Kent replied.

"Good. I, um. I quit the job, like we talked about. I have a new one. It pays better. There's good security, and I'm happier there. It's not permanent, but it's a big improvement."

"That's great," his brother said, sounding relieved. "I'm really glad. And my offer still stands if you change your mind. I can cover any costs you can't, and I can set you up with an interview at my company, even if it is super lame and unexciting. Just promise me one thing, okay?"

"What?"

"Figure out a goal. Just one. At least one. And go for it. Don't get bogged down in where you are now. There are so many other places you could go."

"Okay. I can do that."

Kent sounded concerned, like he always did. Kerry was quite familiar with that concern. It had dragged him to therapy, paid for by his parents who hadn't known what to do or how to help. Kerry struggled to accept love from people who only knew him through the lies and pretending that had defined him since fear drove his truths deep within. It wasn't self-indulgence or naiveté but pure survival. If he let those truths slip out, he suspected his family's concerned love would pull quickly and permanently away.

It was their idea of him that they loved, not the reality. The more he let them help, the further he felt from where he needed to be. He knew he needed to stop letting others define him. Distance was making a difference, even if it left him wandering alone.

"Thanks for checking in. I love you, little bro. Let's do coffee soon."

"We will. Soon. Thanks, Kent. Love you too."

Steam covered part of the mirror, clouding the view of the bathroom around him. The clean skin of his face seemed too bland, lacking the definition and drama it had when he was in costume getting ready to dance. Without letting himself think much about what he was doing, Kerry found some dark eyeliner in his duffel bag and used it to outline his eyes. Next, he applied some black lipstick before using a tissue to rub most of it off.

There was only a trace of stain left on his lips. He smudged the eyeliner so it was smoky on his eyelids. He wrapped a powder-blue towel around his hips.

For a long time, Kerry just stood there, looking at himself in the mirror. Shifting his stance, he brought his legs closer together. His shoulders rolled back a little, the tension drained from his body.

Rearranging the towel, he unfocused his eyes, letting the image linger without detail, pretending the fabric wasn't terrycloth.

Maybe, if he was thinner, less muscular, it wouldn't look so off. Because it did. The image wasn't right.

The blue laid beautifully on his naturally pale skin. The darkness of his inky black hair stood out. His violet eyes added softness.

Something was wrong with him. His parents, his brothers, and Jamie had always said so. They'd all been right. There it was, standing self-conscious and desperate in the mirror's reflection.

But what would fix it?

He glanced around the empty apartment, then at the closed, locked front door, and finally at the windows, covered in curtains. No one else was there to judge. He was alone. For once, there was no one to impress or satisfy other than himself. That freedom to be introspective was terrifying. With a squirm of nervousness down low in his gut, he drew the towel higher, across his chest. Heart pounding, he pulled it tight and pinned down the edges under his arms, then drew in the middle to nip in by his waist. Tilting his head to the side, turning slightly sideways, he indulged for just a moment. No one had to know.

He thought of Destiny, of Ashley — some of the friends he'd made while attending a local transgender support group with Jamie. The sewing skills he'd picked up after having to make his own costumes for Savage Men had led Kerry to offer discreet tailoring or dressmaking services to those in need in the support group. Sometimes he tried on the things he made for friends, and not just to check the hems and fit.

He thought of Dmitri, aka Dima, who was Kerry's closest friend and who refused to dress solely in men's clothes or conform to gender norms. Dima had recently ordered a dress from Kerry, designed by them both, which Kerry still needed to find both the time and the courage to make. Every time he started to work on the dress, he wound up sketching things he wanted to make, and not for a client. Each sketch took Kerry one step closer to a revelation he wasn't ready to confront, so he'd left his friend hanging, making lame excuses for the delay.

He didn't know why something that seemed so natural in those he knew felt so dangerous. Twisting the other way, Kerry pushed out his chest, sucked in his stomach, and tipped up the curve of his ass.

Studying the image, his vision sharpened, and he saw it clearly. There he was — no gauzy daydream — just a broad-shouldered former military brat who hadn't been man enough to satisfy his lover, pretending his old, fraying towel was a fucking dress.

Jamie would have been shocked.

Kerry's family would have been disgusted or furious.

His friends would have been worried.

Ewyn would likely have been scared away.

Dropping the towel, Kerry slung it over his shoulder and bowed his head, trying to control his racing heart, to calm down. Averting his gaze from the mirror, he dropped the towel and grabbed a bar of soap to wash his face.

After his shift was finally over, Kerry's legs ached. He was exhausted and wanted to not have to stand up for days. The light sheen of sweat all over his body made him extra self-conscious. When Ewyn leaned in for a chaste kiss by Blaze's exit, Kerry dodged it at first, saying he needed a shower and to brush his teeth.

Ewyn just grunted, looking down his nose at Kerry's fidgeting, then kissed him anyway. One of the other dancers wolf-whistled at them.

As Ewyn followed Kerry to his apartment, Kerry thought about how being in his own place definitely helped give him confidence in testing his own boundaries. He was able to be more self-assured in familiar surroundings, where he knew what worked and what didn't. It was home. Still, it was far from perfect.

They pulled up and parked a few yards down from the building. The cloudy, oppressive night meant there was hardly any moonlight. The air was thick. Streetlights cast dim, eerie amber light on the sidewalks, but darkness crowded in on all sides. In the blackness, shadows moved.

"Oh, this was a bad idea," Kerry groaned, shutting off his car and palming the keys. Something told him to suggest they go someplace else, but where? Not only would it be rude to invite himself over to Ewyn's instead, but doing so required more brazenness than he suspected he possessed. It was already the middle of the night. Going over would mean staying until morning, with all that it implied.

Ewyn knocked on Kerry's window. With a tense sigh, Kerry got out of the car and shifted a step out of Ewyn's reach, just in case of onlookers.

"What's wrong?" Ewyn asked, frowning.

Kerry just glanced around, willing his eyes to adjust, feeling observed in ways that set him on edge, all of his body hair standing on end.

"Let's just, um," he cleared his throat and jumped a little at a sound to their right, where it was pitch black. "Let's just get inside, okay?"

There were people on the porch. Kerry walked as quickly as he could without breaking into a full run, sensing Ewyn right at his back. The nearness of him only pushed Kerry to go faster, not wanting it to seem like Ewyn was anything other than a friend.

He was nearly at the foot of the stairs when a tall, dark shape moved to block his path. He stopped short and felt Ewyn do the same.

"Hey, check this out! He's wearing a skirt. A fucking skirt!"

"It's a kilt," Kerry retorted, too softly. The voice was Victor's. There was a click as a flashlight turned on, shining right in Kerry's face, then sweeping down his body. From the porch, there was low, masculine laughter from several voices.

When the light shined on his bare legs, dusted with glitter, someone on the porch said, "Look at him! He's a fucking fairy."

"Do we have a problem, here?" Ewyn called out loudly, with authority.

The light shifted to Ewyn instead. Kerry glanced over and saw Ewyn's hand palming something from his belt.

"Nah, man. No problem," Victor chuckled.

Ewyn moved closer to Kerry. "Let me get you out of here," he said under his breath.

"This is my home, Ewyn. I just want to get inside. It's fine."

Kerry moved to the steps, going around Victor, who stepped back as he got closer. Kerry took the stairs quickly, jogging to the top, hearing the chasing echo of Ewyn's steps behind him.

"Hey, Sanderson! Is your boyfriend staying over again? You know I can have you evicted for that, right?" Victor called from below, the flashlight's beam searching for them on the stairs. From the porch, there was more insidious laughter.

A deep voice added, "Evicted? That's what we're calling it now? You think he screams like a bitch, too? Should we check? I think we should check."

Kerry was at the top. Key in hand, he moved to unlock the door, hand trembling, heart pounding. It wasn't the first time something like that had happened. At least there was less worry about Victor and his friends getting the jump on Ewyn the way they always tried to do with Jamie, whose smaller, slighter build endangered him more than his training as a boxer helped. At least Jamie hadn't gotten into the habit of stopping by, now that they'd split. He was better off far away from that place. Kerry knew he could take care of himself, but being responsible for the unpredictable actions of others and their consequences made him panic.

Ewyn grabbed his arm, spoke in his ear. "I can't let you stay here."

"Yes, you can," Kerry argued. "And I'm sorry, but I think it's best that you leave. If you stay…"

"I know. They're watching. Kerry, this isn't safe. I'd never forgive myself if something happened."

"I've lived here for two years. I'll be fine. They're just trying to scare me. It's what they do. They're idiots. They hang out down there because of the landlord's kid, Victor. I've been through this with him before."

"But the landlord would have a copy of your key. You're not safe. Please — "

"I'll bolt the door from the inside. I always do. No one will get in. Promise."

He looked up into the shadows of Ewyn's face, wondering what it would have shown if he could see. He was used to people worrying about his living arrangements. His many arguments on the subject with Kent had taught Kerry how to stand his ground.

The tension between them charged the quiet moment.

"Okay, get inside. Bolt the door. Hell, push a piece of furniture against it if you can."

"I will. I'll call you after I shower, okay? Let you know I'm fine. I'm sorry."

"Just be careful, all right?"

"I will. Thanks, Ewyn."

Ewyn let go. Kerry unlocked the door, went inside and gave Ewyn a smile through the doorway before closing the door again and engaging all of the bolts. Then he pushed the couch in front of it for good measure, just in case Ewyn was listening from outside.

Kerry sat on the edge of the bed and waited a while, but there were no other sounds from the staircase. Once he was satisfied, he went to get his shower, then ate a simple meal of leftover salad. After that, he gave Ewyn a quick call.

"Hey. I'm still fine. I'm heading to bed. You don't have to worry."

In a hushed voice, Ewyn replied, "I'd like you to stay at my place tomorrow night, just for my own peace of mind. Would you consider it? There's only one bed, but there's a couch, too. I'd just like a chance to spend time with you without having to worry about a repeat incident like tonight."

There was a long pause as Kerry thought it over. He was tempted, but what would it say about him if he agreed? He would be proving to Ewyn that he couldn't take care of himself, that he was nothing but a hassle and a mess. He'd also be opening himself up to even more intimacy with someone who had already proven he knew how to take what he wanted.

"Would you think I'm a whore if I said I was interested?"

"You're a virgin, not a whore."

Kerry breathed out a surprised laugh and blushed, his pale skin shifting pink, heating up.

"Tomorrow, I'll take the couch, okay? No pressure. Just want to see you safe. Wish I was there, so I could kiss you," Ewyn admitted even more quietly. Kerry could barely hear him. Wind blew against the phone. Maybe he was outside his home, standing by his bike. Kerry pictured it easily, and found himself yearning to be there with him.

"Me too."

"There's nothing wrong with what you want, if it makes you happy. Okay?"

"Okay," he replied reluctantly.

"Bring some extra clothes. Not that you'll need them."

"Said the voyeur to the exhibitionist." Kerry smiled.

"Oh, Kerry," Ewyn groaned. "Sleep well."

"You too. See you tomorrow."

Ewyn hung up and slipped the phone back into his pocket. Farther up on the staircase, he saw the light through Kerry's window switch off, the apartment going dark.

Switchblade in hand, Ewyn made himself comfortable on the step he sat on, and waited.

Below, on the lawn, dark figures moved around, their voices too low to carry up to him. He knew they could see him, sitting there.

He liked it that way.

There wouldn't be any sleep for him that night, but at least he could feel confident no one would get the chance to hurt Kerry. Over Ewyn's dead body would he drive home and leave Kerry's fate to chance with monsters circling, hungry, in the dark below him.

Some people needed protecting. It was Ewyn's job to step up and protect those in need. It didn't necessarily mean he was falling back into old habits. He was doing what needed to be done.

Two flights below, a tall male form paused near the bottom of the steps, peering up his way. The razor-sharp blade in Ewyn's hand spun in slow circles. He was calm. Ready.

A moment later, the lanky shadow moved away, then vanished by the porch.

Wordlessly, Ewyn dared them to try and catch him off-guard, but hours passed, peacefully.

Chapter 9: Questionable Choices

Sitting at his sewing machine in the corner of his studio apartment, Kerry slipped the last pin out of the shift's hem. He stuck it between his lips with a few others and carefully fed the folded cotton edge through. The sunlight there at his sewing table was golden, streaming through flimsy curtains on tall windows. The curtains didn't give much privacy — not that he needed much anyway, being three stories off the ground — but they did help obscure the metal bars on the windows, allowing Kerry to pretend he was anywhere else other than where he really was. The cathedral ceiling was one of the best features of his modest home, leading the eye up away from disappointing reality of being stuck down on the ground. It also lent a deceiving sense of space.

A bang shook him, far away but not nearly far enough.

"Backfiring car," he told himself. "Or maybe fireworks."

He knew better, but the lies helped him put it out of his mind. A few minutes later, sirens could be heard a few streets away.

A chill in the morning's air made him shiver. It slipped in around the old windows and beneath the door leading out to the stairs. Kerry was only wearing boxers, but as soon as he trimmed the thread connecting his creation to the sewing machine, he quickly straightened the shift and held it up.

He'd made one already for Ryan, a friend from the trans group Kerry had been introduced to thanks to his relationship with Jamie. Kerry tried it on himself as he worked to check the fit and length. Then, without thinking about it much, he made a second one with the extra material.

It was knee length, slate grey, with a wide belt to wrap the hips. He slipped it on and stood in front of the tall, framed, and narrow mirror propped against the wall to his left. After checking the evenness of the bottom hem, he tied the belt. The gray looked good against his ivory skin. The shoulder straps hung nicely from his muscular shoulders. The sides of the shift barely skimmed his thighs. Wearing it, he felt comfortable, as if he could move and breathe after being bound too tight for years.

He checked the mirror again.

Boots. It needed boots.

He would have liked something slimmer and simpler, but his footwear selection was limited, containing mainly pieces of his costumes, and all of his costumes were designed to appeal to straight women, who were an audience he didn't necessarily dress for in private moments. Plus, buying the shoes he had in mind would have taken a spurt of the particular sort of courage he didn't have quite yet. He found his knee-high black combat boots and sat to fasten all of the buckles.

For once, Kerry didn't feel like he was wearing a costume. Even if no one else understood, at least he knew he wasn't lying or pretending. That was his main issue with working at Savage Men. Every night, he had women of all ages and types throwing themselves at him, shoving money down his shorts or grabbing at his exposed flesh simply because of the false ways he was marketing his body to them.

When he was younger, wearing slacks and button-down shirts with polished shoes, combing his hair just so and keeping it short — it had all been to see that tight nod and smile of approval from his parents. It didn't matter that the collar choked him, or that he thought the haircut looked ugly, or that he felt like he was playacting instead of being.

At the club, all of those unknown women slipping dirty, sweaty bills in his thong made him feel like a sellout and a fake. The truth was he felt no desire for them in return. He was only there for cold, hard cash. Seeing their lust for his body didn't make him feel good; it only brought shame and more confusion. Their camaraderie didn't include him. It pushed him away. It isolated him further. They weren't his people and he didn't belong with them. He was only something painted and dressed to please, to do only what was expected and what he was told, to shut up, perform and go away before they saw his exhaustion and unease.

He was tired of feeling excluded. He was fed up with doing things only for the approval of everyone but himself.

Things were better at Blaze, but they weren't perfect. Being surrounded only by other men didn't help as much as he'd hoped with combating the feeling of disjointedness that followed him constantly. Now, he felt more included, but he still didn't quite fit. The problem wasn't Blaze. He saw that now. It was him.

The problem was on the inside. The dress helped, but it was only clothing. It was surface decoration, not a solution with any depth at all. Plus, he couldn't even leave the house wearing it, or let anyone see him dressed in such a way.

It was too dangerous.

The voice of his stepfather whispered in his ear, warning that he was being foolish, that he needed to snap out of it and be a man, or else. It didn't carry the weight of threat it once had. Though Michael was technically a stepfather, he was the only father figure Kerry had. His biological dad, Kurt Sr., had left when Kerry was a baby, full of the same impractical sorts of dreams Kerry had — or so his mother told him. Maybe someday Kerry would go searching for Kurt Sr., but in the meantime, he had more than enough of everything else to figure out first.

Ignoring learned instincts and heeding others that came from deeper places had gotten Kerry out of a job he'd grown to hate, and had earned him closeness with Ewyn. No one had to know what he did inside his own home. Today was the first day of the rest of his life, and he was trying to use it in the most authentic ways possible, even if it meant doing so initially in private.

Once he'd finished with the boots, he stood scrutinizing his reflection, trying to understand it. Each time he stood in that spot at the mirror, faced with himself, there was always a duality — inside and out. Did they match? Did it matter? There were always so many layers. It was difficult to know what was right or wrong anymore. No matter what he did, he knew he'd be upsetting someone. So far, he'd been more concerned about *not* upsetting others. But, that morning, that day, for possibly the first time, he tried to only listen to instinct. Reaching down into his gut, he realized he felt relieved.

Kerry had a muscular, masculine body, and he was wearing a dress. Some of his friends, his family, society — they wouldn't have understood. He could see himself the way they would have. He could see the way the pieces didn't seem to fit.

Yet, he felt a strange peace with the way he made his own picture for once instead of theirs.

He finally wasn't pretending — he just was.

Maybe he was a monster. A disappointment. A freak and a lost cause. But at least that knot in his stomach had loosened a little.

At least he could look at himself without feeling ashamed of how much he was lying. Without hating himself.

Studying himself, Kerry thought his skin looked too pale. He thought of how he put on stage makeup each night, and how doing so brought out his features. Those moments at the mirror, wearing costumes he'd made by hand, using his imagination as he painted up his face, had been some of the best parts of his days, without fail. The club, the other dancers, the questions and responsibilities all faded back and he was just happy.

Wanting to own that same kind of happiness again, he reached for the eyeliner from the plastic case he kept his stage makeup in.

Pulling off the plastic cap, he stepped closer to the mirror. Widening his violet eyes, swirled with a touch of blue, he outlined them with the black pencil.

Satisfied, sighing, he set the pencil down and ran a hand through his short, black hair. It always managed to look windblown even when he'd been hiding away inside for days.

"What the fuck's wrong with me?" he asked himself, his gentle whisper of a voice vibrating the air.

Just trying to get the outside to match the inside, his desires whispered back.

But what was on the inside anyway? He didn't always know how to interpret the confusion he felt. Nausea was a faint tickle, trying to stir his hard-won sense of comfort and taint it.

Old reflexes, he thought, trying to dismiss them. The boy he'd been wanted to go cower in the corner, hands over his head, begging for forgiveness for wearing the wrong things — things boys weren't supposed to wear.

He'd been trying to change himself for so long; he wasn't sure how to stop now.

The scissors were right there. He stared at them, knowing he could cut up the shift, tear it to ribbons. It would be easy. The fabric was so soft, yielding. Denial had been one of his biggest coping mechanisms for a long time.

"I can't do it anymore," he murmured. The words were pulled from his core; past all the ways he'd tried to please everyone else for so many years.

The shift wasn't completely right. The picture was off, but he didn't know why or how to fix it.

Not for the first time, he admired Jamie's decisiveness, how he'd managed to do the same thing Kerry was attempting — looking for truth in the mirror — and see through all the bullshit clouding the picture.

Eyes wide, pulse racing, nothing certain, Kerry pulled up to a small, well-maintained, single-level house. It was tan with white trim and a large window overlooking the front lawn. Ivy climbed one corner of the house and a giant palm tree soared into the air behind the property. Neatly sculpted hedges lined the front of the house to the side of the off-center front door. There was a one-car garage and a small driveway with a curving path that led to the home's entrance. Cameras were mounted on both sides of the house, with another by the door.

Security. No big surprise.

Ewyn pulled up close to the garage door, then waved Kerry in to park behind the bike in the driveway.

Kerry cut the engine.

He was about to go inside Ewyn's house — Ewyn who was... what? Potential boyfriend? Actual boyfriend? — and Kerry was doubting himself even more.

Michael had been in his head in a big way lately, not like he'd been since Kerry was a teenager.

Resting his forehead on the backs of his hands which wrapped the top of the steering wheel, Kerry muttered, "I'm so fucked up."

There was a knock on the window's glass.

"What are you doing?" Ewyn asked Kerry.

"Doubting myself," he answered, too quietly for Ewyn to hear through the closed door. Ewyn looked so big, so masculine, standing

Lynn Kelling

there in his motorcycle jacket, with his piercings, his feet planted widely, and his eyes as alert as ever, like he never stopped watching for threats, even at home, which Kerry guessed might be true.

Am I really doing this? Am I really going to let this guy fuck me? Make me his bitch?

The conflicting sides of his personality warred over the idea. The part of him that was his stepfather's son was horrified at the notion and wanted to throw it in reverse, to drive all the way back to his childhood home and apologize to his parents for everything before starting over completely. The rest of him that was only Kerry was frozen, held still by all of the confidence and strength he saw in Ewyn. There were no bigger turn-ons than those two qualities. Ewyn was the first person he'd been close to who wasn't asking Kerry to be anything other than himself. If anything, Ewyn asked only for Kerry to let go of all of his confusion and fear, to follow his own instincts for once and stop pretending. It was dangerous. The biggest temptation of all.

Ewyn was patient. Finally, Kerry unlocked the door. Ewyn opened it.

"Lemme guess," Ewyn said. "You just realized you let a guy take you home?"

"Something like that. Sorry."

Holding out a hand, Ewyn pulled a reluctant Kerry from the driver's seat. They stood facing each other in the middle of the night, crickets chirped all around them.

"Okay, I'm making a rule. Our very first one," Ewyn said, with a flicker of good humor in his tone. He caressed back over Kerry's cheekbone, into his hair. "No apologizing. Ever. Especially not for the way you feel."

Closing his eyes, enjoying the warm touch of Ewyn's hand, Kerry hummed and replied, "I still like the accent." With effort, he raised his gaze, looking Ewyn in the eye. "That's gonna be a hard rule for me to follow."

"I can tell. We'll work on it."

"Okay."

Ewyn took Kerry's hand, weaving their fingers together. Chewing at his lip, Kerry looked down at the sight of that with a little wonder, and started to smile despite himself. Quickly kissing Kerry's cheek, Ewyn tugged his arm. "Come on. I'll show you around the place."

70

Chapter 10: Taken In

After unlocking the door, one-handed, Ewyn stepped inside, his gaze sweeping from right to left. Kerry followed along. Ewyn punched a code into a small box by the door. It reminded him of Michael. He'd had a security system installed on their old house, too.

For just a second, his worst memory became real again.

His arm was pulled so hard it dislocated at his shoulder as he was dragged out of the car. The pain was monstrous. Michael's knuckles connected with the bones of Kerry's face as he was backhanded hard enough to knock him onto the wet grass. Michael stepped closer, drawing back his foot and spitting, "You're sick! I'll beat the faggot out of you, god help me!" then —

There was a tug at Kerry's arm.

"Come on," Ewyn said, turning on a light by a switch on the wall. He caught sight of Kerry's expression. "Everything okay?"

"Sure," Kerry lied. "Cute place."

He tried to shut down the memories, but every step he took, every second he kept letting Ewyn hold his hand felt like he was just giving Michael more reason to dish it out. There had only been a handful of bad episodes, and always after Michael had returned from a stressful tour of duty. They would happen when most of the other boys were out with friends, or busy with their mom. After Michael would go off on his youngest stepson, he'd be wildly apologetic and kind. The first time, he denied what had happened to Kerry's mother, Debra, and Kerry went along with it, making excuses for his injuries. Eventually, Debra realized the truth, shortly before Kerry's brothers had done the same. Debra threatened to kick

71

Lynn Kelling

Michael out for good. He'd go to therapy for a while, explain it was his problem, not Kerry's. Things would improve for long stretches of time. Kerry's brothers would watch out for him, keeping a wary eye on Michael. For the most part, it worked. But most wasn't all. Michael's last blow-up had been a doozy. He'd beaten Kerry so badly, he'd blacked out. Michael had been forced to move out for a few months until he'd proven himself again and recommitted to therapy. He'd never touched Kerry in anger again. Still, the things he'd said, the things he'd done — they lingered.

"It does the job," Ewyn said, taking them forward into what seemed to be a living room to their right. It had a big screen TV, furniture in neutral white and beige tones and a few framed paintings on the walls that looked like they might be depictions of Ireland, with green rolling hills and dramatic, overcast skies. They kept walking.

"And here's the kitchen," he explained. There was a table and chairs barely big enough for four, with granite countertops and stainless steel appliances. Everything was immaculate.

"Wow. So much nicer than mine," Kerry said, thinking of his crappy little kitchenette with its old two burner cook top and mini-fridge.

The tour continued through a doorway and into a short hall with three doors.

Pushing the closest door open and flicking the switch, Ewyn said, "Bathroom. Just the one." Two steps forward took them to the next door. It opened to a bedroom. "And here's where I see if you're gonna be bolting for your car or not," Ewyn said uncertainly. He left Kerry's side while he went to turn on a couple of lamps.

There were mirrors everywhere — behind the bed, next to the bed, above the bed. The way they were placed appeared to expand the space in all directions, multiplying their reflections, and gave Kerry a little bit of vertigo.

"It's not a vanity thing," Ewyn explained. "Like I said, I like to watch. It's also hard for anyone to sneak up on me this way."

The bed was queen-sized, with a low, wooden headboard with vertical rungs and a matching footboard. The colors of the space were dark with cloudy blues, dark floorboards, and dark wood furniture.

Kerry stared at the mirrors, his body feeling a lot warmer all of a sudden. Swallowing hard, he stayed still as Ewyn stepped up close into his personal space. His hand skimmed the side of Kerry's thigh, over the wool of the gray kilt he wore. One hand clasped Kerry's hip, his thumb moving over the top of the bone in a smooth arc.

He guided Kerry backward, slowly, until his back was to the wall. In the mirror behind the bed, he saw himself. Ewyn brought both of Kerry's arms up above his head, guiding his wrists together. Holding Kerry's wrists in one hand, Ewyn slipped the other up his kilt.

Kerry whimpered as soon as Ewyn's fingers grazed Kerry's dick, palming and lifting his balls. He could see all of it happening in the mirror, watching as he let himself be fondled and held down. The indulgent voyeurism of it was making him hard, fast.

Ewyn scraped his teeth over the edge of Kerry's jaw when Kerry tipped his head back, resting it against the wall, his hips tilting into the fondling touches between his legs.

"Shower," Kerry protested. "I need — "

"I remember." Gazing down Kerry's body, Ewyn lifted the front of the kilt and tucked it into the pinned-tight waist to keep it raised. With the toe of his boot, he nudged Kerry's feet into a wider stance, then just watched as Kerry gazed at their reflection. The back of Ewyn's index finger stroked up and down the underside of Kerry's dick as it swelled and rose.

"You're not bolting," Ewyn noticed. "I take that as a good sign. But this is a lot for you, isn't it?"

Kerry exhaled heavily, frowning against how hard he'd become, so fast. It made him want to squirm, having his perverted lust so exposed and undeniable. To have Ewyn want him so much that he'd spread and pin him there, just to watch, just to play with and get off with — it sounded too good to be true.

Faggot, Michael whispered in his ear.

"There's a lot I haven't done."

"Like take a cock?"

"Yeah. Like that."

Ewyn watched his hand work, tracing Kerry's reddened cockhead with his thumb. His gaze flicked up to Kerry's eyes, then down again as he said, "It's okay to like it. This wouldn't work if you didn't, would it?" He took hold of Kerry's cock from above and wrenched it down. Kerry cried out a hard moan, tilting his hips to try to relieve the pressure. Ewyn whispered, "It's fucking hot how hard I make you."

Kerry tried to take a deep breath, blowing it out across his lips. Ewyn's hand idly slid up and down Kerry's cock, catching fluid at the tip and slicking the way for the next pass. Squeezing it, he caught Kerry's next whimper with a kiss, taking it deep and giving Kerry his tongue.

Ewyn then broke the kiss and shifted to pin Kerry's arms against the wall with both hands, looking deep into his eyes. Kerry kept glancing past Ewyn's face to the mirror. He could feel how obscenely erect he was, and how close he was to begging for more.

"One more room to see. Then we talk. But first, you'll shower."

The command worked on Kerry's weaknesses. He tried to thrust, to rub off on Ewyn's hard body, but it was too far away.

"You like that? Being told what to do?"

Ewyn started to back off, to let go, so Kerry pleaded, "Don't go."

"I'm not done with you," Ewyn promised, trying to caress away Kerry's frown, running the pad of his thumb over his lower lip and then kissing him. "Got no plans to be done with you."

Ewyn untucked the front of the kilt, letting it fall back into place and giving Kerry back his privacy.

Kerry rested a hand on Ewyn's broad chest, another on his hip. The kilt was tented now over his hard-on. Rolling his eyes at himself, he tried not to show he was ashamed and upset.

Ewyn tugged on the hem, slid his hand down the side of the kilt, and asked, "Who hurt you, Kerry?"

Kerry shook his head.

"I can see your pain," Ewyn persisted. He tugged again at the kilt, and when Kerry didn't answer, asked, "I've never seen you in pants. Does it help? Wearing this?"

Debating his answer, Kerry wound up nodding, admitting, "I don't know why. My family doesn't like it. Jamie didn't like it. He —"

"I like it," Ewyn interjected. "Suits you. And I like you."

"I like you too," Kerry murmured, his chest feeling tight and more dangerous emotions chasing up on him. He tried to push them down and fight them back the way he'd been trained to do since he was a small boy. It wouldn't work. They wouldn't go. Not all the way, at least, which just caused his panic to spike.

Ewyn gathered Kerry up in a hug, which Kerry returned forcefully, grabbing hold of Ewyn tightly. After a long moment, he let out a breath and felt steadier. Ewyn caressed down Kerry's spine repeatedly, smoothing his shirt to his back.

"Does it bother you when I call you 'boy'?"

The question startled Kerry enough for him to break out of the hug. Was it a joke? A jab? But then he saw that Ewyn's expression was serious, waiting, searching. Kerry opened his mouth to speak, then shut it again when no words came out.

The whimper that slipped free instead shocked him.

Ewyn took Kerry's face in both hands and kissed his forehead before pulling him back to his chest again. Kerry couldn't breathe. Panic strangled him, and the more he tried to show nothing, feel nothing, the more it got away from him. The only thing that helped was how Ewyn was holding him in the hug, like he was physically holding him together.

"I'm sorry," Kerry mumbled.

"Don't," Ewyn growled. Kerry hid his face against Ewyn's neck and let out a choked cry full of all of his confused struggles to deny everything he feared he really was. "Don't you dare apologize." After a moment, he narrowed his inquiry, but did so gently, tenderly. "Do you feel like you're not a boy? Not male?"

The questions loomed huge between them, around them, and in Kerry's mind. His anxiety ratcheted higher with those words hanging in the air. He answered honestly, the words hurled from him to chase encroaching danger away.

"I don't know. I don't know! I don't know! I don't — "

"It's okay. It's okay, love," Ewyn repeated, kissing his cheek and cradling the back of Kerry's head.

Kerry stood in the hall, hugging himself with one arm and biting the end of his thumb. His lovely lavender eyes were wide with alarm and exhaustion. Already, now that Ewyn was really looking, and especially because of the light gray kilt that hung from Kerry's narrow hips, he could see it. How Kerry had edged over a line cleanly separating one gender from another. More than that, he'd done it without even realizing it. There was a soft beauty about him, a demure, submissive charm that belonged to the female, yet it was

Kerry's too. Hadn't that been what had drawn Ewyn to Kerry in the first place?

It brought out fierce, protective instincts in Ewyn, making him want to stand between Kerry and the world trying to deny all of his softer qualities.

Ewyn hadn't loved as he knew he could. There had always been, with each relationship, something held back out of duty or reluctance born of worry that not all was as it should be. Standing there, in the cramped hall beside Kerry, Ewyn was afraid. Because he felt it — how easily his need for Kerry and emotional investment in protecting him could cause him to fall, especially with how much Kerry seemed to need the protection and attention, and how there wasn't any ground to crash onto. Ewyn would just tumble down, down, down… forever.

And that meant the fear would never go either. He would never be able to stop shielding Kerry once he started.

But wasn't it already too late? Could he really walk away when predators like Victor were waiting to pounce and sink in teeth to tear and rend?

At the same time, was it fair to Kerry to give in? When Ewyn knew his inclination to be overbearing and overprotective? Would he hurt Kerry more than help by holding on?

With a shiver, Ewyn cleared his throat, straightened his shirt and led the way into the second bedroom.

Before he spoke, he let Kerry look around at the gym, the weights and exercise gear.

"Nice set-up," Kerry said.

Laying a hand on the front of the safe, Ewyn explained, "This is where I lock up my gear when I'm not on the job. I never leave weapons lying around."

"Can I see them?" Kerry asked curiously.

"Of course." Ewyn fished out his key on its chain around his neck and got the door open. He stepped aside to give Kerry a better view of the contents. There were handguns, shotguns, an automatic rifle, ammo, clubs, knives, tasers, even a pair of razor-sharp swords.

"Jesus," Kerry breathed.

"I've had plenty of training with them all. I usually only carry a knife or two on me when I'm not working, not the guns. Do they make you uncomfortable?"

"No. Maybe. It's complicated. My dad — stepdad — he had weapons. Not like this. Not as many."

Ewyn locked the safe again and studied the tiredness seeming to weigh down Kerry's shoulders.

"Come on. Into the shower ya go. Can I get ya something to eat? Drink?"

"Maybe a piece of fruit? Some water?"

"Coming right up." Ewyn pulled a clean towel and washcloth from the linen closet in the bathroom, handing them over. Taking them, Kerry leaned in and kissed Ewyn's cheek before he could pull away.

Ewyn closed the door, trying and failing to hide his happy grin.

Chapter 11: Helpless

Dried off and dressed in a pair of black briefs, Kerry sat on Ewyn's bed with his knees drawn up, holding a big, red-gold honey crisp apple. Seeing the unsettled quality of Ewyn's expression, Kerry swallowed his bite of food and asked, "Should I put more clothes on? I usually sleep naked, but I figured..."

"No, that's fine. You should be comfortable. I can be a gentleman. You wear less at work, so I should be used to this by now, shouldn't I?"

Kerry kept glancing up at Ewyn, just to check, to anticipate. Ewyn was pacing. Kerry liked facing away from the mirror behind the bed. It helped him convince himself he was in a normal bedroom instead of a display case.

"If you'd prefer I sleep on the couch..." Kerry offered.

"No, you're the guest. I'll take the couch."

"You don't have to. It's your house. Your bed. I don't mind," Kerry said. Even his terror of his own lust was unable to hide his sense of disappointment.

"I don't want to make you uncomfortable. And seeing you like that, in my bed, makes me...."

"Horny?" Kerry guessed.

Ewyn laughed, but it turned into a groan. He tried to discreetly adjust himself and it made Kerry grin behind his apple.

"It's okay. Come on. I don't bite."

"Don't bite? I don't even think you have teeth."

Kerry screwed up his face, scrunching his nose, then broke out laughing.

Ewyn hesitated a moment, then pulled his shirt off. Next he opened and pushed down his pants, leaving on his boxer briefs which hinted at every inch of his pierced cock and the heavy swell of his balls. Working only on instinct, though fighting the urge to tense up and over-think what he was doing, Kerry let his legs fall open as Ewyn knelt on the bed, then crawled up it. The closer he got, the more Kerry spread. His heartbeat sped up, his breath quickening.

With a moan, Ewyn moved on top of Kerry, pressing him back to lay on the bed, the apple still loosely held in his hand. Nudging Kerry's chin with his nose, then nipping at it, Ewyn thrust lightly against Kerry's groin, provoking a small gasp and a counter-thrust from Kerry. He felt as helpless as a lamb pinned down by a ravenous lion, but in ways that only excited him. Shouldn't he be more scared? Shouldn't he want to fight back or say no?

Caressing up the outside of Kerry's thigh, up the side of his torso, over his chest, Ewyn exuded ravenous hunger that nothing as simple as an apple would sate.

"I keep thinking of you as a kitten," Ewyn admitted, breathing harder, speaking in a gruff whisper. "All soft, playful and innocent, with your wide, pretty eyes and that purr of a voice. Drives me fucking mad."

"Are you saying you want me to be your sex kitten?" Kerry smirked.

"God fucking dammit," Ewyn moaned, his brogue thickening along with his cock which pressed against the inside of Kerry's hip. "I did intend for us to talk, you know."

"That scares me more than this does," Kerry admitted.

Ewyn's hand pushed down inside Kerry's briefs, grabbing a handful of him. It was a crossed line that helped encourage Kerry to surrender a little more. He let out a shaky exhale and tried to relax as Ewyn fondled him.

Hooking a finger in Kerry's briefs, Ewyn yanked them down far enough to expose him. He searched Kerry's eyes while brushing his fingers over Kerry's sac. His legs nudged Kerry's thighs farther apart. Kerry knew all of his nervousness was written all over his face. There was absolutely no power or leverage in his position. He was pinned down, his most vulnerable parts exposed and actively toyed with. His briefs were caught just below were his balls hung. When Ewyn's finger slipped in through the side of the briefs' leg opening to rub firmly over Kerry's pucker, a hard shudder and a small gasp broadcast more of his helplessness.

Staring down at where his hand worked, and where Kerry's arousal was on full display, Ewyn said, "I know you're exhausted. Let me help you feel good. Then you can get some sleep."

His gaze lifted to Kerry's eyes again, just as the finger pulled at Kerry's rim, then pushed just hard enough to fit barely inside his rim. It made Kerry grunt and flush. His cock began to drip. Desperate for an anchor, he reached for Ewyn, holding on to his shoulder in order to feel steadier. But when Ewyn nudged the finger slightly deeper, Kerry found himself falling apart even more. He spread wider on his own and tried to push down on the finger. Ewyn's hand pivoted, his thumb brushing the patch of skin just behind Kerry's sac. When he started to press there, Kerry clenched and let out a gruff, desperate cry.

Panting, pleading, Kerry fought for sense to speak. "I, uh, don't... don't want to sleep yet. And I don't want this to be all about me."

Ewyn leaned in closer, brushing his lips over Kerry's gasping mouth, inhaling his breaths and small, frantic sounds. The finger pushed a little deeper and the pressure just behind his sac got more intense, causing his cock to drip more. Kerry gathered some courage, and slid his hand inside Ewyn's boxer briefs. Touching him nervously, Kerry cradled Ewyn's thickness in a hand. When he felt the metal piercing, he rubbed over it, curious about how it shifted and moved.

"I'm saying yes, okay?" Kerry told him shakily. "It'll be easier for me to talk after."

"You need proof I'm not just in this for your ass?" Ewyn challenged. He thrust slightly inside Kerry's grip and tugged his finger in a slow withdrawal that Kerry felt all the way from his head to his toes.

"N-no, but..."

"We have time. We could take it slow. Get off just like this."

But Kerry knew what they were doing was just the tease before the real thing. He'd been running from the real thing for years. It scared him more than anything, but he was so sick and tired of being tormented by the idea of something he knew he had to try.

The argument flowed free, uncensored, since too much of Kerry's focus was on the ways Ewyn was touching him, and the firm weight of Ewyn's dick inside Kerry's fist. "But I don't even know if this is going to work for me, and I won't know until I try. Do you even know how long I've been scared of an idea instead of reality? Hiding, and lying, and — "

"Okay," Ewyn relented. "Okay. Just know... it'll hurt," he warned.

"I'm not scared of that. You wouldn't hurt me in any way that matters."

Ewyn freed his hand, took a deep breath, then sat back on his heels. Without a word, he tugged at Kerry's briefs and pulled them off. Once they were free of his feet, Ewyn tossed them aside. Being completely nude again banished all of Kerry's weariness, fast. Anxious but thrilled, he felt exposed and overpowered, knowing Ewyn intended to get inside him, permanently crossing a line that had taunted Kerry for too long.

In a drawer in the nightstand was lube.

"Roll over. Get comfortable. Spread your ass for me. As much as you can."

Kerry set the apple on the other nightstand and rolled to his stomach, getting his knees under him but spreading them so wide, his stomach nearly touched the bed. Gathering a pillow under his chest, he made himself comfortable and tried not to feel self-conscious about how pulled open his ass was in the pose.

He'd insisted on the shower for this reason. He wanted to go all the way, to see if receiving was going to do for him what he hoped it would, so he'd cleaned up, washed himself out, and gotten as ready as possible.

"No fucking hair anywhere on you, is there? Except for your head."

"I get waxed, for work." Something wet smeared over his hole and he grunted in surprise.

"Easy," Ewyn soothed. "The wetter the better. Take deep breaths, relax and try to enjoy it."

A realization occurred to him. "Have you done this before?"

"Not with someone with your particular set of parts."

Somehow, knowing this was new in one way for Ewyn, too, helped ease Kerry's nerves.

A long, slick finger slid into him to the last knuckle and he couldn't hold in his groan, or stop the quiver that raced through him.

Skin heating, embarrassment rising, he clenched on the finger a little, then tried to stop, to just let it slide. Lowering his head to the bed, he panted and arched into the invasive probing.

"Can't fucking wait to get inside you," Ewyn said, sounding wrecked. "So fucking tight, the way your ass grips just one finger, how soft and warm you are in here.... You had this bleached, didn't you?" Ewyn pulled out, rubbed Kerry's hole.

Kerry didn't answer. He let his silence answer for him.

There was a squirt of lube and then two fingers were gently pressed through his rim. Kerry hummed through the ache, hiding the way it showed on his face.

"That's two," Ewyn said, sliding them deeper, past his outer ring, letting Kerry's ass pull them in.

Kerry whined, low and soft.

"If you need to stop, tell me. That's an order."

"I'm all right." He shivered as the fingers pulled back, the friction intense. He dared to take one glimpse at the mirror beside the bed. Ewyn knelt behind Kerry's ass, his left hand resting on the base of Kerry's spine, watching hungrily, avidly, as his fingers pressed to nestle inside him again. "Do you think I'm vain?"

Ewyn laughed a little, briefly catching Kerry's eye in the mirror. "The farthest thing. I think you're fucking perfect. So much, it scares me a little."

For someone who'd always felt wrong and damaged, to be called perfect was the best kind of compliment. Hiding a smile, Kerry lowered his head again, breathing through the stretch. Ewyn buried his fingers, then spread them, twisting them around. The lube helped, but Kerry's body had never experienced such a thing before. It felt wrong; dirty and shameful. Kerry told himself it was all in his head, just because he was scared. Ewyn wanted this from him — wanted him in this particular way — and Ewyn had already done so much in showing concern for Kerry's wellbeing. This was a way Kerry could give something back, to make Ewyn happy.

All he had to do was relax and let it happen.

The fingers withdrew. With more lube, they reentered him and spread apart right away. He made a small, hurt sound of protest.

"Just pressure, okay? Lots of pressure. You'll stretch. It just takes time. Here. Let's try this." Ewyn had reached for Kerry's cock and began to tug on it while pumping his two fingers, slowly fucking Kerry with them.

Kerry moaned, his hips snapping, the fingers riding him no matter the angle of his hips.

"Push your ass back into it, just a little."

Kerry gave it a try, sitting back, pushing into the next in-stroke, while Ewyn kept giving him long, complete strokes. The tugging was everything Kerry needed, and he rocked against it, wanting more. He focused on that instead of the building ache in his ass.

"Fucking hell," Ewyn moaned. "Moving easier. You feel that?"

"Yeah," Kerry answered, the roughness of his voice conveying everything he was feeling.

The fingers withdrew completely before rubbing over his rim. He stayed still, enjoying the pulling of Ewyn's hand, and realized he wanted the fingers back, that he felt strangely empty without them. Fingertips rubbed over his opening, paused, pressed, then only the tips breached him.

He clenched, a thrill shivering up his spine.

"Beautiful," Ewyn sighed. Kerry tried to push back to take the fingers deeper. "No, stay still. Stay just like that."

The fingertips rubbed a little at the inside of his stretched rim, but stayed where they were, barely inside him. Kerry shivered. Pre-come pulsed from his cock, which jumped in Ewyn's grip. Kerry's balls drew up, feeling heavy and swollen. He moaned and fought not to writhe.

"That's it." The fingers slowly sheathed in him again, going as deep as they could. Ewyn rubbed through the wetness soaking Kerry's cockhead, like he was letting Kerry know he felt it and knew how much he was enjoying being fingered. "I should just get you off like this. Let you rest."

"Please, I can do this. I want it."

"You want it, or you think you owe me?"

Kerry didn't know what to say in reply. He shut his eyes as another tremor worked its way through his spread and claimed body, clenching on the fingers, his cock dripping. It felt like his body answered for him, sense overriding sensibility.

"Let me see your face. Let me see you."

Kerry turned his face to the side and opened his eyes. He could see their reflections in the other mirror. Ewyn looked so big, so hard and ready behind him. The obscene sight of his left hand buried inside Kerry's asshole and the slide of Ewyn's right hand wrapping around Kerry's erection was something he couldn't look away from.

Ewyn watched him watching, then let go of Kerry's dick in order to pull out his own cock, letting the elastic of his boxer briefs hug under his balls, his cock curving up in front of him, huge and ready, the piercing gleaming in the light. Stroking himself instead, Ewyn resumed finger-fucking Kerry, who couldn't hold back a low moan of pure need.

"You want this? Should I give it to you?"

He felt his reaction studied closely. Anguish creased his brow, his lips parted on his gasps. "Yeah," he panted.

"Feed it to your pretty ass?"

"Mmm. Please."

"Gonna be my girl, Kerry?"

A wild moan slipped free.

"Say yes."

"Yes... Please..."

Ewyn gave him a third finger, squeezing it in beside the other two on the next in-stroke. The hurt showed plainly in the quivering gasp of Kerry's lips. He made a short, panting whine.

"Easy. Stay open for me, now."

"Hurts."

"I know."

The three fingertips didn't go deeper, they just stayed inside his rim, stretching it too wide. Kerry convulsed a little, then tried to push back, or pull forward. Ewyn just followed him, rubbing more lube around where the fingers were lodged.

"Try to relax," Ewyn urged, his voice rougher, his breathing harder. The fingers slowly pulled out and Kerry's hole closed up again. Ewyn rubbed in a circle over it, then slowly filled it with the three fingertips, popping them through. "That's it. Good girl."

Kerry, crying out in low, rasping grunts, couldn't stop.

It went on and on. Ewyn did the same thing a few more times, making Kerry endure that still, unbearable stretch for minutes at a time, watching closely as he fought to bear it before giving him a moment's relief. Soon, Kerry was sweating, breathing even harder, and overwhelmed. The pain was different than anything he'd ever felt before. It was focused on such an intimate, shameful spot, caused by someone Kerry desired so strongly, and trusted to hurt him more. The pain twisted around on him. The guilt he could never escape was calmed by the pain, was happy about the pain. It was punishment. It was deserved. In fact, the more it hurt, the more Kerry wanted it to hurt.

His erection had wilted, but the pain was bringing it back. Soon, Kerry had to reach beneath himself to jerk off a little just to ease the pressure somewhere.

He caught a dangerous flash of Ewyn's eyes in the mirror, like Ewyn knew Kerry was getting off on the pain and humiliation for the wrong reasons.

Finally, the three fingers pushed deeper. With the side of his face resting on a pillow, his lips parted as he panted, Kerry tilted his hips a little higher and whimpered, but his tugging sped up.

"That hurts?" Ewyn asked.

"Yeah," Kerry sighed.

"You like that?"

He nodded.

"No, say it."

"Yeah."

"You think you deserve it?"

Kerry caught Ewyn's gaze from over his shoulder for the first time, and couldn't hide everything behind his stare.

"Yeah. I do. Punish me."

Ewyn sighed. He pulled out, stopped touching Kerry and sat back on his heels, frowning.

"Come on!" Kerry yelled, his soft voice breaking.

Ewyn folded his body around Kerry's and growled in his ear, "This isn't punishment! I'm not doing this to hurt you!"

But Kerry was delirious, dazed, everything in him surging with pure, powerful need. He reached behind his shoulder, holding Ewyn there, scratching through his hair and nuzzling against him, purely begging, "I want it. *I want you.* Please, I want it so bad."

Ewyn tore open the condom, rolled it on. Kerry sighed, eyes closed, rubbing himself back against Ewyn. The thick, soft mat of his chest hair tickled Kerry's back. The heat of him soaked into Kerry's skin. He rubbed his ass, dripping with lube, back against Ewyn's hand and dick.

A hand braced under Kerry's abdomen. "Up on your knees. Come on."

Kerry lifted up. Ewyn pressed up close, between Kerry's spread legs. There was blunt, wide pressure against Kerry's sore, throbbing hole.

"Yeah... please... more..." he begged, breathless.

"Look at me," Ewyn ordered. "Kerry, look at me now."

They locked eyes in the mirror behind the bed. Ewyn bared his teeth and pushed, pulling Kerry back onto him by a hand wrapping his hip.

There was a sudden gasp at the huge flare of pain, the profound sense of being trapped in a way he hadn't felt with the fingers. Then he could only frantically struggle for air, mouth agape as Ewyn entered him.

Layered, strong uncertainty overwhelmed Kerry's system, causing him to question everything. He'd been wrong. He'd always been wrong.

"Easy. Easy now, a *mhuirnín*. Stay open for me. If you tense up, it'll hurt more."

Ewyn's cock pushed to work its way deeper than the fingers had reached, making Kerry feel breathless, frantic, impaled so deeply on someone so much stronger than Jamie, someone who easily held him still with an arm braced across Kerry's hips, unable to pull forward and off. He couldn't escape it. He was forced to face it and give over to it.

Nuzzling the side of Kerry's face with his nose and bearded chin, maybe sensing his panic, Ewyn pressed a trail of kisses, hushing to him. "It'll ease. I swear it will."

For a moment, Kerry fought, trembling, trying to pull the arm from across his hips, to move, to get away, but he couldn't budge and gradually, the tenderness of Ewyn's kisses distracted Kerry from some of the shame.

He realized Ewyn was panting, too.

"You're killing me," Ewyn moaned. Finally, after an eternity, he drew back, his cock withdrawing inch by inch.

Kerry let out a heavy moan and grabbed for the headboard. With rough gasps, he felt the thick column expel from him only to press back into his ass. The movement never stopped, the constant push and pull taking Kerry apart, fast, in primal ways.

He was grunting, crying out, trembling, and Ewyn only took him faster. Teeth gritted in a snarl, Ewyn straightened, staring at the sight of Kerry taking Ewyn's cock. Growling, fucking, Ewyn rode him in shuddering, hesitant thrusts. Soon, he came with a gasping cry, his hips gently slapping Kerry's cheeks.

"Ahh, fuck," he hissed. "Oh god dammit."

He nuzzled Kerry's neck, reaching for Kerry's soft cock.

Whimpering in anticipation, Kerry didn't realize how good it would feel once Ewyn began to furiously jack him, his hand still slick with lube. In no time, Kerry was hard again, clenching constantly on the cock stuffed up his ass. The perversity of it had him coming in almost record time, shooting over Ewyn's fingers, convulsing in his arms.

Ewyn pulled out, driving a startled yell from Kerry. Manhandling him over to his back, Ewyn lay fully atop him, pressing Kerry into the bed. Catching his mouth in a hard, hungry kiss, Ewyn moaned, "Absolutely fucking glorious."

If Kerry was afraid everything would be different between them after they'd had sex, he was right.

That evening, he barely had the energy to wash up in the bathroom while Ewyn changed the sheets. Then he collapsed, naked, in bed and was out in seconds.

He woke many hours later with Ewyn naked but awake beside him, under the covers.

As soon as Kerry's eyes were able to stay open, he watched the fiercely protective way Ewyn gathered Kerry close, spooning up behind him with an arm looped in front of Kerry's chest to keep him there. Right away, Ewyn's cock began to swell, nudging Kerry's ass insistently.

Everything about Ewyn's look, his energy, spoke of a powerful beast — a lion or bear, guarding its stake, ready to tear off heads if any other creature dared to approach. It was overwhelming but strangely enthralling, especially in how it pushed Kerry to give over and give in.

"Was it okay?"

"Was it okay, he asks," Ewyn groaned, kissing the back of Kerry's neck. "I have *never* in my life come that hard, or felt this way about someone I'd..." he sighed. "Can I have you? Are ya mine, now?" he whispered heatedly.

Kerry smiled, his cheeks aching as his happiness grew so big. "Yeah," he agreed. "It's a deal."

"Are ya sore?"

"Yeah."

"It'll be easier next time. It won't hurt as much."

"Okay. Good."

"Did you get off on it?"

Kerry thought about it. "I got off on you. I liked having you like that, and seeing what it did to you, how much you liked it."

"Who hurt you, Kerry?"

The suddenness and seriousness of the query stopped him short.

"Please tell me who hurt you so I can hurt them back."

"It's not — "

"Just tell me," Ewyn demanded quietly. "Don't you think I can see it? It's there, in your eyes every second, and to not know why or who — "

"Ewyn, please — "

"Tell me who hurt you so I can fix it. I need to fix it, Kerry. I — "

"I did," Kerry blurted, just to make him stop, then instantly tried to shrink down and lose himself in the embrace, melting into Ewyn. "It's me, okay?"

"No."

"It's always been my fault."

"Kerry..."

"And it's a long, long story."

Chapter 12: Stories of Scars

They sat at the kitchen table with coffee and oatmeal for breakfast. Kerry had slept well, but suspected Ewyn had not. Kerry was having trouble making eye contact or thinking of where to start. Ewyn remained perfectly silent, just waiting.

In the middle of the night, when Kerry had awoken to see Ewyn dozing, he'd crept out of bed and retrieved the white candle hidden in his bag. He'd lit it, set it in the window by the kitchen sink, in a dish. Then he'd gone back to sleep. The candle was still there, a little shorter. They hadn't talked about it.

"Why do you wear the kilts?" Ewyn had asked.

Kerry tried to figure out how to explain.

"I have three older brothers – Kurt, Kipp, and Kent. My bio dad wanted to preserve his initials, I guess. Big fan of K. My oldest brother, Kurt Jr., is seven years older than me. I used to wear his big shirts with a belt tied around my waist. Mostly it was when I'd be playing alone in my room. If I walked around like that, I'd get yelled at and sent to get changed."

"By who?" Ewyn said, his eyes narrowing.

"Michael, my stepdad."

Ewyn was silent for a moment before asking, "Did any of them know you like men?"

"We didn't talk about it. Hell, I didn't even think about it. I'd have crushes on people. Boys, girls, anyone cute. I didn't think it was weird until one day I said out loud that a guy in a music video was cute. Kipp heard me and told our stepdad. I don't think Kipp was trying to be cruel. We had been arguing for a few days over stupid shit, just basically getting on each other's nerves. It probably started with this stuffed rabbit our bio dad had given Kipp when he was younger. I liked it, so I kept taking it. It pissed him off. I think he was just trying to get back at me, continuing the fight. It wasn't until afterward that he realized what he'd done, and that it was a really big deal. I could tell from his face how sorry he was, though he wasn't able to actually say it."

"What happened? What did Michael do to you?"

"He, um, came after me, pulling his belt out of his pants. He grabbed me by the arm, yanked me backward, away from the furniture and TV, then whipped my back a few times. Kipp watched from the doorway, his eyes bugging out of his head in shock. Michael was so angry. He yelled, 'You are to never say anything like that again, do you hear me? Are you a faggot? Are you?!'"

"Jesus wept," Ewyn breathed. "How old were you?"

"Eight. Kipp left the rabbit in my bed that night while I pretended to be asleep. I never said anything like that out loud again. Not at home. Not around friends. I'd learned."

"Fucking homophobic rotten piece of shite," Ewyn seethed, looking ready to smash the table just to vent some of the boiling frustration inside him. "He fucking beat you?"

"No, I mean, it wasn't something he did regularly. I think any sign of weakness set him off, triggered his own issues. It was just that one time, until... well. I did still like some guys. I couldn't escape that once I got older. The first person I kissed was a guy. I dated a few, secretly, but they were never out either, so we couldn't go anywhere. It was basically just making out and hiding from everyone."

"What about your mother? Did she know about any of this?"

"I don't know. I don't think she ever found out about that time when I was eight. I didn't tell her, because I didn't want to get in more trouble with Michael. As far as I know, Kipp hadn't talked about it either, and Michael..." Kerry shook his head. "He and my mom fought all the time. If she'd known about that, he'd have been out on his ass."

"But it's her job to protect you, Kerry. You should have given her the chance!"

"Maybe. It felt like it was something I had to figure out on my own, though. He'd gotten so mad at me, obviously it meant I'd done something wrong, or been something wrong. But to fix it?" He shrugged. "I had no clue how. I tried to do everything I could to please Michael. He's a Marine. He had a really stressful job, came home mentally drained. He needed complete control, always. It was how he coped. When he wasn't overwhelmed, he was always a great, caring guy and a good dad. He made time for each of us; made sure we got good grades and had help if we needed it. He let us know we were important to him, and loved us like we were his. We *were* his. After the first couple of years, my bio dad didn't even visit or call. But that control element was always there. We had to make our beds with military corners. Our rooms had to be spotless, perfectly organized down to our fucking sock drawers, sorted by color and style. We practically wore uniforms. Button-down shirts in solid colors like blue, gray or white. Khakis perfectly tailored and pressed. Our shoes always had to be shined, and no sneakers allowed except for exercising. Hair cut the same way, by the same barber. No jewelry.

"Order and appearances were everything. I wanted him to be happy with me, so I tried to follow all of the rules, to be exactly who Michael expected me to be. But... I slipped up. I tried to keep the guys secret — to keep Michael happy but have something for myself in private now and then. So... I was making out with this kid from my science class, Jakob, in my car, parked behind the house. Everyone was supposed to be out at an event at the base. It should have been fine. Jakob was on top of me, hand down my pants, jerking me off while we kissed. My hand was in his pants, too, playing with his ass.

"I wasn't paying attention. Didn't even hear him coming," Kerry sighed. "Michael ripped the door open, yanked me out by the arm, dislocating my shoulder. Dragged me away from the car. Jakob ran off. Michael pulled my shirt off, ripping it right open. I got on my feet, tried to say something. He backhanded me across the mouth, spitting, 'You're sick! I'll beat the faggot out of you, god help me.'

"I tried to apologize but he backhanded me again, hard enough to knock me over. I could taste blood. My head was spinning. My arm was in agony. He kicked me in the stomach a few times while he got his belt free. I mean, you can guess what happened. He was in a rage. He couldn't stop and I couldn't move. Mostly, the welts were over my back, but he got me across the head once or twice and I blacked out."

Ewyn's face was mask-like in its composure, which was somehow more worrisome than when he'd just looked angry. It felt like it had gotten away from Kerry somehow, like he'd said too much and shifted something between them, forcing Ewyn into a decision Kerry knew nothing about.

Ewyn asked, "Why did he come back? Why was he there?"

"He'd gotten drunk at the event, started shouting at people. So Mom put him in a cab and sent him home to sober up."

Ewyn grunted, his jaw clenched. "Did they even fucking take you to the hospital? Bet I can guess the answer."

"I know they thought about it." Ewyn let out a miserable chuckle, shaking his head, his eyes gleaming with glints of cold fury. Kerry kept explaining. "I think it was my mom who brought me into the house. Or maybe my brother, Kent. I never found out for sure. I've thought about that night so many times, trying to make sense of it all. When I came to, they were both there, asking me where I hurt. Someone had cleaned me up. My arm was back in the socket and in a sling. Michael was gone. Mom had asked him to leave. But... I think they didn't take me to the hospital because she was afraid of people finding out what he'd done, and the professional consequences for him if the hospital got the military police involved. We never really talked about any of it. Ever. I could kind of tell from my mom's face that Michael had mentioned Jakob, maybe to defend himself, but she never asked and I didn't want to confess to anything that might upset them too. But I knew not to give Michael a reason to react that way again."

"I thought you said he'd been kicked out?"

"Oh, yeah. He was, but it was their pattern. He went to therapy again, took some anger management classes, and a few months later he'd done enough to be allowed to move back in. He did seem better, but I avoided him, mostly. It seemed safer that way. My brothers kept him away from me too."

"How old were you that time?"

"Seventeen. It fucked with my head for a while. Anyway, it was safer to date girls, so I started seeing Haley. She was a tomboy, which I thought was sexy. I, uh, I just wanted things to get easier. Simpler."

He breathed out a bitter laugh and shook his head.

Ewyn took his hand, studied his expression.

"Tell me, love. Please," Ewyn begged.

"No," was all Kerry could manage, shaking his head again, biting down on his back teeth and denying all of it, pushing the pain way, way down.

"Please. You're safe here. I swear it."

"No. I... I need some air. I can't, I..." He stood and glanced toward the back door leading to the back patio. Ewyn moved before Kerry, opening the door and holding it for him as he walked outside, hugging himself, rubbing his arms. Once out on the patio, he took a deeper breath, looked up at the sky and tried to slip free of old grief.

Ewyn waited patiently. "What do you need? What can I do?"

The heavy weight in his chest, the instinct to lie or run from what was real, even though he knew it was impossible, left him drained. Some things were too precious to lie about, so instead he just didn't talk about them. They stayed inside. Protected. Secret.

"I need a little more time before we get into... that. Everything with Haley, and with... I can't go there right now."

"Not a problem," Ewyn frowned. "I'm not going anywhere. The last thing I want is to upset you."

It was hard to focus as an unwanted slideshow of his worst memories flickered across his vision. It robbed him of the sliver of hope he'd begun to find since meeting Ewyn, leaving him hollow and defeated. Whenever Kerry tried to meet his own needs, it always ended in failure or nightmares. Maybe what he was doing now would end up the same way. Ewyn might not think he deserved punishment, yet punishment had always found Kerry in one way or other.

Ewyn folded him into a hug that Kerry melted right into, holding on tight to Ewyn, taking his comfort there.

"Whatever you're carrying," Ewyn told him softly. "I know how that is, to have something you feel like you can't get out from under. Give it time and keep trying. You'll be okay."

Will I, though? He wondered. Resting his head on Ewyn's shoulder where it was warm and reality was more powerful than regret, Kerry wanted to believe Ewyn was right. He didn't see how. He hadn't felt okay in a long, long time.

"Whenever you're ready to talk, I'll listen."
"Thank you."

Chapter 13: Warped Mirrors

"Jamie doesn't seem to fit your pattern at all. How'd that come about?"

"I lied about Jamie. A lot. The whole time."

Ewyn raised an eyebrow in question.

"After Haley, I moved out. Couch surfing, living with friends. That's how I met Jamie. We were just friends for a while, but then... It was before he had transitioned. He'd still been identifying as a girl, mainly because his family wasn't supportive and kept trying to hold him back, but I..." Kerry breathed out heavily, found himself smiling. "I don't know. Jamie gave me hope. He was magic. He felt different than people saw him too, and lied about who he was all the time, just like I did. But he also made the impossible seem possible, and I... I loved how he had this need to be something else. He really believed he could do it. But he had no real support and wanted someone to be on his side, and I was happy to do that. I helped him get away from his mom and got away from my parents at the same time, even though we were only teenagers. We leaned on each other. It got me out of my head, and away from everything that sucked in my past. I did everything I could for Jamie as he started to transition. It made me feel like I was doing something good. Something that mattered. I was helping. I was appreciated. It gave me something positive to focus on. He was always bad at being sensible and careful about things. He'd get so emotionally invested in something, he couldn't see any other way to handle it than to barrel straight through. He'd throw himself into ideas without looking to see if there was even anywhere to land. And that's always where I was really good — being organized and planning ahead — so I watched out for him. We balanced each other out. We were both kind of broken in different ways."

Kerry sat next to Ewyn on the couch in the living room, a glass of water in his hands.

"And your family? Michael? What did they think of all this?"

"They didn't get to hear much about Jamie being trans. They met him accidentally a couple of times at the beginning, when they were hunting me down to see where I was and running into him in the process. After that, we were more careful. I deliberately kept Jamie away from them. It was better that way, and Jamie didn't mind. He likes his privacy."

"Denial that big? Sounds like a recipe for disaster if you ask me."

"Oh, yeah. It was," Kerry agreed. "Kent was the only one who knew what was going on. He checked on me, and I knew he wouldn't tell the others more than he had to. All they cared about was that I had a place to live, that I was eating and all of that kind of stuff. I took whatever jobs I could, but they didn't pay much. We were dirt poor. I'd started to strip when Jamie and I began to fight on a pretty regular basis. We'd been dating a few months. I was eighteen. Dancing was my escape. Just another way to rebel against my circumstances, but it only made things worse. Our sex life was a mess. We were both frustrated, neither of us getting what we wanted and without a single clue where the middle ground was supposed to be. When Jamie found my sketches of kilts and..."

"And?" Ewyn prompted when Kerry hesitated.

Kerry dropped his gaze, feeling truly embarrassed for the first time since they'd started their talk.

"Um... dresses. Dresses on guys' bodies... My... my body."

He glanced up nervously at Ewyn's face, but saw only curiosity and care, so he somehow kept going, even though his face was heating up. Kerry had never opened up so fast about so much to anyone before. He decided to trust it and not let his tendency to overanalyze trip him up.

"Anyway, it only pushed him farther away. He didn't get it. I had learned to sew for work, to make my costumes. Then I'd helped Jamie tailor his clothes and did some projects for friends for some extra cash but... this was different. He knew it was personal. It scared him, I guess. Made him feel like he was losing me, which I guess was the truth. He'd tell me I was confused, that I hadn't gotten over Michael's shit, and that I was just acting out and making a fool of myself. Maybe I was. I... I don't know."

"That's a lie. Yes, you do."

Kerry looked over at him.

"You do know. Don't let someone else's opinion override your own. You know yourself. Don't let other people tell you who to be and what you're allowed to feel." Ewyn was gritting his teeth, biting off each word. "Even if Jamie was scared of losing you, what he said was fucking cruel."

"It's not his fault," Kerry tried to explain. "I think he just sees everything feminine — dresses and makeup and physical weakness — as a bad part of his past. The worst part. A boy in a dress, right? That's what he'd been his whole childhood, basically against his will. His family never understood. Not really. His mom eventually helped fund the transition process, but it was only after Jamie tried to run away a few times and wound up homeless. She was trying to keep from losing him. We met before he'd gotten anywhere near the finish line he'd been killing himself to get to his whole life, then literally as soon as he found what he'd been looking for, the identity he'd always wanted, there I am. Who was I, deep down, beneath the bullshit? Since I was a kid? A boy in a dress. I don't blame him for being uncomfortable. Our differences just kept getting more extreme and we couldn't fit together at all anymore, so he left. One day, in the middle of an argument, he packed a bag and walked out. That was it. We just weren't meant to be."

Ewyn took Kerry's hand, urging him to turn sideways so they faced each other. "Listen to me. None of this was your fault," he insisted. "Everything you've said so far... I can hear it in your voice, see it in your face, and I haven't even known you long. There's nothing wrong with you. You're perfect just the way you are. I've never met anyone like you, but now that I have you... It makes me angry that you can't see yourself the way I see you. You're a beautiful person, Kerry. Your environment and circumstances have kept you on the defensive for far too long, left you questioning yourself for the wrong reasons. None of the things that have caused you pain were your fault."

"No. I don't agree," Kerry argued, shaking his head. "Ever since I was a kid, everything that's gone wrong, it was all just a series of

97

rebellions. Against the way they told me to dress, the way to act and be. Against not being able to like boys. Against being told to get a girl and what happened with Haley. Against not giving Jamie my whole heart and complete attention when I should have and making that really difficult time for him about *me* instead. Being a disagreeable little shit comes back to bite you. I get that now."

"No way. No fucking way," Ewyn growled. "They all got in your head, love, convinced you everything natural about you was wrong. Being who you are isn't a rebellion. It's truth. It's the right thing to do, the only way to be happy. Doing things to find happiness isn't a cause for punishment, especially if no one gets hurt. All that matters is what you want, what makes you happy."

"But that's selfish. The way I acted did hurt people. It hurt my parents, my lovers — "

"Who were not tolerant of you! Michael was cruel! Jamie was selfish! He should have let you go instead of making your life a series of guilt-trips."

Kerry took his hand back from Ewyn, running his fingers through his hair, trying to find a way to explain so Ewyn would understand. "Michael's not a bad person. He's my dad. I love him. He's been to war, for fuck's sake. He's allowed to have a bad day once every ten years. In his world, it isn't acceptable to be gay, or dress outside of gender norms. That has nothing to do with me."

Ewyn gave a bitter laugh and stood up. He began to pace, biting his lip, rubbing his mouth.

Kerry continued, "We still talk. We're fine. Maybe I'm not as close to him as I am to my brother, Kent, but that just comes down to a clash of personalities. I don't tell him things that I know will set him off, but I do let him know how I'm doing in general. Michael cares about me."

"If Michael can't accept you just the way you are, then no, he doesn't care about you. He cares about an idea that doesn't actually exist. And that's his problem, not yours," Ewyn insisted, his brogue thickening with his temper. "Taking care of people doesn't mean you get to forcibly change who they are. As far gone as I've ever been when at my most idiotic, I'd never crossed those types of lines. I can't even imagine... You're one of the sweetest people I've ever met and to think he dragged you out of a car and *beat you*! Just for kissing someone!"

"It wasn't just kissing," Kerry argued softly.

"Kerry!" Ewyn snapped.

"Sorry."

"No apologizing, for fuck's sake!"

Kerry burst out laughing. He couldn't help it, especially since there was a really strong urge to keep apologizing about apologizing. Ewyn's no apologies rule would have really pissed off someone like Jamie, whose persona revolved closely around pride and strength, but Kerry appreciated it as a way to start to unlearn a bad habit. Having Ewyn call him out helped Kerry see where he'd been giving away pieces of himself by letting misplaced guilt win.

Staring at Kerry's laughter with astonishment, Ewyn said slowly, "Yer making me crazy, do ya know that?"

"Likewise," Kerry replied, without bothering to hide the warmth behind the word. His smile lingered, but he dropped his gaze, and watched his fidgeting, twisting fingers instead. It was strange how, even after only a couple of days, there was nowhere he'd rather be than in that living room, with Ewyn too upset to sit down.

"The candle you light, with the J on it," Ewyn asked. "Is that for Jamie?"

"What? No," Kerry said abruptly. "No."

"Okay."

Remembering how good it had felt to have Ewyn overpower him in bed the night before, allowing him to vent some of the built-up pressure inside, Kerry now felt even more pinned down, but in more complex ways.

Even without Ewyn holding him, Kerry knew he would never be able to go now, unless Ewyn gave the okay. Simply listening and showing understanding had already won Ewyn more of Kerry's loyalty than he likely realized. No one else in his life had demanded Kerry to drop the act and own the truth the way Ewyn did. The urge to obey and surrender to those demands was frighteningly easy to do.

"Can I just ask... of all things, why dancing? Stripping?"

Kerry hesitated. "Things with my family — it's years of drama and bad decisions with repercussions. Even with Michael cheating on her, Mom wouldn't go, but she kept yanking at Michael, never letting him stray too far. They were really good at knowing just how to torture each other. It's one of the reasons I moved out so fast instead of going to college. My parents never forgave me for that. They'd had a college fund for me, all saved up. I told them to keep the money. When they heard I was stripping, dancing, I was glad it upset them and that they couldn't stop me for once. I know what it says about me and the kind of person I am, but yeah, I did it in part to hurt them and Jamie. They always needed me to be someone I never was and it sucked. So I acted out. Dancing got me attention, made me feel sexy and good about myself in a way that had been totally missing. Dancing was always just about me, no one else. I liked that."

Ewyn had stopped pacing. Now he was just standing there, towering over Kerry sitting on the couch, hands in his lap. In a strange way, it made Kerry feel like he was back at home, being made to explain his behavior to his elders. Only now, the person judging him was having the exact opposite reaction than anyone had had so far. It left Kerry feeling profoundly confused.

Ewyn stepped closer, and the silence drew out. It was a weighted sort of quiet, packed full of all of the things Ewyn was deciding about Kerry — opinions Kerry had no way to affect.

It made him feel very self-conscious.

"Does it make you happy?" Ewyn asked, like he sincerely wanted to know, without judgment. "Dancing. Does it make you happy? Because your parents aren't here anymore, watching over your shoulder. Neither is Jamie. Now it's just you making these decisions. Is this still the right one to make?"

It was a hard question. Kerry chewed on his lip, feeling the ache in his body from their lovemaking, liking that Ewyn hadn't been scared off or gotten bored listening to Kerry's story.

He thought about dancing, how he felt doing it, the excitement and dread just before going on stage and the questions that swirled in his head after leaving it, too.

"I don't know, honestly. I'm not sure it does make me happy anymore. At first it was fun, but the initial rush is gone. It's not a rebellion anymore. No one gives a shit. Now it's just my job, you know? And that's a good and bad thing. It's not something I do for kicks. It's the way I support myself. I have no other skills."

"I doubt that, but I won't press the issue for now." Ewyn looked briefly around the house like there might be answers to all of his questions peeking around the corners or window frames. "Okay.

Okay, don't worry about it now. You're not working tonight, are you?"

"No."

"Good. Let me take care of you today. Make sure you rest. I don't have to work until much later, and only for a few hours. You can stay here while I'm gone if you'd like. It would make me feel better, knowing where you'd be, that you were safe."

"I don't know. I really think I should head home soon. Take some time to think about everything for a while," Kerry admitted. "You've been so generous, Ewyn, but I can't impose on you. It means a lot to me that you've let me get so much off my chest, but I have to let you get back to your life. There's a lot I'm trying to work through and figure out right now, but none of those things are your problem."

"I'm not a wall, Kerry," Ewyn said decisively, looking stubborn as hell. "When you tell me this shite, the words don't bounce off, they stick. One thing I've learned about you is that you're terrible at being kind to yourself. That stops now. I'm making it my responsibility to help you become aware of how you're hurting yourself so it stops. You deserve to be happy, to have some peace so you can figure out who you are and what you want."

Kerry didn't know what to say, so he said nothing, slouching down a little farther into the couch. Ewyn stepped forward until he was so close, he was able to trap Kerry's left knee between his legs, standing on either side of his foot. Almost automatically, Kerry leaned forward, touching Ewyn's thigh. Ewyn caressed through the hair at the back of Kerry's head, then down his neck to his back. Being touched like that, with unspoken tenderness, made Kerry feel safe in a way he didn't even realize he'd been desperate for. He rested his head against Ewyn's hip, a smile playing at the edges of his lips.

"Do you know what drives me out of my mind, every bleeding day?" Ewyn asked passionately.

"No. What?"

"Knowing there was something I could have done for my brother, Darcy. I could have done *something*. He was such a gentle soul, bless him. Like you. But I lost him. It's too late to act differently, to try to save him somehow, but it's not too late for you."

"Ewyn…"

"It makes me happy to see you safe, okay? That's all. It's selfish. It makes me feel like maybe it'll be easier to look in the mirror if I follow my gut on this, instead of turning a blind eye like before. I know there'll be consequences. I've never had a male lover before. I'm not interested in hiding that I want to be with you. Friends, colleagues, and family members of mine will judge me for this. I'm not kidding myself about that. But, honestly, I don't give a fuck. I want you."

Kerry was holding on to Ewyn's thigh with his right hand, and caressed Ewyn's other leg with his left, liking the firm feel of his muscle under the denim, and the natural scent coming off his body. Every second they spent together felt like a decadent indulgence someone would try to drag him away from at any moment.

But Michael wasn't allowed in. Kerry made his own choices now, even if they scared him.

"I don't know what to say."

"Say okay."

Kerry hesitated, then caressed over Ewyn's groin. Shivering, Ewyn clasped Kerry more tightly to him, possessively so. Kerry nudged up the fabric of Ewyn's shirt with his nose, then kissed the small patch of exposed, bare skin by his hip and whispered, "Okay."

"Hey! Where's your boyfriend, Sanderson?"

"Better watch yourself, now."

Kerry blocked it out. Head down, eyes forward, he ignored the small group of men on the porch with Victor Hammerstein in the center. He jogged up the steps, not letting fear win, just doing what he needed to do and get inside. It had been a mistake to bring Ewyn to the apartment. He knew that now, but there was no taking it back. He needed to ride out the consequences.

Once he was inside, with no sign anyone had followed him up the steps, Kerry bolted the door and slid the couch in front of it again, just in case.

His phone buzzed.

There were a couple of messages. One was from Kent, just checking in to see how Kerry was doing. The other was from Jamie, asking to stop by.

"Fuck," Kerry sighed.

He dialed, and not because he necessarily wanted to talk to Jamie. With Victor's recent attempts at intimidation and threats, which seemed to have escalated way beyond what they'd been while Jamie had lived there too, Kerry didn't want him coming anywhere near the place. It was way too dangerous.

It was a small miracle he'd even gotten Ewyn to agree to let him leave. Kerry had lied to alleviate Ewyn's worries, saying he was going on errands and not back to the apartment, that he would check in later before thinking of going home. The way Ewyn had reacted to Kerry's determination made him half-suspect Ewyn would try to stop by to check on him if he did admit he was headed back to the apartment, which might only make things worse.

Kerry knew he would have been better off staying somewhere else, but where? Instinct said it was too soon to foist himself on Ewyn and there was nowhere else he could go without undoing all of his hard-won progress. It was a situation Kerry didn't know how to fix.

"Hey. What's up?" Jamie said in greeting, his voice sounding relaxed and positive.

"Hey. I got your message. I, um. Can we talk? Is this a good time, or..."

"Yeah. Hold on a second." Kerry heard low rustling and voices from the other end, too distant and muffled to make out. The was a soft thud and the background noise stopped. "Okay. What's going on?"

"Nothing," he lied. "I, just..." he blew out a breath, stared at the sight of the couch barricading the door. "Promise me you won't come over for a while."

"Whoa. Did I do something to piss you off, or — "

"No. No, it's not you. It's not a big deal. I just don't want you to get involved, make it more complicated."

"What the hell is going on?" Jamie demanded, getting riled.

"It's stupid. It's Victor."

"Oh, fuck. What now?"

"Nothing. He's just started saying shit to me, in passing. And I'm fine. He can't get in, and I'm staying clear of him as best I can. But I'm just worried about you, and him catching you alone or something."

"Kerry, I can take Victor if I need to."

"No, you can't, Jamie. Please don't be cocky about this. It's not just him. He's always got his buddies around now. They could gang up on you."

"They could gang up on you, too!"

"I know! I..." He groaned, floundering.

"Do you need me to move back in? Watch your back?"

Kerry had an instant, negative reaction to the offer, as kind as it was. He'd just started to take forward steps with Ewyn, feeling like he was being more authentic than ever before. He couldn't go backward now, and invite Jamie back in to confuse him again, bringing back all of the old patterns of pleasing and pretending that had been bringing him down. Not even as a friend, for safety's sake.

"Kerry?" Jamie asked, when he said nothing.

"Yeah. Yeah, I'm here. I hear you. I don't think that's a good idea, but I appreciate the offer. I... I'm kind of seeing someone. And..." he cringed, felt for a moment like he was going to swallow his tongue. The dreaded pronoun choked him, lodging in his throat. He fought it free. "He works in security. He's been watching out for me. I'll figure something out, okay? I'll find someplace else to stay for a few nights, until Victor cools down or gets bored."

"What's his name?"

"Jamie..."

"It's just a question."

"Yeah, I know."

"Is he trans?"

The floor was quicksand, sucking him down, preventing escape.

He just blurted it out. "No. No, he's... he's not trans. And no one knows. No one but you. I haven't... told anyone. So don't, please. If you ever loved me, promise me you won't out me with this."

"You really think I'd do that to you? Jesus, I didn't know it was this bad, Kerr. I'm not the bad guy. I've got you, okay?"

Kerry ran a hand through his hair, blowing out a breath. Calming down. "Okay. Thanks."

"What do you need? What can I do?"

"Nothing. I really am fine. I just wanted to make sure you knew it wasn't great here and to steer clear for a while. I've got my hands full trying to figure out my own shit. I didn't want to have to worry about you too."

"You're getting out of there, right? Go stay with Kent or something. Or Dima. Somebody."

Kerry glanced around at his stuff, mentally packing it up in bags, carting it the place of someone he trusted. He hated the thought of running scared. It felt like he would be letting Victor win.

"Yeah, I'll go."

"Promise me, Kerry."

"Okay. I promise."

"The new guy..."

"Ewyn."

"Ewyn. He makes you happy?"

"So far, yeah. It's different."

"I bet." Jamie sounded sad and worried, but also like he really did wish Kerry the best, which made his heart ache a little. "Text me later? Just so I know you're okay?"

"I will."

They hung up. Kerry flopped down on the bed behind him and groaned.

Chapter 14: Exposed

It wasn't even a choice, really. Kent had his own life. So did Dima. Kerry wasn't close enough with his other friends to ask such a huge favor. His lease wasn't going to be up for a couple of months and he didn't feel comfortable crashing somewhere that long unless the other person was getting something out of the deal, too. He didn't have the money to pay anyone for letting him stay. Not while trying to cover expenses at an apartment he didn't feel safe in.

So, he made a choice.

He wanted to make the offer in person rather than over the phone, so he texted Ewyn to see if he had a few minutes later in the day to grab dinner or something. Ewyn responded saying he had another security gig that evening for a few hours, so dinner was out, but that Kerry was welcome to come over before, whenever he liked.

In his messages, Kerry specifically avoided saying anything about Victor. He didn't want Ewyn to worry. It would have just made things worse.

By mid-afternoon, he knew it was time to go to Ewyn's, but he hesitated for strange, superficial reasons. Something prevented him from packing up everything and bringing it with him. It felt too presumptuous, and like he might jinx the whole thing if he did so. He knew, logically, it made the most sense. If Ewyn wasn't okay with Kerry's offer, it left Kerry able to try one of his back-up options without having to stop back at the apartment again.

Still, he just couldn't do it.

He'd worked so damned hard at independence. It had been his primary goal since he was seventeen. Now, he finally had his own place, a job that wasn't completely terrible, a car, and freedom. If he loaded up his trunk with all of his possessions, or even most of them, and ran off looking for rescue, it would have been the same as admitting defeat. He'd be nothing but a failure. A fuck-up.

Maybe it was dumb, but even if his place wasn't perfect, at least it was his. If he had no choice but to walk away from it, he was going to need to do it in phases, just for the sake of his own sanity and pride.

But it wasn't just packing that was tripping him up.

His lengthy conversation with Ewyn added other complications.

Kerry ran the gray shift he'd made through his hands. How funny to have so much mental and emotional energy invested in a small scrap of cotton.

He'd told Ewyn about sewing and about designing dresses. Ewyn hadn't balked or seemed put off. In fact, so far Ewyn had seemed to love the kilts Kerry had been wearing daily, when it was safe. He hadn't been able to keep his hands off, in only good ways.

Maybe it would be okay.

Maybe he could try.

Deep down in the back of his mind, he wondered if the desire to wear the shift in front of Ewyn was just a way to self-sabotage the deal he intended to propose. It would be a way to really test Ewyn's loyalty and open-mindedness. If he was put off by the dress, it saved Kerry grief in the long run.

Maybe it was better to know than not.

If Kerry scared Ewyn off just by doing something that made him happy, it spared him the pain of investing anymore in someone who would have only hurt him in the end.

Kerry slipped on the shift, then tucked the skirt up into the belt to hide it, wearing a jacket on top and zipping it up. Then, he put on a pair of jeans and slipped on some half-laced black workboots. Some lip gloss and eyeliner went into a pocket of the jacket. In another pocket was mace and a pocketknife, just in case.

He pushed the couch out of the way, unbolted the door and left an overnight bag ready to go on the bed. Bracing himself for trouble, Kerry left the apartment, locking it behind him, and headed down the stairs to his car.

There was no sign of Victor, or his friends. For once, the porch was empty.

Breathing a sigh of relief, Kerry got behind the wheel and took off.

When he pulled into Ewyn's driveway, Kerry slid his seat back for some extra leg-room, then pulled off the boots and jeans before putting the boots back on. The jacket got tossed into the passenger seat. He applied some lip gloss and eyeliner, his hands trembling just a little, his gaze failing to stick too long on his troubling reflection. It felt like wearing his heart on his sleeve, exposing it and him to all sorts of harm. All of his inner alarms were blaring. He kept checking the side and rearview mirrors for Michael, coming to drag him onto the pavement for another beating.

Maybe Ewyn would laugh. Maybe there would be some disgust hidden behind his gaze.

But he had to know.

Kerry wasn't exactly sure what plan B was, but he expected whatever was about to happen with Ewyn to fail miserably. He had no hope at all. Feeling nauseous and unsteady, his face pale and his gaze failing to lift from the ground, Kerry got out of the car and walked to the door.

His heart was in his throat, his entire body tensed for a fight as he knocked with a shaking hand.

"Coming!" Ewyn called from inside.

"I'm screwed," Kerry breathed, his eyes closed. "I'm screwed, I'm screwed, I'm screwed."

The door swung open. The instinct to run was nearly overpowering. When there was an awful, nightmarish second of perfect silence as Ewyn looked at him, Kerry took a backward step.

"What happened?" Ewyn demanded. "What's wrong? You look petrified. Come in. Sit down. I'll get you some water."

A nervous laugh escaped Kerry and he chanced a look up at Ewyn's expression.

All Kerry saw was pure worry, which stunned him for a second. He just stood there on the stoop, staring.

"Kerry..."

The waiting — for a punch, a kick, a threat, a laugh, a sneer — paralyzed him. There was nothing in him able to trust the evidence of acceptance.

Ewyn wasn't even looking at the dress. It was like he didn't even care. He only studied Kerry's face, his eyes.

"You're scaring the life out of me, love. Please." He reached out, took Kerry by the arm and drew him closer, bringing him over the threshold and into the home. When the door closed behind him, Kerry tried to catch his breath, to focus. When Ewyn's hand slid lightly down the side of Kerry's arm, Kerry flinched.

"Kerry..."

He folded Kerry into a hug. The compassion and tenderness in the enveloping embrace was a steady shore he broke himself against. Eyes staring, breaths coming in shallow gasps, hands in fists, Kerry was locked within his own anxiety. It trapped him.

"God, you're shaking. It's only been a few hours. What could have happened? You didn't go back to that damned apartment, did you? Did Victor try something with you? Are you okay? Are ya hurt?" Ewyn let go to look for wounds or bruises. His hand slid down Kerry's side, then came up to clasp under his chin, tilting his face up for a better look. "You dressed up for me? You look beautiful, a *mhuirnín*."

The breath left him in a rush. The feel of Ewyn's hands on him, steadying him, helped anchor him down against a tide of painful memories threatening to carry him away. "You're not... you don't hate it?"

Ewyn frowned. "Oh, Kerry. What they've done to you, love... No, I don't hate it. You thought I would?"

"I-I don't know."

For a moment, he tried to see if from Ewyn's point of view. Ewyn, who admitted to holding on too tightly to people. Who had never dated men, only women. Who could have had anyone at Blaze, but chose the one person mostly likely to implode in a fit of pure self-doubt and fear. Maybe it should have been a warning that Ewyn fed off of Kerry's weakness. That it allowed Ewyn to feel more powerful, in comparison. Maybe Ewyn liked Kerry to remain at his most vulnerable, so Ewyn could keep playing the role of savior.

It didn't feel that way, though. The undiluted concern in Ewyn's reaction to Kerry's case of nerves only made Kerry want to give in and lose himself in Ewyn's steadiness — consequences be damned.

"Sit down. You look like you've been terrorized."

Ewyn drew him to the couch, where Kerry sat. Ewyn brought a glass of cool water from the kitchen and handed it to him before sitting by his side.

"What happened after you left?"

"Nothing," Kerry said, falling back on the safety of denial once more.

"You went back there, didn't you?" Ewyn guessed, his expression darkening. "Why would you do that to yourself?"

Kerry sipped the water, shook his head. "I didn't want you to worry, and I guess I've just been kidding myself about how bad it's gotten. I should have listened to you. Victor..."

"What did that bastard do now? Did he touch you? Come after you?"

"No. He... said some things, when I got home. Him and his friends. They asked where my boyfriend was, said I should watch myself. Called... called me a..." The awful word wouldn't come out. "But I got inside the apartment okay. I called Jamie. Told him to stay away from the place, because I know how impulsive he is. He wouldn't see how dangerous a drop-by could become. And I — "

"You can't stay there," Ewyn told him. "I won't have it."

One of Kerry's eyebrows rose. A surprising urge to resist the order struck, even though asking to stay with Ewyn was the whole reason for the visit. Maybe Kerry's inner rebel was coming to the surface again.

"Are ya honestly telling me you feel comfortable staying there?" Ewyn challenged.

"No! No, but... where else am I supposed to go?"

"Here. With me."

A warm swell of mixed emotion spread through his chest, steadying his breaths, unknotting his stomach. It felt strengthening, all-encompassing, invigorating, and alarming. Something about having Ewyn basically demand Kerry stay with him struck him differently than the idea of asking to stay. He found himself arguing against the very thing he'd hoped for. Kerry's rebellious side took temporary control.

"But Ewyn, we just... It's too soon. I can't ask that of you."

"You didn't ask. I'm telling you to stay here."

The urge to smile almost got the better of him, but he fought that down too.

"I'd feel like I'm taking advantage."

"You, taking advantage? Coming here, looking as irresistible as you do, giving me a chance to keep you close, keep you safe? There's no taking advantage in that."

"What if we're moving too fast?"

"If you start to feel so, tell me. It can be a safe roof over your head, if you'd like. That's all."

Staring into Ewyn's dark eyes, feeling a dangerous tickle of want stirring, Kerry stammered, "I-I swear I'd do my part. I could help clean, cook, any... anything you need."

Something dangerous and animalistic moved behind Ewyn's gaze. His chest rose and fell more heavily. Kerry swallowed and became overly aware of the size difference between them, compounded by the ways the dress made him feel more helpless and bare.

There was scorching heat in the way Ewyn's gaze swept down over Kerry's body, lingering.

He felt it — how Ewyn wouldn't hesitate to consume him if given the opportunity, how his hunger was the most dangerous thing in the room, but Kerry was nothing but enthralled by it. To give as much of himself as he had, just in coming there dressed as he was, and be met with only pure, raging lust and heartfelt concern weakened all of his defenses.

He shifted sideways, facing Ewyn, drawing his left leg back onto the couch cushion. The twisting movement spread his legs, pulling the skirt high on his thighs. Ewyn's gaze went right there, to the shadows below the skirt's edge.

"Anything," Kerry offered softly. With one hand, he drew a handful of the skirt towards him, just a few inches, exposing more of his thighs.

"Stop," Ewyn commanded. Kerry froze, his breath quickening, his body trembling slightly. "Lay back."

There was no resisting, no protesting.

With a shaky exhale, he lay back on the couch, against the armrest.

"Hands off. No touching," Ewyn told him, his voice gruff and growling.

Kerry let his hands fall to his sides, away from the skirt. The sound of his own heartbeat filled his head.

"Look at me."

Ewyn reached for him, wrapping a hand under Kerry's right ear in a slow caress, the fingers then drawing lower. The first two pressed under his jaw, right at his pulse point, making him conscious of how hard his heart was beating. But he did as ordered, and looked only at Ewyn through half-lidded eyes and dark eyelashes.

When Ewyn, turned to face him, pushed the skirt up with his free hand, Kerry's breath caught. He wasn't wearing underwear and now that choice left him even more self-conscious as Ewyn pushed the material up to his waist.

"No, look at me," Ewyn said sternly after Kerry closed his eyes in embarrassment.

Breathing hard through parted lips, he forced his eyes open, glimpsing how flushed, swollen and erect his cock was before focusing only on Ewyn's dark hunger once more.

"Shift your leg beside me," Ewyn told him, nodding to Kerry's left leg, bent in front of him at an angle, the one thing standing between Ewyn and Kerry's body. Slowly, Kerry shifted the leg to stretch along the back of the couch instead, opening himself entirely to Ewyn.

With soft, barely audible whines, Kerry fought for control of himself as he was pushed hard into accepting his submissiveness. He watched Ewyn gaze down at Kerry's cock, straining up to his pelvis, his balls heavy and drawn up tight. Kerry was dripping. Couldn't stop it. The fingers pressed harder at his pulse point, telling him Ewyn knew exactly how fast Kerry was falling apart.

"Anything I want?" Ewyn asked, with every single thing it implied right there in the growl of his voice.

Kerry shuddered, then managed a whispered, "Yes."

"Grab your legs under the knees. Draw 'em back. Spread yourself for me."

He obeyed before he could over think it, drawing both legs back as far as he could while keeping them as spread as his position on the couch would allow. Ewyn took a moment to fix Kerry's skirt, bunching it up even further. His hand slipped underneath to find his nipple, twisting and pulling it sharply. With a quiver and a grunt, Kerry felt more of the clear fluid drip down his cock at the jolt of stimulation.

"Like that, do ya?"

"Yes."

112

Ewyn twisted even more, and Kerry cried out roughly, his back arching. When his cock jumped in delight, he felt a twinge of shame and excitement, all swirled together. If Ewyn didn't touch him there soon, Kerry felt he might die.

Ewyn let go of the nipple, rubbing over it and the swell of Kerry's pectoral muscle. He gave it a hard squeeze, kneading. Kerry pulled at his legs, undulating.

"Be still."

"Please..."

"Patience, now. I'm in no rush."

Kerry panted, closed his eyes.

"I didn't say you could look away," Ewyn warned.

His nipple, slightly sore, was twisted again, held like that, and Kerry moaned, forcing his eyes open, letting Ewyn see all of his struggle to have his obvious arousal exposed for scrutiny. Somehow, as he lay there, panting, spread, the most delicious pain shooting through his chest, Kerry managed to get even harder, his cock a purplish-red exclamation of just how much he loved everything Ewyn was doing.

Kerry's control slipped as Ewyn let the moment draw out, the pain in Kerry's nipple spiking. He fucked the air, rolling his hips in desperation for relief.

"Be still," Ewyn scolded, twisting the flesh in his grip even more, drawing a wild cry from Kerry, who shivered and tried to force himself still.

"Please," he whimpered, begging.

Ewyn released him, caressing him, humming, "Mmm, I like you begging."

Kerry's heart pounded, beating against Ewyn's fingertips. He felt dizzy. Lightheaded.

The hand on his chest caressed down his stomach, then the side of his hip.

"Please," Kerry keened, desperate.

Ewyn's hand brushed the inside of Kerry's thigh. The pad of his thumb skimmed over Kerry's sac, driving the air from his lungs in a shuddered breath. It brushed again, more firmly.

"Ewyn..."

"Easy now, love," he crooned with a pivot of his wrist, pushing his index finger all at once through Kerry's rim and sheathing it in his ass.

Kerry grunted, panting, quaking. The dry friction burned and the penetration made him feel even more indefensible, stripping away everything but his wild need for more of everything Ewyn was forcing him to feel.

"Deep breaths," Ewyn urged, the hand at Kerry's jaw moving, the thumb brushing over his bottom lip.

Inhaling, then blowing out the air, Kerry tried to comply.

A few moments later, his breathing more regular, two fingers fed between Kerry's lips, riding his tongue. He sucked on them, moaning, frowning as he was rubbed from the inside in two places. A convulsion worked through him, there and gone.

The fingers withdrew. Ewyn pulled a condom from his pocket and ripped it open, rolled it onto Kerry. He leaned down over Kerry's body and fed a finger slowly back through his rim. Cupping Kerry's balls, he took a long lick up the underside of his shaft, provoking a guttural moan. Kerry's cock chased the press of Ewyn's tongue. Kerry's balls were gently squeezed and the finger up his ass drew a few inches out. Throwing his head back, he panted.

Ewyn sucked a kiss to Kerry's tip, then licked across it, moaning, "God, I want to taste you."

"Ewyn... please..."

"You wet for me, kitten?"

"Yes... please... more..."

The finger pushed back into his ass, all the way, and Ewyn moved to suck on Kerry's cockhead, taking the whole thing into his mouth for the first time.

Crying out, it was all Kerry could do to grip his legs and stay in the pose instead of grabbing the back of Ewyn's head and thrusting deeper. His balls were rolled, then squeezed again as Ewyn sucked. It fried Kerry's senses, emptied his mind, left him wanton and desperate, willing to do anything Ewyn said, if only he wouldn't stop.

Ewyn took a few deeper pulls, his head bobbing. Kerry whimpered and fought to stay still. The suction and grip of Ewyn's warm, wet mouth was all he knew. Nothing else existed except that one point of connection. His balls were pulled away from his body. The finger twisted in his ass. Kerry trembled and gasped. As orgasm hit, he bucked a little, his voice breaking on a cry. He felt Ewyn sucking harder, the contraction of the muscles of his mouth around Kerry only intensifying everything. Ewyn stroked him through it and withdrew his finger to rub over Kerry's rim.

Kerry panted for air.

Ewyn let him go and guided Kerry's trembling legs back down. He caressed over Kerry's stomach, smiling, biting at the edge of his lip.

"Ask me again if I like the dress," Ewyn dared.

"Why does it feel so good to let you take control like that?" was Kerry's reply.

"You like it?" Ewyn said, more of that hungry darkness revealing itself again, enough to make Kerry shiver a little. "Tell me you like it."

"I like it. I really fucking like it."

Ewyn exhaled heavily, his gaze sweeping all over Kerry's body as if mapping it and claiming it in new ways. "It doesn't scare you?"

Kerry detected Ewyn's fear there, private and ingrained. "No," Kerry swore. "I love it. I love how you make me feel. How you get me to let go."

His need shifted on him, then. It wasn't just sexual anymore. The ways Ewyn had already shown his interest and care pulled at the core of Kerry's heart. He didn't just want more of what Ewyn offered — he needed it. So much so, it scared him. Privately, he vowed to show Ewyn his gratitude and loyalty, however he could.

"Thank you for taking care of me. For… everything," Kerry told him.

"Say you'll stay," Ewyn commanded, bearing down on him, touching and holding in ways that made Kerry feel for the first time like all of the softness and vulnerability in him not only wasn't his failing — it was what made him right.

"I'll stay."

Chapter 15: Undone

The dress had been laid carefully aside on the bed. Ewyn was glad it had stayed clean, because he intended Kerry to wear it for several more hours before Ewyn could personally remove it from him again. He'd had no idea seeing Kerry dressed in such a way could have such a strong affect on him. The dress, the makeup — they were outward signs of the vulnerability Ewyn was so attracted to, hidden within Kerry's spirit. The indulgence of seeing him appear physically in a state truer to the way Ewyn felt Kerry probably existed beneath his many masks lit up the core of Ewyn's being with excitement. In fact, Ewyn suspected all of his many layers of security and protection existed solely for this reason — to help pure, fragile honesty shine its brightest. It was everything that mattered to Ewyn.

He wasn't expecting anything other than to help Kerry clean off and maybe enjoy the view as he soaped up and rinsed off. Just having him there, consenting to stay and let Ewyn indulge in doing everything he needed to help safeguard the new treasure in his life gave Ewyn more peace than Kerry could ever know. All of his persistent frustrations from feeling like everything was getting away from him, like every move he made to do the right thing, for himself and for others, only made things worse, were finally letting go. It made Ewyn feel steadier than since before Darcy had been killed. The possibility he saw in Kerry felt too good to be true, for mainly selfish reasons. So, Ewyn just prayed not to screw it up like he always had before. Luck had never, ever been on his side. It was only sheer, ballsy determination that kept him fighting the odds.

But after they were both standing in the two-person shower, Kerry quickly got on his knees at Ewyn's feet, looking nervous as hell.

"I haven't ever..."

"You don't have to, kitten," Ewyn assured him, extending a hand to help him back up. "Having you here with me is more than enough."

Kerry didn't take the hand. Instead, he reached up and took hold of Ewyn's cock, stroking it experimentally. The pad of his thumb rolled over the piercing in the head.

"You have another condom?"

"Yeah." Ewyn inched the glass door open and grabbed one from the cabinet in arms' reach, trying to limit the amount of water that sprayed out onto the tile floor. Ripping it open and rolling it on, he kept a careful eye on Kerry. He seemed determined, staring at Ewyn's dick now that he was facing it. Ewyn couldn't remember the last time he'd had someone on their knees before him, so desperate and nervous to suck him off.

"If I'm not doing it right, tell me?"

"As long as you don't bite down, you'll do fine. Honestly, it's a turn-on that you haven't had a cock in your mouth before, said the voyeur to the exhibitionist."

"That's my line," Kerry grinned.

"Good god, you're beautiful," Ewyn said softly. It made Kerry shy again, lowering his gaze. The demure reaction pushed all of Ewyn's buttons, making him only more eager to have Kerry close and keep him there where Ewyn could ensure everything would be all right.

Kerry stroked Ewyn through the condom, then opened up. Extending his tongue, looking bashful and wanton at the same time, he took his first lick.

"That's it. Nice and wide, now."

The sight of his pierced cockhead on Kerry's pink tongue was one Ewyn would never forget. Ewyn caressed the side of Kerry's jaw, enjoying the heat and energy radiating from him in waves. Kerry kept his eyes on what he was doing. Opening even wider, he wrapped his lips around the head, sucking a kiss to it, as if worshipping Ewyn's cock in just the right way was the most important thing in the world to him. Ewyn realized how good it felt to have a lover take just as much care as he usually did in how they pleasured him. It only made Ewyn want Kerry more.

"Christ," Ewyn groaned, palming the side of Kerry's head. "The sweetness of you, love. Go slow, now. Don't take it too deep just yet. Use your hand for the rest."

Kerry was tentative. He only tried to suck a couple of inches of Ewyn's dick, his hand circled around the shaft to ensure he didn't take too much in and choke himself. The sexiness of seeing Kerry suckle Ewyn's thick cock when he'd never done such a thing before for anyone else drove a hard surge of pure lust and possessive need through Ewyn. He would have loved to see his come on Kerry's lips and tongue, but knew better than to take such a foolish risk and jeopardize Kerry's health.

Kerry moaned, sucking more intensely, quickening his pace. Breathing harder, Ewyn refused to thrust, giving Kerry time to adjust and explore. He pushed the dark hair back from Kerry's face, watching his full lips stretched wide and wrapping tightly to the dark shaft as it slid and pumped between them.

"Perfect. Just like that," Ewyn urged.

Kerry started to play with Ewyn's balls as he suckled, fingering the piercing there. It was the innocence of him that tipped Ewyn over the edge. He came and Kerry kissed him through it, licking at the come through the condom.

Pulling off almost reluctantly, Kerry gazed up and asked, "We can go get tested, right?" He nuzzled Ewyn's thigh, water raining down upon them.

For how long had Ewyn looked for someone willing to trust in him as freely as Kerry did already, so quickly? Ewyn grinned down at Kerry. Perhaps he really did have other sorts of luck than bad.

"Abso-fuckin-lutely we can. Come here so I can kiss you already."

Ewyn left for work shortly after their shower, making Kerry swear to stay and rest until he returned. It was a short job, only three hours in length. Kerry settled in on the couch, sketching design ideas on a pad of paper while he listened to music on the stereo. He loved the faith it showed in him to be allowed to stay behind in Ewyn's home, plus there was nowhere else Kerry would have wanted to be.

Before he knew it, three hours had flown by. Ewyn returned with a jingling of keys. He came in, disarming the house alarm system, dressed in a slim, tailored gray suit which worked on all of Kerry's weaknesses. The suit made Ewyn seem professional, confident, capable, intimidating and sexy as hell.

"I have a favor to ask," Kerry began. He was reclined lengthways on the couch, almost in the same pose he'd been in when Ewyn had proceeded to take him so easily and thoroughly apart. The only difference was this time Kerry's legs were crossed rather than spread wide.

"Name it, beautiful," Ewyn replied as he unfastened his holster.

"I need to pick up some things from my apartment if I'm staying the night."

"The night? You'll be staying longer than that." He seemed to read Kerry's expression, his tone changing as he added, "Didn't you bring what you need?"

"No," Kerry admitted, worrying his bottom lip. "I thought it might jinx the whole thing if I came prepared. Sorry."

"Eh! No apologizing."

Kerry pressed his lips together to keep from apologizing for apologizing. When the urge passed, he continued. "I really am a pessimist sometimes. I swear I'm working on it. I didn't bring a single thing with me, but I did pack some things up before I left."

"Okay then," Ewyn shrugged. "Let's go. I'll take you on my bike."

"Your bike?" Kerry blinked.

He saw Ewyn's gaze slip down to the skirt of Kerry's dress.

"Oh, I did bring jeans. I should probably wear them so I don't flash the world."

"Well..." Ewyn's eyebrow rose in consideration, like he was imagining Kerry's bare ass on the back of the bike, flying down the road, the skirt blown up well past his waist.

Kerry hurried up and started toward the door. "I'll get the jeans."

Ewyn chuckled.

It was a twenty-five minute drive from Ewyn's place to Long Beach and traffic was light. The sun started to set and shadows stretched as dusk fell. But, because it wasn't what you'd call dark, and Ewyn's loud motorcycle wasn't exactly inconspicuous, Kerry asked him to park down the block and wait there while he went to grab the bag he'd packed in advance. The last thing he wanted was to provoke a confrontation between Ewyn and Victor.

"How long do you think you'll be?"

"Not long. Five minutes at most."

"How about I follow at a distance, walking, just to make sure — "

"I'll be fine, Ewyn. I live here, remember? Plus, even if fate's on our side and Victor isn't stalking from the porch, the rest of my neighbors are intensely nosy and I'd rather not give them something to gossip about."

"Yeah," Ewyn said warily. His sideways glances indicated he was noticing all of the less savory aspects of the area which Kerry wished he wouldn't. The abandoned, empty buildings, the trash, the people sitting on their stoops, staring, and the general air of dejection and oppression seemed to argue against Kerry's good intentions.

Kerry turned to go, giving Ewyn one last glance from over his shoulder. Ewyn had his arms folded and was leaning back against his bike, watching Kerry go. Satisfied, Kerry hurried up to the building.

There weren't many cars around. The porch was almost completely empty except for one guy on his phone who Kerry knew was friends with Victor. Kerry could sense eyes on him as he climbed the steps and passed the windows of other apartments.

Nearing the top, he dug out his keys, palming the one for his door. But, when he reached for the doorknob, the door swung right open.

"Shit," Kerry breathed, pulling his arm back, caught between the instinct to run and the shock of seeing the state of his apartment.

Furniture was overturned, the bed covers ripped off. Things were broken or smashed. Someone had trashed the place. Had they been looking for money? What had they taken? He did have a small fold of bills from tips tucked behind a loose floorboard near the bathroom, so he went to check it. It wasn't really the money he was worried about though. There were pictures hidden there too and —

"AAAH!"

A hard blow across the middle of Kerry's back sent him flying into the kitchen cabinets. His head hit the wood before he could bring his arms up to block the impact.

A voice he didn't recognize growled, "We don't want your kind here! Don't you know that, you stupid piece of shit? Yeah, we know where you work, what you do, you fucking pervert. Filthy cocksucker."

Something glinted as it swung with vicious force, coming right at him, whistling through the air. It was a bat. A metal bat. Kerry saw it clearly right before the bat connected; he felt a snap, and an explosion of agony in his lower leg consumed everything, whiting out his vision.

He screamed, trying to curl up.

"Maybe this'll help the message get across, huh?"

A booted foot kicked the side of his face, and things got fuzzy. It was all he could do to turn onto his side. His eyes barely cracked open, Kerry saw the person standing over him, wearing a hooded sweatshirt, their face in shadow. The opened door, filled with the view of a rosy purple sky, was just a few feet away. It promised escape, but might have been in a completely different universe. He'd knew he'd never get there. Letting go of hope, he passed out, seeing the bat swing again. It all went black.

Chapter 16: Caught

Ewyn tracked Kerry to the apartment, staying well back, just wanting to keep him in sight. Instinct and persistent, pessimistic terror drove him. The old nightmare haunted him for what seemed to be no reason at all — Darcy lying on the pavement with a plastic sheet over his bloody corpse, just because Ewyn dropped his guard for a moment.

Maybe that made him paranoid. Maybe his exes had been right about him all along and he really couldn't let go. Maybe by following Kerry, Ewyn was betraying him and smothering the trust they'd built, but he couldn't drop his guard again.

He wouldn't.

It could scare Kerry off, causing him to accuse Ewyn of being too overbearing, just like Isla, Jessica and Gen. If so, there was no helping it. Ewyn had to stop fighting his intuition, for good or ill. He was only too happy to sacrifice pride and happiness for the health and welfare of those for whom he cared.

Guilt and regret would always be the heavier burdens.

He stayed by a telephone pole when Kerry went up the steps, watching him push the door open. That's exactly what it looked like — he'd pushed the door open instead of using the key to unlock it. Right away, Ewyn's alarm bells went off, so he moved closer. By the time he heard a startled, pained cry, sounding like Kerry's worn-smooth voice, Ewyn was sprinting up the steps.

Then he heard Kerry's scream, unmistakable and chilling.

Ewyn forcefully let go of his own fear as soon as it began to wash through him, freezing him up. Training and practice took over with astonishing ease.

Palming the knife out of the sheath strapped to his ankle as he climbed, he then flicked out the blade.

A different voice — not Kerry's — shouted roughly, but Ewyn didn't stop to try picking out the words. When he got to the top landing, he didn't pause, but zeroed in on the two bodies in the dark. The larger one, standing above the person on the ground, wore a black sweatshirt with the hood pulled up over their head. They were swinging a baseball bat in a downward, driving blow.

Ewyn moved as the figure on the ground grunted thickly with the impact, the sound of it meaty and flat.

Fury fueled him as he cleared the landing and dashed into the apartment. The bat pulled back, ready to make the same downward arc again, smashing down on Kerry's helpless body on the floor. Pushing himself forward, Ewyn got his left arm around the attacker's chest from over his shoulder at the same time as his right hand, holding the knife, jabbed up into his throat.

"Drop the weapon," Ewyn said, repeating the instruction naturally, without having to think or feel, only react. It helped him speak more calmly than he might have, "or I'll jab this so far into your carotid, you'll be dead before you can blink."

For a second, all Ewyn heard was heavy breathing. The person he held was tensed up, sweaty, jittery and running on adrenaline.

"This is none of your fucking business!"

Ewyn twisted the blade, punching through the top layer of skin.

"Okay! Okay! Stop!"

The bat clattered to the floor. Most of the light in the tiny apartment came in through the opened doorway, a single fading shaft in the gloom. Ewyn reached into his memory of looking through Kerry's kitchen for supplies. That had been when he'd wanted to make breakfast, but he'd done a more thorough mental inventory than eggs and coffee warranted, just out of habit. Now, tapping into that, he recalled there was duct tape in a drawer a few feet away.

Keeping his tight hold on the guy in his arms, he pushed to the side.

"Open that drawer," Ewyn growled, twisting the knife a little more, just to show he wasn't to be screwed with. Once the guy had opened the drawer, Ewyn said, "Grab the tape, then get your ass on the ground. Flat to your stomach. Hands behind your back."

After that much had been done, Ewyn snapped into action. Quickly, he sat on his captive's hands and back, taping the man's feet and wrists together.

Only then did Ewyn divert his attention to Kerry and the cell phone in Ewyn's pocket. He had it in his hand with 9-1-1 dialed as soon as he had slid across the few feet of floor to Kerry's curled form.

A visual scan told Ewyn that Kerry had been kicked in the face and would need stitches. Blood seeped from a cut across his left cheek, under his eye. It was the most noticeable injury. The entire area was swelling up, darkening with a nasty bruise. Kerry wasn't moving, but his chest rose and fell slightly with each breath he took. Ewyn reached to feel for Kerry's pulse as the operator picked up, needing the steady beat beneath his fingers.

"My friend's been robbed and beaten. He's unconscious and needs an ambulance. The attacker has been immobilized but is unhurt."

What damage has the bat done? How badly is Kerry hurt?

It was impossible to guess. All he could do was stay by Kerry's side and pray the ambulance came quickly.

Stuck in limbo with no answers or reassurance, Ewyn sat on a stiff couch in the hospital while Kerry was taken for CAT scans, MRIs and God knew what else. Though Ewyn had been asked to stay in the waiting room while they attended to Kerry, a nurse had been kindly keeping him informed of what little she could. They'd stitched up the wound on Kerry's cheek, but the internal injuries needed to be either found or ruled out. Blessedly, Kerry had regained consciousness shortly after they'd finished his stitches. When he'd been wheeled out for tests, he made brief eye contact with Ewyn but either hadn't tried or hadn't been able to speak. The police lingered, though they'd already questioned Ewyn about the incident. Now, they needed to speak with Kerry once he'd returned.

Ewyn held Kerry's phone. It was an older model than his own, the case color an earthy green. The decision to call a family member was a bigger one than Ewyn was comfortable making, especially given what he'd heard about Kerry's family.

The youngest of the three brothers, Kent, seemed the safest bet. Ewyn knew of the bond brothers shared. Thinking of Darcy, Ewyn trusted that brotherly connection to lead him through the mess they were in, hoping Kerry would forgive him for acting without permission. If Ewyn called Kent, he was sacrificing part of Kerry's privacy. Still, Ewyn felt Kent needed to know.

After finding the name in Kerry's contacts, then dialing, Ewyn took a deep breath. He leaned forward, his knee bouncing restlessly, thankful that the waiting room was empty of eavesdroppers for the moment.

"Hey, kid, how's it going?" was the response when the call was picked up.

"Is this Kent Sanderson?"

"Yeah," was the tense, defensive reply. "Who is this? Why do you have my brother's phone?"

"My name's Ewyn Garrity. I'm a friend of Kerry's. I'm calling because he's in the hospital."

"Fuck. What happened now?"

Ewyn filed away the comment for later scrutiny. Then he said, "Someone broke into his place and beat him. I stopped it, but now they're trying to determine how hurt he is."

"What do you mean, they beat him?" Kent asked with quiet horror in his voice.

"I mean they had a baseball bat."

"Oh fuck, no. Oh, Kerry," Kent groaned. "Shit! I knew I should have forced him to get out of that apartment."

Ewyn heard a bang, like Kent was kicking things. He knew the feeling.

"Do they have the bastard who did this?"

"Yeah. I'm in security. I made sure he didn't get away. The police have him in custody. Didn't recognize the guy, but I'd bet anything he knows Victor Hammerstein."

"Hammerstein's his landlady's name, isn't it?"

"Yep. That's the one."

"The Hammer. That's what he always called her. So you think this ties back to her kid?"

"I do. Him and his friends have been giving Kerry a hard time. Should have known. Should have kept him clear of there."

"Hammerstein constantly gave him a hard time too. Not surprised her kid's even worse." Kent said flatly. It was funny, he kind of sounded like Kerry, only with a much stronger voice. "Let me guess, this attacker didn't even take anything?"

"From what I've heard so far, they can't tell. But it looks like it was more a direct attack against Kerry than a robbery, especially with the homophobic shite that motherfucker was saying as they loaded him into the cop car. The apartment was smashed all to hell, most of his things too." He added more softly, "Most of him."

The emotion caught up with Kent, surpassing anger. "Did... he have any head injuries, or..."

"Needed some stitches. Got hit in the face good and hard, so he looks a wreck. But he took several body shots with that bat, and..." Ewyn sighed. "We'll know more soon. We're at St. Vincent's Hospital."

"Okay. I'm on my way. Thanks." Kent almost hung up, but came back to ask, "Oh, what do you look like, so I can find you? You'll be there, right?"

"I'm not going anywhere. Big Irish bloke. Got some piercings and a beard. Hard to miss."

"Okay. Thanks. See you soon."

About a half hour later, a taller, stockier version of Kerry with more roughly carved features hurried out of the elevator. Kent's hair was a little lighter, his eyes hazel instead of violet, but the resemblance was there. Ewyn paced in the hall, still waiting for Kerry to return and too on edge to sit anymore.

Kent stopped short when he saw Ewyn, measuring him a bit.

"Kent, right?" Ewyn guessed. "I'm Ewyn." He held out his hand for shaking, and Kent took it.

"Is he here?"

"Not yet. Soon, I hope. Worried out of my fucking mind." He rubbed a hand through his hair and tried to calm down and not project a pessimistic outlook on something that might be fine.

"Thank you for stopping that guy," Kent said, still looking at Ewyn like he was trying to figure him out.

126

"Just wish I'd gotten there sooner. Kerry didn't want to be seen with me, or else I'd — "

He stopped himself there, silently cursing his stupidity.

But it seemed Kent was more savvy than Ewyn would have liked. "Why didn't he want to be seen with you? I thought you said you were friends?"

Eyes closed and trying to think his way out of the problem he'd just made for himself and Kerry, Ewyn fought not to let on but he knew his silence didn't work in his favor.

"Oh, Kerry, forgive me," he murmured regretfully under his breath before meeting Kent's gaze. "He didn't want to give his landlady any more ammo against him, not that it was needed, it seems."

"Why would she..."

Ewyn sighed again, waiting for Kent to figure it out. He averted his gaze and slipped his hands into his pants pockets. Because he'd come right from a job, he was dressed more nicely than he would have been otherwise. The suit's sleeve now stained with some of Kerry's blood, Ewyn guessed he made quite a picture, though not one Kent was prepared to understand.

"He's not," Kent laughed uncomfortably. "He's not actually dating you."

Ewyn gave him a sharp glance.

"Oh my god. He is," Kent realized. "But he's not... he doesn't... Oh."

"Look, I don't have his permission to talk about this with you, and I know he values his privacy. But, like I said, I work in security. My place is secure. That's where he's staying. He's not going back to that fucking building."

Kent cleared his throat, looking even more uncomfortable. He slipped his phone out of his pocket and tapped at the screen a few times, probably checking his messages. "My, uh, my father is on his way here. I think it'd be better if I left out your specific relationship to Kerry for now. And, if you'd rather go, we can take over from here."

"No. No way. I'm not leaving until he's discharged."

Kent didn't reply. Putting his phone to his ear, he said to Ewyn, "If you'll excuse me a moment," and walked away.

127

Kerry returned, wheeled back into his room on a bed just when his father arrived. Ewyn hung back as Michael Sanderson and Kent rushed in to get the latest news from the nurse. As much as Ewyn wanted to know if Kerry was all right, he stayed away. Though visiting hours were going on, he wasn't sure he was welcome in the room, plus the last thing Kerry needed was more complication — having to explain Ewyn's presence on top of everything else. Telling himself it was the respectful thing to do, Ewyn gave the family some space.

He could just see them through the opened door. Mr. Sanderson gave Kerry's hand a squeeze, and Kent was talking, but Kerry wasn't looking at either of them. Exhaustion, agony, fear — they were an ache in Kerry's expression, unbearable to witness.

Rubbing a hand over his mouth, Ewyn forced himself to stay where he was.

But then Kerry seemed to glimpse him. He said a few words, then Kent came out into the hall.

"He's asking for you," Kent told Ewyn.

"Oh. Okay."

Once he'd caught Kerry's gaze again, Ewyn didn't let it go. Closing the gap between them, he paid no mind to the others for now, even when Michael left the room just before Ewyn entered it. He let Kerry's beseeching draw him in. The nearer Ewyn got, the more Kerry reached out, until his hand lifted off the bed, stretching toward him.

Ewyn took it up in both of his and whispered, "Oh, Kerry, I'm so damned sorry."

Kerry's fingers tightened around his, like he was afraid of Ewyn pulling away. His arm tugged Ewyn even nearer, his terribly bruised, beautiful face impossible to look away from.

"Ewyn," Kerry said, sounding shaken. "My leg. There's something wrong with it. The pain isn't going away."

Ewyn clasped Kerry's hand in both of his, trying to show Kerry his steadiness to help anchor him. "Look, whatever it is, we'll handle it. You're awake. You're talking. That's all that matters."

"But my job…"

"I know. It'll be okay."

"I should have known better. I should have asked you to come with me. I'm so stupid," Kerry's voice was paper thin, his face too pale. He cringed and then cried out, his free hand going right to his back.

Envisioning the bat swinging through the air, hearing it connect in his memory, Ewyn silently cursed the fucker who'd beaten Kerry.

"What can I do?" Ewyn asked.

"Nothing. Just stay? Please?"

"Okay," Ewyn told him. "Okay."

Kerry's father lingered out in the hallway, watching them. The descriptions of Michael Sanderson's former mistreatment of his youngest son were too fresh in Ewyn's memory. It kept his guard up, but instinct wasn't helping him figure out what to do anymore. He didn't know what to say, and Kerry was in too much agony to worry about an explanation or introductions.

Luckily, they were spared further social discomfort when a doctor walked in, carrying test results and x-rays.

"Okay, Mr. Sanderson," she said, clipping the x-ray to a board and turning on the light so they could see. "The good news is, despite your extensive bruising, the only break you've suffered is in your fibula." She pointed to a tiny white line, cutting straight across the middle of the bone in Kerry's lower leg. "And luckily it's undisplaced, so your recovery time should be on the shorter side. You'll need a full leg cast for about four weeks. After that, we'll put you in a below-the-knee brace for a further six weeks. At first, I'm going to ask that you stay off your leg as much as you can. Don't put any weight on it. I'll have you come in for new x-rays at four weeks when we remove the cast, and make a judgment call from there based on how you've healed. Once you're in the brace, you'll want to gradually start putting weight on the leg, using crutches or a cane. I recommend you work with a physiotherapist after that. There's one who practices out of this hospital and is excellent."

She went into more detail about treatment, how they would put Kerry in touch with an orthopedist for the casting and bracing. Ewyn took notes on everything with the notepad function in his phone, just in case Kerry had trouble remembering later.

"You'll need plenty of bed rest for several weeks, so I hope you'll have some help at home, preferably someplace without stairs to navigate." She looked at Ewyn, who was still holding tightly to Kerry's hand.

"No problem," Ewyn told her.

"I can't ask you to take care of me," Kerry protested.

"You don't need to ask, I'm telling. It's done."

Kerry's expression twisted. He made an effort to smile a bit, despite his obvious discomfort. "Thank you." He squeezed Ewyn's hand.

"You'll have a safe space, no worries, and no stress. Okay?"

"Okay."

The doctor said, "We should be able to discharge you in a few hours."

"Great. Thanks," Kerry told her.

Once she'd left, Kerry seemed to realize his father and Kent waited nearby.

"That's Michael. I asked him to wait in the hall. I don't know what to tell him."

"I know. Leave it for another day. He'll understand."

Kent, however, returned a moment later, leaning through the doorway. "Kerry? Let us take you home, huh?"

Kerry shook his head, his eyes downcast.

"Please, Kerry. We'll make sure you're taken care of, and get your rest. You won't have to worry about anything."

Kerry blew out a breath, his whole body trembling and strained. "I can't. Thank you, but no."

He looked almost panicked, like everything was starting to get away from him. Ewyn couldn't help remembering the descriptions of how Kerry had suffered at his stepfather's hands. It made him glad Kerry was trying to avoid going back to the family home, where the was no guarantee he would be completely safe. Not with Michael there and Kerry's relationship with Ewyn hanging over them.

"Kerry," Kent said with more aggravation. "I'm not leaving you with a stranger! Enough is enough. If you won't go with Dad, then come back with me. I have the room. I — "

"I have somewhere to stay," Kerry cut in weakly.

"But — "

"Kent, I have somewhere to stay, but thank you for the offer."

Kent, however, wasn't done. "You can't run anymore. These choices you're making are putting your life at risk! Please, it's enough. It's more than enough. Mom's rushing here from Aunt Kathy's place upstate to see you. This is the better choice."

"It's my choice, not yours. Let it go."

The silence drew out as Kerry lay there, holding Ewyn's hand, looking at nothing but his broken leg, covered in a sheet.

Finally, Kerry added, "I'm really tired. I'd like to get some rest."

There were footsteps from just outside the room. Ewyn glanced up just as Michael walked out of sight, headed toward the waiting room and the bank of elevators.

"I'll talk to Dad. I'll keep him out of your hair, okay?" Kent finally offered.

"Okay. Thanks."

"And I'll stay until you're released, just to make sure you're okay. Is that all right?"

"Fine," Kerry relented.

"I don't have my bike," Ewyn realized. He'd ridden in the ambulance with Kerry. Speaking to Kent, Ewyn said, "Any chance you could give us a ride back to my house? It'd be much appreciated."

Seeming to jump at the chance to help, Kent eagerly replied, "Of course. No problem. It would be nice to see Kerry get settled before leaving him."

Eyes closed now and some of his frown melted away, Kerry was nearly asleep. Thinking of Darcy and all of the conversations they might have had should he have survived, Ewyn could only imagine the physical pain, not to mention the emotional torment Kerry was going through. Caressing his cheek, Ewyn felt him press gently into the touch. Kerry settled a little more and dozed off.

Chapter 17: Picking Up the Pieces

"You're not going to believe this, brother, but I'm at the hospital. The guy I'm seeing, Kerry, was jumped and beaten with a baseball bat. It happened in his own goddamned apartment. Some piece of shite who knows the psychotic son of the landlady, trying to scare him off for being gay. I stopped it as soon as I could but — "

"Jesus, are you serious?" Trevor exclaimed. "Is he okay?"

"Not yet, but he'll get there. Look, I'm calling because I need a couple of favors."

"Name it."

"I'll owe you, but you know I'm good to pay you back. My bike is over by Kerry's place, where this all went down. Can you swing by with Caelab to get it?" Caelab was Trevor's collared submissive. They both rode Harleys, too. Ewyn's gut told him he could rely on his old friend to help him get out of the sticky situation he found himself in.

"I could if I had the keys," Trevor replied, pointing out the obvious.

"Well, that leads me to my next request. Kerry's brother is coming back with us to make sure Kerry gets settled. I'm going to be calling my mum, too, and there's also the issue of Kerry having bruises all over his face and body from the attack. This kid lives on his image, you get me? He's a dancer. It's his life. You've seen my bedroom."

"Oh," Trevor said, finally getting it. "You need me to take 'em down?"

"Yes. Take down the ones you can, cover the rest with some fabric. There's a screw gun in my garage, some old curtain rods, curtains and fabric, as well. All I'm looking for is a temporary solution."

"I can handle that. I've got my spare key to your place, but you'd need to give me the code to get in."

"And you'll have it. I'll text it to your phone. The bike keys are hanging by the door. Thank you. You're a life saver."

"No, I think you have us confused," Trevor said easily. "It'll be done. I'll text you once it is, okay?"

"Thanks."

Several hours later, exhaustion had set in. They'd gotten lucky with an emergency appointment with a nearby orthopedist who fitted Kerry with a full leg cast. It had been applied without anesthetic, given the nature of the break, and Kerry's insistence that he could stand the process without drugs.

They'd hung his lower leg over the side of the bed, allowing gravity to keep it straight. The cast was applied from toes to knee in that position. Then they'd lifted his leg onto the bed and the cast was continued up above the knee, bent at a forty degree angle to allow the leg to swing through when crutch walking.

Having the leg so thoroughly confined and unable to bend, the skin inaccessible if he needed to scratch, and doctor's orders to stay completely off of it made Kerry panic. He was claustrophobic in his own body, with no ability to move from where others set him, no idea how he was going to get dressed or bathe or function. His independence had been the most important thing in his life. Now, that was gone.

Ewyn sat in the passenger seat of Kent's car, while Kerry was in the back where he had more room to extend his leg. They were driving to Ewyn's house. As freaked out as he was, Kerry didn't have much energy left to focus on worrying about practical things. His head wouldn't stop spinning and he was bone-tired. All he wanted was to sleep for days and to forget everything until the pain lessened. But when Kent stopped for gas and left them alone for a moment, some of Kerry's tried and true practicality kicked in anyway. He asked Ewyn, "Is this a good idea? My brother seeing what's in your house? Your bedroom?"

"I took care of it," Ewyn assured him.

"How? I thought you were waiting for me at the hospital the whole time? We've been together since they released me."

"I've got my ways, love. Privacy's important to me too, but your family deserves a little assurance they aren't leaving ya in a questionable situation. I don't intend to keep them out if they want to visit you; if you allow it, of course. That's your call to make."

Every time Kerry moved, it hurt, and it wasn't just his leg. His neck, jaw, cheekbone, back — all of it ached. The more time that passed, the worse it got. The dose of Advil they'd given him was the only thing helping him keep it together.

When they arrived at the house, Kent didn't say much as he and Ewyn helped Kerry out of the car. Ewyn had helped Kerry clothe himself in a set of old scrubs that a nurse had given them since his jeans had been cut off of him in the emergency room. The leg of the pants were sliced open to fit over his cast. The dress Kerry had been wearing was concealed beneath the baggy scrubs and Kerry's jacket. The destroyed jeans had been given to Ewyn in a plastic bag along with Kerry's wallet. Hiding the dress was all that mattered.

Ewyn unlocked the door and held it open while Kent aided Kerry with his new crutches. Groaning at the way they pressed at his underarms, aggravating the discomfort that was already in his chest and back, Kerry realized the doctors had been right. As headstrong as he could be, he really wasn't going to be moving around a lot if he could help it.

"Just come lay down in bed, okay?" Ewyn urged. He went ahead of them, opening the bedroom door, then turning down the bed.

Kerry had barely enough in him to realize the bedroom looked a lot different. The mirrors were gone and fabric was draped prettily over the ceiling above the bed and down the walls behind the bed and directly in front of it.

"Ahh, fuck," Kerry cursed at all of his aches, stopping by the bedside and trying to ease off the crutches and turn to lay down.

"Easy now. Nice and slow."

Ewyn braced Kerry's arm, helping him. With a pained groan, gritting his teeth, Kerry tried to settle. He lay on his back with fluffy pillows under his head and his broken leg propped up on another pillow to help the swelling go down. Ewyn covered him with the sheet and blanket. Then he left the room. Kent stood there at the bedside, biting at his thumb and watching Kerry.

"Mom wants to see you, but how about we let that be tomorrow instead? So you can rest?"

"Yeah. Please."

"Kurt and Kipp also want to see if you're okay, but they didn't want to crowd you. They know you don't like that, so they'll come tomorrow instead, too, after Mom." Softer, he asked, "Are you really okay to stay here, Kerr?"

"Yes," Kerry answered. "I am. I'm staying here."

"Okay. If you say so."

Ewyn returned with a tall glass of water, setting in on the bedside table. He leaned in, kissed Kerry's forehead, and said, "Sleep. You're safe."

"Thank you," Kerry murmured, overwhelmed by the sudden chaos his life had devolved into. The destruction of his home, his body, his ability to do his job, and his privacy — it all threatened to drag him down. The only thing steady and strong was Ewyn.

At first, Kerry slept in small gasps of time. Discomfort, stiffness, an inability to change position much, and racked with pain from head to toe, deeper rest stayed beyond his reach. Whenever he opened his eyes, the light slipping in under the bedroom doorway helped him remember where he was. He wore the comfortable, gray shift dress — washed by Ewyn — and nothing else, though most of him was hidden beneath the bed covers. The strangeness of being in the room without the mirrors kept confusing him. He'd awaken, then have trouble placing where he was, or what had happened. Next, the pain would set in, mainly in his head, back, and left leg. And he'd remember.

Dancing was over for him. In an instant, the way he supported himself, the way he'd been defining himself, was gone. A man he didn't even know had taken the choice out of his hands with a few swings of a bat and plenty of blind hate. Kerry would quickly lose his new job mere weeks after beginning it and finally getting out of Savage Men and into a better situation. Who knew if he'd be able to get hired again there, or somewhere as good? He'd heard his spot at

Savage had already been filled, so he couldn't even go back there out of desperation.

He also couldn't go back to his apartment — that much was beyond doubt. Not having a home or a job made him feel like he was floating, with nothing holding him down, and nothing stable to call his own. He was worthless. A burden to those around him. His resistance to rely on family because of his reluctance to discuss Ewyn or other recent developments also didn't help. He was nothing — not a dancer, not independent, not able to provide for his own basic needs, not a dutiful son, not straight, not masculine — just a battered reject without reason to believe things would improve.

Logically, he knew it was the shock making him depressed, the pain shattering his positivity.

He hated being in the bedroom alone with his pessimism and pain.

When Ewyn came in to check on him, Kerry was ready.

"Is anyone else here?"

"Nah, just you and me. Kent left right after you dozed off. I called out of work for a couple of days, to keep an eye on you. Your phone's been ringing a lot. Your mom. Michael. Your brothers. Jamie's tried a few times, too. Saw his photo come up on the caller ID."

"Okay. I'll, uh… I'll have to figure out what to tell Jamie. There's no way he could have found out what happened. He's probably just checking in with me. He's not in contact with my family and I don't think he'd find out through Victor or The Hammer. No one else should have heard. But eventually I'll need to call Jamie back. Fill him in. Make sure he protects himself."

"Do you want me to text him for you? Just to say you're okay and will call back soon?"

"Yeah. That would be great, actually. Thank you."

"No problem. I can call Cory at Blaze, too. Fill him in on what happened and explain you won't be able to come back for a while. Say you'll give him a call once you're feeling up to it."

"Would you? Please? That's a conversation I'm not ready for right now."

"Of course."

Kerry blew out a breath, then said what was really concerning him. "It's dark out, but you haven't come to bed. You're sleeping in here, right?"

"I was gonna stay on the couch. I don't want to accidentally bump you or your leg and — "

"Please sleep in here," Kerry said, directly.

Ewyn seemed to read Kerry's expression. He sat down on the edge of the bed, taking Kerry's hand. "What's wrong? Talk to me."

Kerry sighed, biting his cheek, searching for the words to properly convey his feelings. His body, his confidence, his life — it was a mess. Sheer force of will was the only thing keeping him in one piece. He wasn't weak. He couldn't be weak.

That's Michael's brainwashing talking.

"I'm, uh," Kerry said, struggling to explain, "having a hard time with all of this. I mean, I just lost my home, and my job, and — "

"Hey," Ewyn hushed, caressing Kerry's arm. "You have a home — a safer one with someone who would do anything to take care of you, no matter what that means. And that job wasn't right for you anyway. You said it yourself. It was a way to make ends meet. Think of this as an opportunity to have a new beginning. You can finally pursue your dreams without the pressure to keep a roof over your head. But these are all things that can wait you've rested, and healed."

Kerry took a deep breath. What Ewyn had said helped, more than Kerry expected.

"I can't imagine what my family's thinking right now, about me and you. I didn't know what to tell them. Was it terrible to ask Michael to leave the room? Do you think he hates me for it?"

"No. I don't. I think he understood how much you're going through. He must know by now how you value privacy. But we'll deal with all of that later, too. Taking care of you is the priority. They know that. They're worried about you, but we'll just have to reassure them that you're comfortable here. Okay?" Ewyn caressed Kerry's hand, gazing into his eyes.

"I haven't known you very long. I've hijacked your life. I'm asking too much."

"You're not. You're surviving. Healing. And let's focus on the quality of our time together, rather than the quantity, all right?"

"Yeah. All right," he allowed, reluctantly.

"All my life, I've gone where I'm needed most. It's what drives me. It's who I am. You need me. I'm happy to be here for you. Helps me feel useful. Like I'm making a difference. Like maybe some of my overbearing qualities can be used for good instead of evil for once."

Kerry smiled, squeezed his hand.

"What else is on your mind?"

He thought of Jonah, another important piece of him that had gotten lost in the confusion. Jonah deserved so much better. Kerry knew his duty, and living up to the role he would always play in relation to Jonah was still a priority even if it wasn't easily defined or explained. Thinking about it was emotional quicksand, so he pulled back, shut off the endless sorrow. It wasn't the time to talk about that. But not being able to explain only made it feel worse, sinking the pit in his stomach and his spirit.

"Please," Ewyn begged. He caressed Kerry's non-bruised cheek. "Don't close me out."

"I need to light my candle," Kerry admitted, praying to avoid explanation.

"I already lit it for you. It's in the window in the kitchen."

Eyes stinging with a hard rush of gratitude, Kerry knew he would have hugged Ewyn if moving didn't hurt so much. So, all he could do was squeeze his hand again. Kerry still felt he needed to impress Ewyn, so to have nothing to give, not even pride, cut deep.

"Whenever you're ready to tell me about the reason why you light it, I'll listen," Ewyn said.

"I hate you seeing me like this. I'm a mess. I'm useless."

"Kerry, I still have you. You're still alive. The last time I went through this, not so long ago, I lost one of the most important people in my life." Pain of a different sort than Kerry was enduring reflected in Ewyn's dark eyes. There was depth to it, and layers. It was the sort of weight that stayed for a long time, unshakable, inescapable. There was no way to explain it until it had fallen upon its next victim. And Kerry had been there. He was still there. "I know the stakes. I've been terrified for hours of how easily I could have lost you, too. When I think of what could have happened if I hadn't come for you? I mean, my god. Please don't worry about anything else. Just be here. Rest. That's more than enough."

Holding tight to his secrets, Kerry could only try to draw comfort from Ewyn's steadiness.

"Get some more sleep," Ewyn told Kerry, kissing his forehead, gently smoothing his hair back. "I'm going to call Cory and shower, then I'll be joining you."

"Okay."

Just a little while later, Ewyn lay next to Kerry. To not be alone, and have Ewyn's right beside him, made Kerry feel a lot better. In his apartment, it had been so lonely at night with Jamie gone. And years before that, the loneliness had been worse. How many times had Kerry sat up in the hospital, on his own, holding Jonah's hand, wishing there had been someone there for him to lean on when he felt weak?

Despite his predicament, his injuries — everything — Kerry knew he was lucky.

Ewyn saved me. He stayed with me. I need to stop questioning things. If you sent him to help me, Kerry prayed to Jonah, then thank you.

Maybe it was a sign. Maybe, for now, he could stop trying to be what he wasn't, and hadn't been for a long time. He was just so tired. He didn't have the strength to pretend anymore, consequences be damned.

It was late in the morning when Ewyn brought in a plate of hot breakfast and coffee. Kerry shook off his sleepy doze and shifted further upright as Ewyn set down a tray. Earlier, Kerry had washed off at the sink rather than attempt to shower or use the bath. The awkward balancing act and unshakable dread of catching sight of his reflection had left him weak once more and eager to crawl back in bed.

"What's up?" Kerry asked, frowning when he noticed the puzzling expression on Ewyn's face. "You look like something's up."

"Well..." Ewyn exhaled heavily, avoiding eye contact and biting at the edge of his lip. Kerry hid a small grin. He didn't even know Ewyn was capable of seeming bashful. "I have to go to work today, but I can't leave you alone. Kent said he'd be coming by later. He's packing up your things from the apartment and bringing it all over here. I cleared out space for boxes in the garage and we can put your dresser right over there, so you have access to your clothes.

The other furniture will go to Kent's place for now, if that's all right with you. But, in the meantime…"

"What?"

"My mother is here," Ewyn said, his face scrunching up with embarrassment.

"Really?" Kerry said somewhat excitedly.

"You're happy about this?" Ewyn said cautiously.

"Why's she here?" He perked up, forgetting some of his worries.

"I asked her to be here, and stay with you. She's a fusser, though."

"A fusser?"

"Yes," Ewyn said heavily. "Why do you think I moved the hell away when I could? The woman won't leave me alone."

Kerry smiled, his own troubles forgotten, distracted by wonderful visions of what Ewyn's mother could possibly be like.

"But in this situation a fusser can be put to good use. I'll make sure she knows to let you sleep and to not tell embarrassing stories about me."

Kerry had only one concern about the idea, but it was enough to leach some of his joy away, especially after the disastrous family situation at the hospital. "Does she know you're dating me? Is dating the word we're using? I know we haven't talked about it much."

"Yes, she knows. I think she could tell from the look on my face when I answered the door."

A thickly-accented woman called from the living room, "Ewyn Garrity, are you going to keep talking about me in there or are you going to finally introduce me already?!"

Kerry chuckled, then groaned as a twinge caught him, lacing through his back.

Ewyn moaned. "This was a bad idea."

"Are you kidding? This is the second best idea you've ever had."

"Oh, is it? And what are we calling number one?"

"Well, I always wanted a hero. Did I ever tell you that?" Right after he'd said it, shocked at his own brazen honesty, Kerry started to blush.

"Fuck, you're adorable," Ewyn sighed. "Okay. Let's get this over with."

He went to open the bedroom door. A short, plump and curvy fifty-something woman stood on the other side, her hands on her hips. She had a cloud of curly light brown hair around her head and dark brown eyes. The resemblance was hysterically obvious. Kerry's heart ached with affection to see it.

"Mum, this is Kerry. Kerry, my mum, Erin Garrity."

"Oh Ewyn, he's just lovely, isn't he?" Erin said fondly, giving Kerry a smile and coming over. She took his hand, giving it a pat. "It's so nice to meet the young man who's stolen my boy's heart. He really is done for. I can tell."

"I really don't want to be a bother," Kerry started.

"Nonsense," she scolded. "Ewyn may call me a fusser when he thinks I'm not listening — "

"Mum — "

"But he will always be just as much of a fusser, in his own special ways." She gave him a deceptively sweet smile from over her shoulder.

"I think I love you already, Ms. Garrity," Kerry chuckled, seeing Ewyn's mortification as he lingered over by the door with his hand over his mouth.

"Oh, it's just Erin, sweetheart. Ewyn, I can see," Erin continued, "that you finally found someone worth fussing over." She glanced down at Kerry's untouched plate full of breakfast. "But here we are, chatting, and this child is fading away to nothing. You need to eat, Kerry. You're far too thin."

"Yes, she's one of those," Ewyn warned from his corner.

"Oh, don't even pretend you wouldn't enjoy it if Kerry had some more meat on his bones," Erin said with a cheeky grin.

"Oh, Jesus." Ewyn wiped his hand over his eyes. "I'm not going to survive this."

"And if I hear you're underfeeding him — " Erin started.

"I'm the one who cooked him the breakfast in the first place, woman," Ewyn complained.

"Egg whites and toast," she scoffed.

"He likes egg whites and toast!"

Wearing a huge grin, which actually hurt his sore cheek a little, not that he cared, Kerry kept glancing between them. The whole thing was priceless.

"Kerry," Erin said, turning back to him, "How about I fry you up some sausages to fill out that pathetic breakfast my poor son put together?"

"Mum, do not start offering my boyfriend sausages, for Christ's sake. We don't even have sausages."

"Oh, I doubt that."

Kerry burst out laughing, even though it made his ribs ache, then tried to clamp his lips together to hold in the sound.

"You, don't encourage her," Ewyn warned Kerry.

"Don't call him you. Where are your manners? This poor child has been seriously injured, Ewyn, and — "

"I know he's injured! I was there. Come on. Out." He took hold of Erin by the shoulders and guided her from the room. Closing the door behind her, Ewyn said to Kerry in barely a whisper, "I am so sorry."

"Are you kidding? This is amazing. She's amazing. And you're adorable when you're embarrassed."

Ewyn seemed content with that, but still looked disturbed in a way that made Kerry's grin hard to lose.

"I'll have my phone on me the whole time, and I'll leave your phone right next to you. If she's too much, tell me and I'll handle it."

"She's your mom. I'll be fine," Kerry smirked.

"Well, I'm glad to see you smiling," Ewyn allowed.

"Let him eat his breakfast, child," Erin yelled from the next room.

"I'm a grown man, not a child," Ewyn called back. Then he swore under his breath, "Jesus. You, don't let her talk to you like that."

"My dad was a Marine. I'm kind of used to bossy people. And, trust me; they're not all as sweet as her."

"Okay," Ewyn relented. "Eat. I'll kiss you goodbye before I go."

"Okay," Kerry smiled back.

Chapter 18: Outside In

After breakfast and almost an hour after Ewyn left for work, the doorbell rang. Kerry heard Erin curse the noise. He'd been quietly paging through a book to keep his mind occupied, so perhaps she thought he was napping and the visitor would be a disruption. Silently, Kerry waited to see who it was.

When Erin crept into the room, Kerry had set the book set aside and smiled to show her he was awake. She was carrying a huge bouquet of flowers in the colors of white, gold, and violet. Erin placed them next to Kerry on the table, and handed him the card.

I hope these keep you smiling.
Counting my blessings today
and so glad to have you at my side.

Love, Ewyn

"Aww." Shyly, Kerry confessed, "They're from Ewyn."

"I guess I did something right, then," she said with a wink. "And how are we holding up? Can I make you anything? A nice snack or an early lunch, perhaps?"

"No, I'm good, but thank you, Erin. I'm still mainly tired, I think. It's tough being stuck in bed, being a dancer and a runner and a generally active person. But I think it might be good for me too. Kind of a forced vacation."

"How lovely, to be a dancer! Of course, you'd miss it, but you'll be dancing again soon. We all need reminders now and then to take

Lynn Kelling

it easy and rest. It feels like Ewyn's been trying to get me to rest since the day he was born," she chuckled. "Don't you worry your pretty head about a thing, all right? Take your rest. It's well earned. Anything you need, just let me know. It's no bother at all. It's just so nice to be included for once, to be honest. Fussers like me and my boy can never rest until we've ensured everyone's cared for."

"I hope you know how much I appreciate you being here," Kerry told her. "And your open-mindedness. Your acceptance. Feels like it's been hard to come by lately in other parts of my life, so yours is like a breath of fresh air."

Erin sat on the edge of the bed, taking his hand. "Oh, people do get stuck in their ways, don't they? What a sad thing for them, to lose out due to fear, especially when they're losing out on someone as sweet as you. Don't let their loss be your heartache. If anyone's giving you a hard time, you just let me know. I'll show 'em who's boss! I'm all too happy to help, as Ewyn kindly warned you earlier."

Kerry smiled over at her and gave her hand a squeeze. "Thanks, Erin."

"If there's anything on your mind, I'm told I'm a fine listener. Known for my discretion. And my cooking, though judging by my sons' skinniness, it hasn't been so easy to tell. But are you okay, dear? You've been through so much!"

"I'm okay, really," Kerry protested. "But maybe I could ask…"

"Name it. Anything at all."

"Did you ever get to meet Ewyn's girlfriends? He hasn't told me much. I'm not trying to pry. Just wondering how I measure up, maybe," he said self-consciously.

"Oh, yes. I met them a few times, though Ewyn has tried his best to keep me portioned off in a separate space in his life. Needs his privacy, and deserves it, but I think he always knew I felt they wouldn't go the full distance. He hoped so sweetly they would, but sometimes a mother just knows." She gazed over at him with a keen eye. "You're so much different than them, Kerry. And not for obvious reasons. I knew, as soon as I saw you. Like letting go of a heavy weight. As fretful as my boy may be over your condition, it's only because he's so devoted to you, and for the right reasons. He's fighting to protect instead of fighting to keep or fix. Before, it was so plain. Bad matches. But we're not supposed to let on we think so. Just drives them closer together in the end." She tisked. "I hope you

144

won't think less of me, Kerry, for running at the mouth, so, or being a hopeless gossip, but a mother just worries for her own."

"What did you think was off with them?" Kerry asked, driven to find out what Erin's perspective might have been.

"Ewyn always had this picture in his head, you know. Nothing like Darcy, who chased dreams and never stayed put for an instant. No, Ewyn was so traditional. By the book. Channeled his frustrations into orderliness and control. Wanted the wife and picket fence and all the trimmings, but he never listened to his own urgings. His heart. Let his head take the reins and led him right to people who didn't want anyone telling them what to do or how to take a safer path. Was it self-sabotage, maybe? Who knows."

"You think he knew they weren't a good match for him?"

"I do," Erin agreed. "Deep down. Like he wanted to build in safeguards just in case his mission was too successful. Darcy and I always tried to tell him differently, but Ewyn knew himself too well. Wouldn't be told otherwise."

"He's blamed his over-protectiveness for the breakups. Which is funny, because that's what I blame my last breakup on too."

"So you cared too much?"

"In a way. It's just always been so dangerous. Where we lived. My ex's status as trans. The people he surrounded himself with. His brazen attitude. Maybe I was self-sabotaging too."

"Could be. Sometimes there's a lesson to be learned, and the only way it'll sink in is to be knocked flat on our arse with the truth."

Kerry sighed, "Oh, I so agree. Why do we try to save people who don't want to be saved?"

"We all have a streak or two of romanticism hiding in us. Figuring ourselves to be a hero in a fit of foolish pride. But look at you and my boy! When two people only want to save each other, that's when the scales balance. When the paranoid devil on the shoulder calms a bit in facing someone relatable."

"You really do think we're a good match? Me and Ewyn?"

"I do," Erin said warmly, patting his hand. "You give him something to stand up for, which is all he wanted all along. Especially after losing Darcy like we did."

"I'm so sorry about that. What a horrible thing to have happened."

"Yes. Thank you, sweetheart. But we've made our peace. Or have made some progress at it. Gives me hope, really, to see Ewyn with someone like you, who wears their sweetness on the surface. Who defies expectations. Shows me his heart wasn't hopelessly damaged from loss, and that maybe this means our days will be filled with some color and light again, like they used to be."

"I hope so too." He struggled to say what sat on the tip of his tongue, wondering if it was too much to share so soon. The plain acceptance in Erin's spirit tempted him onward.

"What is it, dear?"

"My family doesn't accept that I'm not straight. That I'm... different than expectations."

She leaned in a little, whispering, "You can't control the expectations of others. It's a battle no one can win. We're made the way we are for a reason, far be it from us to guess. You're a beautiful soul, Kerry. You're doing just fine. If they can't see that? More's the pity for them."

"You really think so?"

"Of course I do. To love is our only job in this life. To love! Whomever we can, as much as we can."

"Wow," Kerry sighed with awe. "I like that."

"And I like you."

"I like you too," Kerry said shyly. Erin gently touched his cheek, her eyes shining as if tears were close.

"Oh, Kerry. I do see why he fell for you."

"I wish my parents were as accepting as you are," Kerry yearned, lowering his gaze as he admitted the painful truth.

"We can't help who we are. Just what we do with what we have. Ewyn told me how worried they've been about you. That means a great deal. Don't count them out yet."

Distantly, there was a knock at the door.

"Oh, I'd better get that," Erin said, shifting up off of the bed and onto her feet. "Excuse me, dear."

"Of course. Thank you, Erin."

Just a moment later, Kerry braced himself as soon as he heard his mother's voice. He hadn't gotten a good look at himself yet. That had been intentional. However, he could imagine his injuries were upsetting to behold. He was also horrified to be facing his mother while wearing a dress, even if the dress couldn't be seen thanks to the bed sheets pulled up to his chest. Scanning the room again, even though he knew nothing inappropriate was in view, Kerry felt distinctly ill at ease when his mother walked into the room.

"I'll bring in a chair," Erin offered as Kerry's mother, Debra, stood in the doorway. She wore one of her trademark power suits, with an A-line skirt and pearls ringing her neck. The color of the suit was a pale pink. Her long hair, dyed black to hide the gray, was gathered to fall in a pretty, curling cascade over one shoulder.

Her shocked expression said everything.

"Oh, come on," Kerry said, quickly losing any semblance of levity, feeling mostly ashamed. "It can't be that bad."

"Not that bad?" Debra stood stiff as a board. "They beat you with a baseball bat. You're living with a stranger."

"Ewyn is a good friend and former co-worker. He's the farthest thing from a stranger. Plus, he saved me. I might be dead if not for him," Kerry said, trying to fight for sense. There was so much to be ashamed of, but Kerry's exhaustion overpowered most of his self-consciousness. He couldn't hide that he was with Ewyn the way he'd always tried to hide Jamie. It was time to defend his choices.

Erin carried in a chair from the kitchen. She seemed to sense the tension and stayed silent as she hefted the chair, almost as big as her, setting it next to Kerry's side of the bed.

"You all right, dear? Need anything to drink or eat?" she asked Kerry in a whisper, setting her hand gently on his arm.

"No thanks, Erin. I appreciate you asking, though."

"Such a polite boy," she said, giving Debra a smile as she showed herself out and quietly shut the door.

He realized then, the stark differences between Erin and Debra. Not only had fortune smiled on Kerry when he met Ewyn — the source of astonishing, unexpected happiness and possibly the only reason he still drew breath — but also in knowing his mother. She gave him healthy perspective on the power dynamics at work in his own family, but also showed him the tension between them wasn't an unavoidable burden due to limited options. Support was available in other places. Kerry's family had grown that day to include a lovely, kind-hearted, fierce Irishwoman who proved to him that even if his heart wasn't fulfilled by the tender understanding he'd always found lacking in his parents, others were there to care for him in their stead.

"I guess Erin introduced herself. I'm sorry you won't get to meet Ewyn today."

Debra gave him a tight smile, which indicated her doubt that he was as sorry as he claimed.

"She's an angel," Kerry said. "She's been really great, taking care of me."

"How much pain are you in?"

"Enough."

She looked at his leg, enclosed in the bulky cast. "You'll lose your job."

"Yeah."

"You're not going back to live in that place, are you?" It sounded like a rhetorical question.

"No, of course not."

"And your father told me you're not coming home, either."

"I'm happy here. I'm safe."

"So, this man — Ewyn — is going to provide for you and act as your caretaker? After knowing you how long? And I can probably guess what he gets out of this arrangement."

The insinuation stung enough to bring out a more direct response than he would have given otherwise.

"Look, Debra, I've got more than enough to deal with right now and who I choose to be close to isn't anyone's business, especially if you're going to say things like that."

"I'm your mother. I've been with you through everything with Jonah, and stripping, and God knows what else."

"He's not a weapon you can use against me. And I'm not asking you to save me from this. These are my choices. They're mine. I'm owning them, all right?"

"Those choices are why you're hurt right now, and that disturbs me. How am I supposed to sit back and watch you put yourself in dangerous situations? I'm just supposed to allow it and not object to your behavior?"

"That's right."

"Someone has to try to show you how immature and reckless you're being."

Feeling the throbbing of his broken leg and the many bruises all over his body, realizing any movement would only add to his pain and that he was trapped in that room and that conversation, Kerry said softly, "It's my life to fuck up, not yours."

Debra sighed heavily. She came over, sat in the chair, dropping her purse and leaned over, holding her head in her hands and rubbing her forehead like a headache was forming.

"I just never know how to do the right thing with you," she lamented. "You make it so difficult."

"Yeah, sorry for getting beaten and all."

"Don't spin this around," she argued, sounding hurt. "You're living with a man. This is his bed, isn't it? You're sharing a bed with a man, when you're physically unable to defend yourself or — "

"Please stop."

"Is this really who you think you are?"

"He makes me happy. He's a good person. The one thing he wants to do, more than anything, is to protect others. That's the man whose bed I'm sharing. That's all that should matter to you."

"Does he even know you? Does he have any idea what you've gone through?"

Kerry had no comeback for that. He turned his head away, but then he felt his mother staring at the bruises across his face, which he refused to see, and he sensed her hurt for him.

"Pretty flowers," Debra murmured. It sounded like a peace offering.

"Ewyn sent them."

"That was nice of him."

"Yeah, I thought so too."

"Your father and I will cover the hospital bills and any expenses you might have. If you need physical therapy for your leg, or... I don't know. Pocket money. A line of credit for emergencies. I just want to make sure you have what you need. Okay?"

He knew he should refuse, but the reality of his financial situation held him back. "Okay. Thanks."

"Would you look at me for just one second, please?"

He hesitated, then looked. She appeared so worried, and older than her years.

"All of this... is this because of Michael? Because he really has changed. I promise you he has. He's trying. He worries about you just as much as the rest of us. Just... tell me how I can fix this. Are you just staying here with this man because you don't feel welcome or safe at home? Or is this what you really want?"

"He makes me happy," Kerry said, looking right at her, searching for the right thing to say and trusting his gut. "He saved my life and stayed with me in the hospital. He opened his home to me, and asked his mom to take care of me when he's at work, and he thinks I'm beautiful."

A tear slipped down her cheek. She quickly wiped it away and reached for a tissue. Nodding and lowering her gaze, she said, "Okay." She tried on a smile, and reached out to hold his hand. He wrapped his fingers around hers. "Okay."

Chapter 19: Reinforcements

The soldiers, as Kerry sometimes thought of them, arrived a couple of hours later. Erin gave them a wider berth than Debra, letting them file into the bedroom without commentary. Once Kerry glimpsed the looks on his brothers' faces, he understood why.

He wished Kent was there to act as an intermediary. Kerry never knew what to say to his older brothers.

"Hey," he said, feeling awkward; even more than he'd felt in the hospital with Michael scrutinizing him and his injuries. As Kurt and Kipp glared at their youngest brother's broken leg and visible bruising, not to mention the stitches across his cheek, Kerry once again wrestled with the particular type of anxiousness he always suffered in these moments. He felt the need to pull up straighter, to mask emotion or thought, to deny everything true and carry on all the old lies. But it just wasn't in him that day.

There had always been a breadth of space between Kerry and Michael. Yes, Michael had raised him, but they weren't blood relatives and never would be. In the absence of that, as well as of Kurt Sr., Kerry always sensed his brothers trying to assume the responsibility for his care without quite knowing how to follow through.

One of them stood on one side of the bed, one on the other, surrounding him as if using defensive tactics like this was a battle instead of a conversation. There were chairs, but Kerry knew without asking that his brothers wouldn't sit.

They looked angry.

He sensed them looking at each other, communicating wordlessly, devising a strategy. What made it hard, as it always had, was that though they were brothers, they were strangers, too. Kurt and Kipp had never really understood Kerry — not even a little. The roles they played effectively hid the human beings within.

"How the hell did this happen?" Kurt asked.

Kerry tried to control the urge to roll his eyes. "Is that a rhetorical question, or…?"

The two eldest Sandersons didn't share any of the same facial features. Kurt resembled their mother, where Kipp took completely after their absentee father. Kerry and Kent were differing mixes of the two, though Kerry had always been the most delicately and femininely appointed. At the moment, Kurt and Kipp were both wearing the Sanderson uniform of khakis and polo shirts, their close-cropped haircuts identical, just like their nearly black hair and light eyes. With their intentional cookie-cutter appearances, hyper-masculine physicality, decisiveness and willingness to follow instructions, they were everything Kerry wasn't.

"I'd just gotten home. Saw that my place had been trashed," Kerry explained. "I didn't see anyone. I just wanted to make sure the box with Jonah's things wasn't — "

"You should know better than that," Kipp cut in. "People matter more than things. You matter more. And you know to do a visual scan of the area first when you suspect there might be a threat present. I know you know that, Kerry."

He was right, of course, but Kerry's priorities had never quite meshed with the family directives. Sentimentality was more prized for the youngest Sanderson than the rest of them would ever know.

"I'm not you. Either of you. I know that stuff, but my instincts are different. They just are. Yes, he got the drop on me with the first swing, and it sent me flying into the cabinets. I hit my head and he kept hitting me."

"We should never have let you live there," Kurt said.

"I don't tell you where to live, do I?"

"Kerr, are you only staying here because of Michael? Tell the truth," Kipp pressed. He sounded more shaken than Kurt, but that was usually the way. Kurt was in charge as the aggressor and decision maker. Kipp, the bigger of the two both in height and bulk, questioned things and took more of a supporting role. "Because he hasn't done anything like that since. We've kept an eye on him. He's retired now. He's not a young guy anymore. Michael just wants the family to be together and to fix this."

"This isn't about Michael. It's about me. That's the truth."

"This Garrity guy's a friend of yours?"

He could feel them crowding in, even though they hadn't moved an inch, flanking his bed and staring down at him, their arms folded tightly over their chests. They were trying to frame this in the old terms and take it to a more familiar place. From deep down, Kerry felt the need to push them away and establish his new ground. Quietly, he asserted, "He's my boyfriend."

For a moment, neither of them said anything. Then Kipp said to Kurt, "Well, no wonder then."

Kerry glanced up, feeling defensive and tired.

"Michael wouldn't do anything to hurt Kerry," Kurt replied to Kipp.

"You're the one who forced Michael out of the house last time. I was there, you know."

"It's different now. He's different."

"He beat Kerry unconscious. Maybe not with a baseball bat, but is the difference really that significant?"

Kerry kept looking between them, trying to read between their lines. They were both so good at remaining composed and calm under pressure, but their cracks were showing. He could tell how afraid for him they were, and it played at all of Kerry's weaknesses. It made him want to placate them, just to ease their concerns, but he wasn't sure how to do that without sacrificing things he cherished.

"I don't remember most of that night after Michael started attacking me," Kerry said, his soft voice cutting through the tension in strange ways.

They had never spoken of it. Not in detail or directly. Part of him had wanted to ask, but he decided it was better not to know what exactly had happened after he'd blacked out.

Kurt's hand covered his mouth but he locked eyes with Kerry. He felt how badly Kurt wanted to grab Kerry up and take him out of there, bring him somewhere safe where no one could ever hurt his baby brother again. But there was no such place. It didn't exist.

"Kurt pulled Michael off of you. Punched him in the face," Kipp said almost reluctantly. "We got your arm back in the socket while

153

you were out, so you wouldn't feel it. We made sure Michael left while Mom sat with you and cleaned you up."

"You could have died," Kurt said accusingly. He wasn't talking about Michael anymore. "This guy might be in police custody but there are plenty of others like him out there. You need to be more careful."

In barely a whisper, Kerry told him, "I love you too, okay?"

Kurt turned his back, wiping a hand over his face and hanging his head. Slightly disturbed, Kipp stared at their oldest brother, waiting and uncertain.

Testing the waters, Kerry said, "You guys would like Ewyn. He's like you. He's strong. Smart. Loyal. He takes care of people. Don't worry so much, okay? Please?"

"What do you need?" Kipp asked. "What can we do?"

"I need... some time to get my life in order, at my own pace."

"Do you need money, or help with getting your things out of the apartment, or...?"

The practical things had never been the real problem. Money didn't matter. Just the endless, seemingly futile quest to feel at home in his own skin, and no one else could help him with that.

"No. I'm okay, but thank you. Kent's getting my stuff from the apartment, I think, so maybe you could help him with that."

"Okay."

"Thank you for coming by and thank you for... you know. Before, with Michael."

Kurt finally turned back around. He came over, gently grasping Kerry's shoulder, looking right into his eyes. There were creases in his brow and tightness at his mouth, his body tensed like he saw that metal bat hitting Kerry over and over again, without any way to stop it.

"Take care of yourself, little brother. Please," he asked.

"Okay."

"If you need anything, just call," Kipp offered.

"I will."

Like so many other things, Kerry had been avoiding making the call, but there had been several messages from Jamie. It was only the knowledge that Ewyn had passed along word to Jamie already to stay away from the apartment that fed Kerry's hesitancy. Because, with Jamie safe, ignorant of the attack and unable to respond as Kerry feared he would, things were stable. Jamie was protected from the truth and Kerry was able to avoid the murky consequences. He could lie forever, keeping Jamie in the dark, shutting him out. A voice whispered to him to try it and take the coward's way out, for Jamie's protection from himself.

But Jamie was more than worried. He was freaking out. He knew Kerry was avoiding him for a reason, and couldn't find out what it was. Kerry, of course, was worried Jamie would sense just how fucked up things were from his voice alone.

But how was Kerry supposed to keep Jamie in check when he didn't even know where Jamie was and no longer had control over Jamie's life or choices? How was he supposed to protect someone who no longer wanted his protection?

Kerry was still more invested in Jamie's reaction to the news he'd been hurt than his own family's. The distance with Jamie was new, whereas with his family it was comfortably old. Kerry feared the difficult conversation that couldn't be avoided any longer.

Maybe it was all just deflection, though, from the real issues plaguing Kerry — his struggle with his identity, the brittle tension with his family, and his inability to put his needs before others' wants.

Without knowing what to say or what to do, he picked up the phone and dialed, bracing himself.

"Hi."

"Why haven't you called me back?" Jamie asked with plenty of wounded accusation. "Do you have any idea how worried I've been? You disappeared! Weren't at the club. Weren't at the apartment."

"Why'd you go there?" Kerry blurted instinctively. "Don't go there."

"The hell do you mean, don't go there? Do we have a problem here? Is that why you haven't called me? I did something to piss you off?"

Kerry knew he deserved the recrimination and all of Jamie's ire, and that it was all too easy to step into an emotional trap and continue the argument. It was their pattern, and why they broke up. He resisted the comfortable urge to counter each accusation with effort, taking a deep breath instead. When Jamie fell silent for a long moment, Kerry took the opening.

"I'm sorry you've been worried," he started, softening his voice. "I wasn't closing you out intentionally, I just have had a lot going on. It's been urgent necessities only for a few days."

"What happened?"

The denial sat on the tip of his tongue.

Nothing. Nothing happened.

Such an easy lie, and he'd never have to explain, or deal with the emotional fallout, or worry about Jamie going after Victor for payback.

But there was no containing juicy gossip, like a local hate crime where the perp actually got caught red-handed. Kerry and Jamie still had friends in common. He'd find out eventually, somehow, and it would make it so much worse if Jamie heard it through someone else.

"What is this, Kerr?" Jamie tempted. "You know I love you. Whatever trouble you're having, you can always call me, ask for anything — "

"No. I can't. I can't lean on you anymore. We broke up. I'm on my own. I have to deal with shit on my own now."

"Tell me what happened. Is it the job? Michael? The Hammer? What? Are you okay?"

He really could hear how worried Jamie was through the tension in his voice. Kerry felt the instinct to placate and confess to everything, then did his best to conquer the urge. Concern over Jamie's possible reaction to finding out Kerry had been beaten within an inch of his life far outweighed Kerry's worry of Jamie getting his feelings hurt over a white lie or two. He knew Jamie would have to go confront Victor, that he'd never let it go, so Kerry had to chance it. "Yeah, I'm okay. Or, well, getting there, I guess. Could be worse. But I'm not staying at the apartment, so there's no point in going there, okay? I'm staying with a friend instead."

He knew Jamie couldn't push for details, since so far he hadn't given many of his own either.

"This a temporary thing?"

"Not really. And my family knows, so it's turned into a huge deal, but I'm handling it. I just tend to not answer the phone as much as I usually do. So don't take it personally. I have people taking care of me. It's going to take me a while to get things sorted and settled, but I'll do it. So don't worry so much, all right?"

Jamie sighed uncertainly. "Yeah, I guess. Look, I'd love to get together for coffee or something if you're ever looking for a friendly face. Just let me know. I don't wanna overstep, but I'm still figuring out how to let go too."

"I know. Thanks. I'll check in soon. Take care of yourself," Kerry told him, then ended the call.

Chapter 20: Seen

"Come on, I'll help you into the bath."

Kerry's eyes widened but avoided Ewyn entirely. He bit his lip and bowed his head. He exuded more bashfulness than since the moment they'd first met by the dressing room at Blaze, with Kerry in nothing but a thong and shoes he could barely walk in.

Weeks had passed, and the bruises on his face had faded. The dark, reddish-purplish-blacks had shifted to a mottled dark yellow. Now, they were almost completely gone. The stitched wound was healing fast. The stitches themselves had been removed weeks ago.

But Kerry had been careful to not be undressed around Ewyn. He'd also avoided being touched, even as he struggled to get around the house on his own with the crutches. Erin had only been able to help minimally by bracing Kerry as he moved since she was so much smaller than him, and Kerry had gotten tired of lying in bed endlessly with his sketchbooks and restless thoughts. When Ewyn was there to help, Kerry shrugged off offers much more often than he accepted them. Kerry also constantly tried to talk about anything but himself, what he was going through, and the repercussions of the attack. Ewyn sensed Kerry pulling as far away as he could, a defense tactic that Ewyn didn't believe was doing him much good at all. The further away Kerry remained, the more his spirits fell. His body was steadily healing and he was getting plenty of rest, but Kerry seemed worse by the day.

Ewyn couldn't stand by and do nothing to help any longer. It was time to press Kerry to let him back in, even if it resulted in an argument between them. At least the back and forth of a disagreement would enliven Kerry's disturbingly faded soul.

Ewyn knew the strategy was risky. It had lost him lovers before. Some people just didn't want their boundaries tested, even in the service of pure concern. But past failures didn't dissuade him in the slightest.

He could tell Kerry's reticence came from shame and self-consciousness. Ewyn intended to prove to him that he was every bit as beautiful as he'd always been, if not more.

The full leg cast had come off that day, replaced with a below-the-knee brace. Ewyn intended to take advantage of Kerry's newfound freedom and coax him to celebrate a little.

"Nah. Thanks, but that's okay. I'll just wash up on my own, later."

"With the lights off, balancing on one foot and a crutch?" Ewyn asked.

Kerry shot him a sharp look. Ewyn met it with ease. "The soak will be good for your muscles. I'm not taking no for an answer."

Kerry said nothing, but twisted the edge of the bed sheet. Eventually, he retorted, "Whatever you're expecting is misguided. I don't exactly look good right now."

"A mhuirnín," Ewyn warned, "I've got my own perspective. I know what I see and what I want. I won't have you tell me otherwise. You're finally free of that damned monstrosity you've been lugging around and moving a little easier so I'm more confident you can climb into the tub without hurting yourself. It's time to treat yourself and relax."

The attack had happened so soon after they'd first started getting close, and it was clear Kerry didn't trust Ewyn was really in it for the long haul. He still wanted to impress instead of be himself. Trouble was, Kerry didn't have the strength to keep up the act.

"Shall I strip you down and carry you in, then?" Ewyn added.

Kerry's eyebrows rose and a blush stained his pale skin pink. "Funny."

"Oh, I'm not kidding," Ewyn assured him. "I'll keep hands off if you'd like, but I'm determined to see you unwind a bit."

Ewyn walked to the side of the bed and Kerry swung his legs to the side. The movement was slow, careful, with a gradual bend of his left leg, like he didn't quite trust his knee to work.

"I'll, uh..." the words were stammered softly but filled with a lovely hint of defiance. "I'll walk."

He got up on one foot, his left leg bent at the same forty degree angle the leg cast had been set at. Ewyn steadied him right away and Kerry let him take his weight, one arm slung tightly around Ewyn's back for support. Tensed up and moving awkwardly, he kept leaning on Ewyn as he hopped from the bedside to the bathroom. Each step away from the bed felt like a victory.

"Oh my god," Kerry chuckled upon spying the set-up Ewyn had arranged. He'd turned off the overhead lights in the bathroom but had set candles everywhere. It gave the room a romantic atmosphere, but also lessened the temptation for Kerry to look in the mirror at himself if he didn't want to.

Ewyn had been paying attention. Each time Kerry went into the bathroom he meticulously avoided lifting his gaze and kept his back to the mirror. Most times he didn't turn the light on at all, using only the sunlight filtering through the narrow window above the shower to see by. Ewyn didn't think it came from a place of vanity, but rather from trying to avoid deeper sadness. Kerry's looks were the way he'd supported himself for a long time. When many other parts of his life and identity left him floundering, that had been the one constant.

Someone's prejudice and rage stole that from him. That was a hard thing to face when you were still trying to pick yourself back up.

Ewyn kissed Kerry's cheek.

"I like it," Kerry admitted with a shy smile.

"Good," Ewyn replied tenderly. "Okay. I'll pull this off. Tell me when you're steady."

There had been only a couple of shift dresses Kerry had been cycling through to wear each day, though he meticulously hid them beneath the bedclothes and tried not to get out of bed if someone was watching. Erin's determination to stay on top of the laundry pile meant she'd likely found out about the dresses in no time at all, though Ewyn had no way to know for sure. His mother had never mentioned a word to him about it. Still, Kerry seemed to avoid being out of bed when Ewyn was around. Ewyn figured being seen in the dress was another reason Kerry had hesitated on the offer of the bath.

The black, silky fabric floated away from Kerry's body, hinting at curves and planes of muscle Ewyn longed to caress. He knew the convenience of the garment was only one of its appeals. He only wished Kerry would stop awaiting a reprimand for dressing in such a way, and would at least trust Ewyn to accept a preference that clearly brought Kerry much needed comfort.

"I like you in this, by the way. You should make more of them. Just make it a little shorter, maybe."

Kerry glanced up at him, perhaps to see if Ewyn was making fun. But he wasn't. Not in the way Kerry suspected at least.

"Or, you know, a lot shorter."

A hint of a smile twisted up the corner of Kerry's lips.

Ewyn caressed the edge of Kerry's jaw and murmured, "Such a beauty."

Kerry leaned slightly against the vanity, his good foot solidly planted. "Okay. I'm ready," he said, his voice a little stronger, his posture a little straighter.

Ewyn took hold of the bottom hem of Kerry's dress and pulled it over his head.

Kerry wasn't wearing underwear. For a moment, he seemed to shrink in on himself to be so suddenly naked. With the arm that wasn't keeping him steady, he rubbed at his side, the arm crossed in front of him, goosebumps coming up on his fair skin. Even in the dim lighting, Ewyn could see Kerry's blush deepening. It took every ounce of willpower Ewyn had to refrain from touching and shifting the mood to a more intimate place than he sensed Kerry was ready for.

"This is embarrassing," Kerry murmured under his breath.

"Maybe you haven't realized this," Ewyn said, "but I actually prefer you naked. Shocking, I know."

Before the attack, Kerry had always been perfectly hairless. Now without access to wherever he'd gone to be waxed, his hair was growing back in. The dark fuzz begged to be caressed. Ewyn itched to feel it against his palms.

"I haven't had anyone help me take a bath since I was little." Kerry's violet eyes flashed, a tease and a lure, working on all of Ewyn's weaknesses.

"Well, you've been missing out."

Kerry sat on the edge of the already filled, steaming tub, then carefully swung his good leg in.

"Easy now." Ewyn braced him, helping him sink into the hot water, making sure his broken leg stayed dry. He set out a folded, thick, fluffy cream towel to prop up Kerry's lower left leg.

"Oh god," Kerry moaned as the water enveloped him.

"Good?" Ewyn smirked.

"So good."

While Kerry closed his eyes in something close to bliss, his guard dropping, Ewyn looked him over. He needed to see.

Kerry's back was still marked in two spots from direct hits from the bat, the bruising finally fading away but still defined enough to show the blows. Rage blurred Ewyn's vision, but he quickly fought to get it under control. This wasn't the time or place. However, next time he was in the gym, that would be his fuel to fight and move.

Kerry's leg was just as bad, with deep bruising on his thigh that had not healed as quickly as his face.

"Maybe a spray tan would help hide them," Kerry commented, eyes open once more and following the direction of Ewyn's gaze.

"Don't you even think about it. You're perfect just the way you are." His touch feather light, Ewyn stroked Kerry's thigh, over the bruising. "Does it hurt?"

"Nah."

"Your back?"

"It's a lot better. I just get stiff from lying in bed. I've been stretching and doing some light exercises during the day, which has helped."

"Well, if you're more mobile now I can start giving you light massages, work out more of the stiffness."

"Yeah, I bet you're good at that," Kerry smirked, flirting. He leaned back, reclining in the water. He looked like he wanted to let his legs fall open but wasn't sure if he should.

Acting on the evidence that Kerry's instinct wanted him to let go, Ewyn caressed up Kerry's thigh, his hand twisting to palm under it. The closer his fingers got to the junction of Kerry's legs, the more Kerry's cock twitched, slowly filling. His legs shifted wider.

Kerry spoke up, his voice tensed. "You know that thing we talked about in the bedroom about you keeping hands off?"

"Yeah?" Ewyn pulled his hand away, ready to apologize.

"Don't. It's nice to feel you touching me. Makes me feel like less of a monster. But you don't have to if you don't want to, I — " Kerry gasped, quivering as Ewyn grabbed hold of his dick and tugged.

"Rule number two: you're never to say you're a monster. Ever. Or anything similar. You're strong, and brave, and unbelievably gorgeous, inside and out."

He tugged steadily, just a few pumps. Kerry rocked counter to each one, lips parted, brow furrowed.

"Stop!" Kerry gasped.

Ewyn let go.

"I was gonna come already," Kerry groaned.

Ewyn breathed out a wicked chuckle, caressing Kerry's inner thigh instead, his flushed, rigid cock bobbing in the water.

"And then I'd have to get out of the water and it feels too good in here to get out yet."

"Okay then." Ewyn soaped up a washcloth, getting it thick with suds, then began to wash Kerry's body. The cloth glided gently over his tight muscles. Kerry hummed with pleasure, his head rested back against another towel. The soft splash of the water as Ewyn's hand moved was the only sound in the room.

He took his time, drew it out. Kerry's legs fell open widely, his cock still stiff minutes later.

Ewyn dropped the washcloth and grabbed some waterproof lube. After applying some to his fingers, he reached down between Kerry's legs, his arm plunging into the water up to the elbow. Rubbing the slick over Kerry's hole, he studied Kerry's reaction. He'd bit his lip, let his head tip back a little more. His chest rose and fell a little more heavily.

Ewyn teased his fingertip through Kerry's rim. Sweet little frown lines instantly creased his brow, his expression pleading. His cock gave a twitch, begging. Ewyn fed the finger deeper, sliding it in to the last knuckle.

Kerry moaned softly, his ass gripping the finger. Heat rose fast in Ewyn's body, making his pulse quicken. He leaned in and lightly kissed Kerry's lips. His right hand played with Kerry's dark hair, combing through it.

After withdrawing the finger completely, Ewyn pushed it back inside. Kerry reacted beautifully, pushing down a little into the thrust to take it, so Ewyn kept going.

"More. Please," Kerry begged, so softly Ewyn had to strain his ears.

"Yeah?"

Ewyn pulled out, then began to work both his index finger and middle finger inside. Kerry frowned harder, groaning through the stretch. When the fingers were buried, he gasped slightly, lips parted, and let his head fall to the side. Ewyn kissed his temple, petting his hair.

"I want you," he said, his lips moving against Kerry's warm, soft skin.

"I want you too." The fingers pumped, impaling him. Kerry reached into the water, playing with himself a little and pulling on his dick.

"Good, it's settled then. Time to get out."

Ewyn helped him out of the bath, towel drying him a little, but in too much of a hurry to linger. Leaving the full tub, the candles — all of it — he picked Kerry up and carried him back to bed.

After a near-miss with the doorframe and Kerry's braced leg, Ewyn set Kerry down near the edge of the bed, damp, naked, fingered, and flushed with desire. As much as he needed to touch Kerry and get inside him the fear of hurting him lingered, making Ewyn uncharacteristically hesitant. While he tried to figure out the best positions given Kerry's injuries, Ewyn pulled out his cock, slicking lube over it. When he shifted closer to the bed, Kerry spread his legs to make room. Ewyn hooked his arms behind Kerry's knees and carefully folded Kerry's legs back. Kerry kept his left leg stiffened and extended at first, as if fearing any contact with Ewyn's body. Luckily, he was flexible enough to manage even as Ewyn spread him wider.

"Try to relax your legs," Ewyn urged. "I want you comfortable. I'll be careful."

"I know. I'm just — "

"Nervous?" Ewyn guessed.

"Yeah."

"Give it a try."

Kerry slowly relaxed his leg, letting his brace rest against Ewyn's arm. Moving in a gradual slide, Ewyn shifted closer to Kerry, lining up to enter him. Holding there, he watched for signs of pain or strain in Kerry's expression or body language.

"Okay so far?"

"Yeah," Kerry nodded, biting at his lip again.

"Good. I need to feel you," Ewyn growled. "Really feel you. Been dreaming of it."

Kerry had gotten tested as part of his medical work-up at the hospital. Ewyn had done likewise shortly after. The need for condoms was gone.

As Ewyn let his cock press against and begin to enter Kerry, feeling all of the resistance of his near-virginal opening, he could see shyness winning over in Kerry, especially to be taken while they were face-to-face. His gaze fixed on the ceiling, his head thrown back, Kerry bit at his lip and cringed as if anticipating pain. The braced leg now rested more firmly against Ewyn's arm, as if forgotten.

"This okay, love?" Ewyn asked, nudging Kerry's jaw with the tip of his nose and then scraping his teeth gently against it. "Do you want it?"

"God, yes," Kerry groaned so quietly, swallowing the words.

"Then tell me so again. Let me see you."

Ewyn pushed through, his cockhead breaching Kerry's clenched rim just as Kerry made hesitant eye contact with him. A startled whimper escaped Kerry, his mouth falling open around panting breaths. Ewyn savored all of the bare, open, honest emotion reflected back at him in each small cry and each subtle shift within Kerry, seen so clearly through his lovely eyes. He held Kerry down more firmly to the bed, guided his legs back farther and pushed in deeper.

Kerry gasped wildly. Then Ewyn felt Kerry's hands clasped tightly to Ewyn's ass to pull him in more.

"Don't stop," Kerry begged. His brace now lay against Ewyn's back, the rough straps rubbing there as a reminder of just how fragile Kerry truly was.

"Relax yourself, now. Bring your hands up above your head. Stay open for me. If you want me, then let me take you."

Ewyn sank in the rest of the way as Kerry obeyed, letting his arms come up to rest on the bed above the tumble of his inky hair. He felt Kerry clench up on the cock buried balls deep in his ass. Then, the muscles relaxed. Kerry let out a heavy sigh as the tension drained from him.

Careful of the injuries, not jostling him at all and focusing most of their movement on where their bodies joined, Ewyn drew back, then pushed in, setting a slow, deep rhythm. He studied each little reaction caused by the steady friction as Kerry was gently ridden and undone. The reticence fell away, leaving only anguished delight at the pleasures overwhelming his body.

The house was silent around them, so Kerry's small, desperate cries seemed unnaturally loud. Ewyn watched him trying to hold them back, and failing completely.

Ewyn bent to trail rough kisses along the underside of Kerry's jaw after he threw his head farther back, arching into the next long thrust and pushing down to meet it. Ewyn quickened to feel that private encouragement, asking for more, showing how much Kerry wanted it. Letting his lips brush against the soft skin by the top of Kerry's throat, feeling the vibrations of his next low, hushed exclamation, Ewyn murmured, "Louder."

He guided Kerry's legs farther apart, taking hold of him by one ankle and the underside of the brace, testing his flexibility. Then Ewyn withdrew until he felt the ridge of his cockhead catch on Kerry's rim. He paused a moment, then drove in hard.

Kerry's yelp climbed in strength and volume. Ewyn felt him shudder, fucking air. A downward glance showed him the rigid, dripping state of Kerry's cock.

Wanting to see more of that, Ewyn straightened up and tugged Kerry with him, closer to the bed's edge. Keeping tight hold of Kerry's widely spread legs. Ewyn resumed riding him harder and faster. He could see everything now — Kerry's erection, his entire slim form spread so completely, taking Ewyn's thrusts so easily. He could also see Kerry's struggle to hide his expression, even as his cries continued to grow. He stared at the sight of Kerry's pink hole taking the dark, swollen column of Ewyn's dick, felt how soft and warm Kerry was inside, hugging so tightly and pulling Ewyn in on each push.

Ewyn gave it even harder, felt Kerry bear down and struggle for breath, his hands fallen so gracefully by the sides of his sweet face.

"Please..."

"Louder."

"Please!" Kerry cried, his voice breaking.

"Look."

Kerry's head tipped down, their eyes meeting again, briefly, before Kerry shifted his gaze to where Ewyn's cock plunged into Kerry over and over again. A convulsion shook Kerry, there and gone, and with it a hard moan.

Growling, Ewyn felt his orgasm begin to catch fire, lighting him up. He gave Kerry a few last hard thrusts, pumping come deeply into him and shuddering with each push.

"Please... please..." Kerry beseeched, writhing and undulating, rocking against the last few thrusts as if to draw as much pleasure from them as possible. "I need..."

"Shh..." Ewyn shifted them further onto the bed without pulling out, then let Kerry's legs come back down to rest. The weight and bulk of the brace pulled the left one down first, and Kerry seemed glad to let it lay comfortably against the soft bedding. Propping himself up on a hand, looking down on Kerry from above, Ewyn brushed the backs of his fingers over Kerry's sac, drawn up tight to his body. Another shiver shook him, his hips rolling slightly. "I know you do."

He traced with his thumb through the clear, wet drips soaking Kerry's hard-on. Each light touch drew a soft gasp and a twitch. Ewyn played him like that for a while, gently petting the skin by the root of Kerry's cock and the short stubble there, or the underside of his sac, or the tip of his cock.

Kerry was restless, unable to stay still, but he obeyed the orders and didn't move to touch himself or ask for more than he was given.

Soon, the quality of the sounds he made sharpened even more, pushed past shyness. They became loud, unfiltered. His whimpers stirred Ewyn's cock, struggling to harden again and to take Kerry once more. Ewyn stayed silent, listening to the music of Kerry's need.

It went on and on. The lighter he touched, the more frantic Kerry became, twisting on the cock impaling him, struggling to thrust against the fingers toying with him. He grew wetter and Ewyn painted Kerry's crown with the fluid gathered there.

He rubbed the spot just under the ridge of Kerry's crown, triggering the nerves, and watched him shiver. It shifted into a sob, so Ewyn took hold of the base of Kerry's sac and tugged, drawing his balls away from his body, stretching the skin and pushing against where he was still buried in his ass.

167

Lynn Kelling

"Deep breaths, love. Nice and deep. I see you. I have you."

Kerry moaned, the sound choking off as Ewyn squeezed ever so gently.

Tears slipped from the corners of Kerry's eyes. He inhaled, chest rising, then let the breath out, though it hitched once.

Ewyn caressed Kerry's sac, relaxing his hold. Then he made a loose fist around Kerry's erection.

"Go on. Go on, now," Ewyn urged.

Trembling, Kerry rocked into the hand, rubbing off on it. Ewyn caressed Kerry's shaft with his thumb, squeezing a little more on the withdrawal. Grunting, panting, Kerry fought for his climax. When it came, he was strung tight. An arc of pearly white come shot up over his stomach and chest. Ewyn gripped in a few tight strokes to see him through it. Kerry convulsed again, making sweet, plaintive sounds.

When Kerry's body grew still and his breathing slowed, Ewyn pulled out and fetched a warm, damp washcloth to wipe Kerry down while he recovered.

After that was done, he reclined at Kerry's right side, a hand resting on Kerry's chest. His eyes were closed, his breathing deep and even. At first, Ewyn thought he may have dozed off.

"I've never felt like that before," Kerry said in barely a whisper.

"Felt what?"

Violet eyes opened to catch and hold him. Kerry overlaid Ewyn's hand with his own. He didn't try to close his widely spread legs or cover himself. He was totally, beautifully relaxed.

"Cherished. Free. Like being and living in the moment, and nothing else, was all that mattered. Thank you for that."

"Well," Ewyn replied, kissing Kerry's temple, "thank you for trusting me, and giving me so much of yourself. You're a gift, you know. Priceless. Rare."

He felt Kerry studying him, the tables turned.

"It can be a curse," Ewyn admitted, "to care so much. A hell of a curse. Especially if the care isn't wanted or returned."

"I thank god you do," Kerry murmured. He turned, seeking Ewyn's lips with his own. "I'm tired of always pulling away. I need the ways you lure me in."

"A mhuirnín," Ewyn sighed, "I could fall for you so."

"What does that mean? Is it Gaelic?"

168

"It is. Means 'sweetheart'."

Kerry rolled onto his side, lifting and carefully placing the brace down again. He shifted closer, putting himself right against Ewyn's body and looping an arm around to keep him near.

"I'm so used to people I love pushing me away," Kerry said.

"Me too, love. Me too."

"I don't know how to pay you back for how much you've given me. I have nothing."

"Give me your heart. Your honesty. Stop hiding yourself away. I want you free. I want you to be you."

He felt the rise and fall of Kerry's breaths.

"I like you in your dresses. You'll keep wearing them, won't you?"

There was another pause, giving off waves of fear and worry that Ewyn would have happily banished forever if he could.

"Okay," Kerry finally agreed, his voice hushed.

"Remember," Ewyn said, enfolding Kerry in an embrace, "whatever you feel, is right. It's you. And I adore you. Does it make you happy to wear them?"

Kerry hesitated. "Yes. Yeah."

"Good. Trust that. Promise me you will."

Kerry peeked up at him, smiling. "I will. I'll try."

"Good girl," Ewyn praised, letting all of his love fill the words. He leaned down closely, kissing Kerry's cheek.

Strengthening his hold, Kerry clutched Ewyn to him like he didn't want to let go.

Chapter 21: Devotion

The best thing about Erin Garrity, in Kerry's opinion, was that she was a mom, but not his mom. While Kerry's mother had always stayed strong by building walls, Erin navigated with sly wit and brazen yet humble self-confidence, weaving in, out and around anything in her path. After a few weeks in her company, Kerry found himself savoring their time together, where he was never doubted or criticized.

He was inspired by the selfless nature of her nurturing qualities and how she never questioned herself or took the easy route to do something if the longer path did a more thorough job. He'd never met anyone quite like her — her fearless direct eye contact just as impressive as any Marine's, but coupled with a tremendous desire to set her company at ease, and a determination that reached far beyond her size. And yet, Erin was gentle, sweet, and seemed to know how to dispel Kerry's stubborn worries with just a smile.

There was no judgment in her. She didn't bat an eye at his dresses or makeup. She hadn't pried about the candle that always sat on the windowsill. She'd listened to Kerry vent about his decision not to tell Jamie about the attack, giving her input only after Kerry asked for it. Her advice had been to trust his instincts but to realize the way news travels might work against him sooner or later. She'd told him about when Darcy had passed, and how she'd tried to keep certain details of what had happened from a more closed-minded branch of her family, only to have it all come out anyway in drama she refused to take part in.

That day, Kerry had asked again about Ewyn's exes, and in particular whether Ewyn had ever dreamt of having kids someday. The reason for his concern was obvious, given his biological limitations. He'd told her if she wasn't comfortable speaking without Ewyn's permission to forgive the question.

"Oh, sweetheart," she'd sighed, sitting down beside him on the couch where he had propped his leg up on a pillow set on a chair while he searched for design inspiration on his phone's browser. Though it was getting easier to get around with brace rather than the cast, using crutches or just hopping around on one foot, his left leg still felt like the biggest hindrance he'd ever experienced. It got in the way. It ached. It made everything more difficult. Yet, his slightly increased mobility meant he didn't really need Erin's help as much anymore, as much as he dreaded admitting it. Not that his opinion on the matter could persuade her or Ewyn to leave him all alone every day.

He clutched the phone, the screen dark, fearing the emotions that might hit depending on her answer. She set a hand on his arm. "If it's meant to happen, it will, one way or other, no matter what. I do think, years back, Ewyn bought into the more traditional idea of happiness and family for a short while there."

"By traditional, I guess you mean straight?"

Erin gave him a commiserating glance, rolling her eyes a bit. "Yes, that's the one. Darcy had already covered the wild and gay carefree lifestyle. Poor Ewyn felt that left him no choice but to go the other direction. Take responsibility for us all. But reality is different than a picture painted by other people. He always had to work so hard to be happy. It never got easier and the more he held tight to what he thought he wanted — the girl, the home, the nine-to-five job, children — the more it got away from him. It wasn't his picture, you see. His dream. Not really. Having things doesn't necessarily mean they're the right ones for you. Honestly, chasing the white picket fence type of happiness made him miserable! I knew he believed it would all fall into place if he hung in there, tried harder. It just never did. Isla — always sharp as a tack — and Jessica, who was more shy and cerebral, they all did him a favor by leaving without giving him a say."

"It must have been quite a shock for him," Kerry guessed. "He had to have been frustrated and hurt."

Lynn Kelling

"He was bewildered! You know how he gets. Always keeping tabs. Always making sure. And then... left alone, just like that. With no way to argue the point or convince."

"Sounds a little like me and Jamie. I wanted it to work, even though on a basic, practical level I knew it never really would. I just had such a hard time giving up hope until Jamie left. Right in the middle of a fight during a romantic date-night dinner at our apartment. Packed a bag and walked out. Wouldn't hear a word about it. His mind was made up."

"You can't keep someone who won't stay, but it's a blessing in disguise. Pushes us closer to where we need to be, as much as it pains us to endure it."

"So you don't think it disappoints him that I can't give him a family?"

"Oh, Kerry, of course you can. Just not the way Ewyn might have expected. But it sounds like the two of you aren't afraid of some hard work, and that's in your favor. If you want your dreams desperately enough, I have no doubt you can make all of them come true."

He smiled over at her. "You really are amazing. No one's ever said anything like that to me before. Like they just believed in me completely, for no reason at all."

"I have plenty of reasons. The best ones. I see your heart, Kerry Sanderson. It's a good one."

He twisted at the waist, slung an arm around her shoulder, and gave her a hug. "Thank you."

"You're very welcome, dear," she replied, pecking a kiss to his cheek.

An hour later, Kerry stood in the kitchen while Ewyn finished cleaning up in the shower. He'd just returned following a shift at Blaze. Erin had gone home once Ewyn had returned. Balancing on one foot and the slightest amount of weight on his brace, Kerry felt pulled by old promises and parts of the past he couldn't let go.

Ewyn and Erin's encouragement to just be, to listen to himself and trust his instincts, seemed counter to all of the other choices he'd made. There was good reason for it. For so long, Kerry had fought himself at every turn, doing what others thought was right rather than heeding his own inner voice. Of course it seemed wrong and overly self-indulgent to stop fighting so hard.

More than anything, Kerry wanted to listen and take care of himself for once. But there were pieces of who he was he knew he couldn't part with. Would those pieces fit if he changed? How did he move ahead without moving on?

Kerry leaned against the counter by the window with pitch black night beyond and an unlit candle on the sill. Before, it had felt better to keep the past to himself, and to push it back inside. He hadn't ever been able to talk about it much with Jamie, and opening up to his family only led them to try drawing him back in where they could control his every action.

When he heard the bathroom door open, he knew it was time to share the biggest secret of who he really was. Ewyn deserved that much. All Kerry could do was hope it wouldn't come between them the way it had with him and Jamie, muddling previously defined roles and responsibilities, exposing weaknesses he knew he'd carry for the rest of his life.

Going by the sound of his footsteps, Ewyn went into the bedroom first. Then he turned right around and came out, as Kerry expected.

Kerry turned his back to Ewyn's approach.

"Hey." Ewyn wrapped a hand around Kerry's waist and kissed the side of his head. The affection in the gesture made the pure, full-bodied sadness chase up. It would have been so much easier to have that kind of acceptance to strengthen him years ago, when he was in the thick of it.

"You feeling all right? Or is this about the candle?"

Kerry reached out, picked up the candle and turned it over in his hands.

"Jamie never understood why I did it — lighting it every night. And I didn't know how to explain in a way that wouldn't make me seem weaker or lesser to him. He needed me to be strong, and sometimes — a lot of times — I just wasn't. This — the candle — was my weakness. It's all I allowed myself. But it's more than that. It was my promise. Letting down people who love me... it's the worst feeling in the world, but I keep doing it, over and over again, and... Out of everyone, to know I let down Jonah...."

His vision blurred. Instinctively fighting back the emotion, the clear sign of weakness, something forever forbidden at home and with Jamie, Kerry felt ashamed. He rubbed his eyes dry and cleared his throat.

"I'm listening," Ewyn promised. "If you need to let this out, let it out. It's okay."

"This was mine, Ewyn. He was mine. No one else has had to carry this. I know I need to tell you, but I don't know how."

"I know," Ewyn told him, pressing his warm lips to Kerry's hair. "That's why I haven't asked. I would never judge you for showing pain or hurt. Do you really think you need to pretend to be stronger than you feel you are with me? That I would criticize you for it?"

"No. No, of course not," Kerry realized.

"Who did you lose, love?"

"Jonah." Kerry stared at the candle. "He was the best of me. He was all promise, hope, and love, but he never really got a chance. It's so unfair. It's..." He stopped the train of thought, the indulgent emotion. "There's a box. Carved, polished wood. It's under my side of the bed. Kent brought it to me when he packed up my things."

"You want me to get it?"

Kerry nodded. "Please."

It only took a moment before he heard Ewyn's footsteps returning. Kerry didn't turn to look.

Ewyn sat down at the table.

Kerry grabbed the lighter on the counter, but he didn't light the wick. He waited.

He'd memorized and obsessed over everything in that box. When he heard Ewyn open the lid, Kerry hung his head, knowing he was too young to feel this old. Silent tears gathered.

On top was a quilt he'd sewn together from clothes and gifts family and friends had given him. Beneath the quilt was a tiny purple and blue hat. It was one of the things he'd crocheted, painstakingly, with much trial and error, over the countless hours he'd sat in the NICU, listening to machines beep and hum. Under the hat were photos, most framed, but some collected in a small album.

"Christ," Ewyn said quietly. "Ahh, fuck. Kerry...God, I'm so sorry."

He got up and walked over, enfolding Kerry in an embrace from behind. Ewyn's strong arms crossed Kerry's chest, gripping him by shoulder and arm. His lips were pressed against the side of Kerry's tear-stained face. Kerry just stared straight ahead, failing to keep it in control, stuck on the thought of promises unfulfilled and chances lost. And not just for Jonah. He had been failing himself, too.

"I wanted it to be a lover, or even a brother. I hoped to heaven it wasn't this. I really did," Ewyn confessed.

"Haley got pregnant," Kerry said. "We were barely seventeen. It was a rebound relationship after the whole debacle with Michael beating the piss out of me when he found me with Jakob. It was just supposed to be fun — a way to get away from our parents and be wild together. As soon as she realized what had happened, she freaked out. But she didn't believe in abortion, so she didn't terminate. Jonah... he was born too early. Haley couldn't handle it. She had been prepared to surrender her parental rights anyway, before he was born. At first she'd talked about adoption, but I always wanted him. Always."

Kerry remembered old arguments with Haley, standing outside of one of their homes or walking around their neighborhoods together, trying not to be overheard. They'd been desperate attempts to stand up for himself, trying to convince her he could handle raising a child on his own when he had no such faith in himself. "She wasn't ready to be a mother. I knew I was going to be a single parent, but I didn't know it would be that hard. I... I did what I had to do. *My* life didn't matter anymore. All of my issues, everything that had made me feel so confused and unsure — none of it mattered. And I was glad. The one important thing was taking care of him and making sure he knew I was there for him, that he wasn't alone. He was my life. I was supposed to take him to school, teach him to tie his shoes, watch him graduate. He was supposed to be my *whole life*."

Ewyn kissed him again. "I'm so goddamned sorry."

Refusing to give in to the urge to crumble, Kerry said defiantly, "I stayed with him every night. Every night, as long as they'd let me. I didn't sleep for months. I sat in the NICU, watching him breathe, holding his hand with one finger, or feeding him bottles. His tiny body would be tucked against my arm, my chest, right here." Kerry palmed beneath his heart. "Skin to skin."

"He had your hair. Blue eyes. He was so beautiful, love."

"When he was three months old, they let him come home with me at last. He had issues with his heart, but they had done surgeries and he'd progressed really well. He was breathing on his own, gaining weight."

Lynn Kelling

"You don't have to say it."

Kerry shook his head. "No. I do."

Ewyn caressed Kerry's chest, right over his heart, right where he could still feel Jonah, clutching so gently to him.

"He was four months old. He'd fallen asleep on my chest, while I was sitting in a rocking chair in his nursery at my parents' house. That was it. He just... he just stopped..."

"Kerry, don't. Don't do this to yourself."

Kerry inhaled deeply through his nose, then blew out the breath. "I had it all planned out, Ewyn. I was going to be a good dad. I was going to take such good care of him, like I'd always wished Michael had done with me. I was going to give that back to the world, set that right, and help that little boy know he was loved *so much* by his dad."

"You weren't just his dad. You were his mother. You were his everything."

"I could have done it, for him," Kerry told him, feeling the truth of it all over again. It was a hopeless, foolish yearning. "I could have ignored all of the shit I didn't understand about myself, and just lived my life for Jonah. But then he was gone and I was even more fucked-up. I still am, and I'm sorry for that... for you."

"Don't you dare," Ewyn scolded. "Don't you ever apologize for that to me."

Kerry looked up at him, steadily. The more he let out, the better he felt. Everything he'd kept so far down inside had been weighing on him. Setting it loose left him lighter, clear-headed.

"I sat with him every night so that if he woke up, he wouldn't be alone, and the night wouldn't be so scary. But then he was gone and I couldn't stand thinking about him being... somewhere... without me to show him it was gonna be okay. So I lit the stupid candle. I lit it to show him he's still with me and it's gonna be okay. For both of us. That there's still hope. Just because I lost him doesn't mean I won't find him again, someday."

Ewyn turned Kerry around, manhandling him into a hug, holding him against his chest by the back of his head and his waist. Some of Ewyn's tears dampened Kerry's neck, and he felt Ewyn's deep sigh.

"That's fucking beautiful," Ewyn said thickly. "You have so much sadness in you, love. Thank you for letting me understand it a little

176

more, so I can take better care of you. You deserve that. This isn't something you should have to carry on your own."

"I know it's just a ritual. It's a coping mechanism. Jamie didn't really get it. But I haven't lit the candle for weeks, and I don't know what it means. Am I forgetting him? Am I failing the one person who needed me most?"

"You're growing, love, that's all," Ewyn said. "You'll always keep him in your heart, but now your hope can take other forms. You can own it for yourself. Use it to make Jonah proud of the person you're becoming."

"You really think I can move on from this? How?"

"One step at a time," Ewyn told him. "Believe me, I've been through it too with losing Darcy. You need to be kind to yourself and forgive yourself. None of this is your fault, Kerry. You did right by that boy. You did right by Haley and Jamie and your family and all of them. You did your best. That's all you could do. Let Jonah be your blessing instead of your pain."

He grabbed a chair, sat down and pulled Kerry down with him. Kerry straddled Ewyn's lap, facing him. Ewyn pulled him back into the hug.

"When Darcy got shot in the chest and beaten to death outside that club, it sent me to a dark place. It really did. Luckily, I had my mum to keep my head on the right way. I had to take care of her, make sure she was going to be okay. It tore her up, in similar ways that you were torn up, I guess. Her baby was gone, yet he'd lived a happy life. He was fortunate there. Still... I tried to turn it into a positive. I'm still trying. Working at the club, helping other people like Darcy, that's how I cope, and move forward. Mum scolds me for trying to take on too much, pushing too hard and winding up blinded to what else I'm losing because I won't let go. I'm trying to stop making that mistake. So if you ever need something different than what I'm giving you, please tell me. I'd love to help you figure out how to move on in your own way. Darcy, Jonah — they're with us always, no matter how tight we might try to hold on to their memories. We don't really have to work so hard to keep them. They're ours. Always. No matter what. So, carry him with you, as I know you do, but take him to a happier, more peaceful place, okay? Let his presence in your heart fill you up instead of tear you down."

Kerry took a deep breath and slowly let it back out. He kissed Ewyn's neck, felt it cause him to shiver. "Thank you for that. I love you."

"I love you too."

Chapter 22: Color

The more Kerry began to move around and do things for himself, the more his spirits were raised. Using only one crutch while putting just a little weight on his brace allowed him to carry things again and feel more self-sufficient. He unpacked his sewing materials and machine. Ewyn set up a worktable for him in the living room by the front window. Not wasting any time, Kerry set his sewing station up there and got to work finishing projects he'd promised his friends and co-workers.

The need to fulfill those responsibilities was what initially drove him on, though he hadn't expected the surge of positive energy that filled him, something he hadn't felt in a long time. It was close to the feeling of bringing his paychecks to the bank to be cashed and knowing they would help pay his bills and fund his independence. But creating his designs felt even better, giving him a purpose in new, wonderful ways. He didn't have anyone's disapproval over the blurring of gender roles to worry about. He knew Ewyn supported his efforts by his words and the practical ways he helped to get everything set up. Having that to lean on made Kerry feel like he could do anything.

Erin spent less time visiting once Kerry began doing better, though she did stop by daily with a hot, homemade lunch that always tested the strict boundaries of his usual diet. That day, she came with corned beef sandwiches with steam still rising from the fresh-baked bread. Kerry's mouth watered as soon as he caught the rich, warm scent.

"What's this now?" Erin wondered, peeking at Kerry's worktable. His sketches of a purple shift dress and some reference photos were tacked to a cork board propped against the wall, while the half-finished piece lay in a silky puddle beside the sewing machine. "Oh, how lovely. Ewyn, have you seen this! It's incredible!"

"Yes, woman, I've seen it," Ewyn cried from the kitchen as he grabbed a mug of coffee and nearly dashed for the back door to escape. But when his hand rested on the knob, he paused and asked, "Please tell me you didn't bring another old photo album. I won't be held responsible for the ridiculous things you made me wear."

"You loved that little sailor suit!"

"Oh, Jesus," Ewyn groaned, hanging his head.

"Kerry, look. Here, on the second page," she directed, swiftly pulling out a small album from her purse and flipping it open. She pointed to a photo of a severely frowning child of about six in a big, floppy sailor hat and suit that was about two sizes too small, his little arms folded sternly over his chest.

Kerry burst out laughing. "That's priceless."

When he caught Ewyn's eye, he saw a hint of that same stubborn frown, now softened dramatically. He set the coffee mug down and hurried over. He slipped the album gently from Kerry's hand and closed it, holding it high out of reach when Erin made a grab for it.

"That's enough for today, I think," Ewyn said diplomatically. "Thank you for the sandwiches. I'm sure you're very busy and can't stay long."

Erin set her hands on her hips and squinted up at him. "Yes, you do put on a good show, don't you? And when I tried to take the suit away from you, I'm sure you'll claim you didn't sneak it back out of the donation pile and set it in a deep corner of your closet to hide away? And that your grumpiness in the photo wasn't because of the suit at all but because I kept trying to give it away?"

Ewyn opened his mouth and closed it again. Kerry's grin widened.

"Thank you for stopping by, mum. We are very busy. Why don't you ask Kerry about his new designs before you go? Far more interesting topic."

"Oh, of course you are terribly busy, dear. Don't let me keep you," she said, shooing him away, letting him take the album with him. When he'd gone to reclaim his mug and left through the back, she winked at Kerry and slipped a second album from her purse. She handed it to him. "Always keep a spare or two of the really important things."

"That's great advice," he agreed, flipping through the pages.

While he did, Erin peeked at what he was working on, complimenting fabrics, his stitching, and his various ideas.

"I could make you something too, if you'd like," he offered. "Think it over and let me know what you might like. Colors, styles, anything that comes to mind."

"Ooh, that'd be lovely! Kerry, you're such a sweetheart." She gave him a sideways hug, barely having to bend down even though he was seated on a low chair. "I've never had any custom clothes. There's just so many possibilities. My…"

Erin's face lit up as she began to dream and imagine.

"How lucky are we to have such a talent as you," she told him. "Such creativity! Well, I have plenty to think about now, don't I? I won't keep you, dear. Look at the photos as long as you'd like, just keep them away from that one," she asked, pointing to the door through which Ewyn had disappeared.

"Will do," he promised. "I'll keep them safe and get them back to you next time you visit."

"No rush. No rush at all." She shifted her purse strap higher on her shoulder and moved to the door. "Have a lovely day, Kerry."

"You too, Erin. Thank you."

Seeing Erin had livened his spirits, as it always did. She was a breath of fresh air. Everything Kerry usually felt self-conscious about — his clothes, makeup or physical weakness — somehow never crossed his mind in her presence. Privately, he attributed that to Darcy. Maybe she saw a little of him in Kerry, or maybe she was just better at seeing people for who they were instead of who she wanted them to be.

But the more Kerry let go of the old, restrictive parameters that defined him, slowly allowing deeper instincts to guide his choices in ways that were visible to others, the more disconnect he felt with the remaining intact, though disparate, facets of his life. Ewyn and Erin had been understanding, but what about everyone else?

Sometimes on phone calls, Kerry mentioned Ewyn directly or indirectly to his brothers when asked about how things were going.

He'd feel the loud pause as they debated whether to say something or not. They were never were critical or gave Kerry a clear sense that they disapproved, yet the question of Kerry's sexual orientation was something that was clearly not on the list of comfortable things to talk about.

If Kerry's brothers actually stopped by, Kerry always made sure to be in bed or on the couch, covered in sheets or blankets so they didn't see the dresses. He was willing to hide them from sight for the time being, but he found he wasn't willing to dress differently just to please family members. It was a new revelation but one of which Kerry was surprisingly proud. He also only applied makeup when he knew he wasn't going to be seen by anyone other than Erin or Ewyn, but felt his personal boundaries surrounding that choice beginning to soften. If things kept going well, who knows what he might be willing to do?

He found himself smiling more.

He sang softly while working, sometimes even dancing a little, as much as his brace would allow.

Overall, he felt much lighter, like the world had opened up and brightened in color.

After he'd eaten the delicious lunch Erin had provided, Kerry gave his friend Dmitri a call. He was eager to talk to someone who he could be certain would understand and support his new choices.

"Hey, girl, why you been dodging my calls?"

Kerry grinned despite himself, flushing with joy to hear Dmitri's voice.

"Hey, Dima. No, I swear I haven't been dodging you."

"You lying bitch," Dmitri accused lightheartedly, sounding bored out of his mind. "It's because you haven't made that tunic for me, isn't it? I'm just another client for you know that you're on your way to becoming a famous fashion designer."

"My specialty is stripper costumes. That's a far cry from being a famous fashion designer."

"You never know unless you dream, baby. What on earth has happened to you?" Dmitri asked. "Where have you been hiding? Are you all right, darling?"

"I'm all right. Been finally getting things done, actually. I have that shift for you. If you can stop by my new place sometime, I'll fit it, make any little adjustments I need to, and then it's yours."

"I can come by Sunday if you want."

"Yeah, that works."

"What's this new place of yours?"

"Well, uh," he chuckled nervously.

"Uh-oh. I know that sound. Just please tell me you didn't move back home."

"Are you kidding? I'd never."

Dmitri laughed. "Well good. So, you've finally moved on from whatshisface?"

"Finally, yeah," Kerry nodded, glancing around the living room of Ewyn's house. "I'm living with someone new. He's taking care of me while I recover. I mean, he's not my nurse or anything. He's just... good for me."

"*He* is taking care of all of your needs? Is it time for me to finally mourn your stubborn cherry?"

Shocked, Kerry let out a belly laugh.

"I'm taking that as a yes. Congratulations, my dear."

"Thanks, Dima. It's a momentous occasion."

"Are you kidding? For you, yes. It is. You're the queen of blue balls. Does this mean I get to meet him?"

"Yeah, I think that could be arranged," Kerry teased. "As long as you're nice to him."

"Does that mean he's easily intimidated by fabulous gay boys?"

"No," Kerry grinned. "He works security at Blaze. I'm pretty sure he's a pro at handling fabulous gay boys."

"Mmm, I like the sound of that."

Dmitri's shift was draped on a male dress form in the corner of the living room by Kerry's sewing station. Kerry checked the hem again to ensure it was even when Ewyn walked in. Ewyn had been exercising and just finished with his post-workout shower. Wandering over to Kerry, he said, "Now that's more like it. Finally, some color."

Kerry's lips twisted up in a crooked smile. "It's not for me. My friend Dima ordered it. Before, with my dancing schedule, I never seemed to have enough time to finish these projects, but now I do. He's paying me, and it's not a ton of money but at least it's something."

"But you enjoy it, don't you?"

"Yeah, I love it," Kerry answered honestly.

"Then you should keep doing it. Expand your business. Find a way to advertise. See if any stores would carry your work."

"Maybe," Kerry said thoughtfully, looking over the shift. "What I do is kind of specialized though, for people who need things outside the typical norms."

"All the more reason to pursue it," Ewyn encouraged. "If it's something hard to find, and isn't readily available already, people will want it. You just have to know your clientele."

"Hmm," Kerry glanced between the dress and Ewyn's adorably confident expression. "You really think I could do it?"

"I know you could. Trust me, as a firmly non-creative person, I know real talent when I see it." He looped an arm behind Kerry's lower back and kissed him lightly on the lips. "I do think you need more clothes in violet, though," Ewyn said slyly. "I've noticed you like your earth tones, but you could handle something a little more… vibrant. Don't hold back on us now."

Hiding a smile with a dip of his head, Kerry bit at his lip. He wasn't used to men in his life encouraging him to dress more vibrantly. Even when he tried to detect anything mocking in Ewyn's words, Kerry couldn't find a thing. It sounded genuine.

Kerry's parents had invited him and Ewyn to dinner a few times in the past week. As nice as it was to have a fantasy of being one big, happy, inclusive family, Kerry knew it would never turn out that way — not with Michael's history and not with his other relatives' tendency to avoid talking about everything that Kerry was afraid to bring up himself. Michael hadn't even had a conversation with Ewyn yet, and things had been uncomfortably tense at the hospital.

So Kerry always declined, knowing he couldn't and wouldn't dress in the polo shirt and khakis he had always worn around family. It was too late for that. He'd come too far to go back. He was done pretending he was something he wasn't. Maybe it had taken Ewyn to show him that things could be different, and that he could be accepted by someone who was important to him.

But at the same time, Kerry couldn't quite face the idea of showing up to dinner at his parents' home with his boyfriend while wearing a dress and makeup. Even if he was becoming more comfortable with himself, he still wasn't *that* brave.

184

He kept telling himself time would help. If he delayed sharing the truth with them just a little longer, at least until he was more comfortable owning it, maybe the hope of having a happy resolution could hold out. At the same time, he knew he couldn't keep declining their invitations and still expect the invites to continue coming. As patient as his parents were, their tolerance would run out eventually.

It left him feeling stuck in all kinds of ways, with no idea how to get free and constantly second-guessing his tentative steps at establishing new boundaries.

Ewyn rubbed the back of Kerry's neck. "What're you thinking about?"

"Nothing."

"Tell me."

"Just those dinner invitations from my folks, I guess. I'm just glad you're okay with this part of who I am, because they're not."

"Well, you can't know that for sure. Not until you give them a chance to prove themselves."

"Maybe. I mean, I appreciate that they're trying to be inclusive with you, but it's not just about me being bisexual. The fact that I'm dating a man is only one of the elephants in the room." Gesturing to the dress on the form, and the one he was currently wearing, he said. "They have no idea about this. At all. And it's a much bigger deal than my love life. My strategy for coping has always been to just avoid telling them and act the way they expect when I do see them. I just don't think that's going to work anymore but I'm not sure honesty is going to be worth the hassle and fallout. Does any of that even make sense? The whole thing makes me feel like I'm thinking in circles."

"If they love you, they need to love you for who you are, not who they want you to be."

Kerry hummed, closing his eyes as the neck rub loosened some of the tightness there. He leaned into Ewyn's touch, loving the inviting heat coming off of his body.

"If you want to talk about it with me, I'm here for you, you know," Ewyn offered.

Kerry's eyes opened again, doubt sinking into his stomach.

"I don't scare off easy," Ewyn added. "Plus, I'm observant. To say the least. Anything you tell me probably isn't going to come as much of a surprise. Kind of part of the package when you're dealing with a paranoid son of a bitch."

"No, I get that about you. I do. I think it's why I've felt comfortable embracing who I am lately. You make me feel wanted, even when I'm not trying to impress you."

"Good," Ewyn said tenderly, giving Kerry another light kiss.

"I just... haven't said it out loud before."

"Didn't think so. But there's gotta be a first for everything, right? Have you said it in your head, at least?"

"I have," Kerry said, lowering his voice as apprehension caused a riot in his stomach.

"Also good."

"I, um..." He stopped, took a deep breath, and started again, aware of how strange and tense his voice sounded. "I used to go to this trans group meeting with Jamie, and I thought I was just being supportive of him. I was lying to myself. As soon as I started to really listen to what everyone was saying there, I felt how their experiences echoed things I'd gone through too, and... I wasn't just going for Jamie. But it's not the same for me as it was for him. It's not just that he was assigned female at birth, and I was male. That's not what I mean. It's... It's not something I need hormones or surgery to address in order to feel at home in my body. I'm okay with my body. It's more... everything else. The way I dress. The way I'm expected to act. The way people want to lump me into this one narrow category of 'male' where if you deviate from acceptable, rigid rules at all, you're scorned and mocked and — "

"Hey," Ewyn said gently, laying his hands on Kerry's shoulders. "I get it."

Kerry blew out a breath, surprised he'd gotten riled enough to raise his voice.

He felt the word sitting on his tongue, but he still wasn't sure, even after everything he'd already done and said, that he could actually say it without spontaneously combusting in an explosion of nervous energy.

"Fuck, this is hard," he groaned after the silence had drawn out too long.

"Kerry," Ewyn said, drawing Kerry's gaze up to his warm brown eyes. "I love you. It's okay. You're okay, just the way you are. If you aren't ready to say it yet, I can wait. I won't leave you as long as you need me with you."

"I think I'll always need you, Ewyn," Kerry managed, his heart feeling full to bursting with all of the devotion that incredible man had so generously given him. "So I hope you didn't make any other plans."

Ewyn laughed. He caressed Kerry's cheek and kissed him slowly.

The kiss ended gradually, but Ewyn didn't pull away. While his mouth was still only a breath away from Kerry's, he asked, "Should I switch pronouns for ya?"

A shiver of pure, delicious delight raced down Kerry's back, stirring his cock. Moaning softly, he kissed Ewyn again, with force.

"Shall I take that as a yes?" Ewyn asked, grinning.

"Yes," Kerry replied with passion, slinging his arms behind Ewyn's neck and kissing him again. Ewyn gave Kerry's ass a squeeze through the dress, pulling him flush against the firm length of Ewyn's muscular body.

"What am I switching to then, a *mhuirnín*?"

"She," Kerry breathed, afraid to pull away and unable to let go. The word was so close. It was right there. She nuzzled the side of Ewyn's neck, breathing him in, trying to calm down. "I…" Maybe it was too soon. Maybe she should wait a little longer.

Maybe she was just a coward after all.

"I know people like my family won't adjust well to switching pronouns," Kerry said, staying too close for Ewyn to be able to scrutinize her face. "But for you… I'd like it. If that's okay. And…"

"It's okay, love. I promise it is," Ewyn said, caressing repeatedly down Kerry's back, smoothing the soft dress to her skin.

Tears burned, and she thought of all those times she'd hurt, and been so confused, so lost, so torn up inside, and had to bury it, or pretend it away. To man up and act like it didn't matter that she was different, that she felt no one would love her if she was honest. Real men didn't cry. Real men didn't desire other men. Real men didn't want to wear dresses.

She'd been so lonely in her isolation, for so very long.

"Why is this so hard?" Kerry gasped, holding on so tightly to Ewyn.

"Because it's important, that's why. Because this is everything that matters. It's your life. Your heart. Your truth."

"I'm…" she blew out the breath, tried again. She spat it out, needing to be rid of it, tired of hiding it. "I'm genderqueer."

She was trembling. Ewyn held her in a fierce hug, kissed Kerry's hair. "I'm so proud of you."

The tears fell, soundlessly, and she loved Ewyn so much in that moment. She gave over her heart and vowed to herself to strive to somehow make Ewyn as happy and appreciated as he'd just made her, even if it took the rest of their lives to accomplish it.

"Say it again," Ewyn said eagerly, happily.

Kerry found a smile threatening. "I'm genderqueer. I'm not just a boy. I'm not a girl. I'm myself. I'm…"

"Abso-fucking-lutely breathtaking, is what you are," Ewyn growled, scooping her up. Kerry let out a laugh as Ewyn picked her up, lifting her from the ground and pulling her in for a deep kiss. "Fair warning," Ewyn said between gasps for air. "I may need to take this dress off ya and kiss you for a while. In a few different places. To start with."

"Yes, please."

"Please, she says," Ewyn grinned. "Well then…"

He palmed Kerry's ass, hitching her up around Ewyn's waist. Kerry yelped, doing her best to wrap her legs around Ewyn's midsection to help hold on as he carried her out of the living room, through the hall and into the bedroom.

Chapter 23: Letting Go

Kerry felt light as a feather in Ewyn's arms, his — *her*, he corrected himself — slim, toned frame holding little weight, and Kerry's evident efforts to hold herself up by her grip on Ewyn's shoulder and back, using both arms and legs, spoke of her dancer's physique. The soaps she used had a neutral scent rather than a masculine one. Her voice, demeanor, smile, posture — they all blurred lines in the loveliest ways.

For Ewyn, who had always been drawn to explore a sexual and romantic relationship with a man, but held back when he couldn't ever seem to find the right counterpart for his admittedly demanding personality, being with Kerry had felt thrillingly easy. The pieces to their distinct identities somehow fit perfectly together, creating a bigger, better whole in which they were both happier and readier to take on the world.

Kerry's gender issues were not an obstacle or challenge for Ewyn at all. He'd never seen Kerry differently, and had always felt how she needed to live beyond others' expectations. It wasn't just the wild choice of being an exotic dancer after being raised in such a strict household, or the rebellious side that pushed her to take chances in love and living. It was all of the subtleties like her preference to speak softly, to be held and comforted, to follow her dreams without facing doubting questions.

In fact, Kerry's desire to capture an existence that borrowed from both male and female worked for Ewyn's romantic needs too. He got to enjoy Kerry's masculine body, but fill the caretaking role in the relationship. The need to dominate was gratefully accepted by

Kerry's submissive, quiet nature. Kerry had been neglected for so long in such important ways that the craving for attention exuded from her with strength.

It woke Ewyn up, made him feel needed, alive, and ecstatic in ways he hadn't experienced since before he'd lost his brother.

That was another thing he shared with Kerry. They knew loss. They saw how it magnified what was important and allowed everything else to drop back. They each carried a pit of sadness in their hearts, but were able to bring the sort of comfort only found in someone who understood and had lived through a similar set of trials.

So many of Ewyn's exes had lacked that type of maturity. They were baffled by his constant gravity and seriousness. They didn't see that he couldn't lighten up if circumstances provided valid reasons to worry.

Not only did Kerry understand the way the others hadn't, but she naturally encouraged Ewyn's proclivities without judgment and only tenderness.

It made Kerry feel like more than a lover, more than a friend.

She felt like home.

The more Ewyn felt how right they were together, the more it scared him. Because a miracle found could so easily be lost.

Darcy had taught him that.

The attack in Kerry's apartment had confirmed it.

But Ewyn knew it was futile to lock Kerry away in a cage. She'd be protected that way, surely, but she would stop flourishing. She would wilt and die, kept away from the light and energy of a world waiting to hurt her.

It was a trap. A different sort of cage.

But Ewyn just held Kerry tighter, kissed her longer, and tried to show what was in his heart as clearly as he could in the time they were given.

He laid Kerry down on the bed, pushed his hands under the dress to bunch it up and slipped it over her head. Made bare beneath Ewyn, Kerry was all smooth, pale skin. Ewyn had seen waxing supplies stashed in the bathroom, but must have been at work when Kerry had done it, stripping all signs of hair from her body from neck to ankle. Intensely tempted by such an exquisite canvas, and heartened to see the bruising had all but faded away, Ewyn began to kiss her. His lips dragged light kisses down Kerry's neck to her chest, from the spot above hearer to the dark tan of her nipples, from the rippled muscles of her abdomen to the hollow of her narrow hips, from the root of her cock to the inside of her thigh. And on he went.

Kerry tangled her hands in Ewyn's short hair, holding on and breathing harder. She spread herself wide, without shyness, though her skin pebbled with goosebumps and small shivers shook her. She squirmed on the bed, her cock thickening, rising up and demanding further attention from Ewyn's mouth.

But first, Ewyn slipped the lube from where it sat on the nightstand. Kerry's eyes were shut, her lips parted on soft sighs, so Ewyn felt sure she hadn't noticed.

After slicking some over his fingers, he leaned in again to kiss over Kerry's thighs and up to her pelvis. He kissed the soft swell of Kerry's sac, then her root, then dragged his lips up to the tip and kissed there last.

Kerry let out a moan with a shudder. Her legs drew back, her chin tipping up, her back arching off the bed. Her hips rolled slightly.

Ewyn couldn't stop watching.

"I miss the mirrors," Kerry groaned.

"Oh, me too. I'll bring them back if you're ready."

"I'm so ready," Kerry sighed. Her fingers scratched lightly over Ewyn's scalp as a long lick up her shaft was taken.

"Your wish is my command. Pull your legs back for me. That's it. Even more. Perfect."

He swallowed Kerry down, gave her intense suction and rubbed over her hole at the same time.

Kerry tensed, groaning, pushing down onto the fingers and up into Ewyn's mouth.

With his free hand, Ewyn held Kerry's pelvis down to the bed to still her. His fingertips traced the flushed pucker of Kerry's knot, teasing it open. It caused her to gasp. Ewyn kept sucking her steadily, going slow but wrapping his tongue tightly around Kerry's shaft and hollowing his cheeks.

Unable to ride Ewyn's mouth, forced to lay still and endure it, Kerry grunted, convulsing slightly. Ewyn tasted the salty drips from Kerry's slit. He pulled off, then sucked even harder, just on Kerry's tip. Two fingers eased through Kerry's rim, staying just inside her,

Lynn Kelling

going no deeper. Kerry whimpered, dripped again, her cock twitching.

Ewyn let Kerry's cock slide back into his mouth, over his tongue and simultaneously pushed hard to stuff her full, sheathing both his index and middle fingers to the last knuckle.

Moaning, Kerry tried to buck, but Ewyn held her down. Inside her, Ewyn twisted his wrist, knowing what he searched for and determined to find it. He pulled off and just watched Kerry's face as he rubbed and stroked with his fingers. Kerry stared, wide-eyed, at the ceiling, her mouth fallen open around soft cries. Ewyn mouthed over Kerry's sac, playing it between his lips, using his tongue.

Then he found it — the hard little gland. His proof was in Kerry's desperate gasp, followed by a sharp whine as Ewyn kept up the pressure on the sensitive spot.

Ewyn focused so hard on just feeling and listening that the whole world fell away. There were no worries, no cares. Just him and his love. He wasn't mapping possibilities or strategies, marking the exact risk of danger or compiling various tactics or plans if someone happened to threaten them, or Kerry specifically. He wasn't thinking of work, or the past, or even the future. He just was, and it was everything.

There was no overcompensating or second-guessing. He simply played Kerry's beautiful body to create the greatest possible pleasure for her, and so stimulate his own need to witness and watch as only a natural voyeur could.

The more Kerry responded, trembling constantly under Ewyn's hold, her cries growing desperate, rasping and breathless, the more Ewyn gave her. He rubbed back and forth over that spot, unable to tear his gaze away. Fluid ran down the side of Kerry's cock, milked from her. Ewyn licked at it with the tip of his tongue, giving Kerry as little friction as he could to keep her from tipping over the edge just yet.

The longer it went on, the more he saw Kerry giving over to exhaustion, so he spaced out the triggering taps more and more. Kerry would lie still, then shiver and grunt with each one. Her head fell to the side, her face flushed pink, a sweet frown creasing her brow and pouting her lips.

Ewyn could hold out no longer.

192

He moved swiftly, pulling out and freeing his cock. Sitting on the bed, Ewyn gathered Kerry up and manhandling her closer to straddle Ewyn's lap. She was light enough to lift and position. Ewyn lined up and relaxed his hold, letting Kerry sink slowly down.

When Ewyn's crown popped through, Kerry made a wild cry, gripping hard at Ewyn's shoulders to try to control her fall, but with the brace, Ewyn knew it was difficult to find leverage against the bed. She was helpless, being slowly impaled on the end of Ewyn's dick.

Kerry hid her face against Ewyn's neck, her begging mewls loud in the quiet room as she was taken, inch by inch, gripping so hot and snug with such yielding softness to the rigidity claiming her.

Ewyn kneaded Kerry's cheeks, spreading them, squeezing them. With one last upward thrust and a grunt of effort, he bottomed out.

He rubbed at Kerry's stretched-smooth rim wrapping the thick shaft. He caressed up and down Kerry's back and nipped at her earlobe.

"Gonna ride me while you come. Need to see you. Feel you. You want it?"

Ewyn's teeth scraped over the edge of Kerry's jaw as she leaned back, arching her spine. He nipped lightly at Kerry's chin as she leaned even further, her head tipping back to expose her throat. Ewyn felt her begin to move.

The sensual swiveling started small, hesitant, but the more Ewyn's cock slid in the snug glove of Kerry's ass, the more Kerry let go.

Ewyn lay back on the bed, making sure Kerry saw what he was doing. Easily, Kerry swung her legs around and bent them at the knees. She kept the weight off of her broken leg, but immediately began to ride Ewyn harder. Her eyes squeezed shut, a furrow of concentration running down her brow, Kerry began to bounce. Skin slapped skin. Ewyn first palmed each of Kerry's cheeks, urging her on, moaning hard at the slipping and sliding of his cock within Kerry's tight ass. He thrust up into the downward pushes, taking her faster. They found a good rhythm and Ewyn reached instead for Kerry's wet, red, straining erection. Fondling it, rubbing firmly over the head, letting it squelch obscenely within his fist, Ewyn saw the effect it had.

Anything else Kerry had held back was released. She pleaded wordlessly, riding Ewyn like she needed to feel taken even more than he needed to come.

She shot, gasping, her body clenching in spasms as climax hit. Ewyn held her still, then thrust hard enough to knock the breath from Kerry, over and over, slamming in and in and in.

"Oh, Jesus..." Ewyn moaned, quivering as he orgasmed, pumping into Kerry until he was spent.

He let Kerry fall, exhausted, to the side to curl up on the bed, guiding herself down with a contented hum.

But Ewyn didn't intend to let her go far. He shifted to curl up behind Kerry, palming the overheated skin over her heart, measuring her pulse.

There were things to do, but they could wait.

Breathing in the sweat and perfume of Kerry's skin through her dark hair, Ewyn felt her slip into a doze, her breaths even and shallow. Ewyn caressed the silken skin around Kerry's left nipple, brushing over the tip as it stiffened. His cock lay between Kerry's cheeks, waiting.

Minutes slipped away. Ewyn began to scratch instead of just brush over the sensitive skin. He pulled and twisted when he felt Kerry suck in a breath. Exhaling in a rush, Kerry pushed back into Ewyn's crotch, her face turning toward the bed.

Ewyn reached to steady his swelling erection, pushing it into Kerry in a slow, squelching slide. There was hardly any resistance.

"Ewyn," Kerry whimpered.

Ewyn hooked his arm under Kerry's legs, curling them up to her chest and holding them there as he began moving in long, complete thrusts. He savored the way Kerry's ass pulled him in, the way she stayed relaxed and open the whole time, inviting it, the roughness of her breaths as Ewyn had her.

But, sensing something in the way Kerry carefully kept her legs folded up, her fingers tensed where they clasped her thigh, Ewyn asked, "What do you need? Tell me."

Kerry stayed silent, though she turned her face more fully away from Ewyn's scrutiny.

"You want it sweeter?" He watched Kerry's reaction. "Rougher?"

He felt Kerry clench, her sigh shivering out. So, Ewyn reached for Kerry's sac, gathering it up in against his palm, and pulled. Squeezed.

Kerry made a rough cry, her whole body clenching even more at the blast of pain.

"More," she panted. "Please."

Ewyn kept thrusting slowly, all the way in, almost all the way out, the friction more intense as he squeezed Kerry's balls in gentle pulses, stretching them away from her body.

"Deep breaths," Ewyn told him. "Nice and deep."

He pulled harder. Kerry grunted and pushed into the next thrust.

"No. Be still."

It went on for minutes, Ewyn's stamina increasing and Kerry's body straining with the waves of pain. For Ewyn, it was gloriously good, and he fought against the climax rushing up at him. But it was futile. There was no denying how Kerry made him feel. It was right there, taking his breath away.

He kept squeezing gently every few seconds as he came down, liking the way it caused Kerry's inner muscles to contract around him.

Then, spent, he rubbed over Kerry's sac, soothing.

"Please," Kerry begged suddenly, almost sobbing with need. "Can I, please? I need..."

"Yes. Go on."

Kerry lifted her leg, grabbed her cock and began jerking off frantically, panting. Ewyn kept rubbing, rocking shallowly in and out. He felt Kerry convulse with her second orgasm moments later.

"Hands off now."

Ewyn rubbed up from Kerry's sac over the underside of her cock, flattening it to her pelvis, spreading the hot come spurting from the tip.

"That's it. Good girl."

Kerry moaned.

"Please..."

"Shah. I've got you."

He pulled out, propped himself up on his elbow, then leaned over Kerry to catch her mouth and tongue her while she caught her breath and came down. Kerry surged up into the kiss, grabbing the back of Ewyn's head to keep him near, opening wide for his tongue.

195

Ewyn fed three fingers into Kerry's swollen, throbbing hole and drank down her whimper, the sweetest nectar.

Chapter 24: Out

The next morning, Ewyn helped steady Kerry as she got dressed in the bathroom.

"Do you think we could maybe..."

"What?"

"Go to the fabric store?" Kerry glanced up at Ewyn's face. Going out in public at all while owning her full identity and battling her injury would be a trial. If it was to attain something that Kerry would use to take a forward step toward better things and bigger goals, she'd have that much more motivation to do it. "I want to make some more dresses, for myself and other people. I'm going to take your advice, make some samples to shop around. Maybe get the word out that I can make custom pieces for order."

"Mmm, absolutely," Ewyn said with a sleepy growl, brushing light kisses to Kerry's lips. "I'm glad you've been giving it some thought, and you're ready to go after what you want."

"Well, I already have some of what I want," Kerry teased, biting down on Ewyn's lip.

Chuckling, Ewyn said, "What did I tell you, kitten? You can nip, but I'm the one who bites." He went for the side of Kerry's neck, biting gently, then sucking at the spot. When he pulled back there was a mark left behind. "So they all know who you belong to," Ewyn whispered. "And who takes care of you." He pecked a kiss to Kerry's nose, then helped her down.

The dress Kerry was wearing that day was army green with asymmetrical black straps crisscrossing the bodice. For the first time in weeks, she put on a shoe, going with a combat boot which she hoped would steady her as she attempted to move around in spaces much bigger than Ewyn's modest home. She was also wearing makeup, with lavender eye shadow, black eyeliner, mascara, powder

Lynn Kelling

and some bronzer to even out her skin and nude lipstick. The stitches in her cheek had dissolved, but the scar was still there and visible. She hoped the makeup would cover most of it. After she'd applied it all, using as much as instinct tempted her to, she couldn't help but smile at her reflection.

Gone were the old worries she'd always carried when getting ready to go out. She didn't have to be concerned about attracting the wrong attention from people in her old neighborhood. Ewyn's neighbors seemed more the live and let live variety. She wasn't worried about running into family, and even if she did run into them, she felt better equipped to deal their response. And she wasn't screening her emotions through the filter of Jamie's opinions and personal preferences. Ewyn was supportive. He was providing Kerry with an environment in which she really could listen to herself and take cues solely from that.

Sure, there was always the wild card factor. There would always be people who didn't approve of how Kerry liked to dress. She couldn't anticipate them and expect to avoid them entirely, no matter what she did. All she could do was be mentally prepared to stand up for herself or ignore rude commentary, depending on how the situation played out.

At least Ewyn would be there. It would be a good test run, since Kerry had no plans to stay hidden away inside Ewyn's home forever.

The makeup made Kerry feel like she was presenting her best self. It took away some of the self-consciousness her injuries conjured. She looked better with it on, closer to the middle of the gender spectrum, where she knew her heart lived. It wasn't a mask, or a costume. It was merely a way to be more herself. The polo shirts and khaki pants were the costume. The straight military brat was the act.

It should have been enough to be happy with herself, and not care what others thought, but she knew it was going to take a while before she actually got there. Deep down, she was always going to assume the worst and second-guess her choices.

Seeming to sense Kerry's introspective thoughts, Ewyn asked, "You all right?"

It all twisted around in Kerry's mind and heart. She tried to smooth it out, but it wouldn't quite go.

"It's hard for me."

198

"What is?"

"The noise in my head. Doubts about myself."

"Planted by other people," Ewyn guessed.

Kerry rolled her eyes slightly, then dropped her gaze.

"Do you doubt yourself as you stand there? Or are you too worried about the opinions of people who don't get to have a say in who you are?" Ewyn paused, waiting for Kerry to think it over.

"I'm sorry I'm making my issues your problem."

"Eh! What the hell is rule number one?"

Kerry smiled sheepishly.

"Do you doubt yourself?" Ewyn pressed.

The answer was easy. She knew what she wanted, but she had trouble letting go of people she knew did doubt her. Especially Jamie. Kerry owed him another call. She needed to check in. It had been too long without word that Jamie was okay, and Kerry needed reassurance that Jamie hadn't found out about the attack or gone looking for revenge.

It had been a pattern in their relationship for Jamie to somehow always discover things Kerry tried to keep private and sacred, no matter how hard she tried to keep Jamie from them. It had always felt like fate itself was trying to out her, undoing all attempts to conceal truth whether she liked it or not.

Moreover, Kerry still worried about Jamie's innate lack of fear. Given Kerry's history of getting hurt over and over despite all of her precautions, a deep, dark terror warned her Jamie's boldness would catch up to him eventually. She didn't want it to be true. She wanted Jamie to exist as a heroic example of what was possible, despite the odds stacked against them.

Jamie was a living, breathing symbol of hope thrown in the face of the massive doubt and lack of confidence embodied by Kerry's family. Jamie had been Kerry's first big step away from them. Her independence after the breakup, her new life with Ewyn, and finally owning her true gender identity were further steps setting her on a path where she felt her family could never fit.

If not just to see if he was okay, Kerry also needed to thank Jamie for everything he'd done to coax Kerry along. Later that day, after the trip to the store, Kerry told herself, she would make the call.

"No."

"Well then. There's your answer."

Enjoying the fresh air on the drive to the fabric store, Kerry left the window down to let the breeze blow through her hair and warmed at the feel of Ewyn's hand resting on her thigh.

At a red light, Kerry looked sideways at him. "It's so strange how easy it is to be with you. Makes me think I was making things harder than they had to be for a long time."

"Likewise, love," Ewyn smiled. "Is it good to be out?"

"Really good," Kerry agreed. The sky was a bright, clear blue with bare wisps of clouds. The breeze was cool, the air warm. It was the kind of weather that begged for picnics in the sun or a drive to the beach. As intimidating as it would be to be out in those kinds of places, dressed as she was and with her boyfriend, the appeal of the idea was stronger than her fear, maybe for the first time in her whole life.

"Then we'll have to get out more often."

"Yeah, that'd be nice." Kerry caressed the top of Ewyn's hand, wrapping her left thigh through her skirt.

Ewyn parked as close to the store as he could, but it was still a process to get out and up on the crutch, then to hobble across the road and up the sidewalk before even getting inside. On the way, Kerry passed an elderly couple who stopped in their tracks to gape at her, plastic shopping bags dangling from their hands. The man muttered to the woman, "Huh, take a look at that. You think it's a sissy boy or an ugly girl?" The woman hissed at her companion, giving a tug at his arm. Kerry just kept going, focusing on getting there without falling.

On Kerry's other side, busy watching out for driving or reversing cars, Ewyn told her, "Doing good, love, just a little further." He nodded subtly to the storefront as if to encourage Kerry to pay attention to the destination rather than things like the other pedestrians.

Air-conditioned coolness blasted her as they entered. A clerk called hello and a few customers turned to look. Kerry couldn't tell if it was because of the crutch or the appearance of her that caused it. She was somewhat relieved to be inside rather than out on display in the wider world, but the fabric store was sure to be its own testing ground.

"Can I help you with anything in particular?" the clerk asked. She was nearby, stocking a rack of seasonal decorations.

"Nope, just browsing. Thanks," Kerry replied.

"Well, if you need help with anything at all, just let me know."

It was difficult to navigate the narrow rows, but Kerry tried to just take her time. Once she got deeper into the store, others stopped glancing her way as much. Ewyn helped her pull bolts of fabric and set things aside to be purchased. For the most part, Kerry tried to stick to what was on sale, but she also couldn't sacrifice taste for cost — not if she actually intended to sell the things she made.

Soon concerns over what and how much to buy with her limited budget clouded out any of her other current challenges.

She picked out a few vibrant colors in soft, easy-to-work-with fabrics like jersey, but also stocked up on more neutral, earth toned colors as well. Mostly, she stuck with solid colors instead of patterns. After she had matching thread, elastic, and zippers, she was ready to check out.

The total cost made her feel certain she was spending way too much, especially since she was out of work.

"Maybe I should put some of this back," she wondered quietly, her anxiety cranking up.

"You have to spend money to make money. Let me get this," Ewyn asked. "I'm an investor in your business."

"No way. I can't let you do it. It's too much. I'll just put it on my card."

"Sweetheart, let me get it," Ewyn insisted.

Kerry sighed. The check-out clerk smirked at them.

"Okay, but I owe you. I'll pay you back."

"We'll see about that," Ewyn argued, smiling up at the clerk. If her expression was any clue, she was definitely entertained by the back and forth.

Shifting her grip on the crutch, Kerry balanced there as Ewyn completed the transaction and took the bags from the clerk.

"Thanks for shopping with us. Have a great day. You two are such a cute couple."

Kerry felt the blush she knew was turning her pink.

"Oh, that's all her. Makes me look good," she heard Ewyn say to the clerk in response, which of course only intensified Kerry's blush and brought out a helpless, huge smile she tried to hide from view.

It was still on her face as they got back to the car. Even worries of encountering other judgmental pedestrians couldn't stifle it. Ewyn jogged ahead to quickly load the bags into the trunk before coming around to help Kerry with the door and the crutch.

"I see that smile. You can't pretend it away," Ewyn warned.

"I can try," Kerry huffed.

"Well, you're not succeeding," Ewyn teased. "Nor should you." He loaded the crutch into the back seat and moved to briefly caress Kerry's dimpled cheek beside the happy grin that wouldn't fade away. "If there's anything the world needs, it's more of this."

Kerry gave up the fight, beaming at Ewyn, who bent to give him a kiss.

"Love you," Kerry murmured.

"Oh, but I love you more," Ewyn grinned with a wink. He closed the passenger door before Kerry could counter him.

Kerry had many of the fabrics they'd purchased spread out on her worktable. Walking up behind her, Ewyn slipped a hand around her waist and brushed his lips over the shell of Kerry's ear. With a little shiver, Kerry hummed and leaned into the touch. Ewyn reached out and tugged at a folded length of deep purple fabric. It was incredibly smooth and soft to the touch.

"This one's going to be for you, right?" Ewyn asked hopefully.

"You like it?"

"I do," Ewyn said eagerly, thrusting slightly against Kerry's ass. The way her dress draped over it was driving Ewyn wild, especially with how the straps crisscrossed her narrow waist. He caressed down over Kerry's hip to her thigh. Sensing something in Kerry's attitude, as if she was withdrawing a little, Ewyn turned her around just to make sure nothing was wrong.

Kerry kept her chin down, his eyes lowered.

"Everything all right? You look like you're worrying about something."

With a shrug and a half-smile, Kerry acted like she was trying to play it off. "Nah, just a lot on my mind, I guess. A lot to figure out."

"Like what?"

"It's nothing." She shrugged, then caught Ewyn's gaze at last. Ewyn could feel her swallowing an apology for something. "I'm just used to not talking about things. Especially the types of things that would start a fight with Jamie. Or things I couldn't tell Kent, or the rest of my family. And I do want to tell you things, but I don't know if I'm complaining too much or being too much of a hassle."

"Just tell me," Ewyn insisted, brushing his thumb by the corner of Kerry's rosy lips, which were quirked to the side with worry. He could hear in Kerry's tone how she'd played off her concerns over and over again with her ex and her family, burying her feelings for the comfort of others and to avoid causing any disturbances. It was a terrible way to live — always feeling like you mattered less than everyone else. Ewyn had no intention to let her get away with it anymore.

"That elderly couple in the parking lot at the store. Did you hear what they said?"

"They said something to you?"

"Yeah. Well, about me, not to me. I guess you didn't then."

"No. Kerry, you should have said something earlier if they were harassing you or — "

"They didn't. They made a comment, and it wasn't nice, but... I have to get used to it. If I'm going to live like... this," she gestured to her dress, "I'm going to get that kind of thing all of the time. It's a given. So I was just thinking about it. The trade off. Freedom in exchange for additional negativity."

Ewyn had seen Darcy face similar conundrums. His brother, however, had decided early on to counter such bigotry and ignorance with a solid front of good-natured, friendly, confident charm. It had worked well for him until he'd been met with violence well outweighing his capability for self-defense.

Maybe it should have caused Ewyn to question Darcy's approach, but it never had. He wouldn't have dimmed Darcy's inner light for any of the bullies and murderers in the world. Darcy's fate had not been a failing of his, but of the world he lived in. As much as it scared Ewyn to see Kerry facing discrimination — and it surely did terrify him — he would no sooner lock Kerry away or change who she was then he would have done with Darcy.

With a twinge of pain mixed with fear, Ewyn said, "Love, just try to think about it this way. You're brand new. Like a bird that hasn't been discovered yet. Some exotic species. Will some of the less enlightened folks out there say some stupid shite now and then, just from failing to understand at first glance how wonderful you are? Of course they will. It doesn't mean you're any less wonderful. It's not your job to make everyone love you. You aren't playing for tips like you did at the club. If they don't like it, they can fuck off."

"It upset you when people called Darcy names, didn't it?" Those soft violet eyes held him, peering into Ewyn's heart. Helplessly, Ewyn drew Kerry closer, his arms wound around Kerry's lower back. He felt each breath Kerry took, the heat and the life burning in her. Feeling so grateful for it, Ewyn prayed silently for Kerry's continued safety.

Maybe Darcy could help watch out for her.

Maybe Jonah could as well.

At first Ewyn wasn't able to answer. 'Upset' didn't come close to touching how it had made Ewyn feel to witness others' blind hatred of his little brother, just for being different. It was possibly the biggest challenge of his life. It had defined Ewyn, guiding his purpose, causing him to feel like everything he did to try to help and make a difference for his brother would never be enough to counter the many strangers trying to bring him down.

Losing Darcy had proven that suspicion. It had heightened Ewyn's determination to be the sole protector of those he loved, even though sometimes it was truly a futile endeavor, or entirely unwanted. In response, some sadness stayed with him, as well as the need to live in the moment, and never take anything for granted.

"You don't have to talk about it if it hurts too much," Kerry said softly, frowning sweetly at Ewyn's inner battle with his emotions. "See, this is what worries me too. I don't want to keep bringing this pain back into your life."

"That you remind me of him is not something you should worry about. I love that you touch the same part of my heart as he did. Protecting you isn't a burden. It's what I do. It's who I am."

"But how am I supposed to protect you from feeling this way when I can't control what they're saying about me?" Kerry asked almost desperately.

"You can't. Kerry, you can't. You know that. And I don't want you to even try. Did it tear me apart to see Darcy navigate through hatred and ignorant scorn? Yes. But it was my lesson too, not just his. He got good and fast at not letting the negativity touch him. He just lived. He laughed, and danced, and did exactly whatever it was he wanted to do, even if it didn't make any sort of sense to anyone else." The words lodged in his throat, which closed up, choking him. He blinked too fast, the pain rising without warning. Kerry just laid her head on Ewyn's shoulder and gave him a hug.

For a minute, Ewyn endured the struggle, holding Kerry close, caressing her dark, soft hair. The tension in his chest and throat slowly eased. He let out a deeper breath and then went on, his voice rougher.

"Darcy lived a good life. He was a good man. What a tragedy it would have been if he'd done anything differently, dulling his shine just to appease the closed-minded people of the world. Just the thought of that is horrendous. *Please*, love. Be yourself. Don't let them take that away from you."

Kerry pulled back just far enough so that she could try to read Ewyn's eyes again. "So I'm not hurting you?"

"Hurting me? You've stolen my heart. Ripped the bloody thing right out of my chest so you can carry it around with you. It's the best kind of hurt in the world. I know how incredibly lucky I am to be with you. Darcy was an amazing person, and I miss him constantly. I'll carry him with me for the rest of my life. But that I get to have you now, despite all of the closed-minded idiots of the world? And be with you every day? With the ways you make me smile, and laugh and want and need to just grab life by the balls, that's everything that matters. That's the whole world, held right in my hands."

He clasped Kerry's firm back through the soft fabric, feeling her breathe, the warmth and vitality of her soaking into Ewyn's palms.

Kerry bit uncertainly at her lip, her eyebrows tilting slightly in question. "Do you ever wish I was a woman? It would be easier. And that's what you've always wanted before. I — "

"No, it's not what I've always wanted," Ewyn said firmly. "It wouldn't be easier. Take this as you will, but I understand you much better than I ever did them. I wouldn't change a single thing about you. It's you I'm attracted to, not the idea of something else. Have I ever done anything to cause you to question my desire for you and your body?"

"Well... no."

"If I ever do, I demand you tell me, right away. All right?"

"Okay."

205

"Have I ever caused you to question how much I love the way you dress and present yourself?"

Kerry laughed at that. "Oh, no. No, I definitely don't question that."

Ewyn slipped his hand up Kerry's skirt and gave her bare ass a squeeze, provoking a soft yelp from her.

"Honestly, I don't have a single clue why…"

Chapter 25: Found

It was late, and work was done for both of them. The quiet of the darkness around them and the comfort of what they'd talked about earlier made Kerry feel a little more brazen.

"What's up with all the piercings?" Kerry asked. She played with the silver stud through Ewyn's left nipple. Feeling the soft, pliant flesh around the hard silver embedded within made all sorts of questions spring to mind.

"I just like them," Ewyn shrugged. "It's a rush to get them done, and I like the way they look. Growing up, I was always encouraged to express myself in whatever ways felt right, and this did. The one in my dick has some benefits during sex, plus it just feels good to have the metal rubbing, especially when it rubs against my clothes.

"Mmm. Yeah, that makes sense. I hadn't thought of that." Kerry reached lower to touch the piercing. She ran her fingertip over the silver ball tucked under the ridge of Ewyn's cock, feeling the stud move slightly. She tried grabbing hold of it with two fingers. The longer she played with it, the harder Ewyn became.

"Do you like them?"

"Yeah," Kerry confessed, biting her lip. "I really do."

Soon, Ewyn became restless, so he rolled to his side, pushing Kerry to lay flat on her back. He arranged Kerry's hands above her head, then caressed down the underside of her right arm. His knuckles skittered over the hairless skin of Kerry's underarm, down her chest to brush over her stiffened nipple, along the center line of Kerry's torso to her navel, and finally to the bare skin where her pubic hair would have been.

"You're so smooth everywhere. Makes me want to lick you for hours, head to toe," Ewyn said softly. His knuckles paused at Kerry's stirring cock before sliding down her hairless thigh.

"I might grow my hair out a little. On my head," Kerry said, tossing the thought out there while they were discussing appearances. It seemed the safest time to mention it.

Ewyn glanced up at her face, then caressed around the side of her jaw, fingering through the strands of hair curling around the edge of her ear. Tucking them back and playing with the ends, Ewyn said, "Good. You've got lovely hair."

Kerry smiled helplessly, warming at the easy response and tender nature of the touches. "Okay. I'm glad you don't mind."

"Course I don't mind," Ewyn countered. "It's your hair anyway. You should do what you like with it."

The encouragement made warmth swell and grow in Kerry's chest. Moved to express her gratitude to Ewyn, Kerry surged upward, kissing him with a happy hum.

Ewyn dropped his gaze as their kiss ended. He nuzzled the side of Kerry's neck, his face hidden from view.

"What?" Kerry asked.

Ewyn shook his head. "Don't mind me."

"No, what? What's wrong?"

There had been too many times when Jamie would seem upset for no reason, without explanation. Jamie's instinct had always been to solve his own problems, not share them. That streak of independence had served him well in achieving his goals, though it hadn't led to great emotional intimacy between him and Kerry. It had been one of the behaviors that had driven a wedge between them, especially when Kerry became so reluctant to ask about the reasons for the seemingly bad moods. She had resolved since then to listen to herself more and speak up if something seemed off.

"Is it something I said?" Kerry wondered, feeling the urge to pull back, stop touching, which she'd never had before with Ewyn.

Ewyn propped himself up on his arm, bowing his head, brow furrowed. For an awful moment, it felt like a standoff. Neither of them moved or said anything, and Kerry's heart spiked with anxiety.

But then she saw Ewyn's eyes were bloodshot and the muscles in his jaw twitched.

"Ewyn..."

"Sometimes, when you smile," Ewyn said, stiltedly, "it just makes me angry, thinking about that son of a bitch beating you with that fucking bat. And your body, looking so small and helpless, lying on the ground, not moving, and the sound of the goddamned bat hitting." His jaw clenched. His eyes closed. His head shook slightly back and forth. "I wish it just made me angry," Ewyn said quietly with a strained voice. "It fucking *hurts*."

"I know."

With tender ache, frowning heavily, Ewyn said, "Course you do." He winced and seemed to bear down on the pain. Kerry pulled him close and down into a hug. Ewyn's strong arms wound around her, holding on.

"He hurt you for some of the same reasons why I love you so much, and knowing there are so many other assholes out there who'd do the same in a heartbeat if given the chance..."

"No, you were right earlier. You were right about Darcy. I won't live in fear of them," Kerry told him. "As tempting as it is sometimes, I can't let fear guide my choices. Because if I did, I'd never step foot outside the house. I'd never see my family again. Sure, it scares the hell out of me, but I don't have a choice. That doesn't mean you're going to lose me, okay? I promise."

Ewyn exhaled heavily, his grip tightening.

He looked up at Kerry's face again, all of his dread right on the surface, making him more vulnerable than Kerry had yet witnessed. "Do you swear you'll keep letting me protect you? Please, love?"

"Yeah. If it helps you feel better."

"It does."

"But, you know," Kerry said quietly, caressing through Ewyn's sandy colored hair. "Even if you lose me, it doesn't mean you won't find me again, someday."

Ewyn's breath caught. He gave Kerry's cheek a hard kiss, the heat of his breath warming Kerry's skin. "I won't lose you, too. I won't." It was said with determination. His reddened eyes shone as they bore into Kerry. He looked so young, then, and scared. It was a glimpse of the same stubborn little boy who had hid away a beloved outfit he'd outgrown, unable to let it go.

Thinking of Jonah, all of those long, lonely nights in the hospital, Kerry enjoyed how nice it was to be held so lovingly by someone who wanted to stand between Kerry and everything that might hurt her. "I won't lose you either. And you already have me."

Ewyn shifted higher, leaned down and began to kiss Kerry. The passion of his emotions burned in each brush of his lips and the scratch of his beard against Kerry's skin. His hand slid over Kerry's body with the desperation of someone who'd lost too much and held on that much tighter to everything he still had. There was nothing held back in Ewyn's grasping, caressing and kneading touches. He was all open and asking, giving Kerry an idea of all of the ways he still wasn't healed or recovered from the trauma of loss.

"You have me. I'm yours," Kerry promised. "And I have you too. Do you feel it? It's all okay, Ewyn. I love you."

The caressing, kissing and shared glances in the shadows, filled with understanding, went on and on.

Ewyn reached between Kerry's spread legs with wet fingers. Two entered her in a steady push and Ewyn just kissed her more deeply, licking into Kerry's mouth, opening her there as well. Each whimper was swallowed, chased. When the pumping of his fingers became steady, the muscles loosening, Ewyn drew back so the kisses were lighter teases of Kerry's lips as she quivered.

Pulling his fingers free, all it took was for Ewyn to press Kerry's leg higher, to lean in closer. Ewyn breached her in a swift thrust. There was no pain. In fact, the easy slide of Ewyn's cock was a comfort, filling Kerry and proving their connection in tangible ways. Pulling her leg higher still, staying open and relaxed, Kerry sighed with pleasure as Ewyn sweetly made love to her. Leaning in, he kept brushing kisses to Kerry everywhere he could reach, his breathing heavy and his strong, muscular body covered in downy, soft hair, pressed into her, trapping her to be worshiped and undone.

Ewyn shuddered, holding deep as he came with a small cry, his eyes closed with bliss.

"Touch yourself. Come for me, beautiful," Ewyn panted.

His eyes flashed and Kerry shivered with lust at how intently Ewyn watched. Somewhat self-consciously, Kerry grabbed hold of her own cock and began to stroke it. Ewyn gave her little pushes, riding her just a little. He rubbed Kerry's chest, and Kerry stroked faster. Ewyn's lips brushed Kerry's temple in a kiss and she came with an anguished, breathy gasp, spilling hot over her fingers, the shivers hitting her over and over as Ewyn kept up that wonderful, gentle thrusting inside Kerry's ass. Relaxing into it, letting out every purr and sigh, Kerry soon let her hand fall away.

Ewyn kissed Kerry's forehead, murmuring, "Oh, love." Folding his broader, larger body over her, Ewyn seemed to try to shield Kerry, or, rather, contain her in a cocoon of care where everything was right and nothing was wrong.

"I just want to stay here forever," Kerry said, fingering through the hair at the nape of Ewyn's neck, kissing his warm skin. "You make me feel like everything will be okay."

And for a precious little longer, they stayed just as they were. It healed places inside that Kerry thought were past hope, or even dreams.

Chapter 26: Embracing Truth

The phone rang. Kerry gazed at the newly framed photos sitting on the kitchen windowsill. They'd been placed beside an electric candle set to a timer. She was tempted to let the call go to voicemail.

It did, however, remind her she needed to try calling Jamie again. Jamie hadn't answered the last time Kerry had tried, or called back. Jamie had more than earned his independence and space, and Kerry understood the value in both after fighting so hard for them from her own family, but instinct told her to try one more time, just in case.

One photograph sat on each side of the candle, on which was written in Ewyn's handwriting in permanent marker, 'For Jonah and Darcy.' The photo on the left was of Kerry and her son, sitting at home in an heirloom rocking chair. It was the same one her mother had sat in, holding and nursing her when she was a baby. Debra had gone all out, getting that nursery ready for Jonah's homecoming. Jonah's hand wrapped around Kerry's finger, and he smiled a little as Kerry gazed down at him. On the left was a photo of Ewyn and Darcy. They looked like they were barely out of their teens. Ewyn's arm had been slung around Darcy's shoulders. He had planted a kiss to the side of Darcy's head, who had laughed brightly. It was the only photo Ewyn displayed of his brother. The resemblance broke Kerry's heart. Darcy was a more feminine incarnation of Ewyn, slender and elegant in contrast to Ewyn's bulk and masculine charisma.

Her thoughts were so much with family and how much those connections meant, even when the relationships, nor even fate, were ideal. Kerry answered on the sixth ring.

"Hey."

"It's been weeks, kid," Kent said. "Why haven't you been talking to me? Are you okay?"

How could she begin to tell Kent everything?

"I don't keep my phone with me all the time anymore. And I've just been figuring out a lot of stuff for myself, but I'm okay. I'm actually better than I've been in a long time."

Would Kent agree, though? If he could see, if he really knew?

There was so much doubt. It was bigger than anything. It had always been better to keep her secrets, to hide away in lies. Taking the first steps to acknowledging what was real was the hardest thing she'd ever done.

Imagining the disgust and scorn on her family's faces hurt so much worse than the bat.

"Let me see you, please? Can I come by after work?"

"I don't think that's a good idea."

"Why not? Are you still with Ewyn?"

"Yeah, of course."

"Why don't you want me to come over?" There was suspicion there, and concern. "He's treating you right, isn't he?"

"Yes, Kent, that's not..." Kerry sighed. She remembered saying to Ewyn how she wasn't going to let fear run her life anymore, or decide for her who she was going to be. But to actually be faced with the prospect of seeing Kent, and having to explain herself — that was a whole other story. There would be no taking it back. Whatever her beloved brother's reaction would be — that would be the new reality, for better or worse. "I always feel I need to defend my choices with you guys, so that's why I'm keeping some distance, okay?"

"What choices? About being with Ewyn?"

"No. Not exactly, but that is part of it, I guess. It's more about who I am. I'm never..." she took a deep breath, gathered some courage. "I'm never completely honest, even with you. I haven't been for a while, but I can't lie anymore. I shouldn't have to."

"You're freaking me out, kid. Just let me see you, okay? You don't have to lie about anything. I don't want you to. I just need to

213

Lynn Kelling

see that you're okay and getting better. Mom and Dad, Kurt and Kipp, they're willing to give you your space, but they kind of rely on me to check in, in their place."

"I know." Kerry sagged a little, feeling anchored to the spot, and those photos. "Okay. I'll be here whenever you want to come by."

"Thanks. See you soon."

As Kerry was recovering from the emotional shock of knowing she was going to be facing Kent, revealing her gender identity issues to her family for the first time, the phone rang again.

It was Jamie.

Instantly, Kerry shifted mental gears and answered, even before knowing what to say.

"Jamie?"

"Kerr, I just came from Blaze. I went to see you, and… What is this shit? What the hell is this shit, Kerry?"

Kerry sighed, trying to decide how to react. "I… I don't know what you mean."

"Yes, you do! I have a friend who knows another dancer there. We heard you left. We heard *why* you left."

"Jamie — "

"You were beaten? You were fucking beaten and you didn't even tell me?!"

"Can you just let me — "

"They told us you almost died, Kerry. That they tried to kill you and why the fuck would you not tell me about that?!"

"Calm down," Kerry said, doing her best to sound authoritative. "I'm fine. I swear. Yes, it was scary, but I'm okay now. I really am. I'm safe."

"Were you jumped? Was it on the way home from work? No one could tell me where it happened, or details, or — "

The lie sat right on the tip of Kerry's tongue. She could just agree. Say it was random. Blow it off and hope Jamie would let it go.

"It doesn't matter, Jamie. It really doesn't. What happened isn't on you. It's not on me. It just happened, and I got away from that. I'm somewhere safer now so there's nothing — "

"It was Victor, wasn't it?"

"Fuck. Jamie. Come on."

214

Jamie laughed, but it sounded too tense, too cold. "God, it was. It was Victor."

"No. No it wasn't. It was some other guy, okay?"

"Some other guy sent by Victor."

Kerry pounded a fist against the counter top, her teeth clenched in frustration.

"It doesn't matter," she repeated. "It's over. They got him. He's been charged. There was a witness, and plenty of evidence. You don't have to save me from it, okay? You got away. I got away."

As Jamie spoke, Kerry heard the emotion. The pain. "Baby, they tried to kill you! And I should have been there! I shouldn't have left. I should have gotten the fuck over myself and stuck by you and this is all my fault."

"No, Jamie, in no way is this on you. I'm not your responsibility anymore!"

"I nearly got you killed," Jamie said in a hollow, distant voice. "Because I was selfish. Immature. All we have is the people we love and if we lose them..."

"Jamie, please," Kerry begged. "Please listen to me! We broke up months ago. It's okay! It was time. And life is going to keep happening to both of us. I've been trying to call you, because I do love you and I wanted to make sure you stayed away from there, because they're dangerous. Even more so now. They might want revenge for getting caught and — "

Someone in the background on Jamie's end of the line had been saying something. Kerry wasn't able to catch what it was.

Jamie cut in, his tone different. Calmer. Controlled. "You said you're safe?"

"Yes," Kerry agreed eagerly. "Safe and healing. And happy."

Jamie pulled the phone away, murmuring something, talking to whomever he was with. Then he came back on the line, saying, "Good. That's good. That's all that matters."

"Promise me you'll stay away from Victor. Jamie, you have to swear to me you will."

"Sure. No sweat. Look, I've gotta go. Another call's coming through. I'll check in soon okay? Stay safe. You promise me too."

"Oh... okay..."

Before Kerry could say another word, Jamie ended the call.

215

For several minutes, she debated calling back, or texting, or even asking Ewyn to chime in on whether she should do either when she couldn't make up her mind. In the end, she decided to try to let it lie and leave it alone.

For years to come, she'd think back on that choice. She'd wonder if she had called Jamie back, would it have changed the outcome?

Ewyn had the day off. Kerry couldn't decide if that was good luck or bad.

Out on the driveway, Ewyn worked on his bike. Kerry could hear him banging around, the stereo cranked and playing rock music. Kerry was tempted to keep peeking out of the windows to see what he was up to. Ewyn did look good after all, with his bare chest, tight jeans, work boots, and covered in engine grease.

Wiping his hands on a rag, Ewyn came back into the house, leaving the door open to allow the breeze through.

"Need a drink," he said. "Want one?"

"Sure. Thanks."

"Beer, soda or water?"

"Guess," Kerry replied with a half smile from over her shoulder.

"Okay," Ewyn grinned back.

The fridge opened, then cabinets banged softly as they were opened and closed again. Water ran in the sink.

Close by, a car door shut.

"Shit," Kerry sighed, remembering her phone call with Kent. Ever since, she'd been trying to mentally rehearse what she would say — or not say. Now that the moment was at hand, she drew a total blank.

The doorbell rang. Kerry sat frozen.

"I'll get it," Ewyn called, then jogged back to the door — big as life and twice as dirty. Holding onto the doorframe, he asked, "Yes, can I help you?"

Kerry frowned.

"Well, I hope so. I'm here to see Kerry, but I can't imagine I'm at the right house."

"Dima!" Kerry cried, nearly bursting with relief as all of her tension fled, replaced with giddiness.

Unfortunately, she couldn't jog like Ewyn, or even stand quickly, so it was left to Ewyn to reply, "Yeah, she's right here. Sounds like she was expecting you. Please come in."

Kerry struggled to her feet as Dmitri stepped into the house. As soon as their eyes met, Dmitri said, "You could knock me over with a feather. Is he for real?"

"He is," Kerry beamed. "Dima, this is my boyfriend, Ewyn. Ewyn, this is Dmitri Yaakov, a.k.a. Dima, one of my best friends in the world."

They shook hands.

Dmitri was wearing pale teal skinny jeans and a gorgeously hand-embroidered blouse with vintage lace details, which was falling tastefully off of one shoulder. Dmitri's formerly black hair was currently dyed a cotton candy pink and styled in a tall pompadour. He sported cat-eye shaped pink sunglasses with rhinestones at the corners and plum lipstick. His tall, lean frame looked as elegant as always, but especially lengthened that day by his cream spiked heels.

He came in and helped steady Kerry as she got to her feet. Dmitri gave her a kiss on each cheek, then looked her over. It was the first time he'd seen Kerry in a dress.

"Finally, you silly bitch. This is so much more like it. And color too! Please tell me what miracle has occurred to finally get you out of the damned khaki pants and polo shirts?"

The faint Russian accent was still there, an extra little pizzazz sprinkled over every word.

Kerry wore a dress she'd made the day before, out of the deep purple fabric Ewyn liked. The fabric wrapped her hips, showing off a fairly short, tight skirt though the bodice was baggy. Her non-broken foot was bare but she was thinking of getting some sandals to go with the dress. She'd decided she was ready to start trying less masculine footwear, but she wanted to ease into it gradually.

"It just felt like time. Practically, it makes sense with the brace... and I just like it. But Ewyn's the real miracle, actually," Kerry said, biting at the edge of her lip. "The purple was his idea."

"Well," Ewyn interjected, "you're the one who picked it out at the store; I was just giving my opinion on which I thought would look best on you."

217

"My god," Dmitri said softly, hand to his chest as he looked Ewyn over. "Are you kidding me — he's good looking, butch, and has good taste? I guess this is all of your overdue good karma finding you at last, huh?"

"Maybe," Kerry grinned. "I'm really lucky to have him. That's an amazing blouse by the way."

"You like?" Dmitri smiled, showing it off and doing a twirl. "I'll send you one."

"Really?"

"Of course. A friend makes and sells them out of a fantastic little boutique down in the gayborhood."

"Which one? I'm actually looking to start selling more pieces. I'm not going back to Blaze, so I'm going to try doing this full time."

Dmitri's mouth fell open. He suddenly gave Kerry a big hug, squeezing and gushing, "Oh, that's the best news I've heard all week. Good for you, sweetheart. You're too talented a designer to be wasting it."

"Thanks."

Dmitri fished his wallet out of a cream colored leather bag slung over his shoulder and rifled through a stack of business cards. Handing one over, he said, "Call them, tell them I recommended you. I'll give them a heads up. They'll want to see a few pieces, but they're a big supporter of local artists and also sell everything they carry online all over the world. If you're willing to do custom work on demand, that would be a big draw for them."

"You're amazing, Dima. This is perfect. Thank you so much."

"I'm gonna head back out, keep working on the bike," Ewyn said, excusing himself. Dmitri stopped him with a hand on his arm.

Dropping his chin for a second, Dmitri seemed to collect himself. He said with an emotion-thick voice, "I don't know how much of Kerry's background you are aware of, Ewyn, but as someone who cares a lot about her, I just want to thank you for being there." Dmitri glanced back at Kerry, who was suddenly getting teary-eyed too, but trying to push down hard on the swell of memory and tangled feelings. "To see her come so far in only a few weeks, after years of bullshit and cruelty? Incredible." Dmitri shook his head and let out a gruff, exasperated exhale.

Kerry's eyes prickled, but with joy rather than pain, which was harder to instinctively fight back down.

"Will you hug her for me? I don't want to ruin her dress," Ewyn asked, gesturing at his soiled hands and clothing.

"Fuck. He is perfect, isn't he? Saving the clothes and everything," Dmitri sighed, gathering Kerry in a hug and kissing her cheek.

"Love you," Ewyn smiled. "I'll be right outside, okay?"

"Okay. Love you too."

Dmitri looked at Ewyn, mouth hanging open, no words left to say.

Chapter 27: Heart-to-Heart

"So, be honest with me now," Dmitri insisted. They sat on the couch together, listening to the banging and rock music from outside. Ewyn had delivered Kerry her water before heading out to leave the two friends some privacy. Sipping it, Kerry braced herself for the question. "How is it?"

"It?"

"The sex, sweetheart. I can tell just by the way you two look at each other that this has gone places you have never tried to go before. I'm happy for you, as long as you're all right."

"I am all right," Kerry assured him. "It was a little scary, but I knew it was what I wanted. There weren't any doubts about that. Ewyn just wants to take care of me, and that's all I want too, so it works."

"Better than with whatshisface?"

"My problems with Jamie weren't his fault. Our needs just didn't mesh. But yes," Kerry grinned. "I'm happier now. I mean, I came into this knowing who I was, which made the difference, probably. With Jamie, we were both right in the middle of figuring stuff out and that hurt us in so many ways. The more we realized about ourselves, the more it tore us apart. Jamie's not a bad guy, but we just weren't right for each other. I'll always love him though."

"Did you initiate the gender swap with the pronouns?"

"It was kind of a joint effort, actually. Ewyn read into my reactions after he used more masculine nicknames a few times, and asked if it bothered me. We talked about it a few times. He asked me what I wanted, and I could tell he would be okay with whatever my answer was, so... I told him the truth. Ever since, he's been switching over. But, like I told him, it's not a big deal to me if other people don't use the female pronouns. I'm genderqueer, not a woman. Either one feels okay, but with Ewyn, I like being his girl instead of his boy."

Dmitri cocked his head to the side, "I'm so proud of you, you know. All grown up. Have you addressed the family issues?"

"Partially?" Kerry said with a twist of her lips and a shrug. "They haven't seen me recently, or know anything about my gender issues, but they know I'm living here now. They know Ewyn's my boyfriend."

"Wow," Dmitri said with raised eyebrows. The sunglasses were in his hand and he played with the arms. "How was that?"

Kerry shrugged again. "They were kind of weird about it, but they didn't disown me. They still think I'm acting out and are waiting for me to grow out of it."

"Well, when you show up with boobs maybe *that* will change their minds."

Kerry laughed. "Sorry, no boobs for me."

Dmitri tisked. "Shame. Tits would do wonders for your figure."

Kerry ventured outside the house in order to walk Dmitri to his car, whether he liked it or not. The excuse to feel the sun on her skin was more than enough to make it worth the effort and ache in her arms from the crutches. She tried to put some weight on her broken leg, at least to steady her and take some pressure off, but didn't want to chance it too much.

"When does that fucking thing come off?" Dmitri asked, nodding to the brace and digging out his keys.

"Just a couple more weeks," Kerry said excitedly.

"Then you get to go back to shaking your ass, but for an audience of one," Dmitri said with a wink.

"That's right," Ewyn called. Dmitri laughed.

Kerry was careful not to catch the crutches on any of the divots in the path, and avoid any mud clumps. She was listening but not really watching anything but her feet, so when she heard an all-too-familiar voice say with confusion, "Kerry?" she was so shocked, she almost fell right over.

"Kent?" Kerry fought to stay upright. Kent got to her before Dmitri or Ewyn could, catching her arm and one of the crutches.

"You okay?"

"Yeah. Just clumsy as hell with these things." Her face was turning beet red, and it was getting harder to breathe. She felt Kent's grip on her arm, saw Dmitri coming closer, frowning and tensing up. Ewyn was there too, but looked unsure of what to do or how to read the dynamics of the situation.

Kerry wanted to run inside and slam the door, but she couldn't even take a step.

"Just give me the crutch, okay?" she asked, her voice wavering.

Finally, Ewyn was there, rushing in. He took Kerry's arm from Kent, and the crutch too, saying, "I've got her."

He slipped the crutch back under Kerry's arm, but let Kerry pull him a little closer so they were chest to chest. Hanging her head, Kerry tried to get it together, to calm down and be strong.

Out of the corner of her eye, she could see Kent, who was being too quiet. There was an expression too close to revulsion on his face for Kerry's liking.

Ewyn was cursing his greasy hands and clothes under his breath, so near but reluctant to touch more than he already was. Dmitri was right there, hovering.

She hadn't wanted to do this outside, but she couldn't imagine Kent coming in now that he'd seen and heard everything.

"Is... is this a joke? Why are you in a dress?"

Those words were an angry yank at something in the middle of Kerry's chest, pulling the air from her lungs. But her uncertainty vanished, fast.

"Hey, if you're not going to show Kerry some respect — " Ewyn started, getting riled.

"Let me try," Kerry gently cut in. It was time to open her mouth and defend herself a little. She couldn't look her brother in the eye, but she did have something to say. "Kent... it's not a joke. This is why I didn't think you should come over. I don't really know how to explain this to you, but I won't hide it anymore either. I've been lying for so long; it's exhausting. Mom and Michael always wanted to fit me inside the box labeled 'son of a Marine', but I don't fit in *any* boxes, okay? I never have. I've just pretended, to spare the family's discomfort, but I can't do that anymore. I won't."

"I can help her inside, if you want," Dmitri offered in a quiet murmur to Ewyn.

"Please. Thanks Dima," Ewyn replied. They were almost the same height, but Dmitri was a little taller with the heels.

"If you're uncomfortable, please go," Kerry said, turning around with effort but it helped to have Dmitri bracing her back and ready to catch her again if needed.

"No, you don't get to dismiss me like that," Kent argued.

"She can if she wants to," Ewyn said icily.

Breathing out a humorless laugh, Kent shook his head, "So, you're pretending to be a chick now? Is that what this is? Just because you want to date guys doesn't mean you need to act like a girl."

"Please give me permission to kick him in the balls," Dmitri asked under his breath.

It actually got Kerry to laugh despite the awkwardness of the situation.

It took a few minutes of struggling, but soon Kerry was finally back inside. Ewyn looked like he wanted to go wash up so he could properly help Kerry or at least be better prepared for whatever was happening, but he just stayed there, nearby and on edge. Dmitri stayed with Kerry, helping her sit on the couch again. With a grimace, Kerry felt a twinge in her broken leg — maybe trying to put more weight on it had been a bad idea — and moved to bring it up onto the couch, wanting to raise it to take some of the pressure off. Once he realized what Kerry was doing, Dmitri helped and grabbed a throw pillow to put below Kerry's heel.

Kent was a couple of steps inside the doorway, hands on his hips, dressed in textbook business casual with his button-down shirt, tie, pants, and polished shoes. "Can I please have a minute alone to talk to my brother?"

"No," Ewyn and Dmitri answered in unison.

With a heavy sigh, letting his head fall back on his shoulders, Kent said, "Fine. Kerr, how long has this been going on?"

"Forever? I've always felt this way, Kent. I just knew it wasn't okay to tell anyone I did. Michael made that pretty clear, and no one else helped me stand up to him. I only really started to be honest in the way I dress and present myself in the past few weeks, but this is who I've always been. I hid it from you guys when I still lived at home, especially after Michael got aggressive with me. Jamie didn't understand it either."

Kent looked at Ewyn levelly. "But you do."

"Aye, I love Kerry just the way she is."

Kent shook his head, rubbed his hand through his hair. "Why is he doing that? Are you going to ask me to do that too, now? Use 'she' and 'her' and everything?"

"Like I said, I don't fit in a box. It's not just one or the other all the time, you know. All I know is what feels right. I like Ewyn and my friends to use the feminine pronouns, but I get that it makes you uncomfortable. I kind of expected it to."

"So you feel like a girl?"

"Not exactly. I'm not trans in the same way as Jamie, and I'm not transitioning to female; I don't feel like I'm just a guy. I'm in the middle somewhere. I'm gender fluid, or genderqueer. It's not my body that's the issue, it's who I feel I am inside. That's what I've been trying to figure out, and why I haven't been in touch with the family as much. Obviously, if you guys had trouble dealing with me dating someone trans, me being on the trans spectrum wasn't going to go over great either. I needed to understand it myself before I could try to include you all in this, or, you know... defend myself to you."

"Kerr, this isn't safe. I mean, if you get off on doing this in your own home — fine. But if you go out like this, you're begging to be laughed at or attacked by some meathead."

"You know where I've been working the past two years, right?" Kerry let it sink in before continuing. "I'm used to the catcalls and laughing and comments. I got 'em every single night. And living with Michael for so many years... I'm a goddamned pro at tuning it out when I need to. I'm tired of pretending to be someone I'm not. I can't change myself so I can be who you think I should be, or anyone else for that matter. That's not how this works. The way other people feel about this isn't my problem, unless they come at me. I'm not a wimp, Kent. I can throw a punch if I have to defend myself. Now I have Ewyn to watch my back, too."

"What about the guy who broke your goddamned leg in your own apartment?" Kent demanded.

The more Kent egged Kerry on, the easier the defensive arguments came out. She'd already been through this with Kurt and Kipp. They hadn't been pressing Kerry on this particular issue, but that Kerry had some experience under her belt with standing up to her big brothers about the attack helped more than she had expected.

Kerry knew it wasn't her fault that Victor's buddy had surprised her, or that the guy hated her enough to beat her senseless.

"He was a fucking bigot on a mission from the landlady, trying to convince me to get the hell out. And he came up behind me with a metal bat, so yeah, I'll admit he got the drop on me there, okay? But I'm not going to dress in a way that feels wrong just in case I run into assholes. Anyway, it's not the assholes that are my problem, to be honest. It's this part of it. It's Mom and Dad and the rest of our family, because I realize you guys don't support me in this. I don't know how to explain myself to you in a way you'll accept. I love you all so much, but I'm not sure it's a battle I have the energy to fight. I need some more time. Some space, until I feel stronger."

"That's ridiculous."

"Why?"

"You're part of our family, Kerry! We're not just gonna forget about you! You've been through hell. You're living with this guy you just met a few weeks ago — no offense, man — and doing all kinds of crazy shit. It's our job to make sure you're okay."

"No, I really don't think it is. Not if being okay means doing what you say instead of listening to my own instincts for the first time in my whole life."

"You were almost beaten to death!" Kent yelled, getting red in the face. "And that was *before* you started to dress like this. I'm not going to ignore that and forget that I love you. You've been so wrapped up in your own crap, and we understand why, okay? We know there's a lot you're dealing with, but we're not going to stand by and let you keep risking your life."

Shakily, Kerry ran her hand through her hair, searching for the right thing to say, the right way to feel.

"If my time comes, I'm ready for it. In the meantime, I want to be happy," Kerry said quietly. "I want to be myself, for once."

Ewyn and Dmitri were motionless, silent. Kent looked terrified, his eyes too wide, his mouth a tight, straight line.

"Stop saying that shit," Kent begged.

"You have to let me go."

225

"Stop it," Kent yelled stepping forward. "Just because Jonah died doesn't mean you get a free pass to go kill yourself!"

Ewyn moved before Kerry could even react. He stalked up to Kent, getting between him and Kerry.

"One step too far," Ewyn seethed. The look he gave Kent, which Kerry couldn't see, must have been a doozy. Kent stopped short, then took one step backward, raising his hands in a peacemaking gesture.

"I'm sorry," Kent said. "Kerr, I'm sorry. I just can't lose you too, okay? Please?"

Jittery and upset, Kerry tugged at the hem of her skirt, wanting to disappear, to run from the confrontation. It was too late, though. She was deep in this mess, and there was no getting out. But she didn't know what to do, or how to fix it. She had to try, though.

"I'm not going anywhere," Kerry told her brother. Seeing Ewyn defend Kerry's honor helped calm Kerry down, letting her feel like things were less out of control than she feared they were. Meanwhile, Dmitri was tense as ever. Kerry reached for his hand and pulled him down to sit on the edge of the couch. Holding Dmitri's hand helped Kerry felt a little better. "Kent, you've always been there for me. I know that, and I love you for it. And I didn't..." her voice caught, because she felt how it was all getting away from her. It wasn't just him, either. It was all of her fear for Jamie, too. None of it was within her control anymore, if it ever was. No acting would undo what Kent knew now, and what he would soon tell the rest of their family. "I didn't want you to find out like this. I wanted it to go better. I wanted to explain and show you it wasn't a bad thing. It's always been a bad thing to all of you. But can't you see how exhausting it can be to feel like there's something really wrong with me for my whole life? My *whole life*, I've felt like a mistake. And I'm not a mistake!" Her voice cracked, broke apart and gave out.

It was too quiet. Dmitri gave Kerry's hand a squeeze. Kerry plowed on. "I know it's a lot to process, okay? I know it's a shock and scary, given what I've already gone through. I know you'll need time to get used to it, and that's totally fine. I'm not expecting you to get it right away, but please just try to get there eventually? Please give me a chance? I'm okay. I'm happy. I have a support system. I'm safer. I'm not... stripping... anymore. I'm going to try doing fashion design for a while, see where it takes me. Things are so much better now. I feel like Jonah would be proud of me, Kent. You're not losing me. And I'm not suicidal, I'm just a realist. It's dangerous out there, whether I'm in a dress or not."

Kent still looked flustered and unsure, though he was settling down slightly. "Look, I'll, uh... I'll talk to Mom and Dad if you'd like. They want you two to come over for dinner to celebrate the brace coming off."

With a pained smile, Kerry shook her head. "I don't know how to tell them this, or be myself around them. I don't even know how to start."

"Please, Kerr. Think of all of the shit you've been through with Haley and Jamie and the hospital and... everything. They were there for that. I know we dropped the ball with Jamie. I know we should have done more to accept that too. But you need your family, right? We want to be there for you now. I'm not asking you to change, okay? If this is what you need, then fine. We'll get used to it. Of course I'll give you a chance and I know they will too, okay? I'll talk to them. I'll tell them what's at stake here. Just... please don't write us off yet."

Kerry felt jittery with both hope and fear. She knew there was nothing else she could do but wait and see, to try and keep standing up for herself, no matter what happened. "Okay," Kerry allowed.

"Thank you. That's all I ask."

"Okay."

When Kent didn't move, Dmitri spoke up, saying to him, "That's your cue, hon. We've got this."

With another sigh, glancing warily between Kerry and Ewyn, Kent finally gave a slight nod and turned to go.

"Just don't dodge my calls, okay?" Kent asked Kerry.

"All right."

He stepped through the door. When it closed behind him, they all let out a breath of relief.

"Jesus Christ." Dmitri gave Kerry's hand a squeeze. "And still they wonder why you moved out so young."

"Tell me about it," Kerry commiserated, sinking back into the couch cushions and shutting her eyes. "And he's the *easy* one."

Chapter 28: The Call

Cuddled up close to Ewyn, Kerry slept peacefully until her cell phone began to ring. The sound was shrill and impatient. She thought she'd set it to vibrate before heading to bed the night before, but she must have forgotten.

She had specific ringtones set for different people — Ewyn's was part of the song Superheroes by Irish pop band The Script; Erin's was a bit of the tune from Erin Go Bragh; Dmitri's was a light, sparkling sound; Jamie's was the melody from Bob Marley's Three Little Birds; Kent's was the Superman theme song (part of an old joke about his name); and the rest of Kerry's family was set to play a military drum beat.

The phone wasn't playing any of those. It just rang. It was someone else.

And it was four in the morning.

Kerry startled awake. She sat up and saw it was indeed her phone that was ringing, not Ewyn's.

Beside her, Ewyn grumbled awake. "Who's that?"

Kerry saw the name on his screen — Jamie's mother, Angela.

"Oh no," Kerry breathed, feeling like the floor was falling out from under her. Instinct screamed that something was wrong. Something had happened, she felt it.

Snippets of her last conversation with Jamie floated in her head, haunting her — the upset and emotion in Jamie's voice; the certainty that Victor was behind it, despite Kerry's reluctance to give details; and Jamie's determination that Kerry's pain was his fault.

For a moment, she couldn't answer, couldn't move. She didn't want to know.

"Kerry?" Ewyn prodded, sounding more awake and more concerned.

With a deep inhale to gather strength, Kerry answered.

"Hello?"

She was shaking, having trouble breathing.

Angela's voice was strained, worn out and rasping, as if from overuse, like she'd been screaming. "Kerry? That you, honey?"

"Angela, what's wrong? What's — "

"Are you... you have someone there with you, hon?"

"Please," Kerry beseeched. "What happened?"

"Jamie's gone. Jamie's..."

Distantly, Kerry felt Ewyn sitting upright, staring, trying to hear. Maybe he could. Because Kerry wasn't breathing, and it was so quiet.

Angela made a desperate sound of holding back emotion, or of being too exhausted to process it. She cleared her throat. "I don't even know how to say this... It... it was a few hours ago, the police said. They tried... tried to hide the body and..."

The questions came before understanding or acceptance.

"How? Who? Why?"

"In the... the abandoned house next to the apartment building where you two lived. He was... beaten. Naked. Head trauma. Raped and — "

"No. No, no, no."

"His friend. The, uh, the boy he'd been staying with, from the gym — Mark — said he'd been away, traveling for a boxing tournament out of state. When he got back, Jamie was missing. But Mark knew Jamie had been ranting about someone named Victor Hammerstein, and Jamie had told Mark something had happened to you, Kerry. Mark figures Jamie went to talk to Victor himself while no one could tell him otherwise or hold him back."

"Oh god."

"And the cops found Victor, but he claimed he hadn't seen Jamie in months since he had moved out. They found Jamie's car nearby though. So they questioned Victor and they searched the place. Searched the area. It didn't take them long to find him."

Lynn Kelling

"This is my fault," Kerry realized, horror draining her blood out of her body, leaving her ice cold. "He went after Victor because of me. They killed Jamie because of *me*."

"Oh, Kerry, no," Angela said, her voice thick with tears. "No, honey. They did this because they're sick. Not because of you, and not because of my Jamie. He was tough as nails, wasn't he? Went out fighting. That was the other clue, you know. Victor's nose was broken. He had bruises he'd tried to hide. Plenty of 'em. Said he'd fallen down some stairs, but the police... they knew."

"Angela..." Kerry struggled for her voice. It felt thick, strange. She was disconnected, floating above herself and couldn't remember what to do or how to do it. She also kept seeing Kent's rage and predictions that something bad would happen. He'd been right. Scrambling to think of what to say, how to feel, Kerry told her, "I'm so sorry. What... What can I do? What do you need? How can I help you?"

"I-I'm okay," she told him. "My sisters are helping me with the funeral arrangements. I'll let you know about those, okay? I'll be in touch. Take care of yourself, now. That's what Jamie would want."

Kerry didn't know how to accept that. She heard the words but they didn't make sense.

Jamie's funeral?

Jamie's wishes?

No.

He couldn't be gone.

It couldn't be real.

"Angela?"

"Yes, sweetie?"

"Did they charge him? Victor?"

"Oh, yes. They're still processing evidence, but there was enough to hold him and by God's grace enough to damn him to the hell of prison for life. I pray for it."

They hung up. Kerry just sat there, staring straight ahead, the phone cradled in her palm. The choices she's made and their consequences were thick in the air, choking her.

Right by her side, she felt a gentle touch to her arm. The phone was taken and set aside.

"A *mhuirnín*, I'm so very sorry," Ewyn told her softly. When Kerry leaned into him instinctively, Ewyn gathered her against his chest,

230

kissing her hair. Kerry couldn't return the embrace. She couldn't do anything.

"I-I don't understand. I — " Her voice caught and a pair of hot tears spilled onto her cheeks, carving paths filled with pain. More tears followed.

"You can't. You can't understand it. You never will."

"How is this really happening?"

"I don't know. I don't know why terrible things happen. I never have."

The details ran on a loop through Kerry's head, as if imagining Jamie's gruesome murder might make it undeniable. He'd been attacked, the same way Kerry had, and then also raped, and left to die alone.

It wasn't true. It was a nightmare, not real life.

As if he could tell what Kerry was doing, and wanted to pull her from it, Ewyn added, "It makes no sense, and it's not fair. But I know you loved him, and I know he loved you."

"He went there for me, Ewyn. He went there because they attacked me and then they… they…"

"Don't. Don't even go there, love. Jamie was a fighter, right?"

"I made him swear he wouldn't go there. He promised me. He swore." Kerry wiped away the tears that wouldn't stop. "Why would he break his promise?"

"I don't know. I guess he felt he had to."

Ewyn just held on tighter. Kerry turned to face him, hiding her face against the strength and heat of Ewyn's body, unable to stop shaking or to feel anything other than the need to undo it all somehow. Maybe if she went back to sleep, it would all be just a nightmare. She could wake up again and it wouldn't be true.

But Jonah had shown her the worst could happen. And all that was left to do when it does was endure.

It was a lesson she had never wanted to learn again. Part of her didn't want to. Maybe it was no use to try and fight, the way Jamie did.

Ewyn kept holding her, though. He smoothed back Kerry's hair. He held her in his arms and let Kerry feel loved. The comfort of that led her to think of how her family loved her, and feared for her the way Kerry had always feared for Jamie, who did what he felt was right, no matter what. And for the first time, she really saw how she was terrifying them even more by closing them out and not giving them a real chance to understand the whole picture, or do their best to safeguard her in their own ways.

After many minutes, Kerry asked quietly, "You heard everything?"

"Yes."

"How does this keep happening? How do they keep getting away with it?"

"I don't know, love. I really don't. But at least they have Victor."

"Yeah, they do, don't they?"

"What do you need? What can I do for you? Do you want me to make some coffee? Get some water? Call someone?"

"Maybe in a little while. Can we just lay here a little longer first?"

"Of course."

Silence spun out. Kerry let it all whirl through her head, all of the pieces. She tried to understand how this was reality, how this could have happened to someone as strong and fearless as Jamie. She tried to figure out what it all meant.

Ewyn's voice sounded softly, barely able to be heard. "God, protect Jamie's spirit. Help us realize he's at peace and free now, away from all pain and fear. Please help Jamie's loved ones find peace as well, and show us all how to let go of this awful hatred."

Kerry caressed Ewyn's arm, took a shuddering breath. "Thank you."

The process was horribly familiar, like it had been just yesterday that someone — who should have still been there, who had their whole life ahead of them — was being mourned.

The disbelief remained the biggest challenge.

There was no desire for vengeance in Kerry's heart, whatever that may have implied. Maybe the consequences of Jamie's actions, taken supposedly on behalf of Kerry's honor, sapped it from her. But, whatever the cause, Kerry knew there was no good in chasing after those who had committed such unimaginable crimes against someone she once thought was the love of her life.

If anything, being suddenly denied Jamie showed Kerry even more clearly the things she had left of value, and how important it was to hold onto them. Truth, understanding, and courage felt more crucial than ever.

Any questions or bashfulness previously held concerning her newly revealed desire to own her gender identity in public seemed inconsequential. What good was tearing herself apart over something that she knew made her happy when Jamie was dead?

They might not ever know why Jamie had been murdered, and how big a part his status as transgender had played in the crime. Kerry suspected it was a prime factor. For some, it would be more reason to stay hidden and embrace lies in the name of safety.

Kerry just didn't have the energy to do it anymore.

No matter how much she lied, awful things still happened. Not only would they still happen, but she'd be killing herself slowly in choosing the path of denial and fear. The haters of the world would then win twice over.

Because it wasn't just her appearance that drew danger her way, as it had Jamie. It was her relationship with Ewyn, and Kerry would have sooner lost a limb than lose what she had with Ewyn, especially just to satisfy those who sneered at homosexuality.

Feeling the weight of her certainty and incredibly tired, Kerry sat in a fog.

She sipped coffee made by Ewyn. She picked at some food, but she didn't taste any of it.

She listened as Ewyn made a phone call at Kerry's request.

"Hey, Kent," Ewyn said in a voice even more gruff from lack of sleep and upset. "Kerry's okay, but something terrible has happened. I, uh... I don't know how to say it other than just saying it. Jamie was murdered."

Kerry listened without reaction as Ewyn described the how and the why as best he could. Hearing the words spoken out loud again actually helped them seem more real. Rather than making things worse, listening to the story of Jamie's death repeated helped Kerry begin to come to terms with it.

Ewyn paused, listening to Kent's reaction. He glanced Kerry's way and said, "Well, she's mainly in shock, I think. It's going to take some time." Kerry imagined Kent's reply, probably filled with more questions. Endless questions. "I don't know if she's ready to talk. That's why I'm calling instead, especially with the way things went down here before, and — Yeah. Okay, I'll ask." Ewyn cupped a palm over the phone. "He wants to speak to you."

"Fine," Kerry muttered, holding out a hand.

"You sure?"

"Yeah."

She prepared to defend herself with strength she didn't feel.

"Kerry?" Kent said hesitantly.

"Yeah."

"My God. I'm so sorry, kid. I can't believe it. I just... What can I do? What do you need?"

"I don't know. I need to get through this, I guess. I mean, if not for Ewyn, that could have been me. It was the same guys who did it. These monsters... they did this to shut Jamie up. To make him go away. And I need you to understand something, okay? I can't let them succeed. I'm not shutting up and I'm not going away. Jamie never stopped fighting. I need to learn from him. Fight in his place."

"Kerr..."

"What?"

For a moment, there was silence. He felt Kent shifting around the pieces, making a new picture out of them.

"Let me know when the service is, okay?"

"Okay, but I got a message from the family, and I think it's going to be small. Private. Family and close friends only. They don't want it to be a big scene."

"Well, if you want to get a drink after or something, let me know."

"You'd be seen with me?"

"Kerry..." Kent sounded wounded. Kerry wasn't sure what to make of it. All she knew is how much she hurt, and that she didn't know if it would go away, or if things would ever really be all right again. "I love you, kid. I love *you*."

Kerry let it sink in. She wrapped the gesture of acceptance around her to keep the cold out. The memory of Jamie's spirit, his fearlessness, urged Kerry to try, to hope in the face of seemingly insurmountable odds.

"Can I ask a favor?"

"Name it," Kent said eagerly. "Anything."

"Mom, Dad, and the others — just please... ask them to give me a few days? To process it? They never liked Jamie, or knew much about him and… I can't pretend things were different than they were. I need a little space, just for a week or two. But I promise to keep you posted, and to see you soon. The others… I want to. I want to see everyone, but I'm not up to it right now. Let me try to get through this first?"

"All right. I'll handle it, okay?"

"Thank you."

"Can I ask you a favor, too?"

"Sure."

"Promise me you won't go out without Ewyn, or me, or someone else who can watch your back? Please? Just… to be safe?"

"You trust him to take care of me?"

"Yeah, he seems to be doing a great job. If you trust him, I trust him."

"Okay. It's a deal."

Kent sighed in relief. "Thank you."

"I might take you up on that offer, though."

"Any time."

A few days later, there was a small service at a funeral home down the street from where Angela lived. It was a nicer neighborhood than Jamie's and blessedly free of most of the danger factor that plagued the area — the reason they were gathered there at all. The building was quaint, surrounded by palm trees and pristine landscaping.

Jamie's mother, aunts, and cousins filled the room decorated with photos from Jamie's life. He was there as a child with long braids and in brightly-colored dresses. He was there as an androgynous looking teen, his hair cut short and his dark eyes reflecting some of the battle churning within. He was there as a fighter, post transition, in the ring, in gloves, throwing punches.

He was there.

Kerry felt him, his spirit. It lived on in each of them, and he felt it propping her up when her knees wanted to give out, when the sentimental photographs dealt a crippling blow to the center of her gut. Unable to breathe, wanting to disappear, Kerry felt Jamie there with her, telling her to be strong, to keep going, to show them all she could do it, to let it out and let go.

Ewyn stayed right by Kerry's side, looking like a hired guard and generally setting the whole group at ease to have some muscle on hand, just in case. A few of the papers had run the story and there was always a chance of protestors or reporters.

Kerry had worn one of the outfits Jamie had liked best — long black pants rolled to the knee, just above the brace, on her left leg and a dark plum button-down shirt. She paired them with a discreet but sparkly purple necklace purchased by Ewyn as a surprise earlier that day, and she had made up her face. She painted her nails to match the shirt and thought Jamie wouldn't have minded. All in all, the balance felt right — respecting the past and embracing the future.

The night passed in a blur of tears, hugs and stories shared.

She met Mark, the new man and a fellow boxer who wore his pain right on the surface and looked like he'd walked through Hell to get there. Even in her own grief, Kerry's heart broke for Mark.

Kerry touched the urn holding Jamie's ashes, just to feel it was all real. To prove to herself it was. But Jamie wasn't in it. That, Kerry knew for sure. Jamie was somewhere else, with Jonah and Darcy and too many others. And he was at peace.

Chapter 29: Shoes Stores and War Zones

"Look, I'm just glad you're here at all. You don't have to actually come in with me if you're not comfortable."

"Kerry, don't even start. Of course I'm coming in. And why wouldn't I be comfortable? You'll always be my brother." Kent stopped short, running his tongue over his teeth. Some of the uneasiness was still there, at the edges of things, but Kent was trying to power through anyway. Kerry appreciated the effort. Maybe this really was a beginning instead of an end. "I can still call you that, right? Or is that not okay? I just — "

"It's fine," Kerry assured him. It had been a week since the funeral. Kerry had been working on her designs and had begun to go stir crazy. She wanted to go out and get some air.

And some shoes.

"I don't think I could think of you as my sister. No offense. That would just be really weird."

"Maybe you'll get used to it," Kerry smirked, mostly because of how uncomfortable Kent was. Just the fact that Kent was there, a physical presence for Kerry to rely on, spoke volumes and did a lot to convince Kerry that her brother was really trying his best to come around and be supportive. He'd followed through by keeping the family at a healthy distance until Kerry was ready to engage more closely, and in turn Kerry had called Kent every day just to check in. Since losing Jamie, Kerry felt the mantle of being the brave and self-confident one had been passed to her. She couldn't let the world lose the shine Jamie had added to it as long as she was able to do her part to keep it there. Even if that meant coping with her family's struggle to accept her identity. "Like I said, I know this is a lot for you. But you didn't have to be here today if you didn't want to, so whether or not you use certain pronouns or labels is not a big deal. You've proven you're here for me. And you really don't have to come in. I'm just going to see what sizes they have."

"No. I'm not sending you in there alone."

"It's a women's shoe store, not a war zone."

Kent didn't look convinced. In fact, he seemed certain that the whole world had become Kerry's war zone. He gritted his teeth, leaned forward behind the wheel of his BMW, gripped the steering wheel, and seemed generally constipated.

That morning, Kerry had gone to a follow-up doctor's visit where they'd taken more x-rays and evaluated her progress in recovery. Her leg seemed to be healing well along with her other injuries. She'd been encouraged to keep trying to put more weight on her braced leg. The more active she could be, the better. Going from an exercise schedule including regular runs to near-constant sitting on her ass was taking its toll on her leg muscles. She'd been doing upper body exercises with the help of Ewyn's equipment, but it wasn't enough. She had a long road ahead of her.

Because Ewyn was working an all-day security job, and Kerry wasn't comfortable driving herself yet, Kent had accompanied Kerry for the trip to the doctor's office. Kerry's request for her brother's help had been something of an olive branch, letting Kent be more involved if he chose.

Kerry wore a brown skirt with a lightweight black sweater, paired with a black boot. The desire to have a broader selection of footwear had gotten so strong, she couldn't ignore it any more.

She'd always had small feet. She could wear a women's size ten, so there was hope they'd have something that would fit with no special-ordering necessary. But the store wasn't in one of the gay-centric neighborhoods, so things were not guaranteed to go well.

"Okay, let's do this," Kent decided.

Their mother had wanted to come along to the doctor's with them, but Kerry was still trying to work up her nerve to let her parents see her new, more honest incarnation. She also had no idea how to talk about Jamie with them or the rest of the family. They hadn't recognized Jamie as trans, and had generally ignored the whole relationship between him and Kerry. There was no doubt what had happened to Jamie actively shifted former dynamics, coloring Kerry's family's perceptions of her life and choices. She just didn't know how or what the consequences would be.

"Well, I can't stop you, but I can handle this, okay? Don't make it weird."

"Weird? This is already deep in the weird zone. We were just discussing whether you're my sister now or not."

Kerry shot him a look.

"Oh come on. Did you lose your sense of humor along with your desire to wear pants?"

With a sigh, Kerry relented. "Yeah, fuck pants and jokes."

Kent slowly reached for the door handle. "Okay sis. Let's get this show on the road."

"All right. But be careful on the way," Kerry warned.

"Why?"

"Well, that stick is lodged so far up your ass."

"As if you're one to talk," Kent replied, laughing along with Kerry.

They got out of the car. Kent groaned. Kerry did her balancing act on one foot until she could get the crutches out. By then, Kent had come around and tried to help.

"I've got it," Kerry told him.

She was wearing minimal makeup that day — just a little around her eyes and some lip gloss. Combined with the brown, knee-length skirt, which could almost pass as really baggy shorts, she was definitely less flamboyantly attired. Yet, she was going into a women's store to shop for herself.

Focusing mainly on not falling, Kerry navigated the parking spot and the narrow space between the parked cars, then made her way toward the sidewalk in front of the store.

Next to the shoe store was a bank. As they neared the front door and Kent moved to open it for Kerry, a pair of middle-aged women came out of the bank just a few feet away.

"Do you see that?" Kerry heard, but ignored it, keeping only her goal in mind.

"Yeah? What do you think you're looking at, lady? Huh?" Kent said defensively to the women.

Kerry's heart sank. "Don't. Please?"

"Some sort of freak," one woman hissed.

239

She kept going into the store, nudging the door wider with her arm as Kent was distracted by the female commentators. Kerry caught a glimpse of them in the glass's reflection, and the sneer on the one woman's face. It was aimed at her — her back. Somehow, she couldn't even be mad or upset about it. She just felt sorry for her, and the burden of being someone with such a narrow view of the world. She also understood why Jamie's reaction had always been to face criticism head-on, not that she intended to do the same. Confrontation would never be her thing, but she respected the drive to challenge outdated perceptions.

"Can I help you with anything?" the teen behind the register asked. She came around the counter, doing a quick glance up and down Kerry's body. Her name-tag read, 'Sue'.

"Yeah, actually." The bell on the door chimed as Kent finally followed Kerry into the store rather than remaining to make a scene and continue engaging the women from the bank.

"You all right?" Kent asked under his breath, steadying Kerry with a hand to her back.

"Of course." To Sue the saleswoman, she said, "I'm looking for a pair of sandals. Something neutral in color."

"Um... okay. I don't..." She seemed perplexed, as if wondering whether Kerry was confused or in the wrong store. "We don't carry men's shoes, though."

Kerry scanned the shelves with shoes lined up prettily, hidden lights shining down on them from above. There was a selection of sandals to her right, so she nodded to them. "Those might work," she said.

"Oh," Sue said with confusion. "Okay. Um, are these for you to wear, or..."

"Yeah."

"Oh."

There was a brunette standing by some purses, watching them. A couple of elderly women in floral dresses were seated on chairs, trying on some pumps and paying the newcomers no mind. Other than that, the store was empty.

Kerry slowly approached the sandals with Sue following her. She quickly saw one she liked, made of leather with crisscross straps and no heel. The style wasn't entirely gender neutral, since there was some detail work cut into the sides, but it was close.

"How about those? Do you have any in size ten?"

"These?" Sue picked up the sandal Kerry had indicated. She nodded. "Let me check the back. Go ahead and have a seat."

"Thanks."

Kerry took a seat in order to get off of the crutches, grabbing another sandal she liked on the way, just in case the other wasn't available. Kent stood nearby, biting at his thumb and looking generally like a deer in headlights. Smiling up at him, Kerry was easily able to ignore the brunette's continued staring. She wasn't browsing the purses at all anymore, but just stood gaping at Kerry.

On the chairs across from her, one of the elderly ladies finally noticed Kerry.

"Son, this is a women's shoe store," she told her, as if saving her from an embarrassing mistake.

"Maybe he's shopping for his girlfriend," her companion suggested to her. "You don't know. Leave him alone."

"Thanks," Kerry said politely. "I know what it is."

"He's wearing a skirt," the woman whispered loudly to her friend, patting her leg.

"Kerry..." Kent started, trying to interject and maybe suggest they leave. He was eyeing the door.

"Yeah, do you like it?" Kerry asked the women, smoothing the fabric. "I made it myself."

Covering his mouth with a hand, Kent was obviously paralyzed with indecision, not sure whether to intervene or butt out.

"Well," the old woman with dyed red hair replied, "Boys really shouldn't wear dresses, hon."

"You think so? Why? They're comfortable."

"That's true, you know," her white-haired friend told her quietly. "Those Scots wear them all the time. Nothing at all underneath either!" She giggled, then turned to look at Kerry. "My husband wore a dress for Halloween one year," she explained. "Couldn't get him to take the thing off for hours. Just sat there with his beer and wig, happy as a clam."

Sue the saleswoman returned then, carrying a box. "We had one left," she told Kerry. Opening the lid, she lifted out the shoe for her right foot. Giving her a hesitant, lingering look, she asked, "Do you want to try it on?"

"Oh, try it on," the white-haired woman said in encouragement. The red-head gave her a questioning look.

Kerry glanced at Kent, who was still trying to remain invisible. "Hold these for me?" she asked, holding out the crutches.

Kent took them and Kerry began to remove her black boot.

"That looks like a nasty injury," the white-haired woman said, nodding to her leg. "I had a bad fall once, broke my arm. No fun at all."

"He didn't fall. He was attacked. Beaten for being different," Kent interjected defensively.

The elderly women fell silent, shifting their gazes between Kent and Kerry.

From behind Kent, a voice said, viciously, "Good. The last thing this world needs is another faggot prancing around in a dress."

It felt like all of the blood in Kerry's body drained down to her feet.

The brunette had said it. She surged forward, toward Kerry. Kent dropped the crutches with a clatter, almost knocking over a display of socks. He moved to block her way, snapping to life at last. The woman, halted by Kent, spat at Kerry. The thick wad of phlegm landed on Kerry's arm.

Flashes of images from her imagination distracted her, pulling her out of the moment. She thought of Jamie fighting. Jamie, broken and bleeding, with no one to hold his hand at the end. She thought of the beautiful people that hatred and intolerance destroyed, and wondered why. Why, when there were so many other, kinder choices?

"Ma'am, I'm going to have to ask you to leave," Sue spoke up, sounding irritated, her tone more forceful than before.

"Fucking bigoted trash," Kent seethed.

The brunette flushed an angry red and stalked toward the door, shouting over her shoulder, "I hope next time they finish the job! Maybe take care of your boyfriend, too." She shot glances back their way as the shop's doors slammed open, then slowly closed.

"Sir — miss — um... I'm so sorry about that," Sue said to Kerry, her expression apologetic as she wrung her hands.

"Here," the red-head spoke up. She was holding out a tissue.

Kerry took it, thanked her, and wiped the spit off of her arm.

"I've never seen anything like that. Some people have no manners at all. No common decency."

"I'm so sorry someone hurt you," the white-haired lady told her. "That's terrible."

"Thanks," Kerry said softly. She set down the wadded, dirty tissue and looked down at her foot, the boot nearly off, the laces untied. She suddenly didn't want to try on the shoe anymore. "Maybe we should just go."

She bent to retie the shoe.

"We'll take the sandals," Kent said to Sue then. "I'll pay for them now while she gets ready to go, if that's okay."

Kerry paused, her hands trembling just a little. Her vision blurred and her eyes stung. Her head down, she tried to tie the shoe. It was quiet. No one said a word. Sue took the box, put the sandal back in place and went with Kent to the register, though Kent, first, propped the crutches up beside Kerry and laid a hand briefly on her shoulder.

Kerry got the crutches under her arms and by the time she was at the door, Kent had the shoes in a bag. He hurried in front of Kerry to open the door.

"Thank you for shopping with us. I'm sorry about the trouble," Sue said uncertainly from behind the register.

"That's okay."

"It's not okay," Kent countered gently. "Come on."

They went out to the car. Kent opened the car door as well. Kerry slid the crutches into the back seat, then sat carefully down in the passenger seat, swinging her legs in. Kent closed the door and came around, setting the bag in the back with the crutches.

Kerry tried to say thank you. She opened her mouth to voice the words, but they stuck in her throat.

Kent gently touched Kerry's arm. "Are you okay, sis?"

Surprised into laughter, Kerry shook her head. She took hold of Kent's hand for just a moment, giving it a squeeze. "I'm getting there. Thanks."

"Good. Let's get you home."

They reversed out of the spot. Through the glass windows, Kerry could just make out the shapes of the elderly women and Sue. The brunette was nowhere in sight.

"If they don't fit, I'll return or exchange them for you, okay?"

Lynn Kelling

"Okay." She gave Kent a grateful look, her chest still feeling tight. Kent gave her a small smile, then got them on their way.

Chapter 30: Testing Grounds

Ewyn flipped through some of the photos of Jamie that Kerry had pulled out for the services and then wound up keeping them out just to see and have around. The pair of them sat in the living room. Most of the curtains were drawn, but a few lamps cast a warm, cozy glow. On the coffee table sat a large peace plant sent by Kerry's family with a note of condolence.

"He blamed himself for everything bad that happened to you."

"Yeah, he did," Kerry replied with regret for things she couldn't change. "And he shouldn't have. So, learn from that, okay? I know it's important to you to safeguard, but you can't control the whole world. That's not your job."

"Yeah," Ewyn sighed. "Kind of know where he was coming from, though. Even with going after Victor. I was tempted to do the same, you know."

"But you didn't. You made a different choice. You stayed with me instead of doing something unnecessarily dangerous."

"Wasn't his fault, though," Ewyn commented.

"I know. It just makes me..." She growled.

"I know it does, love. I know."

Changing topics, Kerry said, "Tomorrow, the brace comes off. The night after, my parents are having that dinner. Kent sent me a message with more details, asking me to confirm that we're going to plan to go. I do want to. I think I'm ready to try. At least to give them a bottle of wine or something and talk for a minute, if not to stay."

"I don't trust Michael," Ewyn warned. "If they start to use Jamie's death as a way to scare you — "

"I know," Kerry cut in. "That's why I just want to go to let them see me, let them see us, together, as we are. No more hiding. Not from them. Jamie would have just gone over there and dared them to say a word against him. That's what he did with his own family, knowing they didn't approve. He told them, look, this is how it is. Take it or leave it. I want to be more like that. It's going to be really hard but I'm keeping my expectations low. I don't plan on going inside the house. Once they see, I think they'll get it."

"All right," Ewyn allowed. He caressed Kerry's thigh, trying to read into her body language, determine her needs. "Should I let you get some work done? Focus on those samples for the boutique for a bit?"

"Yeah, if you don't mind," she asked, eyeing the nearly-finished pieces folded in a pile on the work table by the window. "I only have a little more to do and they'll be ready. Getting through that meeting with the shop owner might give me the courage I need for facing my family. And working usually helps me stop thinking so much about everything. There's a lot to make peace with. It'll be even easier after tomorrow." After a heavy exhale, she added, "I hope."

"I hope so too."

It was early, the sun barely beginning to rise. There was so much to be done, such a busy day ahead, but Ewyn knew he had to make time for one thing first.

He set the flowers on the grass in front of the gravestone etched with his brother's name and the years he'd lived.

Thinking of the plant Kerry's family had sent him, and the note expressing their sympathy and love, as well as the subdued emotion provoked in Kerry upon receiving them, Ewyn knew he loved someone with a worthy heart.

There had been so many times in the past couple of months where Kerry had leaned on Ewyn, literally and figuratively. At first, Ewyn felt hesitant and uncertain in how to respond, whether to give in or hold back. He still felt uncertain, but not about Kerry.

He knew Kerry needed support — a lot of it. But Kerry was also pushing herself, going out there to own who she was, no matter what, despite the cruel reactions of closed-minded strangers. Ewyn couldn't and wouldn't stop her from doing that. It was a constant challenge to step back and let it be, to endure the panic it stirred and trust Kerry would be able to handle anything that happened. Ewyn would never stop safeguarding her, but he also knew the dangers of holding her back. That was a mistake he couldn't make again.

Weeks ago, after Kerry returned from a trip to the shoe store with Kent, Ewyn had seen as soon as he'd walked in the door that something had happened. He saw Kerry's pain. When he'd heard Kerry had been spit on and a total stranger had told her attackers should have finished the job, Ewyn had lunged for the door. He'd wanted to speed over to that shop, to find that customer, to make the world pay for the damage it inflicted.

Kerry had stopped him and reminded him the woman was long gone, that he needed to let it go. Kerry's hand on Ewyn's arm, the resignation in her violet eyes, and the scar on her cheek made Ewyn want to rage and scream. It had taken several minutes for him to be able to set the keys down and turn back from the door. Arrogance was a stubborn beast.

Ewyn thanked God for Kerry's wisdom and quiet strength, every day.

"You'd love her, Darce," Ewyn said, smiling a little. "Two peas in a pod, you'd be. Sharing clothes and fashion tips. I'd have to pry her away from you, I think. You and Ma, both."

He breathed out a chuckle, feeling the ache of what was longed for but would never be.

"Just please watch out for her, as a favor to me? Be her guardian angel? It scares me so much, after so much tragedy, knowing she's in danger, but..." He blew out a breath, thinking of what life was like before Kerry Sanderson had shaken it up beyond all recognition. "That she needs me so much gives me a lot of peace, brother. After you left, I felt like I had no direction, like I wasn't doing enough to make a difference. I didn't know my purpose. You... you always knew. So does she. She's a light, just like you. And it's up to me to keep her shining brightly."

Not for the first time, Ewyn thought of how Jamie's loss had been his gain, and felt guilty for it.

"I don't know if I deserve to feel this happy," he confessed. "No matter how much sappy love I pour out for her, she just soaks it all

247

in, like she can't get enough. Does my heart so good, but who am I to be so lucky?"

Like Darcy was really there, Ewyn heard his reply.

Stop doubting yourself, silly. So you're happy? Be happy! So you're in love? Love! We're not guaranteed tomorrow, so live for today.

"Yeah, you're right. You think she'll get sick of me? And my worryin'? My fussin'? Ma's been chasing off men that way for decades."

Somewhere, there was laughing — musical and light. He saw Darcy sitting on top of the stone, legs swinging, throwing his head back with gales of laughter.

"Just a pair of hopeless, co-dependent fools, eh, Darce? And ain't we lucky."

He kissed his first two fingers, then touched them to the stone.

"Love you, brother. If you've got any spare luck, send it our way."

A flock of sparrows stirred, taking flight all around him, soaring for the clouds in a flurry of wings. They lifted up, and carried his worries away with them, for the moment at least.

Pushing his hands into his pockets and whistling Darcy's favorite tune, Ewyn began his stroll to his bike.

There was work to do.

"What if I can't do this?"

Kerry felt like she was coming apart. The worst part was she knew how stupid she was being, and how much what happened in the next hour or so didn't matter in the grand scheme of things. But still, she panicked. She had her completed samples in a garment bag. It was sunny and perfectly warm out. A photo of Jamie was taped to the dashboard as a good luck charm and for inspirational courage. The boutique was right there, only a few steps away from where they'd parked. Ewyn had driven her to the appointment in Kerry's car, promising to wait outside until it was over for moral support. But the idea of what she was trying to do was ludicrous — a Marine's son turned stripper turned genderqueer unisex dress designer.

Maybe they'd all laugh at her.

Maybe they'd be offended, or angry, tearing her designs apart before coming for her next.

Or maybe they'd just give her that look that said only, 'Oh, you poor, delusional boy.'

"You can," Ewyn said severely. "You're brilliant at this, but you'll never get out there unless you try. Plus, these boutique people have nothing on you. You're gonna blow them away."

Kerry was wearing the purple dress Ewyn liked so much. In addition to the collection of separates and dresses in the garment bag, she had sketches and photos of her pieces being modeled by Dmitri. It didn't feel like nearly enough.

"I'm so fucking scared," Kerry laughed uneasily, blowing out a breath and trying to shake off the nerves.

"I've got ya, girl. Do your thing. Believe in yourself as much as I do."

Kerry frowned as her appreciation for Ewyn's steady confidence nearly burst her heart, then kissed him lightly, careful not to smear her lipstick. "Love you."

"Love you more. Go on, now."

"Okay. Here goes nothing." She climbed out of the car, walking uncertainly on her brace, leaning on a cane. Going slowly, not really trusting her weight on the leg, she carried her things into the store. There were gay pride stickers on the doors and windows. Half of the mannequins were male forms in androgynous or feminine clothing. The wide, gleaming windows were full of custom pieces and brightly colored, dramatic accessories. The awning above the entrance was decorated with rainbow colors. If there was anywhere she should feel welcome, it was here, or so she told herself. But appearances could be deceiving.

It was too early for much of a crowd, for which Kerry was glad.

"Hello?" she called, walking up to the register's counter.

"You must be Kerry," a friendly voice called. An attractive woman with a slightly raspy voice walked forward from the back of the store. She had black hair like hers, though pin-straight and long. Kerry couldn't tell if she was trans, and didn't much care, though she did find herself smiling more honestly and feeling much more at home. "So good to meet you," she said, shaking her extended hand. "I'm Sacha Lee."

"Good to meet you too, Sacha," Kerry beamed. "I brought some things to show you, if you've got some time?"

"Absolutely. I loved what I saw in your email, so come on. Show me the goods." She nodded to a back room with a lounge area and desk.

Chuckling at the irony of the request, Kerry followed.

"Well?" Ewyn leaned against the car waiting in the parking spot, his muscular arms folded over his broad chest.

"She's in! She said yes," Kerry cried, dancing a little and bursting with excitement. "I can't believe it."

Ewyn met her halfway, kissing her soundly on the lips and lifting her up in a brief embrace before slipping the garment bag from Kerry's grasp.

"I can," he grinned. "Congratulations, love."

"She wants me to produce some things for the store in multiple sizes, and will list me as one of her designers for custom orders. I'll be in her store, and online. This is incredible." She bounced a little, biting her lip. "Oh my god, I have so much work to do. We've got to get home."

"Easy now," Ewyn laughed. "How about we stop for a celebratory lunch first? I think work can wait an hour longer."

"Well... okay," Kerry relented reluctantly.

"That can be an order if it has to be."

Kerry grinned. "Okay. Let's go celebrate."

Ewyn raised his glass.

"To dreams coming true," he toasted. "And going after exactly what we want, no matter what."

"I'll drink to that."

Kerry clinked her glass's rim against Ewyn's before she sipped the sparkling water, ordered by Ewyn as soon as they'd been seated.

"I think Sacha will be fun to work with," Kerry said. "I really feel like this is what I should be doing. The whole time I was dancing, it always just felt like a step on the way to something else. It was fun for a while, but it's time for something new. Something bigger. I'm so lucky to have you, Ewyn. Thank you for making this possible for me, and for believing in me. I really couldn't have done it without you. You're my hero in so many ways."

"And you're the light that brightens up my world. You're welcome," Ewyn said affectionately, his voice hushed though their table was fairly secluded. "I'm so happy for you, love, but I'm just glad to see something this good come your way. I say my thanks every morning when I wake up next to you. As difficult as the journey to get here has been, now I know how precious each day is, and what's worth fighting for, and what's not." Ewyn took Kerry's hand and brought it to his lips to kiss the knuckles. "There's always going to be both good and bad, but now I have you to keep me going. I'm not just fighting against what happened to Darcy — I'm fighting for something. Someone."

Kerry smiled at him, feeling the need to do for Ewyn as much as had been done for her. "You really mean that? It hasn't been too much?"

"Yes, I mean it. Our trust in each other, how you lean on me without question, your faith in me and our partnership — that's everything. After Darcy passed, I was afraid for so long. That's what kept me going, trying to right those wrongs out of fear. I know you understand that, with losing Jonah, and now Jamie. Those losses — they change us. But you prove to me every day that I'm not alone in this anymore. We get through things together. All I need is to have you at my side."

Kerry sipped her drink and held Ewyn's gaze. "That's all I need too. Before, I was so lost. I don't know if I would have gotten to a place where I was this happy without your encouragement and acceptance."

"No," Ewyn argued. "You give me too much credit. You had to find yourself. That was all you."

"Well, thank you for seeing me and loving me the way you do."

"Always."

Ewyn leaned in, so Kerry did too, exchanging a kiss.

As she sat back, she admitted, "I really don't know what to expect tonight."

"They're your family first, Kerry. They've been open-minded so far, right? They knew they were inviting your boyfriend along with

251

Lynn Kelling

you. They sent that plant and card after you lost Jamie. I think there's plenty to hope for."

"I just don't want to lose them for good. I feel like I just keep losing people. But what if I do this, and I'm as honest with them as I know I need to be, and they reject me?" She shook her head. "What am I supposed to do?"

"We'll deal with that if we have to, but you need to try. You can do this," Ewyn urged. "No matter what, I'll be there for you. My mum will be there for you. Your friends, Kent, your new career — those are what you hold on to. If the rest drags you down, let go of it."

Kerry had depended on the illusion of a supportive family to help her find strength to go on for years. But, even before Haley and Jonah, Kerry had been searching, not fitting in, and not feeling right. Now, at last, her feet were firmly planted. She was understood completely, and her heart didn't belong to her anymore. The responsibility she had toward loving Ewyn was what kept her going, more than designing, more than making up for mistakes and regrets of the past.

If her mother, stepfather, and brothers closed her out, she wouldn't be left in the cold. It would be okay.

Kerry reached over the table, taking Ewyn's hand. "All right. I'm ready."

Chapter 31: Seeking Bravery

For over an hour Kerry sat in front of the opened closet, looking at her dresses lined up on hangers. In the end, she'd decided to keep wearing the one she was in, vibrant and shameless. Maybe the lace was too much for her family's sensibilities, but it was too late for such trifling concerns. The reality was that she was showing up for dinner with the whole family along with her boyfriend, while wearing a dress and makeup. A little lace wasn't going to put her over the edge.

They pulled up to her parents' sprawling estate in Fallbrook at five o'clock. The Spanish style house, ringed with oak trees, the front entrance flanked by impressive columns, the home topped with a red tiled roof, was as pristine and faultless as it had always been.

Kerry also wore the sandals Kent had purchased for her — dainty with narrow leather straps. They were a tangible sign that her family might wind up being more tolerant than she expected. She still didn't trust her full weight on her leg. It always felt like it was going to give out beneath her. Gripping the cane held between her legs, she debated whether she could get out of the car or not.

Ewyn watched Kerry for a moment, the car parked, the night quiet. "Big place," he commented.

Kerry nodded. The house she'd grown up in was enormous, with six bedrooms, five bathrooms, a guest house, and professionally landscaped grounds. The neighborhood was upper middle class. A bright and bold American flag flew from the pole in the front yard.

"It's all right, a *mhuirnín*," Ewyn promised, giving Kerry's shoulder a squeeze.

Kerry loved the nickname Ewyn gave her. But it was soft and tender; too many of the whispered or blatant slurs she'd been called by family or strangers rang in her ears, drowning it out.

Faggot.

Freak.

Fear was a smothering blanket through which she couldn't draw air. As soon as she'd get out of the car, she'd be exposed — outed. She'd never be safe again. She wouldn't be able to hide, or lie. They'd know. They'd *all* know.

They hadn't accepted Jamie. Why would she be any different?

"I can't do it. I'm sorry."

"No apologizing," Ewyn said sternly.

Maybe they could just drive off. Call and explain, make some excuse.

The front door of the house opened. Kerry's stomach dropped. Her heart clawed its way up into her throat. Nauseated and panicked, she froze, dropping her gaze and gripping the cane.

"I'll handle it," Ewyn promised.

He grabbed the bottle of wine from the backseat and got out of the car with it. Then, he closed the door.

In her peripheral vision, Kerry saw Debra walking toward them. Kent was over by the front door, with Michael.

Debra stooped down to peer into the car. "Is that Kerry?" she asked. "Why isn't he getting out? Is he okay?"

"She's having a hard time right now," Ewyn explained. Their voices carried through the car's windows, barely muffled.

"Who is?" She sounded genuinely confused. With all of her might, Kerry wished herself out of the moment and far, far away. It was the last place she wanted to be. The comfort of the old lies tempted her. There was safety in them, and sanctuary. It was false, cold and hollow, but it was dependable.

"Kerry. Facing all of you is a lot for her."

"I can't do this," Kerry whispered, resigned, letting her head fall back against the headrest. "Jonah, Jamie, I'm sorry. I feel like I'm letting you both down."

Someone else was walking closer. Kerry turned her face away, closing her eyes. In her mind's eye, her arm was being yanked from its socket and the blows were just about to fall.

"Kerry, give them a chance! Please!" It was Kent.

Kerry covered her face with her hands.

"Mom, we could have lost him just like he lost Jamie," Kent warned. He stopped, and then corrected himself, saying, "Lost *her*."

Kerry fumbled for the handle. The fear wanted her to protect herself from more pain, but she couldn't live like that anymore. Ewyn and Kent were right — she had to try. She pulled on the handle and felt a blast of fresh, cooler air. She fumbled with the cane, using it and her right leg to boost out of the car. Ewyn came to her, keeping her steady in many kinds of ways.

"Thanks." Kerry smoothed her skirt and tried not to break into a million little pieces.

"Come into the house, Kerry," Kent said.

Kerry shook her head. Ewyn took her hand, weaving their fingers together.

It was too quiet. All that was missing was the pain, the cruel names and threats. An apology for all that she was, all of the complexities and disappointments, sat right on the tip of her tongue. Only Ewyn's number one rule kept it there, held barely inside.

People approached, and Kerry bowed her head, turning her face toward Ewyn.

"We're so, so very sorry about Jamie," her mother told her, from right in front of Kerry, her tone soft and concerned. She heard Debra's fear there, loud and clear. "We were all horrified to hear about it. Please let Jamie's family know we'd love to help them in any way we can."

"Thank you," Kerry told her, keeping her gaze lowered.

"Please come into the house, Kerry," her mother asked. "You shouldn't be on your feet this long. You'll hurt yourself."

"I'm not welcome," Kerry heard herself say.

"Nonsense."

That wasn't her mother's voice. That was Michael.

Kerry's heart stopped. She gripped Ewyn's hand, squeezing it. When her breath caught, Ewyn turned toward her, kissing her forehead.

"Enough now," Michael said, his low voice carrying. "We invited you here for dinner, not to stand in the driveway. Come sit down. I won't be responsible for causing you any more harm."

"I won't apologize for who I am," Kerry managed to say. She glanced up at all of them for the first time. They were all staring right at her. She could see shock, confusion, and sorrow, but their expressions also held determination and the deep loyalty that had kept the family together through so much.

"We didn't ask you to," Debra said. She stepped closer, leaned in and kissed her cheek. With a sigh, she said, "Oh, Kerry. You know what it is to be afraid for your child." Kerry looked down into her mother's eyes, and tried on a smile. "You're part of this family. We need you."

"Why are you afraid for me?"

"We chased you off, into that neighborhood, that place. First it was Haley that you ran to, then Jamie. I can't stop thinking how close we were to losing you forever, all because we chased you off. We won't do it again. Over my dead body will we, for any reason, close you out. Just because we don't understand all of this yet doesn't mean we don't love you more than anything."

"I'm sorry we haven't made this easy for you," Michael said, looking uncomfortable but sounding sincere. "I'm sorry *I* haven't."

"I could just walk away," Kerry told him, a rare show of defiance in her words. "I could walk away and never come back."

It would be easier, at least in the short term. It would dispel the fear she'd had since she was a small child of not fitting in.

Her leg began to ache. Leaning more heavily on the cane and taking her weight off his leg, she saw their anxious expressions and their worry.

"Please don't," her mother asked softly.

There were so many memories, so many years and pieces of herself in that place. She'd been a child there. She'd had and lost a child there. And now she'd arrived again, neither a man nor a woman, but pieces of each, fitted together into a new whole.

It was just a step, a single one. But once she took it, it was easier to take the next. Ewyn supported her and her mother stepped aside. They watched her limp and grimace with flares of pain. The muscles were weak, the bone barely mended.

"Quick, get the door! Get a chair ready!" Michael called.

It was the longest walk of her life. She crossed the threshold, entered the sitting room. Her two other brothers, Kurt and Kipp, were standing by the windows like they'd been watching everything through them, and they turned to stare as Kerry entered but didn't say a word.

Kent stood by the closest armchair. Michael gestured to it, saying to Ewyn, who guided Kerry forward, "She can sit here. Kent, get Kerry a drink."

Debra pulled up another chair for Ewyn, then herself. She gave Kerry's shoulder a squeeze, let out a relieved sigh and said, "Welcome home, honey. We've missed you."

⎯⎓⎯⎓⎯⎓⎯

Kerry stepped outside with Ewyn to take the call. Holding a hand over her ear to block the noise, chatter and wind, she answered and said, "Yeah?"

"Hey," Kent said. "Are you free to come to dinner? I know it's late notice."

"We're out, actually," she explained. "Ewyn and I. But I can come by tomorrow to see you if that works."

"I'm dating this girl, Olivia, and I promised her I'd introduce you. I mentioned your work, showed her that website your stuff is on and she went crazy about it. She thought the whole androgynous thing was really progressive of you, then started asking how I turned out so annoyingly straight-laced."

"Mm, sounds like we'll get along great," Kerry smiled.

"Look, if there's any way you can visit for just a little while, it does kind of have to be tonight instead of tomorrow. Kurt will be here too."

"Does he know I'm coming?"

"Of course. That's the main the reason he's coming in the first place. Is that all right?"

Kurt had been civil at the last few family dinners, though quieter than usual. Ewyn didn't entirely trust him yet, mainly because he hadn't been able to get a good read on him.

"Yeah, I guess so. When's he shipping out?"

"Tomorrow, actually. That's why it's kind of urgent."

"Wow. How long will he be gone?"

"I don't know. He seemed a little nervous when I talked to him. I think he wants some family time, before, you know? Make some happy memories to carry him through."

"Okay. Well, since timing is important, I'll ask Ewyn to drop me off for dinner tonight. We're with his friends right now. I'll let him come back to hang out while I'm at your place. So yeah, I'll be there."

"Thanks, Kerr. See you soon."

Kerry hung up and nodded to Ewyn, lingering a few steps from the entrance to the bar. Ewyn took the phone and slipped it back into his pocket.

"I have a favor to ask," Kerry said, pulling him a little farther away from the crowd noise.

"What do you need? What's up?"

"Kurt's shipping out tomorrow, and we don't know for how long. He wanted to talk to me and have some family time before he left. Kent said he's nervous about going. So Kent invited me to dinner at his place to see Kurt and to meet his new girlfriend, Olivia. She's a fan of my work, from what Kent said. Would that be okay? I know we had a whole night planned here, but if Kurt's leaving..."

Ewyn looked deeply into Kerry's eyes, weighing the facts, probably checking his concerns.

"I can tell it's important to you," Ewyn said. "We can reschedule with Trevor. If your brother's leaving, that's more important."

"Thank you," Kerry smiled, knowing it was never easy for Ewyn to let her go.

She adjusted her leather miniskirt. The corset top was making breathing a struggle, but the pressure on her chest and the way it pushed up her pectoral muscles, making it look like she had cleavage, was thrilling. Her black high heels completed the look, perfect for hanging out with some of Ewyn's kinkier friends, but maybe not so perfect for dinner at Kent's.

"I kind of need a ride," Kerry admitted.

"And a change of clothes?" Ewyn guessed.

"Yeah," Kerry laughed. "I think that'd be best. Do you mind? You can come back here to spend more time with everyone. I'll call you when I'm ready to go."

"I won't mind, but I will miss the hell out of you, especially with how incredible you look tonight," Ewyn sighed. He stepped close, wrapping an arm around behind Kerry's lower back and drawing her in for a kiss. His hand palmed Kerry's ass, giving it a squeeze through the leather. With a groan, Ewyn let her go.

"There's always later," Kerry promised. "I think there's a lap dance that I owe you."

With an even heavier groan, Ewyn slowly mastered his miserable expression and kissed Kerry again. "I'll hold you to that, you know."

Kerry laughed. "I know."

Ewyn took her hand and turned her away from the bustling party. "Come on then, gorgeous. I'm already counting the minutes until I have you again."

Chapter 32: Empowered

In a flowered blouse, a pair of jeans, and her sandals, Kerry waved goodbye to Ewyn and headed up to Kent's front door. She was curious to see whether or not Ewyn would actually drive off, or would sit out there, waiting and watching, just in case.

Kent's home was a much more modest place than their parents', but bigger than Ewyn's. There were three bedrooms, two baths, and two floors. The exterior had grayish-sage clapboard siding with white trim and a tiled roof. The grass was a little brown from lack of water, and the landscaping minimal with no trees at all, but Kent kept the place tidy. There were three cars in the driveway, two of them Kerry recognized as belonging to her brothers.

Taking an introspective moment to pause there, with Ewyn waiting to see if Kerry would make it inside safely, and her brothers waiting inside the house for her arrival, Kerry looked down at herself with a deep, steadying breath. She stepped up to the door and rang the bell.

From inside, she heard, "I've got it!"

The door opened with Kurt on the other side. Kerry smiled up at her oldest brother, whose lips were tightly pressed together, a faint frown line creasing his brow. "Hey," Kerry said, holding out her hand to shake with Kurt.

"Hey," Kurt replied, coming forward and giving Kerry a hug instead.

At first Kerry was too surprised to react. She couldn't remember the last time her brother had hugged her. It might have been two years ago, at Jonah's funeral.

Behind Kerry, there was the sound of a car driving off. When she glanced back, Ewyn was gone.

Kurt let Kerry go and asked, "Can we talk? Before you meet Olivia?"

"Sure. Yeah."

"Thanks."

They stepped into the house. A central hallway led straight back to the kitchen, where lights shone brightly and from which the mouth-watering scent of grilling steak wafted through the air. She could hear a woman's light, musical laughter. Blues played on the stereo. To their immediate left and right were the study and the living room. One lamp was lit in the living room by the couch. That's where Kurt led them after closing the door.

Kerry sat on the couch and Kurt took the armchair directly across from it. He sat leaning forward, his hands clasped between his knees while Kerry sat up straight, leaning back against the cushions and folded her hands in her lap.

"I know we haven't talked much lately," Kurt started. "But I've been thinking about you a lot. Since I'm leaving, I didn't want to go before... I don't know. Understanding what's going on with you, I guess."

The phrasing of that set Kerry on edge slightly. She chewed at her lip, waiting for Kurt to clarify.

"Kerr, I can't stop thinking about what those guys did to Jamie. And I don't know when I'm coming back or..." he left it hanging there, letting Kerry fill in the rest. There was always the chance that Kurt might not come back at all. They never said so out loud, but the possibility was painfully apparent. "I can't be worried about someone attacking you again when I should be watching my own ass and the rest of my men out there. Kent said Ewyn's been making sure you travel safely?"

"Yeah. I don't go anywhere alone. If Ewyn's busy, I call Kent or Dima or Ewyn's mom or someone else."

"Good. That's good," Kurt nodded.

"You seem really tense. You don't have to worry about me. I'm doing fine."

"I know the statistics, okay? I've... done research. I know the suicide rate for transgender people and the murder rate, and it's obviously not just numbers. We've seen it happen to Jamie and — "

261

"Kurt — "

"I know you've always been focused on Michael, and us, too, I guess. I know Michael did shitty things to you when we were younger, and I know we should have done more to help you or stand up to him. But we're trying and he's trying too. He's a different person now. That's not what concerns me, though. It's everything else. It's the unknown. Guys like Victor."

"No one can police the world."

"Kerr, you dress like this all the time now. I get that. And I know there are some neighborhoods around here that are less than tolerant, and I know that you know that, and it scares me half to death to think that while I'm gone someone might — "

"I'm being safe. Ewyn knows the risks. It's not just Jamie. Ewyn lost his brother to hate crime not that long ago, so he's been there. Trust him to watch out for me in your place, with at least as much perseverance and attention to detail. I know you were always the one standing between me and Michael, once you realized what was happening. And I appreciate that, but you don't have to stand between me and everyone who might want to hurt me. I'm just trying to live the life I want to have, while I can. I'll check in with you regularly, as often as I'm able, okay? I'll write you all the time."

"Okay." Kurt let out a heavy sigh, then nodded. "Okay."

"And just so you know... I know we haven't really talked about this as a family yet. Kent knows, but... this is who I am, Kurt. As you see me right now. This is it. I'm not becoming a woman, or wanting to change my body with surgery, or take hormones. I just want to be myself, like this."

"I know who you are, Kerry," Kurt said softly, looking down at his hands. He cleared his throat and blinked his reddened, wet eyes clear. "I've known exactly who you are since you were little. I'm sorry if I ever made you feel like the things that define you are wrong. If I ever do anything that hurts your feelings, you'll tell me, right?"

Kerry sat forward and laid a hand on Kurt's. Kerry's nails were trimmed short and painted a pale pink. She looked at the sight of her fingers atop her brother's, then smiled and teared up a little too as Kurt took Kerry's hand, holding it.

"Love you, Kurt."

"Love you too, Kerr."

They stood up. Nodding to the kitchen, Kurt grinned and said, "Kent made you a steak. That means you have to eat it."

"I eat steak," Kerry argued good-naturedly. "I'm not a vegetarian."

"No, you just eat like a bird. Even Olivia is eating steak, so you have to."

"All right," Kerry laughed. "I'll eat the steak."

Kurt clapped her on the shoulder and led her toward the kitchen. Walking down the hall, he called, "Look who's here!"

"Hey, Kerry," Kent said with a fond, if slightly bittersweet, smile. He'd been stirring something on the stove but stepped away, wiping his hands on a hand towel. "Thank you for coming on short notice. This is my girlfriend, Olivia."

His arm around her back, Kent introduced a curvy brunette with glowing, tan skin and warm brown eyes. She wore purple-framed glasses and had her hair twisted up in a knot on top of her head. With a smile that lit up as their eyes met, Olivia took Kerry's hand to shake it and said, "It's so good to meet you! I've heard such good things from Kent and I wanted to ask about maybe getting some custom pieces from you, because it's really hard to find things that fit perfectly sometimes and — "

"Let her come in first and get a drink before you're both talking dresses in the corner for the rest of the night," Kent chuckled.

"Sorry," Olivia said lightly, biting her lip. "What are you in the mood for? Wine? Beer?"

"Water," both of Kerry's brothers murmured in chorus.

Kerry had to laugh. "Okay, first of all, no apologizing," she told Olivia. "I'd love to talk and it means a lot to me that you're interested in my work. And second... I'll have a glass of wine."

"Wow," Kurt said, looking surprised.

Kerry just rolled her eyes at him. "Well, we need to toast, right?"

Kent poured a glass for Kerry and the others found the ones they'd already been sipping.

Raising her glass, Kerry said, "To my brother, Kurt, may he have a safe trip and come back to us soon."

"I'll drink to that," Kent agreed. "To Kurt."

"To Kurt," Olivia said.

Kurt kissed the side of Kerry's head. "Thanks Kerr."

Later that night and finally home with Ewyn, Kerry was still a little buzzed on wine. They locked up the house, set the alarm, and headed to bed. As much as she enjoyed being in pants again, especially since now there was no brace on her leg to get in the way of pulling them on, she was eager to get out of them.

On the drive home, she'd caught Ewyn up on everything that had happened at Kent's. Now, Kerry just wanted to focus on Ewyn and leave everything else behind, at least for a little while. As difficult, scary, and painful as life had been lately, she had found peace in her accomplishments, her hard-earned blessings, and her appreciation for the people and challenges that had moved through her life. They all added up to a greater strength and a wiser heart. She prayed for Jamie daily, as she did for Jonah and Darcy, knowing they had each taken their own paths, apart from her ability to influence the outcomes, and she was richer for having their memories to carry her on. She was fitting into her family and being lovingly accepted by them. It lifted her up from within — a triumph she never expected to attain.

No one else needed anything more from her than what she had already been giving. She didn't have to perform or pretend. For the first time, she could simply be.

The focus of her being shifted solely to Ewyn. Kerry's responsibilities used to overwhelm, but now those she felt tying her to her love only inspired her to try harder and push farther. She couldn't wait to shower Ewyn with gratification.

"Should I put the corset and miniskirt back on?" Kerry asked as she pulled her blouse over her head, letting it drop to the floor.

"A *mhuirnín*, you'd break my heart if you started to put more clothes on rather than taking them all off."

She toed off her sandals and walked closer to the bed where Ewyn stood, waiting. "So, I'll save them for tomorrow night?"

"You'd better. Have to admit, there is something I've been looking forward to..."

"I wonder what it could be?" Kerry teased, parting her fly. Slowly, she pushed the pants past her hips and down, along with the black lace boy shorts she'd worn underneath.

"God, I love those," Ewyn moaned, eyeing the lace shorts. "But I like you bare even better."

"Mmm." Kerry stepped out of the clothes and set to work on undressing Ewyn next. She pushed the shirt up and took it over Ewyn's head, kissing his chest, covered in soft hair, then the dark circle of his pierced nipple, licking over it with the tip of her tongue, then kissed just beneath Ewyn's pectoral muscle. Her hands went to Ewyn's fly, working it open. As she pulled the pants down, finding him bare beneath, Kerry sank to her knees and lapped at Ewyn's slowly swelling erection. She licked at the shaft and the head, mouthing the tip, playing the end of the metal jewelry with her lips, tugging gently. Mouthing lower, she licked over the piercing in Ewyn's scrotum as well, and the softness of his sac. She stopped to let Ewyn get free of the pants, gazing up at him with plenty of lust.

"Feels so good to be able to move around normally again. I need to touch you. Get my hands on you."

"I'm all yours," Ewyn smiled. He moved to sit on the bed, up by the headboard, where he could lean back comfortably against pillows.

Kerry crawled onto the bed after him, slinking up Ewyn's body and straddling his legs. With a purr, she took another long lick up Ewyn's cock, swallowing the taste of him down. The scratch of Ewyn's fingers through Kerry's hair gave her goosebumps, and the heavy breathing the display caused urged her to do even more.

"Mmm... I love the taste of your cock," Kerry said, flashing a dark look up at Ewyn's eyes. She took the head between her lips, suckling it.

"Jesus, you really are feeling better, aren't you?"

Kerry let Ewyn's shaft slide back over her tongue, filling her mouth and throat. She tried to stay open, to take it as far as she could, then sucked intensely as she pulled back, setting a slow pace. Ewyn caressed Kerry's hair as she moved on him, moaning, pulling Kerry down faster as if desperate for more.

She kept going until Ewyn's sac drew up tighter, his cock stiff as hot iron. Pulling off with a pop, fondling Ewyn's sac, Kerry asked, "Can I ride you? Please?"

"Fuck yes, you can," Ewyn said, sounding wrecked. Drawing it out just a little more, Kerry tongued Ewyn's scrotal piercing while caressing his pelvis and ripped abdominal muscles. Then she licked up the underside of the shaft to the silver stud in Ewyn's cockhead. She sucked on both ends of the jewelry and then took Ewyn's crown between her lips, tasting the pre-come soaking it. Keeping her throat open, she let a few inches slid back over her tongue. Humming at the taste and thick weight filling her mouth, Kerry felt Ewyn watching, felt too his caress over Kerry's jaw and the edge of her stretched lips while she slowly pulled off. Ewyn groaned, "The sweetness of you, love. It breaks me."

With light, teasing kisses and licks over Ewyn's chest and neck, Kerry made her way further up until she knelt over Ewyn's lap with Ewyn's wet, hot, and ready erection nudging between Kerry's cheeks. Ewyn's hands gripped Kerry's hips, then slid roughly up Kerry's chest, kneading her pecs, hooking a hand behind her neck, and drawing her in closer. His thumb brushed Kerry's slightly swollen lower lip. His fingers skimmed the side of Kerry's face. Moving against each connection, pushing into it or exposing more, Kerry closed her eyes and gave over to it.

"We need some music."

Ewyn reached for his phone and a moment later, music was playing with a low, steady beat.

This part came easily, naturally. It was who she was, showing off for an avid audience of one, freed with the knowledge that she was desired exactly as is, unconditionally. She poured everything she was into it, wanting to show Ewyn she could give as well as take.

Kerry started to move, grinding, rolling her hips while touching herself. She rubbed a hand over her chest and up around the side of her neck, then down the center of her body to wrap and tug her cock. Her other hand cupped her balls, rolling them as she let out a low moan. Her hips kept circling slowly, rocking back against Ewyn's thickness, pushing into her own fist to ride it.

Then she leaned in, brushing her lips lightly over Ewyn's mouth and scratched lightly over Ewyn's broad chest, playing with his chest hair. She thrust gently over Ewyn's abs. Ewyn's fingertips rubbed through Kerry's crease, playing at her hole. When one pushed slowly in to fill it, Kerry whimpered against Ewyn's mouth.

It was more fun than any other dancing she'd done, because she knew how much it was appreciated. There was no reason to hold back anything, or to be shy. This wasn't just where she lived — it was where she thrived.

"A *mhuirnín*," Ewyn breathed. "Are ya mine?"

His hand clasped Kerry's thigh. The finger slid deeper into her, claiming. Kerry pushed back onto it with a shiver, still dancing in small movements.

"Always," Kerry answered. "And you're mine, too."

Ewyn palmed Kerry's inner thigh, then rubbed up to the junction of her legs. Gathering up her sac, Ewyn tugged gently and massaged carefully. Kerry's hips circled as Ewyn fondled her. After withdrawing his finger, Ewyn found the lube and opened the cap. Kerry undulated atop him, now riding Ewyn's fist wrapping her cock, rubbing her ass back against Ewyn's shaft as Ewyn got his fingers wet. A moment later, two pushed deep into Kerry, parting her rim and sheathing in her. She clenched on them, looping her arms behind Ewyn's neck and dragging gasping kisses over his lips.

In a whisper against Ewyn's lips as she was fingered open, Kerry said, "Thank you for taking care of me."

"You're welcome," Ewyn replied with a contented hum. "Thank you for lighting up my life. It's never looked so bright. I'd do anything for you." There was an ache in his voice, and need to keep hold of the good while he was able.

His fingers withdrew, rubbed over Kerry's rim, then penetrated again completely. His hand on Kerry's hip pulled her down into the thrust. With a soft gasp, Kerry circled her hips in small pulses, riding the hand inside her, rubbing at her there and stretching her wide.

Hard-up, wet, desperate and blissful, Kerry sucked a kiss to Ewyn's plugged earlobe, then rasped, "I need you inside me. Right now."

"Say please," Ewyn smirked.

"Please," Kerry begged, letting the ache add anguish to her hushed voice. She kissed Ewyn deeply, opening for more of his tongue, twisting both of his nipples and shivered, gasping, as a third finger entered her. "Please."

"Touch yourself," Ewyn asked.

His fingers withdrew. Kerry took hold of her dick by the root, stroking up the shaft. Ewyn steadied himself with a hand and guided Kerry down. The blunt head was against Kerry's opening, parting it as it was fed inside, stuffing her full.

Kerry whimpered and closed her eyes, staying relaxed so that Ewyn could get as far inside as he wanted.

"More," Kerry pleaded. "Please."

With little upward pushes, he worked his way into Kerry, who pressed down onto Ewyn's cock. Stroking herself and clasping the side of Ewyn's neck, Kerry let herself be gradually taken but tried to keep moving, letting the dance play into their lovemaking.

As soon as Ewyn was fully seated, he said, "Okay, stop touching yourself now. You close?"

"Yeah."

Kerry was achingly hard and dripping wet, only a few tugs away from shooting. With a groan, she obeyed and moved to touch Ewyn instead, caressing his abs as they flexed with each thrust. She saw Ewyn watching her soaking cock bob in the air, her slim hips undulating against the thrusting of the cock inside her ass. The attention added another layer of stimulation, prickling at Kerry's skin, charging her spirit and sending warm tingles spiraling deep inside.

Soon, Ewyn was sliding easier. Kerry was able to bounce on him, taking him harder and faster, her dick smacking against her pelvis as she fucked herself down onto Ewyn's thick cock.

"Oh god," Kerry breathed. "So fucking good..."

Ewyn palmed both of Kerry's cheeks, spreading her and kneading the muscle.

"Show me. Show me what you want."

"You," Kerry panted, coming in to bite at Ewyn's lower lip, a frown of need furrowing her brow. "Just you."

Ewyn caught her lip between his teeth, growling as he snapped his hips up into Kerry's downward bounces. They went harder, faster, until Ewyn moaned, pulling Kerry down completely onto him as he came with a shiver.

"Oh Jesus... that was... fucking *incredible*..." He wrapped his hand around Kerry's erection, tugging it hard and slow. "Come. Dance for me, beautiful."

Everything in Kerry, once tight and tangled, loosened and let go.

She wasn't alone. She knew herself, her needs, and her goals.

And she was Ewyn's. Filling Ewyn's life with love was her mission. It was everything that mattered.

Her heart and body were no longer her own. Loving Ewyn and loving himself were the commitments driving her on and helping her grow. Those responsibilities built her up. There was no need to lie or pretend, about anything.

Kerry felt it as she gave over to happiness, laughing with joy. She kissed the side of Ewyn's face and panted quietly as she was taken slowly apart, quivering with the glorious anguish. Bliss crashed through ache. She cried out, desperately. Perfectly alive.

Coming, trembling, Kerry held onto the man who'd opened her up and set her free to become the impossible — herself.

If you enjoyed this story, you can sign up for a free membership at ForbiddenFiction and discuss it with other readers and the author at the *Becoming Kerry* story page.
We do our best to proof all our work, but if you spot a text error we missed, please let us know via our website Contact Form.

Author's Notes

Maybe you're curious as to why I was inspired to write a genderqueer main character. I've been thinking a lot recently about the secrets we keep, and why. Kerry is someone who starts out the story with many more secrets than truths. In some ways, everything she is, is a lie, and it's making her miserable. Those around Kerry can see something is wrong, but they can't figure out what it is either because the answers need to come from within. I wanted to write Kerry as someone who lives between the disparate visions of who everyone else thinks she's supposed to be, and who she feels she really is underneath it all. I think most of us live there, in a middle space where we're afraid to be completely honest and where we adopt roles that don't really suit us in order to chase some distorted notion of happiness.

I chose to write Kerry as genderqueer because there are so many people who don't understand quite what that means, looks like, or feels like, and I needed to explore one instance of what that could be. Because Kerry's goals can't be addressed medically with surgery or hormone treatments, but are also not limited to her sexuality, I wanted to live in that gray area with her for a while to see what it would take for her to stand with pride and certainty.

Kerry is one person in very specific circumstances, with a unique soul and set of goals in life. Her pronouns, her vision of herself, her ways of expressing who she is, and the beautiful imperfections that make up her character are particular only to her, in this life, this place, this age, and this time. She fits in one spot on a broad, colorful spectrum of possibility. Kerry is not meant to encompass everything it means to be genderqueer or bisexual or pansexual, but is only presented in the context of her own story. I strongly believe what is right for one person is not necessarily right for the next, and that's what makes the world such a beautifully diverse and interesting place. No matter who you are, lovely reader, I wholeheartedly support your right to be exactly who you are unapologetically. For me, that's what this story is truly about. Because it's never easy to break away from imposed labels or expectations, we all could do with a little more loving support and understanding from our community.

I wrote this story as someone who only came out as pansexual to my friends and family this year, at almost forty years of age. My experience was one of knowing without a doubt that who I knew I was from a young age was not okay with the people in my world, and most of all with my parents and siblings. I was bullied and abused for reasons that had nothing to do with my sexual orientation, but definitely influenced my comfort level with my ability to be open about it. So, I buried it. I only shared my truth with romantic partners. I have always been drawn to the queer community without knowing exactly where or how I fit in, and my struggle to publicly embrace my truths is mirrored in Kerry's struggles.

I believe we judge from appearances way too much, and I wanted to give Kerry the freedom to defy that. Just because you see Kerry dating a woman doesn't mean you know who she is. The same is true whether she's dating someone trans, or falls for a bisexual cisgender man, or works as an exotic dancer, or has suffered a terrible injury, or has fathered a child, or wears a Marine's uniform, or is seen in public in a dress with pretty sandals. The real story is much more complex and interesting than that, which is what I want to celebrate. Details and secrets are what add magic. They are what defy the odds and expand the realm of possibility more and more.

For Kerry, a series of small steps is what takes her to a fulfilling kind of happiness and peace with her means of self-expression. Sometimes she strictly follows the expectations of her conservative family instead of her own, whether it's in dating, in work, or in the fundamental ways she expresses her identity. Her ability break away from that life of imposed fear is a gradual one, full of missteps and learning experiences.

Another thing I knew going into this story was that my readers would bring with them some expectations for who the main

271

Lynn Kelling

character would be and what kind of romance this book would contain, along with the certainty that I'd be pushing people out of comfort zones and challenging them to embrace all of the many branches of Kerry's path. My sincere hope is that my readers see the value in exploring the particular twists and turns in the long road Kerry has to travel to get to her happy ending. This was her path. We each have our own and our common human need to try and see just how we fit in with our world is what really binds us together.

I never intended to please everyone with this story; I needed only to please Kerry. Kerry is a kindred spirit who spends too long trying only to survive and eek out small portions of contentment. Kerry is someone with a mountain to climb and no guide book on how to do it, only a gut instinct that things forced upon her just don't fit the way they should. Kerry is someone looking most of all for love and safety, but finds more of her fair share of hate and intolerance. Kerry is a parent who has felt what unconditional love is and can be, and this informs her drive to keep trying to find more of it, somehow. Kerry has experience with imperfect relationships and the astounding blessings that can come from them. She spends so much time being forced to present as male that she revels in the ability, once she finds it, to present as female instead. Kerry is still moving forward after we leave her, and she is the only one able to define what her future will hold.

With love of self and love of others, anything is possible. Love is what makes us grow, while fear is what holds us back. By letting go of fear and embracing love, Kerry became her own hero. That's the vision I believe in, for all of us, no matter who we are.

Thank you for reading. Thank you to my wonderful editors for their guidance and patience. Thank you to everyone out there trying to break free of labels and challenge the intolerance that is so painfully visible these days. Believe in yourself first; the rest will follow.

Lynn Kelling

May 13, 2017

About the Author

Lynn Kelling began writing in order to tell stories that aren't afraid of the dark, don't hold anything back and always strive to be memorable, forging lasting attachments between character and reader. Her inspiration comes from taking a closer look at behaviors and ideas lurking at the fringes of life — basically anything that people may hesitate to speak of in mixed company, but everyone wonders about anyway. Her work is driven by the taboo in order to expose the humanity within it. Lynn is an artist, designer and lover of any form of creative self-expression that comes from a place of honesty and emotion, whether it's body art or opera. She has had multiple novels published, has written over seventy works of erotic fiction of varying lengths, and always has several novels in progress.

Other Works by Lynn Kelling:

About the Publisher

ForbiddenFiction.com is a publisher devoted to writing that breaks the boundaries of original erotic fiction. Our stories combine intense sexuality with quality writing. Stories at Forbidden Fiction.com not only arouse readers through sensations, but also engage them emotionally and mentally through storytelling as well-crafted as the sex is hot.

ForbiddenFiction.com is also designed to be a social reading environment. You'll have fun even if just reading the latest post each day, yet you will have the chance for so much more. Readers and authors can be part of ongoing discussions of specific works and individual authors as well as more general topics.

Sign up for a FREE Membership today at ForbiddenFiction.com

Also recommended...

You may also enjoy these other ForbiddenFiction works:

Whatever the Cost, by Lynn Kelling

Liam and Jacen are roommates–and elite prostitutes working for a secret organization, The Company. They spend their lives making fantasies come true for spoiled, dangerous clients. In the midst of daily risk of emotional and physical damage, their friendship has been an island of sanity and safety. When The Company orders them to do a job together requiring them to cross the no-sex boundary that has kept them friends, Liam and Jacen must examine how they really feel about each other, and how far they are truly willing to go. Is this the life they want? Used to offering up their bodies without protest to the mercurial whims of others while fiercely guarding their hearts, the true meaning of love and consent is a challenge neither has ever faced before. (M/M)

Edge of a Knife, by James L. Wolf

Daniil LaChance grew up hard on the streets of the city-state of Allistair. A chance meeting with the shapeshifting Flame known as Knife changed that when Knife took Daniil as her apprentice. The promise of initiation as one of the sexual mystics of the goddess Pelin turned Daniil's life from one of poverty and desperation to one of magic and mystery—one that could last many lifetimes. (M/M, F/F, M/F)

www.ingramcontent.com/pod-product-compliance
Lightning Source LLC
Chambersburg PA
CBHW060526260626
47161CB00003B/781